THIN MOON AND COLD MIST

THIN MOON

A N D

COLD MIST

KATHLEEN O'NEAL GEAR

A TOM DOHERTY ASSOCIATES BOOK

NEW YORK

THIN MOON AND COLD MIST

A Forge book
Published by Tom Doherty Associates, Inc.
175 Fifth Avenue
New York, N.Y. 10010

Forge® is a registered trademark of Tom Doherty Associates, Inc.

Design by Ann Gold

ISBN 0-312-85701-2

Printed in the United States of America

TO

WANDA LILLIE O'NEAL

She taught me to wonder.
And I will never be able
to thank her enough.

ACKNOWLEDGMENTS

I owe sincere debts of gratitude to several people. Linda Quinton believed that a series of heavily researched books that accurately detailed the lives of nineteenth-century women was important. She felt it was time to strip away the Victorian fable and to look upon those women and their times for what they really were: *extraordinary*. So is Linda. I appreciate her more than she knows.

Harriet McDougal has never let me down. Her remarkable insight and skill always leave me feeling deeply thankful that she exists.

W. Michael Gear, my best friend, joined me for long horseback rides, canoe trips, and hours of sitting on mountaintops staring out across hundred-mile vistas—even though he knew the entire time would be spent discussing the minutiae of historical innuendo. Our togetherness is like being on a constant vision quest—searching, soaring. Thank you, Mike.

HISTORICAL FOREWORD

Twentieth-century women tend to view their nineteenth-century counterparts as pitifully oppressed, virtually bereft of any political rights, and, consequently, unable to control their own destinies. This assessment would come as quite a surprise to many nineteenth-century women.

The frontier proved the greatest catalyst for women's rights in the history of this country. It was "out there" that women would undeniably prove themselves equal to men. Any woman who wanted to break free of the chains of Victorian America knew which direction led to freedom: Go West, young woman. *Go West.*

To say that these women faced great odds, and dangers that are scarcely imaginable today would be a grievous understatement. Often they were alone and frightened. Usually they had children to protect. Though they may have come from different races and backgrounds, they shared one personal characteristic: At heart, they were adventurers.

In 1862, Mary O'Kieffe's wayward husband was off on "one of his jaunts." He'd been missing for days—again. She hitched the horses, loaded the cultivator and a cage of chickens, packed up her nine children, and marched five hundred miles to stake her own homestead claim in Nebraska.

Rosie Ise's husband died shortly after the family moved to Kansas in 1873. She didn't give up and go back East. With the help of twelve children, she worked the farm, "proved-up" on her homestead, and managed to put nine of her children through college.

Mrs. E. J. Guerin abandoned the safety of hearth and home in 1857 to lead wagon train expeditions across the continent. "Mountain Charley," as she was called, had a successful thirteen-year career as frontier explorer and guide.

Sara Horton Cockrell of Dallas became a widow in 1858 after her husband was murdered by the sheriff. She took up managing several hotels, a toll bridge, and a lumber mill. She reinvested every cent she could and by 1870 was the largest property owner in Dallas County.

Dona Gertrudis Barcelo, a monte dealer in New Mexico Territory, had become so rich from her gambling and saloon businesses that she lent the United States Army money to pay its troops after the Mexican invasion.

Women participated in the gold rush, becoming prospectors, miners, and entrepreneurs. Mrs. E. C. Atwood studied geology and mineralogy, owned several gold mines, and became the general manager of the Bonacord Gold Mining and Milling Company in Colorado. In 1900 she told the International Mining Congress that gold mining "could be made to pay by any energetic woman who will pursue it in an intelligent way."

Clara Brown, a slave, bought her freedom in 1857 and moved to Colorado Territory where she opened a laundry. She saved enough money to start her own wagon train company, which brought southern blacks to the West.

Biddy Mason escaped from Georgia slavery in 1851, obtained her freedom papers in Los Angeles, and sank what little money she had into two town lots. Later, she purchased another, and then another. Eventually she became a real estate magnate.

Women who *were* born on the frontier already possessed rights the likes of which would have astounded white women. Many Native American tribes granted women the right to divorce, to vote, to control childbearing by using a variety of birth control methods, the right to own property, to own and operate their own businesses, to serve in high political and ceremonial offices. But inevitable culture clashes provided even these women with new opportunities to step out of their traditional roles. At least five Iroquois women warriors received military pensions for heroic service during the War of 1812: Julia John (Seneca), Dinah John (Onondaga), Susan Jacob (Onondaga), Polly Cooper (Oneida), and Dolly Skanandoah (Oneida). Lozen, the sister of the famed Apache Chief Victorio, became a powerful and respected warrior during the Indian Wars. Buffalo Calf Road Woman, a Cheyenne, fought at the Battle of the Rosebud.

Indeed, women soldiers played very important roles in nineteenth-century warfare.

Mary A. Livermore of the U.S. Sanitary Commission, the forerunner to the American Red Cross, wrote that, "the number of women soldiers known to the service" during the Civil War was "a little less than 400," but the real number was probably much higher. Women fought in every major battle from

Bull Run to Petersburg. A few were commissioned officers, and more than a few were scouts and spies.

Nancy Hart had been so effective as a guide for General Thomas J. "Stonewall" Jackson's cavalry in West Virginia that the Union put a price on her head. She was captured by Lieutenant Colonel Starr of the Ninth West Virginia in July of 1862 and sent to prison. There she grabbed her guard's musket, shot him dead, and escaped on Colonel Starr's horse. She returned a few days later with two hundred Confederate troops, devastated Starr's command, and captured him.

Sarah Emma Edmonds, alias Private Frank Thompson, worked as a spy for Generals McClellan, Sheridan, Burnside, and Grant. She penetrated enemy lines by masquerading as a black boy, an Irish peddler woman, a black laundress, and many others. A case of malaria finally put her in the hospital where her sex was discovered and she was dismissed from the army. Twenty years later, however, she petitioned the War Department for a pension and won. After hearing glowing testimony of Private Thompson's bravery from men who had served with her, a special act of Congress granted her an honorable discharge and a veteran's pension of twelve dollars per month.

Black women proved to be extraordinary spies. Elizabeth Bowser infiltrated the home of President Jefferson Davis, working as a nanny to his children, and reported every conversation she overheard to the Union. Mary Touvestre kept house for a Confederate engineer working on the remodeling of the *Merrimac*. When he went out one day, she stole the plans for the remodeling and personally delivered them to Washington, D.C.

Perhaps the greatest Civil War spy of all was Sarah Slater, who served the Confederacy. The Union never even knew of her existence until after the assassination of President Lincoln. While questioning suspects, they heard Sarah Slater's name mentioned repeatedly. It was said that she met with John Wilkes Booth whenever she was in Washington, and we know that she worked with John Harrison Surratt, the son of Mary Surratt who was hung with the other conspirators in July of 1865. Mrs. Slater was sent on a final mission for the Confederacy in April of 1865. She was, once again, supposed to meet with John Wilkes Booth. Whether she did or not, we will never know, because just before the assassination she vanished. She never again contacted her husband, other family members, or friends. It is very curious that she vanished at the same time as John Harrison Surratt, and when she was carrying substantial Confederate monies to England. Mrs. Slater is a fascinating figure—we'll discuss her in greater detail in the Afterword of this book.

Let me say, in conclusion, that the foregoing is not historical revisionism, which implies a political motive for the rewriting of history, it is simply fact. Nineteenth-century women who wanted independence reached out and took it.

The Women of the West series will chronicle the lives of a few of those strong women. I think you will find that most were not "Gentle Tamers." They were bold, courageous adventurers.

They had to be—to chance their wings in the unbelievably stormy skies of a nation being born.

THIN MOON AND COLD MIST

PROLOGUE

The forest is aflame and I am running, alone, my pistol clutched in both hands. Smoky haze envelops me as I break out of the trees into a meadow. I stumble.

Before me, across a beautiful carpet of dogwood and redbud petals, bodies sprawl, twisted at impossible angles. Some curl on their sides in pools of blood, like newborn babies. Others are rag dolls tumbled down the slope. All wear tattered blue uniforms. Frozen mouths open to me in a final cry for help . . .

I grip my pistol more tightly and step back.

From the black spaces between the trees, pale, firelit faces emerge; they float toward me like bodiless ghosts borne on the billows of smoke. I stand there. Unable to move.

Women rush past, their hair wild with sleep, as though dragged from their beds and told to run. Children cling to their calico skirts. Old men and boys carry muskets. Many of them have Indian facial features. Everyone is shouting, screaming. I know because their mouths move, their faces are stricken with terror, but I barely hear their voices over the cacophony of the flames.

"Stop! Wait. You can't go east! You'll be heading into the worst fires!"

No one seems to hear me. I am just a young Negro woman to them, my cries not worth listening to.

I keep yelling, "No, not that way, not that way. Go back!"

They push by as though I am invisible, shoving me, spinning me around, jostling me back into the trees as they flood down through the carnage in the meadow. The stench of their fear is suffocating.

"Stop! You must listen to me, for the sake of God. You're murdering your own children!"

I rush after them. I am still screaming when the roar of the fire becomes so deafening I can no longer hear myself. The tallest trees burst into flame. Orange tongues ignite the grass. The children try to bury themselves in old leaves to hide.

Then . . .

It is dawn and I am sitting at the edge of a charred grove of trees, watching translucent lavender beams shoot through the tattered clouds of smoke. And I know I've failed. I did not accomplish my mission. Because of me a thousand men will die before noon.

My own sobbing wakes me. I sit up, try to catch my breath.

But every time I close my eyes I am alone again, running, running . . .

Robin Walkingstick Heatherton

CHAPTER 1

May 1864.

Robin crawled through the underbrush on her hands and knees, quietly, like a cougar stalking prey, and inched her way into a tangled fortress of deadfall. Logs and other debris lay three feet high. She stretched out and pillowed her head on an old gray trunk. The wood had been weathered by decades of rain and wind. The bark was all gone. Worms had gnawed curving trails in the flesh of the trunk and soft green tufts of moss had taken root; she traced them with her powder-blackened hand. They seemed so delicate, so alien to this battlefield. It took sheer force of will to keep her eyes focused on the loveliness of the moss when, over her head, golden sparks flitted glimmering as they blew through the scrub oak boughs on their way to the fire-dyed heavens.

The blazes had begun at dusk, when the wind picked up, and now burned out of control all over the Wilderness. Billows of orange-colored smoke gleamed above the tree tops. They had a strange, eerie beauty, but exhaustion so weighted her she could barely keep her gaze focused on their sparkling glory. She'd been awake for almost forty-eight hours straight.

"Virginia, my poor Virginia," she murmured in a soft, hoarse voice, and the coughing fit that had been building in her chest erupted violently.

She pulled herself to a sitting position and buried her face in her blue sleeve to cover the sound. The action brought forth an agony of aching muscles. The fit took several seconds to pass, and she was terrified that someone would hear.

Throughout the night, desperate commanders had struggled to keep their lines together despite the darkness and spreading fires. The shells that whined across the sky paid tribute to the few artillery batteries that had managed to get into position. The denseness of the scrubby waters brought enemies face-to-face before they realized it, so the shooting never really halted, and the screams of the wounded and dying formed a horrifying base note to the fire's crackling symphony.

When she could catch her breath again, Robin blinked at the fireflies winking in the branches. So beautiful. Their greenish yellow light contrasted sharply to the red-orange of the sparks tumbling through the sky beyond.

She watched them; they reminded her of campfires she'd shared with her mother when she'd been a child. That seemed like another life. Like another Robin. A child filled with dreams and tenderness, not the cold bitter woman who lived inside her bones now.

Robin sank back against the log. Faces formed and melted in the wisps of smoke that drifted around her. All images from her childhood. Friends from twenty years ago. She whispered their names reverently: *"Ambrose . . . Ivens . . . Wheatley,"* and a smile touched her lips in response to Wheatley's little-girl grin. Robin was so tired she was no longer certain what was real and what imagined. If she cocked her head she could hear voices seeping from those fleeting mouths. Some sounded frail and old, others tight with pain— her mother's most of all.

"These government people, they are hunted by dead voices and mirrors. You must never trust them, Robin. They are liars. Never believe what they tell you. Fight them. Fight them as long as you live. You will have to—if you don't want to be hunted by dead voices and mirrors yourself."

A full-blooded Cherokee, Sarah Walkingstick Porter had been forced from her North Carolina home in 1838 and begun the Trail of Tears. All of her brothers and sisters had died from disease and her parents from starvation—because they had given every scrap of their own food to their ailing children. Though Sarah had married a white military officer and left the Cherokee to live in Richmond, she had always considered Robin to be an Indian. She'd schooled her daughter in Cherokee legends, their knowledge of plants and animals, and warned her "never to forget" what the white nation had done to her people.

Robin let her chin fall to her chest and inhaled a halting breath. *But, mama, oh, mama, I want to go home. I should be taking care of my little boy. I want to go home so badly I . . .*

She jerked when a single shot split the night, followed by a spatter of blasts so near and loud that she dared not breathe. Ragged screams followed the volley.

A riderless horse raced past her, its nostrils flaring as it crashed through the forest and blended with the night.

Robin got on her knees and peered over the fallen logs, trying to see through the blinding gloom. Her blue uniform stuck to her tall, slender body in sweat-drenched folds, making the thick bandage that wrapped her chest and flattened her breasts feel like a band of iron.

Where were the men? *And which army are they fighting for?*

For two days she'd been using her pocket compass to chart a course through the wilderness, hoping that when the time came she would be able to find her way back to her own lines. She'd begun the attempt last evening and had stopped to rest only when she'd felt certain she had made it to safety.

But I may still be behind enemy lines. I cannot rule out that possibility.

The lines had been slithering back and forth like a den of snakes. In the doghair chinkapin, hazel, and head-high berry brambles, a soldier could get turned around and never know again which direction he faced.

This battle bore little resemblance to organized warfare; it was more like bushwhacking on a grand scale. Invisibles fighting invisibles. No one could see more than a few feet ahead. Even a Southern boy, accustomed to moving through such country, often couldn't determine where he stood in relation to his company. But the Southerners fared a good deal better than the Northerners. Half the Union army came from tame farmlands or cities, and this wild second-growth country seemed to have affected them like a hard blow to the skull, leaving them hopelessly dazed. Yesterday, Robin had followed one company as it thrashed through the jungle, firing muskets at nothing until every ball was gone. She'd heard stories of people who shared dreams. These men seemed to be sharing the same horrific nightmare.

More shots. Panic fire, as if from men who'd been surprised by the enemy.

"Cease firing!" someone shouted. "Cease firing!"

"Who gave that order?" another yelled. "Don't listen, boys, he's the enemy, I tell you! Kill him! Kill him quick!"

Robin hit the ground as streaks of flame shot through the dense trees. They came from no more than thirty paces away.

"Cease firing, goddamn you! *You're shooting at your own men!*"

The fire's haze mixed pungently with the smoke of belching muskets; she could taste the bitterness of gunpowder on her tongue. When hooves thundered, Robin rose, braced her pistol on the deadfall, and squeezed the trigger, taking up the slack, ready to fire.

A big bay horse thundered toward her. A Union colonel swayed in the saddle, almost falling off. The horse leaped a sapling that had been felled by gunfire, whinnied, and swung south, disobeying the brutal reining of the man who held on with one hand while he used his other to fend off the overhanging branches. His wound was clearly visible. The minie ball must have struck him in the back, for there was a gaping exit hole in his stomach. Dark blood coursed over his legs, soaked his pants, and trickled down the horse's sides as they disappeared into the haze. Another horse came crashing in nearly on the bay's heels, a sorrel, ridden by a Union lieutenant.

The dark-haired lieutenant saw Robin and shouted, "Where'd he go, boy? Which way did the colonel's horse go?"

"That way, suh!" she answered and ran forward a few paces to show the way through the forest.

"Follow me," the lieutenant ordered. "I may need help." And he vanished. Deadfall cracked like cannon fire in his wake.

Robin shoved her pistol into her waistband, feeling sick, sick to the death of the foul scents and unbearable sights of war. She slung her haversack over one shoulder and trotted through the wind-blown weave of shadow and firelight. She found the lieutenant with his sorrel standing shoulder-to-shoulder with the bay, fighting to hold the colonel on his saddle.

"My God, Colonel," the lieutenant said. His thin aristocratic face had been bleached by the firelight, making his eyes seem huge dark pits encased in an old skull. "I'm sure those were our men. I mean I know the lines are all twisted up in this wilderness, but I thought I saw blue uniforms. I . . ." His voice broke. "I'm sure they must have been ours, John."

The colonel nodded, using what strength he had left to stay on his mount, but it soon failed him and he slid sideways into the lieutenant's arms in a faint.

"John!"

The lieutenant's horse bolted and both men tumbled to the forest floor.

Robin ran forward. "Hyah! Go on, move!" she yelled at the prancing sorrel to keep it from trampling the officers. It dashed away into the thicket as she grabbed for the reins of the colonel's bay.

The lieutenant ordered, "Hurry it up, boy! Tether the colonel's horse and get over here. He's bleeding badly!" He gently lifted the colonel's head onto his lap. "John? Oh, John, good Lord, stay still. Try not to move."

Robin led the bay a short distance away and tied the reins to a tree, then ran back and knelt by the lieutenant. He had a straight nose and wide blue eyes, framed by brown hair. Soot coated his skin and uniform. He'd lost his hat somewhere. The two men shared a resemblance. Cousins? Brothers? Both looked to be around twenty-nine or thirty. Five years older than Robin.

"Don't try to rise, John!" the lieutenant half-shouted when the colonel struggled to sit up. "We're . . . we're safe here. Rest easy, easy . . ." He smoothed a hand over the colonel's brow until he calmed down, then took out his knife and sawed through the man's bloody shirt to examine the injury. Ropes of intestines had been forced through the wound by the colonel's fall. Robin lowered her head as the lieutenant touched them. "Oh, John," he whispered. "I tried to make the men stop firing. They wouldn't stop. I tried . . . don't know why they wouldn't stop. Don't die, John. God, please don't die!"

Robin remained quiet, waiting for orders that never came. Finally she said, "Suh, shouldn't we binding up the wound? To stanch the flow o' blood?" It would do no good, but it would give the young lieutenant something to do while he regained control of himself. And she needed him to be in control, so he could think straight.

The lieutenant swung around with fire in his eyes. "Hell, no, boy! For the sake of God, go and find a surgeon! And bring stretcher-bearers! This wound is no trifle!"

Gently, Robin answered, "No, suh. I can see that, suh. I was just thinking it might be well to bind the wound or it could be useless to go for the surgeon. If you sees what I means, suh."

The lieutenant blinked, and lowered his head. "Oh, yes . . . yes, of course. But . . . he's . . . I don't . . . do you think binding it . . ." His mouth hung open, moving in more words, soundless now, or maybe it was just the effort to choke back the tears that filled his eyes. He lifted the colonel and cradled the man's broad shoulders in his own shaking arms. Water beaded on the lieutenant's soot-coated lashes.

"You keep a holding him like that, suh. I'll care for the wound."

Robin unslung her haversack and took out a roll of bandages. She carried a roll at all times, to disguise the lines of her bosom. Now, she tipped the colonel's torso so she could slide the roll under his back and come up around his torn stomach. The vile odor of ripped intestines forced her to hold her breath. *Will the killing never stop?* Couldn't the Yankees see that the South would fight until every man between the ages of ten and a hundred lay cold and dead—and many women too? Robin knew of at least fifty women, dressed as men, who had taken up arms to fight side-by-side with their male counterparts. Battlefield nurses had told Robin they had treated hundreds of women soldiers.

She forced a breath into her lungs and wrapped the colonel's wound seven more times, before splitting the end of the bandage and knotting it. Blessed Jesus, so much blood. The white fabric went crimson immediately. When she sat back, she pushed her cap up, showing a kinky fringe of hair.

"Did you see them?" the lieutenant asked, searching her face. "The men who shot at us? Were they ours, or Rebs?"

Robin shook her head. "I didn't see nothing, suh. Just heard the firing and hunkered down to wait, that was all."

"You were scared?" It was an accusation.

"Yes, suh." Robin hung her head in shame. "I was scared real bad."

The lieutenant paused, then his voice came out soft, forgiving. "It's all right, private. We're all scared."

He began rocking the colonel in his arms, like a mother trying to get a newborn to sleep. He kept his eyes closed a few moments, then asked through a shaking exhalation, "Where are you from, boy? You're about as black as Mississippi tar."

Robin tucked what was left of her roll of bandages back into her haversack, and her fingers brushed the cool vial of silver nitrate, in weak solution, which she used to turn her skin its rich mahogany color. It didn't take much. Her half-Cherokee blood had given her a chestnut complexion to begin with. But since many of the Cherokee, Osage, and Seminole were fighting for the Confederacy, someone might have been suspicious about her Indian heritage. No one ever thought twice about a young Negro soldier. "That's 'bout right, suh," Robin answered. "I come from the coast o' Luzianna."

"A runaway slave?"

"Yes, suh, but now that I'm a free man—"

"You're not a man, son. You're nothing but a boy. You haven't grown whisker one yet, have you?"

Robin shook her head. "No, not yet, but my brother didn't grow no whiskers until he was 'bout sixteen. So I guess I got me some time."

"Sixteen? How old are you, boy? Fourteen or fifteen? Lord God, how'd you get in this army?" She didn't answer, and he let out a tortured breath as he shook his head. His eyes drifted back to the dying man in his arms. "This godforsaken Army of the Potomac. I wish I'd never—" The shrill screech of a shell cut through the fire's glow. *"Get down!"*

Robin landed on her belly and covered her head while the lieutenant scrambled to shield the colonel's body with his own. The earth heaved and groaned when the shell struck, shaking the ground like a monstrous quake. Uprooted trees and clods of dirt flew through the air, slamming into other trees before thudding to the ground. A rain of dirt cascaded down upon them. The colonel's horse screamed and reared. Tearing its reins loose, it pounded away into the depths of the forest.

Robin started to shake. *I've got to get back to my own lines, or I'll never see my son again.* Before he'd left to join General Nathan Bedford Forrest's command in Tennessee, her husband, Charles, had gotten word to her that he was leaving Jeremy with his mother in Richmond. The child was five years old. *I'm sorry I missed your birthday, Jeremy. I'll be back soon. One trip to Wilmington to meet Rose's ship, then home to Richmond for Christmas. Daddy will be coming home, too, Jeremy. A few months, that's all . . .*

Rose's note from England had boasted that grand news would follow, news that would turn the tide of the war. But Robin couldn't let herself believe it. She'd heard dozens of desperate stories lately, though she had never known the great spy, Rose O'Neal Greenhow, to distort the truth just to bolster the courage of the troops.

At the onset of the war, Rose had operated a spy ring out of Washington, D.C. that included, among many others, F. M. Ellis, a secret service officer on General McClellan's own staff; James Howard, a clerk for Lincoln's provost marshal, M. T. Walsworth, in the adjutant general's office; and Mr. Callan, who worked for the Senate Military Committee. She had also plied her trade with Colonel E. D. Keyes, secretary to General Winfield Scott, then General-in-Chief of the Union Army. It had been Keyes who had given Rose the information on the size of the federal forces that would move on Bull Run, the route of their advance, their battle strategy, and even a copy of General McDowell's actual order to his troops.

No, Rose's professionalism was beyond question. If she said her news might turn the tide of the war, then it well might. Hope, long dormant in Robin, stirred. But just a breath, like a faint whisper . . .

"Forsaken, forsaken," the lieutenant whispered so forlornly that it made Robin roll over to stare at him. "God has forsaken us, Private. We'll all be lost in this struggle."

She sat up and brushed the dirt from her uniform. It took a deliberate effort of will to steady her voice. "We ain't forsaken, suh, not yet. I was listening to some men what come by earlier, running fast from the fires. They was saying that we was winning dis battle. Yes, suh, I heard 'em right, too. They said Bobby Lee would be getting his due in the morning, 'cause Mister Unconditional Surrender hisself had a good plan."

The lieutenant tenderly touched the colonel's pale cheek and his young face slackened in shock. Robin could see the man's dead eyes, open halfway, sprinkled with bits of forest duff. *Lucky, lucky, lucky.* Too often, she'd witnessed belly wounds that brought suffering for days.

"Oh, no . . . God, no, please." In a choking voice, the lieutenant called, *John?* Oh, John, I'm sorry. I tried so hard to make the men stop shooting. I . . . I tried . . ." He clutched the colonel's clothing with trembling hands.

The fire flared somewhere behind them and cast a lurid glow over the tiny clearing where they sat, revealing things Robin had not noticed before: Moldering shreds of uniforms, blue and butternut, twined through the underbrush like perverted vines; tarnished buttons glittered in the leaves, and here and there a dirt-caked bone protruded from the dark forest floor.

Robin closed her eyes. Had a year truly passed since the battle of Chancellorsville had been fought on these very grounds? It seemed just a few heartbeats ago. General Stonewall Jackson had been shot just east of this spot and later died from his wounds. Nearly thirteen thousand Confederate soldiers had been killed or wounded. She'd walked among them, laughed with them, starved with them—those ragged, exhausted, brave men who had fought to the death to protect their homes and families from the Northern invaders.

Robin picked up her pistol and wiped it off with the hem of her jacket before lifting her eyes to the lieutenant again. She ought to kill him . . . But he'd put the colonel's limp hand to the uniform over his heart and seemed to be biting his lip to muffle the mournful sounds coming from his throat. Jackson had said that the only way to win this war was to kill them all . . .

Robin holstered her pistol. This young man might know something that would help her side.

The war could not go on much longer. Southern troops were marching barefoot now and surviving on one-third pound of meat and one pound of bread a day.

The lieutenant's composure broke and he wept aloud. Robin rose and went to him, laying a gentle hand on his shoulder. He looked up at her with swimming eyes. "He's gone. My brother's gone. My God . . . what will mother say?"

She answered, "She'll say she was mighty glad you was here when it happened, suh. Nobody wants to go it alone. Now, please, let me he'p you. Let's be burying this good man so you can get back to headquarters and tell 'em what's happening in this wilderness."

The lieutenant wiped his eyes on his sleeve, smearing the soot into black streaks, and managed to suck in a breath. He sat motionless for another minute before he said, "I would appreciate your help, Private."

They dug the shallow grave in silence, Robin using her tin drinking cup while the lieutenant used his knife, both listening to the far-off cries of men too injured to run as the fires neared. The lieutenant broke into sobs occasionally, but never slowed his labor. The ground was so soft, it took no more than half an hour.

They lifted the colonel's body and eased it into the hole. As they shoved the dirt over him, Robin said, "Have you heard 'bout Gen'l Grant's plans for the morrow, suh? Is the gen'l going to tell us how to whip these Rebs?"

The lieutenant sank back on the old brown leaves as though exhausted. He ran a hand through his hair while he stared at the fresh grave. "Only God knows the answer to that, soldier. My brother told me he'd received some intelligence on troop movements late this afternoon, but not much. It's such a damned snarl out here."

"Yes, suh, that it is. But we must be winning some of the skirmishes . . . ain't we?" she asked anxiously.

"Oh, yes, we are. We are, son. We cut A. P. Hill's corps to ribbons today. I heard tell that those graybacks broke and ran like ticks thrown into a fire." He tried to smile, but it was a wan attempt. "We outnumbered Hill. He didn't have a chance against us. Hancock will be going in to finish him off at dawn tomorrow."

Robin wet her chapped lips. "That so? Hill seems mighty tricky to me. How's Hancock planning on routing him?"

The lieutenant shrugged. "I don't think even he knows for certain. John said something about how Hancock would be moving his men down the Orange Plank Road toward old Widow Tapp's farm. It's the only real clearing for miles. If it can be seized and held, Lee's right can be destroyed, and so will begin the destruction of his army."

Robin grinned. "That sound plenty good to me, suh. I don't like fighting these Rebs one bit. They got more lives than a barn cat."

"Yes, it seems they do, doesn't it?" The lieutenant met her eyes, then looked away.

Lifting her haversack, she slung it over her left shoulder. Firelight penetrated the tapestry of tree and brush and sent long ghostly fingers over the fresh mound of earth. The fingers advanced and pulled back, then advanced again, as though hesitant to touch the grave, but drawn by the scent of death. Her mother had believed that fire had a soul. On terrible nights like this,

Robin half-believed it herself—a greedy, ravenous soul that thrived on the screams and pungent blood. The flames would be here soon enough, and the thin sheath of soil they'd piled over John would not protect him from that hungry beast. At least he was dead. Dozens, perhaps hundreds, lay wounded and alone in the fire-bright darkness, and they would face the beast alive . . .

"Suh," Robin said, "I reckon we ought to be moving on. If you're up to it, suh?"

"Yes, I—I am," the lieutenant replied as he stroked the edges of the grave. The lines around his eyes had pulled tight. "Let's get started before—"

A storm of grapeshot ripped through the forest around them, mowing down saplings and cracking off thick boughs that pounded the earth like the footfalls of a giant. It lasted but a second.

But when it had ended, the lieutenant jumped to his feet, and glared wide-eyed. "Fire!" The shot had sparked off the rocks and started flames. "It's building fast. Get up, boy. Now!"

Frantically, the lieutenant ran northward, searching for a way around the fire, and Robin took the chance and sprinted in the opposite direction. She shouldered into a dense bramble of vines where warm shadows enveloped her. Quieting her breathing, she trained her ears on distinguishing footsteps from crackles of flame.

The young officer yelled, "Boy? Boy, are you all right? You coming, boy? Where are you? Boy . . . you—you hit?" His steps cracked in the dead twigs, going westward now. "Boy? . . . *Boy, the fire's spreading!*"

The wind fanned the flames into a large blaze, but when she leaned out of her shroud of vines she saw no one, nothing, except the fire licking hungrily through the underbrush, climbing tree trunks, singeing leaves. The young lieutenant was gone.

An icy chill settled in her stomach. She had to reach A. P. Hill tonight, to warn him about Hancock's attack plan. But had the mosaic of fires blocked the path she knew? She could not spend all night trying to veer around blazes—it would take too much time.

You're going to have to establish a heading and try to keep to it. Removing her compass, she took her bearings, figuring about where Hill should be encamped.

As she hurried along a narrow deer trail, she pulled off her kinky wig, unpinned her hair, and let the waist-length black wealth fall down her back. She stuffed the wig into her haversack and removed a pink flowered skirt that she slipped on over her blue pants. After rolling up and tying her coat around her waist, she looked like nothing more than a poor Negro slave girl from one of the nearby farms who'd gotten lost in the foray—though they'd think her half-white or half-Indian because of her straight hair and finely chiseled features.

No man worth the name would shoot a woman.

Unless, of course, he discovered her true identity. Then it would be a miracle if she lived long enough to be justly hanged.

She wiped her sweating palms on her skirt and slipped her revolver from its holster. A man might not shoot her, but she'd kill anyone who tried to stop her from reaching A. P. Hill before dawn.

As she broke into a run and headed down a steep incline, the pall of smoke grew thicker, swirling around her in great gleaming tufts. She picked up speed, racing so fast that she barely heard the agonized voices that flitted like elusive wings across the distances.

CHAPTER 2

It's *her!*" Major Thomas Corley stated for the tenth time. "I tell you, she's responsible. I know it."

Colonel George Sharpe, in charge of the Bureau of Military Information, formerly called the Secret Service, leaned forward and propped his elbows on his long oaken desk to examine the man before him. Brilliant September sunlight penetrated the window of his small, cramped office, and reflected in Corley's pale blue eyes; Corley squinted to fend it off. A single chair sat to Corley's left, the only piece of furniture in the room other than Sharpe's desk and chair. Though forty-two years old, Corley looked much younger, perhaps in his mid-thirties. What a giant of a man he was, a full six-feet-six-inches. The medals on his crisp blue uniform clinked as he adopted an at-ease posture. His curly red hair had been trimmed and looked neat and clean, as did the mustache that curved down around the corners of his grimly set mouth. Sharpe vented a frustrated breath. They'd been engaged in this fruitless discussion for more than an hour and he was sick of it.

"You don't know her the way I do!" Corley insisted. "I've studied her. I know how she thinks. She—"

"You're *obsessed* with that woman, Major," Sharpe replied. "Ever since your brother was killed at Ball's Bluff you've acted like a bloodhound, sniffing out every footprint that Mrs. Heatherton leaves—and plenty she hasn't left, I might add. You are *frequently* wrong about her escapades, Major."

Corley stiffened, but said nothing. The photographs arrayed on the walls outlined his massive shoulders. The pictures had been taken by Matthew Brady at the battles of Bull Run, Antietam, and Gettysburg. Many showed the white tents of encampments, others focused on blasted buildings, and a few documented the overwhelming horrors of war: Men sprawled hideously in death, wounded horses struggling to rise from blood-soaked ground.

"I am obsessed with her *capture,* Colonel, not the woman herself," Corley responded. "That is my duty as a provost marshal for this bureau, is it not? To locate, capture, and prosecute enemy spies?"

"That is correct, Major. But your diligence has taken on a hint of the macabre. You see Mrs. Heatherton behind every lost battle, every bit of leaked information, *every move made by the enemy."* Sharpe paused and gave Corley a stern look.

"You are unfair, sir. I—"

"We cannot risk being accused of Machiavellian tactics—not against a woman. Anti-war sentiment is increasing daily across the country. Our operations are already viewed with a good deal of loathing. It would be unwise at this time to generate more hostility."

"We also cannot afford to have enemy spies running freely through our ranks, Colonel. You forget the deaths—"

"I do *not* forget, Major."

Corley's jaw clenched. He turned to stare out the second-story window at the city of Washington. He appeared to be holding his tongue through sheer force of will.

Sharpe followed his gaze, giving them both a respite from this futile exchange. The newly finished dome on the capitol building shimmered in the pale autumn haze. It was cool for September, and the smoke from thousands of chimneys spiraled into the clear blue sky, leaving a thin band of dirty gray to trail over the buildings.

Sharpe considered the implications of Corley's suspicions. It was so difficult to take the man seriously. He couldn't count the number of times that Corley had burst into his office with similar stories about "that dangerous half-breed," Robin Walkingstick Heatherton, and all had proven impossible to verify. Sharpe believed the woman had died long ago, at the beginning of the war. Of course, if she had survived, she had extraordinary skills as a spy. Corley knew just how to pique Sharpe.

He returned his gaze to Corley. "But wasn't it you, Major, who assured me she was killed at the Battle of the Wilderness last May? Your information seemed quite reliable."

"I thought the body was hers," Corley admitted defensively. "I examined it myself. She was badly burned, but she had Heatherton's beauti . . . Indian facial features and wore the uniform of a Union private. Her haversack was filled with suspicious items, a scorched Negro wig, other things that she could have used to disguise herself. I assumed that she had infiltrated our lines, then been trapped by the fires that killed so many that night."

Corley peered down, and Sharpe had to force himself not to flinch. Corley had odd eyes. Piercing, focused only on death—eyes like a hunger-crazed predator's. There had been rumors that Corley used extraordinarily cruel tactics to gain information. Rape, torture, murder . . . Sharpe could never verify the stories; he had also never been able to dismiss, or forget, them. "But now—I'm certain I was wrong. She's alive, Colonel."

"Even if she is, what makes you think she's responsible for the Union's recent calamities?"

Corley took a deep breath, as though preparing himself for incredulity. "I . . . I can't tell you for certain. I just *feel* her here, in Virginia, and if you think that is macabre, maybe it is. I don't know! What I do know is that the defeat at Reams' Station was her doing, Colonel. Our forces were destroying the Weldon Railroad, south of Petersburg, when the Confederates took them by surprise. We suffered more than three times as many casualties as they. It's as though the enemy knew *exactly* where our men would be."

"But, really, Major, you have no evidence that Mrs. Heatherton—"

"I tell you, she's responsible!" Corley shouted. He lifted his huge hands and shook them as if to lessen his rage. "Listen to me. It's not just Reams' Station. During the three weeks prior to the Reams battle, the C.S.S. *Tallahassee* captured or destroyed thirty-one Federal ships. No naval commander could have known the positions of so many of our vessels, not without precise information as to their missions and whereabouts. *Someone* told the Confederacy where they'd be!"

Sharpe massaged the deep furrows that etched his forehead. He was accustomed to acting on circumstantial evidence—often that was all the Bureau had—but Corley had not provided one shred of real information linking Heatherton to the debacles. "Well if that someone was Mrs. Heatherton, she's been a very busy woman, Major. She must have sprouted wings to have been in so many places at once and—"

"Indeed, sir," Corley cut him off. "Sprouted wings and be flying unhindered through the highest circles in Washington. I believe that she has intimate contacts within the Senate of the United States. . . . Perhaps even in the War Department itself."

Sharpe's brows lowered. "Be specific, Major. *Who* are you accusing of treason? Give me names."

"As you wish, sir." Corley let his hands fall to his sides. "Senator Henry Wilson of Massachusetts, at least—and I have, for some time, wondered about Mrs. Heatherton's relationship with Secretary Stanton. I believe that she may have seduced—"

"The Secretary of War, Major? *You're accusing the Secretary of War of treason?*" In his rush to stand, Sharpe shoved his chair back so hard that it clattered against the rear wall of his office and overturned. He ignored it and stabbed a finger at Corley. "You are *never* to mention such a charge until you have evidence, Major! And as for Mr. Wilson—"

"*Mister Wilson,*" Corley shouted, his face livid now, "was most certainly Mrs. Rose O'Neal Greenhow's lover, and we know that Mrs. Greenhow and Mrs. Heatherton are cohorts in espionage! It is quite reasonable to assume that Mrs. Greenhow's contacts also work with Mrs. Heatherton!"

This part made sense. Sharpe continued glaring into Corley's pale eyes for a moment longer, then retrieved his chair, righted it, and dropped to the seat. Cold drafts whispered around the window and fluttered the papers on his desk. He leaned forward and straightened them. Senator Wilson had worked tirelessly for Mrs. Greenhow's 1862 release from Old Capitol prison, where she had been confined for treason, and Sharpe had one unreliable report in his files documenting a conversation between Wilson and Mrs. Heatherton in May of 1862, shortly before Mrs. Greenhow's release.

Sharpe said, "I will grant, Major, the possibility that the Senator is giving aid to our enemy, though I find no support for your idea that the transport of that aid is through Mrs. Heatherton. Are you suggesting that we assign a special agent to monitor the Senator's movements?"

"No, not Mr. Wilson himself, sir, but his contacts."

"Which contacts?"

Corley folded his arms and began to pace before Sharpe's desk. His medals glinted blindingly when he passed through the square of window light. "This morning I received word from one of our agents in Paris that Mrs. Greenhow is returning from Europe. As well, operatives in Liverpool have informed me that Commander James Bullock and Ambassador Mason, both staunch enemies of the Union, gave important documents to the admiral of the *Condor* to be given to Mrs. Greenhow. She—"

"Where is the *Condor* sailing from?"

"Scotland. Admiral Samuel Ridge in command."

"Samuel Ridge," Sharpe growled. Corley knew as well as he did that the admiral's real name was Augustus Charles Hobart-Hampden, hero of the Crimean War, awarded the Victoria Cross, and one of the highest ranking officers in the British Navy, not to mention a scoundrel.

Hobart-Hampden used a variety of aliases: Roberts, Hewett, and Gulick, as well as Ridge. The man had had an illustrious military career, which made his present Confederate blockade-running even more annoying. It was

Hobart-Hampden who, in 1854, had responded to Admiral Sir Charles Napier's challenge of "Lads, sharpen your cutlasses," by leading his troops aboard Russian battleships and to a glorious victory. Not only that, he personally had skippered Queen Victoria's yacht. A strange fellow, indeed—always at the center of adventure—and very adept at deceit. Fortunately, he delivered more corsets to the Confederacy than ammunition.

Corley said, "Mrs. Greenhow must be on that ship, Colonel, and we may assume that the documents she carries contain critical information that will not help our cause."

"Do we have information verifying her presence on the *Condor?*"

"No," Corley conceded.

"Then Hampden may deliver those documents to Mrs. Greenhow at any port between here and Scotland."

"Yes, that's possible, but I don't think so. I *know* she's on that vessel."

Sharpe just stared.

Corley spread his arms in a gesture that begged forbearance. "Well, if she is aboard, Colonel, we want to obtain those documents. Don't we?"

"Of course."

"No matter where else she makes port, the *Condor* will attempt to run the blockade into Wilmington. If we have agents there, we may be able to intercept those documents . . . and capture both the Senator and Mrs. Heatherton when they go to meet Mrs. Greenhow. Heatherton will be there. I guarantee it, sir, though I cannot say for certain about Senator Wilson."

"It's always Heatherton with you, isn't it, Major? Despite the terrifying prospect of a treasonous senator, or the contents of those documents, your real intent is still to capture Mrs. Heatherton."

Corley dropped his gaze, turned his back to Sharpe, then walked across the room to stand before one of the more gruesome photographs, a soldier with his chest ripped open, his musket across his knees, his canteen glinting in the grass nearby. Bull Run. Sharpe had hung that picture precisely to remind himself of the terrible realities of espionage. Sharpe pondered Corley's hidden message. It wasn't so hard to figure. The government suspected the flamboyant Mrs. Greenhow of conveying General McDowell's battle plans to the Confederacy on the eve of the Bull Run attack. That poor boy in the picture had died because of Mrs. Greenhow's treachery—and perhaps Mrs. Heatherton's as well. That Mrs. Heatherton was dangerous, if alive, would hardly be news.

"In the end, Colonel," Corley said, his eyes still riveted to the photograph, "discussions of Confederate espionage always return to Mrs. Heatherton. It is essential that we neutralize her as quickly as possible."

"Major, I want you to listen to me," Sharpe said through a long exhalation. He pushed a quill around his desk with his fingertip. "I will not have Mrs. Heatherton's body found in a backwoods swamp. If we capture her, she must be alive to stand trial for her crimes. I assume that you understand."

Corley strode back across the room and bent over Sharpe's desk. His lean face had a glow, as though his cheeks had been rouged by the exultation of victory. "I'll go to Wilmington myself, Colonel. I'll only need a few men, four or five."

There were so many "ifs." If Greenhow was aboard the *Condor,* and if Corley could get to her, and if he could intercept the critical documents she carried, and if Wilson or Heatherton came to meet Mrs. Greenhow . . . On the other hand, if any of those things could be accomplished, it would be quite a feather in the cap of the Bureau of Military Information.

"I would like a straight answer from you, Major, before I approve this mission. Do you understand that you are not to assassinate Mrs. Heatherton under any circumstances? I cannot tell you how much scorn would be heaped upon this—"

"I won't kill her," Corley promised, but his face remained eager, alert as a cat with prey in sight.

"And what are your plans, Major, if none of those people are where you expect them to be?"

Corley's mouth pursed, as though such a thing were impossible. He clasped his hands behind his back. "If they have not arrived in Wilmington in one month, I will return to Washington at once. But if I receive information that suggests they have been there, and we have missed them, I would like authorization to hunt them down."

"Five men for a full month? We cannot possibly spare so many."

"Just one, then. I must have an aide. Surely that won't cripple the Department."

"I'll assign Cyrus to accompany you. But if you cannot apprehend the criminals in the act of espionage, pursuing them will be a useless waste of manpower. We'll never be able to create a case against them."

"I understand your hesitation to commit two men for so long a time," Corley said hastily. "But if we can apprehend any of these spies we might be able to wring vital information from them. I really believe—"

"Yes," Sharpe granted. "I know you do."

"I won't need Cyrus to accompany me if I am forced to pursue. I'll send him back and I'll go on alone."

Sharpe's gut instincts told him he was just about to authorize another pointless escapade, but if Greenhow, Wilson, or Heatherton arrived with critical information, he *did* want it.

"Just make certain that Mrs. Greenhow's *documents* are your first priority, Major. Your second priority is the senator, and Heatherton's capture your last. I won't have it said that this Bureau specializes in harassing women. We gleaned quite enough trouble for ourselves when we locked up Mrs. Greenhow and her female cohorts in Old Capitol Prison."

"Begging your pardon, sir, but we are in this business to save the lives of our own troops, are we not? If my duties force me to harass—"

"Any injustices that you commit or allow to be committed by men under your command will bring dishonor to this bureau, and I will not have it, Corley! Do you understand me?"

Corley came to attention, his back straight, eyes focused on the wall behind Sharpe. "Justice is always my highest goal, sir."

Sharpe wondered at the cool irony in that deep voice, but he motioned toward the door. "Get to Wilmington, Major. I'll expect weekly progress reports."

"You will have them, sir."

Lieutenant Jonas Cyrus sat on the shores of the Potomac with his arms around his knees. He was a tall, slender man with sandy blond hair and a closely trimmed beard. Today he dressed as a civilian, wearing a black shirt and pants, with a cream-colored kerchief around his throat. Major Corley knelt beside him, in full uniform; in a blazing grove of maple trees; he was staring unblinking at the muddy current before them. Ball's Bluff rose steeply on the opposite side of the river. In between sat Harrison's Island, small and wooded. A mottled blanket of gold, crimson, and pale green leaves sprinkled the hills. The Major had his hands clasped, and looked very much like a reverent giant, praying for redemption. In the brilliant glare of sunlight off the water, his red hair and mustache gleamed brassy. The light made the freckles on his lean face appear large and red. Jonas maintained silence. He did not know what to make of this strange "visitation" ritual. He'd heard from other secret service operatives that Corley came here frequently, but he'd never personally witnessed the event. Fortunately, those men had briefed him on what to expect.

Corley stirred. "Do you know how it happened?" he asked.

"You mean the battle here, sir? Not exactly. No."

The air left Corley's lungs in a painfully slow exhalation. "It was late October. Brigadier General Charles P. Stone commanded our forces here in Maryland. Old Joe Johnston was across the river. Stone forced the engagement . . ." Corley's eyes widened as if seeing it all again. "Stone sent his men across in three small boats, each with a capacity of twenty-five. By dawn, he had one regiment—six hundred men—on Harrison's Island. The men finished the crossing and took a meandering cow trail up the face of the bluff. They heard the Confederate rifle fire. They knew what they'd face when they crested the bluff. By midday, we had a total of four Union regiments on the field of battle. The Rebels held all the high ground." He turned to give Jonas an eerie, almost inhuman, smile. "Johnston had been warned that we were coming. He knew *exactly* where we would ascend the bluff, how many men we would have, and the time of day we would attack."

"Mrs. Heatherton?" Jonas pretended not to know the answer, though Corley had been talking of nothing else the past two days while they readied for this mission.

Corley nodded solemnly. "When the Confederates charged, and pushed our men back, we had only those three small boats to handle our retreat. Our forces panicked. Those who had huddled on the top of the bluff began to break and run. I watched them." His voice became a hoarse whisper. "They leaped, and rolled, and tumbled over the cliff, falling onto the soldiers massing before the boats below. Many died on the bayonets of their friends. Their screams were terrible." He shook his head. "The graybacks whooped as they flopped on their bellies on top of the bluff and poured fire into those boats. They kept firing and yelling like wild Indians."

A pause. Corley's thin-lipped mouth clamped tight.

"Your brother was there wasn't he?"

"Yes. Michael. My brother Michael." Corley bowed his head and picked up a brown autumn leaf, twirling it in his fingers. "When we were little my father used to beat us—beat us badly, with his fists or a buggy whip, often with an iron poker—I still have scars across my back and legs. I used to call Michael 'the Archangel,' because he always jumped in the middle and tried to protect me. Even though he knew my father would turn his wrath on him. Yes, I loved Michael very much."

"I'm sorry," Jonas said. "We've all lost so many precious relatives in this war. How did your brother die? On the bluff? Or trying to cross in the boats?"

"Neither. He . . ." Corley took a breath. "He panicked and dove into the river, to swim across with a hundred other men. It was like a turkey shoot for the Confederates. The river water turned a frothy white from all the bullets that struck it. Reb losses were negligible, but we lost over one thousand men." Corley cocked his head and stared at Jonas. "I watched my brother go down. I saw him struck in the back, watched the water boil up red around him while he struggled. Then, he drowned."

"My Lord," Cyrus said, "it must have been terrible."

"The worst part was that when I looked up, I . . . I saw her, Cyrus. *I saw her.*"

"Who? Mrs. Heatherton? She was here?"

"Oh, yes." Corley extended his arm and pointed. "She stood by that big rock on top of the bluff. She was dressed in a thigh-length gray sack coat and wore a medium-brimmed planter's hat, but a tress of long straight black hair had fallen out and hung down to her hips. She looked *magnificent,* Cyrus. Almost . . . glorious. With that hair blowing in the wind."

The awe in Corley's voice made Jonas frown. "But, sir, if she was responsible for the deaths of so many—"

"She was. Mrs. Heatherton and Mrs. Greenhow worked together here. I'm quite certain they seduced General Stone and that Washington journalist. What was his name? Malcolm Ives, I think."

"*Seduced,* sir? But I thought both women were ladies in the finest sense—"

Corley stood up to loom over Jonas, clenching and unclenching his huge fists. "Mrs. Heatherton is a common *whore,* Lieutenant, nothing more and nothing less, and she deserves to be treated as such. Indeed, I have heard intimate descriptions of the techniques she employs to get information from men. They are *all* devilish, Cyrus. She will perform acts that are not even conceivable to most men." His blue eyes took on a fiery glow. "I swear," he said in a hushed voice. "I often wonder if she is truly human, or a demon succubus sent to drain away men's souls."

Fascinated, Cyrus asked, "What kind of techniques? I mean, I—I have heard of such things, but I—"

Corley gazed down at Jonas sternly. "Do not *ever* ask me about such things again. Do you understand me?"

"But, sir!" Jonas protested. "I was inquiring out of curiosity." Corley brooded as if Jonas' question had intruded upon some private fantasy. Jonas said, "I apologize sincerely. I meant no disrespect!"

Corley looked away.

When Jonas had gathered enough courage, he asked, "Do you . . . do you dream of her, sir? I mean, she is supposed to be a very beautiful woman. I could understand—"

"Yes, Lieutenant," Corley responded as he slowly turned to face Jonas again. "In the dream, I have my hands around her throat. I'm choking the life out of her."

CHAPTER 3

The setting sun washed the ocean with crimson light. Glittering and twinkling, it flashed in the lens of Robin's field glass. She backed away and rubbed her eyes. Anxiety had long ago soured to urgency in her belly—but she did not know why. Except that something was not right. The world had gone too quiet, as though holding its breath in fear. She'd been jumping at every sound—birds chirping, dogs barking. The sudden creaking of wind-blown trees had sent her scrambling for her pistol so often that the grip had grown slick with sweat, even in the chill air.

"There's nobody watching you, Robin," she whispered to herself. "You're alone out here. Stop this foolishness."

For weeks she had been wrestling with the sensation that she was balancing on a silken strand over a precipice and that just below was utter darkness and despair. It was more than the war. More than the constant desperation. This sense of coming catastrophe had a strange sanctity to it, an otherworldliness, as if God Himself were warning her about the end of the world so that she could prepare herself for Judgment Day.

With great care, she scanned the beach, then reached beneath her gray cape and pulled out the hem of her blue homespun shirt to clean the lens. Mounted in the low fork of a gigantic coastal pine, the field glass had remained steady even in the strong winds that had swept the beach last night.

The Condor *will be here soon enough. Tonight, probably. Then you can go home.*

Puffs of cloud scudded across the pink sky. Robin studied them as she drew a piece of dried beef from her haversack and tore off a chunk with her teeth. It felt like desiccated hide in her mouth. She had to chew hard to work any flavor from it, but she needed the strength it would give. She'd been shivering off and on for hours. Her dirty cape, a relic from the early days of the war, was threadbare and mended in over a dozen places. It provided almost no shield from the cold. At least her new skirmish cap kept her head warm—and hid her long hair.

A half mile up the coast, Fort Fisher nestled in a series of treeless, man-made mounds. She could see soldiers moving outside, making preparations for unloading the *Condor*'s badly needed cargo.

"I'm here, Rose, just as you asked. Hurry. Please hurry."

She settled back against the hillside and bit off another chunk of beef. Once before, when she'd been a little girl of nine or ten, she'd felt this sort of inexplicable panic. She'd sneaked out of the house and gone into the dark forest to talk to the owls, as her mother had taught her to do when she was troubled. As she sat among the trees a strange terror had possessed her. Invisible presences had stirred the woods, and after several long moments, the faint howling of wolves had come to her on the cold night wind. When the animals broke into a full chorus, Robin had ran screaming back into the house.

Her mother had laughed. "My silly girl, your soul just heard the wolves before your ears did, that's all. You will learn that there are many things your soul sees and hears long before your body does. If you understand that, and listen very carefully, your soul can warn you before bad things happen."

But why would her soul be screaming at her here, now? The pale scarlet gleam of sunset sheathed the sea and sand, and transformed the sky into a shimmering carnelian bowl that arched into infinity over her head. Yet her shoulder muscles remained clenched.

"You're just tired," she murmured. "Tired and frightened."

Yes, that was it. Fear had been gnawing at her belly for so long she couldn't think straight anymore. She hadn't been home in seven months and the uncertainty about her family had become desperation. She *needed* to know the fates of her son and husband. Had Jeremy been killed in the siege? And what of Charles? Was he still in Tennessee with Forrest? Alive?

Every night she lived their deaths And every day she woke with the terrible fear that Jeremy's childish laughter might be gone, that Charles might have been torn to pieces by a shell and she would never even be able to find his body—that all her dreams might be dead.

She dared not think too much about those dreams, or the terrible ache for her family would sap her will to fight. Death and mutilation were not the real horrors of war. Human beings knew and understood such costs. They even ignored the brutality after a time. But the loneliness . . . dear God, nothing could lessen its pain.

Spies never spent enough time in any one camp to develop friendships. They were always moving, gathering information and riding off to report their discoveries. Especially female spies. A woman could not spend much time with any particular division, lest she be found out, so she had no cushion for the loneliness, not even brief reprieves. After a time, she felt as hollow and rotten as an old log.

Only another day or two. That's all. After I talk to Rose, I'll head home. Home for Christmas.

She forced herself to think of that. *Christmas. Remember how it was? Try to remember. Try . . .*

It took effort to bring up those images. They were buried beneath so many memories of tragedy and horror. She struggled until she found them.

Charles' mother, old Mrs. Heatherton, always decorated her house's broad veranda with pine garlands and mistletoe. Red velvet ribbons wrapped the banister of the curving staircase that led upstairs. A crystal punch bowl of mulled scuppernong wine sat on the serving table near the roaring fireplace, and from the kitchen aromas of roasting pork and mutton wafted to fill the entire house.

Robin found herself smiling, managing to shove away the certain knowledge that such luxuries would not exist this year, could not exist when Grant had a stranglehold on Richmond and people lacked even the most basic of supplies, flour, salt, needles, and thread . . . Still, the spicy fragrances of sassafras tea and sweet potato pie taunted her just as vividly as if she smelled them now.

Out of the depths of those cherished scents came Charles' soft voice: *"The end is coming. Nothing in the world can stop it. You know it as well as I, Robin. The South is dead. We'll have to leave."*

Last Christmas. He'd been standing by the small fieldstone fireplace in their bedroom, dressed in his blue satin jacket, his blond hair shining in the soft glow.

"But where will we go, Charles?"

"I . . . I don't know. But there must be a place that hasn't yet been ruined by the war. Perhaps Colorado or New Mexico Territory. We could start a little business, maybe raise a few cows, or farm some cotton. I love you so much, Robin."

Robin drew her knees up inside her cape and tucked the tattered edges around her black boots. Visions of the western territories, of jagged peaks piercing the clouds, rose in her mind. She had drawn up such soothing images a thousand times, but tonight they only left her feeling empty and, if possible, even more exhausted.

As evening changed to night, the surface of the ocean turned into a sparkling interplay of indigo and the palest of blues. She swiveled her head to peer at the trees behind her. Oaks, willows, and pond pines created a smoky mosaic. Two birds chirped back and forth.

There's nothing there, Robin. Nothing at all.

But a shiver played along her arms and forced her to rub them before it would go away. Hesitantly, she gazed back at the sand and waves. Purple clouds were boiling up on the eastern horizon, sprouting enormous anvil-shaped thunderheads. It looked like a storm brewing.

Hurry, Rose. Please, hurry.

The ship rocked so violently beneath Admiral Augustus Hobart-Hampden's feet that he had to grip the railing surrounding the ship's wheel. Brown hair straggled around his oval face, sticking to his high forehead. On nights such as this not even his oiled canvas coat could protect him. Rain blew into his hood and trickled down his chest, drenching his wool shirt and pants.

"Where *are* they? Blast them! I know they're out there."

"I don't see anything, Admiral," Jonathan Riggs said. The skinny pilot of the *Condor* was staring into dark storm. He had to fight the wheel to keep the ship on course.

Impatiently, Hobart-Hampden answered, "Nor will you, Riggs, until they are upon us and ready to fire. But make no mistake, we are being followed. I think they spotted us when we entered New Inlet."

"Well, if they did, the *Condor* can handle them, sir."

The *Condor* was a new three-hundred ton, schooner-rigged steamer with three low funnels, a long narrow beam and two short masts. She had been manufactured in Glasgow and painted a dull gray. Because she drew only seven feet of water she could traverse almost any channel and sailed with the swiftness of a sea swallow. What she couldn't outmaneuver, she should be able to outrun. But this was her maiden voyage and not even Hobart-Hampden knew exactly what she could or could not do.

He removed his spyglass from his inside coat pocket and panned the seas in a hundred-and-eighty-degree arc, trying to sight Fort Fisher. The last port of the Confederacy could not have been more than a few hundred yards distant, but Hobart-Hampden saw nothing. Angrily, he murmured, "Where's the signal light? Has the whole damned world gone dark?"

Early in the war, the Confederacy had destroyed all other aids to navigation along the coast, hoping to blind the Union, but Wilmington was vital to the survival of Lee's starving army. Fort Fisher had constructed a great mound from which to signal blockade runners . . . yet no light shone tonight. Or none that he could see.

Hobart-Hampden lowered his glass and cursed himself. He had deliberately delayed his passengers in Halifax, waiting for the moon to wane, and the drenching rain had helped tonight to cloak the coastline. While his passengers slept below deck, his forty-five-man crew rushed through their duties, though many stole moments to seek a glimpse of their sanctuary.

"Where is that fort?" Hobart-Hampden demanded of Riggs. "Do you see anything, Jonathan, or hear anything?"

"No, Admiral, nothing but the thunder, the crashing of the waves and creaking of the *Condor*."

"Fort Fisher must be out there."

"Maybe the commandant, Colonel William Lamb, got word that a Federal ship was coming and damped the lanterns."

"Nonsense! They knew we were coming, too."

The Confederacy desperately needed the cargo of pork, beef, bacon, sugar, peas, and onions that he had picked up in Bermuda. The South's agents in Europe had told him that it was hand-to-mouth now, that General Robert E. Lee spent sleepless nights wondering if his men would have food in their stomachs the next day. Not that Hobart-Hampden cared much about that. He had little sympathy for either side. What he cared about was the extraordinary wealth that came from running the blockade. At sixty pounds sterling per ton, plus the expensive commissions and insurance, a man could be rich after just a few trips. Of course, that was if he lived. The Union worked tirelessly to keep men like Hobart-Hampden poor.

Riggs used the back of his hand to wipe his wet brow. "The rain's so thick, Admiral . . . do you think the fort could be signaling us and we'd never know it?"

"It's possible."

Hobart-Hampden lifted his spyglass again. A gossamer blanket filled his view, sparkling as though the storm gave a supernatural life to the night. He felt that "life" in the pit of his stomach, lying there like a coiled serpent, ready to strike.

Over a hundred gulls perched on the masts, their gray feathers slick with rain, heads tucked beneath their wings. Every so often a flurry of wings or chirps would sound, relieving the tension a bit.

Lightning flashed and one of his crew yelled, *"Look! A ship!"*

"Where?" Hobart-Hampden shouted. "Where are they, sailor?"

Jonathan gasped, "O, my Lord Admiral, there! See them? . . . No, sir, not that direction! In front of us!"

Hobart-Hampden had turned aft, expecting to glimpse his pursuers at last, and had to swing back around to see what Riggs pointed at. From the west, a dark hulk swayed out of the storm.

"We're going to collide!" Hobart-Hampden yelled. "Evade her, pilot! Change course before we—"

Riggs cranked the wheel, and the steamer strained and rocked, throwing Hobart-Hampden to the deck where he tumbled across the wet surface until he slammed into one of the masts. Hoarse screams erupted, as if the sailors could see something Hobart-Hampden couldn't. They pointed to the south, and he lifted his head, searching the stormy oceans for more than just the ship to the west, but what . . . !

The shivering crash took him by surprise, ripping the mast from his hands as the *Condor* ran aground with a wrenching metallic whine.

He watched two men tumble overboard into the roiling black waters. "Riggs!" he shouted. "Throw out some lines! Be fast, man! Get those sailors back aboard!"

Riggs' feet thudded across the slick deck.

Hobart-Hampden searched the darkness for the ship he'd seen and found it. Right in front of them, no more than a hundred feet away. Another flare of lightning revealed it as the burned-out skeleton of an old blockade runner. Hobart-Hampden let out a taut breath. She sat canted at an angle, her charred masts thrusting eerily into the sky. Had she been forced aground, then boarded by Federal troops and set afire? Or had she just run aground as they had, and the captain been forced to fire his own ship to prevent the cargo from falling into Union hands?

He pulled himself to his feet; shook the water out of his sleeves, and turned to survey his ship. Lanterns flared to life here and there as men lowered them over the side to find their shouting companions. A wavering yellow gleam flooded the deck. The *Condor* tilted to the port, but not badly. The next tide would free her. Hobart-Hampden walked toward Riggs, who knelt in a crowd of men on the starboard side.

"Jonathan? How many are overboard?" he shouted against the storm as he knelt down and peered into the black abyss below. Pale specks bobbed and vanished.

Riggs' lean face had gone pallid. "I counted seven, sir, but there may be more. Look at them out there!" The waves were so huge they were being tossed about like rag dolls. "It's hard to even make them out. It's going to be devilish trying to bring them back aboard, too. How will they ever swim close enough to grab onto one of our lines?"

"Shall we lower the lifeboats? Perhaps they could grab onto the hulls—"

Riggs shook his head. "I wouldn't, sir. Even if the men could get to the boats, they'd be dashed to bits against the *Condor* before we could haul a single man aboard."

Hobart-Hampden got to his feet and squinted out toward the coast while he racked his brain to devise another method . . .

He heard it before he saw it—an intermittent splashing, giving a different cadence to the roar of the storm and sea.

He whirled around, and saw the ship coming toward them like a great whale riding the waves. The bow bore the name *Niphon.* Hobart-Hampden whispered, "Great God . . ." Then his voice exploded: "*Man the guns!* Where are our gunners? Riggs? We're dead if we don't—"

The *Niphon*'s rockets flared in the darkness and shells landed all around the *Condor,* sending up great fountains of water. Hobart-Hampden threw up his arms to shield his face.

"Blessed God! Can't we even get one gunner into position? *Where's Davies? Davies? Davies are you on board?*" When no answer came, Hobart-Hampden leaped for the closest gun himself.

The Confederate batteries at Fort Fisher, not more than two hundred yards distant, opened fire.

Hobart-Hampden threw himself to the deck again, terror mixing sickeningly with relief. Another volley let go, whining through the storm. He squinted into the gloom, fighting to see if the barrage had damaged the Union ship. No flames lit the night.

"*Admiral?*"

"What? Who called to me?" He raised himself on his elbows and looked around.

From across the deck a slender figure glided toward him, tall and willowy, a shawl pulled over her head. Hooked to a chain around her neck, a heavy leather reticule hung. Everyone on board assumed that the reticule contained the proceeds from her *Memoirs,* which she had published in Europe, though no one knew for certain. In her right hand, she carried the dispatch bag from Ambassador Mason and Commander Bulloch. She had clutched that bag for the entire journey; even at dinner she ate with it propped in her lap.

"Mrs. Greenhow!" Hobart-Hampden ordered, "Get down!"

She disobeyed, as usual, and kept coming. She knelt before him, her regal face calm. Gray-streaked black hair fell around her cheeks. She had to be over fifty, but no man could see her age when he gazed into those magnetic shining eyes.

She shouted over the yells of panicked sailors and the roar of the storm. "It is imperative that I get to shore, Admiral!"

The *Condor* shifted, reeling sideways as the waves caught her bow, and massive swells of white surf rolled over the deck. Mrs. Greenhow let out a cry of shock as she was knocked backward. Hobart-Hampden dove forward and grabbed her arm to keep her from washing overboard. The action brought them face-to-face, their noses no more than five inches apart. "Mrs. Greenhow, get below deck! I cannot protect you if you insist—"

"I will not, sir!" she yelled in response. "I cannot! I must get to shore. Give me a boat and an escort! You know my role in the Confederacy. I *must* reach Wilmington. There is someone waiting for me, and the news I bring!" She swung around to stare over her shoulder at the bulk of the *Niphon* and dread tensed her beautiful face. She scrambled to her feet and looked down at him with wild eyes. "Get up, Admiral. Get up and order someone to take me ashore. I cannot allow myself to be captured!"

Hobart-Hampden rose to his feet and stood before her stunned. Was she not afraid of drowning? "Madame, look around you. The waves are monstrous! You wouldn't make it ten yards before your boat overturned!"

"I must try, Admiral. *Please help me!*"

In the swaying light of the lanterns, she looked like a statue carved from pale ivory. Hobart-Hampden straightened to his full six feet and shouted, "I cannot, Madame! I will not be the cause of your death. Who is it that waits for you on shore? I will send a message—"

"That is impossible. My 'little bird' will meet with no one but me."

"But Mrs. Greenhow, you must realize that I cannot—"

"I do not realize it, sir!" She slipped the handle of the dispatch bag over her arm and used both hands to pull the soaked shawl more closely about her face. "If you will not grant me a boat, Admiral, I will dive overboard and swim to shore, and when I get there, I will inform President Davis that you refused to render me aid, even knowing that the information I carry is vital to the survival—"

"*Please,* Mrs. Greenhow! I know you spent many months in a northern prison. If you are frightened of being sent back, I assure you we will be quite safe! See for yourself, the *Niphon* is backing off. The guns of Fort Fisher are too much for her. She—"

Mrs. Greenhow turned in a whirl of flowered shawl and stalked across the deck toward the lifeboats. She had squared her narrow shoulders as if to carry a great burden.

"Wait! Mrs. Greenhow, I refuse to let you to risk your life. Wait!"

He rushed after her, pushing through his frightened men, but by the time he had reached her side, she had begun untying the tethers of a lifeboat. "This is madness!" he shouted at her, and grabbed her hands to halt them. "I order you to stop this instant!"

She jerked her hands away. "I am not one of your crew, Admiral! I do not *take* your orders!"

Fort Fisher's batteries thundered again, lighting the stormy heavens scarlet. The *Niphon* returned fire. Mrs. Greenhow glanced up, set her jaw in determination, and shoved Hobart-Hampden aside to resume laboring at a knot.

"Mrs. Greenhow! You are the most stubborn, strong-willed—"

"And you, sir, are a coward," she retorted. Then with a tremor in her voice, she turned and said, "My government and I have both placed the utmost confidence in you, Admiral. I would never have believed you capable of such low cruelty, and to a woman in such desperate need!"

"But, surely you must understand—"

"What I understand, Admiral, is that you refuse to help me. Since that is the case, get out of my way." She rose to her feet. "It seems I must take matters into my own hands. I *must* get to shore! You do not know the grave nature of the documents I carry!"

Hobart-Hampden seized her by the sleeve and held her fast. Her eyes were pleading, if defiant, and they shamed him. "No. No . . . wait," he found himself saying to his own surprise. "If you insist upon endangering yourself, let me send some strong men with you." He turned and waved to Riggs. "Pilot! Mrs. Greenhow has urgent business in Wilmington. You will escort her to shore. Select a man to accompany you."

Jonathan gaped for a few seconds, then fought the cant of the ship across the deck to Hobart-Hampden. His eyes had gone huge. "But, Admiral, look at those waves! The lifeboat is too small to stay afloat. She'll be swamped before we—"

"*I gave you an order, mister! Pick a man and escort Mrs. Greenhow to shore!*"

Riggs saluted and backed away. He cupped a hand to his mouth to call: "Mister Loden? We're going ashore!"

Loden ran to the lifeboat, casting terrified looks at Hobart-Hampden, clearly longing for the admiral to overrule Jonathan's insane order. When he did not, they lowered the boat to the water, unrolled the ladder and descended. The tiny craft pitched back and forth like a twig in a hurricane.

"Forgive me, Admiral," Mrs. Greenhow said as she clutched the dispatch bag and set her foot on the first rung of the ladder. "I apologize. You are a gentleman, after all."

"I pray that you live to say that to me again, Mrs. Greenhow!"

She smiled and climbed down the ladder to sit in the bow of the lifeboat. Another passenger, named Holcombe, and his personal attendant, a lieutenant, shouldered past Hobart-Hampden. Holcombe had boarded at Halifax and had spent a good deal of time with Mrs. Greenhow. Was he a spy, too? Probably.

Holcombe said simply, "We're going ashore as well," before he and his aide joined the two sailors and the dauntless Mrs. Greenhow.

Hobart-Hampden yelled after them: "You go at your own perils! I will not take responsibility for this insanity! Do you hear me? I will not!"

Mrs. Greenhow lifted a hand in farewell, then used it grip the side of the boat.

The tiny craft set off, Riggs and Loden rowing for all they were worth, trying to control the boat as it shot straight up on the crest of a wave, then plunged nose-down like an arrow.

They had gone no more than fifty feet when a massive wave struck them broadside and flipped the craft over. A hoarse cry tore from Hobart-Hampden's throat as he watched Mrs. Greenhow flung headfirst into the water. She vanished into the waves, while the men screamed and thrashed about, grabbing for the keel of the capsized boat.

Hobart-Hampden ran to the rail to peer down into the thundering breakers, searching for Mrs. Greenhow. He saw only her shawl, twisting in the current. He screamed, "Where's Mrs.Greenhow? Do you see her? *Does anyone see her?*"

It took an hour for the storm to lessen so that they could bring in Holcombe, Riggs, and the other sailors who'd been washed overboard. They sprawled on the deck, gasping and staring at the pink gleam of dawn that seeped through the cloudy sky. A fine cold mist still fell.

Hobart-Hampden stayed on the bow, his spyglass up. Far away, near the shore, he thought he saw two brown spots bobbing in a swirl of sea foam. The lieutenant and Mrs. Greenhow? "Precious Jesus, let it be so. And let them be alive."

*　*　*

Robin yawned and inhaled a deep breath of the cool, sea-scented wind. A luminescent pink had taken possession of the water and sky, glittering, flashing in the wings of diving birds. She had waited up all night, praying the *Condor* would survive the battle. The ship still tilted on the shoals, her masts silhouetted against the gleam of dawn, but the tide had started to come in. In an hour or two, if Union ships did not return to finish the work they'd started last night, she would make port.

Amid the fragrances of salt and seaweed, Robin smelled the bread being cooked at Fort Fisher. Her empty stomach growled. She couldn't recall how long it had been since she'd had a healthy plate of ham and eggs. Just a single buttermilk biscuit would be heavenly. The daily fare of the soldier left a good deal to be desired, and even that had been growing worse as the war progressed. In the beginning, they'd had pork and beef, oysters and sweet potatoes, hominy, fresh vegetables on occasion, griddle cakes made of corn and pumpkin, sugar, salt, and coffee—blessed coffee, how she missed it. The last camp where she'd taken meals with the men had been pitiful. They were surviving on a handful of parched corn a day, that and what they could scavenge from the knapsacks of dead Yankees.

The sudden squealing of gulls drew Robin's attention. A large flock had gathered into a swarm down the shore. Fluttering their wings, the birds lunged at each other to protect whatever prize they'd found. She rubbed her bleary eyes.

What are the gulls up to?

Curious, Robin lifted her field glass from the fork in the tree and focused on the flock. Brown showed through the tapestry of feathers, half in the water, half out. Something washed overboard in the storm last night? From the *Condor?* or the Yankee vessel?

She couldn't risk being out in the open for long, but . . .

Tucking her field glass into her haversack, she went to investigate. Cool sand welled up around her boots as she walked, eating at her weary muscles. When the gulls saw her coming, they squawked their dismay. Waves pushed and sucked at the brown object, and something about the heavy way the fabric moved made Robin's heart pound. By the time realization had dawned, she was running.

"Get away! Go on! Goddamn you, get away from her!"

The birds burst upward in a confused whir of wings. She could see the body clearly now. Long gray-streaked black hair flowed out across the sand, mixed with dark fans of seaweed. A slender arm curved over the head, tugged by the weight of a satchel that seemed shackled to the wrist.

Robin raced through the icy surf, gasping, tripping. "Oh, no. God, no . . . how did this happen?" She gripped her friend beneath the arms, and pulled her up onto the beach.

Tears constricted Robin's throat as she fell forward, placing her ear over Rose's heart to listen for a pulse or to feel the rise and fall of her chest. "Oh, Rose, please. Don't do this to me!"

Robin grabbed a hand and pressed the nail of the index finger. The blood retreated and did not return.

"No. No, I—I can't believe this," she whispered as she slumped backward to the sand. Surf washed over her boots and soaked her pant legs. She shook her head, too stunned to feel. Rose must have tried to make it to shore . . .

The very thought made her ill. Rose was no fool. If she had waited a few hours, none of this would have happened. Why hadn't she?

Her gaze fixed on the satchel. She reached over the body and pulled the bag from Rose's stiffening arm. Filled with water, it felt like lead. "How did you manage to keep holding it, Rose?"

She must have fought the sea for as long as she could, trying to swim with the bag weighing down her wrist, then she'd gone under. "Faithful to the last."

Robin opened and tipped the bag to drain it. A single oilcloth bundle spilled out with the torrent of water.

Robin threw the empty bag into the waves and unlaced the cloth. Five damp letters nestled inside. She sorted through them. Each envelope had the words, "Strictly Confidential," scrawled across the top, then below it, "For President Jefferson Davis' eyes only!"

As she shoved the letters down the front of her shirt, into the bandage that wrapped her breasts, she noticed a man on the beach to the south. He was so far away she could make out little about him, except that he was dressed in butternut trousers and a red shirt, and he walked with his head down. He had not seen her yet. At least, she didn't think he had.

Robin brushed hair away from her friend's cold cheeks. "Oh, Rose, why didn't you wait? Our side needed you alive. I—I needed you. I have so few friends left . . ."

She straightened, and strode toward the cover of the pines. Robin would make certain that Rose's efforts had not been in vain. The letters would arrive at their intended destination. It took fifteen minutes to climb to a safe position where she could overlook the beach to see the man. He was very tall. Red-headed. He had stopped beside Rose's body and was in the process of ripping open the front of her brown dress. He thrust his hand down her corset between her breasts, tore off her shoes to look inside, then ripped away her water-logged skirts.

Hunting for hidden papers . . . or just money?

It didn't matter. She could do nothing, not now. She had a long way to go, and then she had to figure out a way through the massive, complicated defensive lines surrounding Petersburg, and get into Richmond to find Jefferson Davis.

Even while her mind began to take up this new challenge, her heart could not, and when she turned her back on her friend and walked away, a sudden sharp thudding, like a hammer striking a rock, began in her chest. It pounded its way up her veins into her brain, and relentlessly, methodically, killed any thoughts other than the terrible fact that her friend was dead.

CHAPTER 4

It is so cold here in this bombed-out husk of a house that I can't stop trembling. Wounded beams dangle over my head, wrapped in soft tendrils of gauzy white mist. I stare at the silvered blur of night beyond. I can't go back to sleep. And I need to—desperately. Tomorrow I must try to penetrate the Federal defensive lines south of Petersburg. But I have been glancing up at the beams since I woke, sensing something . . . as if those shattered pieces of wood were alive and reaching for me with death's own fingers.

A fox sits in the corner. She has moonlight eyes. She has killed a field mouse, but eats it watching me. Other small animals scurry with devilish quiet through the mounds of debris on the floor.

I pull my cloak more tightly around me.

Why can't I weep? My friend is gone . . .

Yet my eyes can find no tears. It is as if my heart has gone dry. Arid as the desert. Thirsty. I have never faced this trial before. Needing to cry and finding my soul too barren to give the emotion a voice.

My mother could cry. I remember those tears. They came most often when she was telling me stories about the tragic burdens of womanhood: The loneliness caused when men went away to war, children born and buried in their fathers' absences, starvation so near and terrible that mothers winnowed horse dung for seeds to feed their children.

But my God, my God, at least she could cry. Women can cry . . .

So, why can't I? What have I become?

I no longer know.

I feel as if I have been somehow stripped of my womanhood, as if God is punishing me by denying me the possibility to redeem myself through my own internal baptismal waters.

Is that why the dream comes? I am always running . . . Has God condemned me to wander forever in a nightmare world of raging battles, fires, and the deafening blasts of cannon? A world where the screams never end . . .

I brace my forehead on my drawn-up knees. The fox has finished her mouse. Now that I am not watching, she bounds through the wreckage and is gone. As though in response, mist descends like a thick white veil, clinging to the walls, twining around me in a shimmering icy blanket.

Rose, oh Rose, did you go through this? You, or Nancy Hart, or Belle Boyd? Please tell me I am not alone—that there are others who have gone before me through this dark night of the soul. . . . Tell me that God still forgives.

Robin sat at the edge of a Negro camp, dozing, her back propped against the pole of a frail open-sided shelter; it consisted of four freshly cut saplings roofed with palmetto leaves, but after three days of hard riding, it felt like the palace of a queen. Especially tonight, with the icy rain and bone-numbing cold.

She tugged on the front of the thin wool blanket she'd knotted around her shoulders, pulling it closed, but it did little good. The storm had blown all the cold off the sea and over Virginia. Nearly everything alive was suffering. The overarching live oaks creaked and moaned in the wind. Owls perched on the branches, fluffed up for warmth, battling to hang on. They looked as miserable as Robin.

Only the black soldiers seemed unaffected. A dozen other palmetto structures dotted the camp, but most of the men stood out in the open. The mist that wafted from the night sky beaded on their canvas coats and glistened like pearls in the firelight. Laughter rang, along with flute melodies, drumbeats, and fragments of gospel tunes.

From the many Negro camps she had shared she knew that this ritual was called a "shout," a time when men gathered into what could best be described as half pow-wow and half prayer meeting. They sang and clapped their hands. Feet pounded the ground in an endless, mesmerizing rhythm. As each song built, and men became immersed in the harmony, the tumult grew . . . and when it ended, a few of the men huddled together and talked about their families and friends.

Robin tugged her skirmish cap down over her ears and exhaled tiredly. The frosty cloud of breath twisted away in the wind. Her eyelids felt as heavy as iron. She had to keep shifting positions to stay awake.

This "shout" had been going on for about an hour, and a dance circle was forming up outside the shelters. Soldiers amiably shoved each other into a line and took up the next song, *The Battle Hymn of the Republic.* "Stoop-rise-and-whirl" seemed to be the basic dance step, but often a man dropped out of the circle and capered sideways, to the admiring cheers and claps of his friends. Calls of: "Wake 'em, brother! Stand up to 'em!" echoed over the rainy camp.

So much laughter, and joy . . . these black soldiers always seemed joyful.

Robin frowned down at the cold coffee in her battered tin cup. How could they be so carefree? Most of these men were runaway slaves who would be returned to their masters if captured, and their fates once they got home would be unimaginable. She had seen one runaway slave forced to pick cotton with his mouth because his enraged owner had cut off both his hands. Ankles shackled, he was a pathetic sight, shuffling down the rows, tripping and falling. He could not even . . .

Without her realizing it, her head inched forward until her chin rested on her chest. Her eyes fluttered closed.

. . . And like wild whirlpools, swirling and eddying, she saw gaps open in the waves of men, yawn, then close convulsively, leaving her surrounded by enemy soldiers. Shouts of defiance rent the air, groans of desperation, and underneath it all a mingled rumble of gasped prayers, the cries for loved ones. Everywhere, everywhere, men staggered, broken and glassy eyed. Some crept through the brush. Others quivered behind trees. The drifting haze of gunsmoke seemed to curl around the dead, waiting to carry away their souls . . .

Robin jerked awake. Her heart thundered as she fought to suck in a breath. When she could fill her lungs, she wiped her sweating hand on her pant leg and forced herself back to this place, here, now. The rain had let up a little. More men had left the dry shelters to join the circle. It appeared twice as large as a few moments ago. Or had she slept for much longer than she thought?

She groped for the flask of whisky in her boot and took a drink. Then another. The liquor burned a path down her throat, and, slowly, very slowly, the serpent that lived in her belly began to uncoil. When she could breathe easier, she returned the flask to its place and leaned her head back against the pole.

War had taught her the benefits of spirits. Often when she lay down on the battlefield after a bad fight, her clothing filthy with dirt and blood, her ears ringing with the cries of the wounded, the only thing that allowed her to sleep was whisky—though she had not even told her husband about the flask she carried. Charles would not approve, no matter that he would understand. To him, Robin was still a "great lady" and great ladies did not drink strong liquor. She thanked God that Charles could not see her now. He . . .

"Hey, boy," a gentle voice said as a hand touched her shoulder. "You awright? You was looking mighty poorly. How 'bout another plate of Bubble-and-Squeak?"

Cato squatted before Robin and smiled. He had a seamed face with a head of white hair, and skin the color of polished mahogany. She had met him when she'd first come in at dusk. In every camp, whether black or white, the men always treated Robin like a brave child, someone to be respected, and, if at all possible, protected.

She returned his smile. Bubble-and-Squeak was sliced beef covered with onions and cabbage and baked in a dutch oven buried in the coals. She'd been so hungry when she first arrived that she'd had three helpings. "No, suh. I done had enough, but I'm obliged for the offer."

The old man nodded. "Well, if you change your mind, you let me know. Boy as skinny as you needs to eat, *a lot.* What'd you do, boy? Run all the way to join up with us? Your massa must of been plenty mean."

"How'd you know I was a slave? Does it show?"

Cato reached out, took her hand, and patted it. "Oh, mostly it's that scared look in your eyes. Like you was afraid the Devil hisself might rise up in a ball of fire and snatch your soul right out of your body."

"I am scared of the Devil. I admit it."

The old man slapped her playfully on the shoulder. "Well, that's awright. In fact, everybody ought to be. World would be a better place. Now, why don't you come over and he'p me with my soap-making? I could use another pair of hands, and I don't like you sitting over here on the edge of the shelter. It's just plain dangerous these days."

"I could use a piece of soap, too. Will you give me one if I he'p you?"

" 'Course I will," he answered with mock indignity. "What you take me for? A gen'ral or sumpin?"

"No, suh," she said. "I could tell you was decent folk right off."

The old man laughed and rose, his joints crackling. "What might your name be, boy? I don't recall you saying."

"Essel."

Cato nodded approvingly. "That's a fine name. You ain't took a last name yet, I guess."

"No, suh." Slaves rarely had last names, though many used the names of their masters as a sign of who they belonged to. Robin shifted uncomfortably. "I didn't 'spect I'd be needing one so soon."

"Oh, in the army you got to have one." He rubbed his wrinkled chin, and firelight glinted in his eyes. She knew he was wondering how a boy had come to own such a fine blue uniform without being a "regular" recruit—but he wouldn't ask. It would have been a waste of breath when so many young black men had escaped bondage and pulled uniforms off dead Yankee soldiers just so they could fight to free their families back home. "Them folks in Washington won't pay you 'less you got a whole name."

"Well, I'd best get one then."

"Don't worry your mind 'bout it. We make such doings a community project," Cato said with a grin. "Come over here by the fire and let me present you to the official soap-makers of the Eighteenth Corps."

She scanned the dark trees as she followed the old man, her eyes searching for the glint of metal or movement. He was right about the danger of sitting on the perimeter in the firelight. A guerrilla war of raid and ambush had been raging for over a year.

Much of the problem stemmed from Davis' policy requiring cavalrymen to furnish their own horses. A man unfortunate enough to have lost his mount was reassigned to the infantry. To avoid this sentence of almost certain death, many deserted the battlefield, joined ranks, and skulked around Union camps until they could steal enough horses to resupply themselves. Isolated pickets were the preferred targets. So much so that Federal brigadier August Kautz had ordered his men to tie their horses far to the rear of their picket positions so that the theft of the animals would not endanger the lives of his men. But any Union soldier was fair game, especially a black one, even if he didn't have a horse to steal.

Cato knelt in an empty space in the circle of men around the fire. "Fellas, let me present Essel to you all. He's 'bout fourteen, I figure, and badly in need of some soap. I told him if he he'ped with the making, he could have a piece."

A middle-aged man with thick black whiskers looked Robin over severely, as though judging her soul, then nodded. "If he'll work for it, I reckon he can have one." His flat nose spread out across his face like a squashed plum. He thrust out his hand to shake Robin's. "My name's Leander Brushy. Come on over here and set yourself down, boy. I'll put you to cutting up tallow."

"Much obliged, suh." She hurried to sit down between him and an old man with silver hair and a long beard. The elder had the kindest eyes she'd ever seen and laugh lines around his wide mouth. "What's your name, mister?" she asked.

"Nate," he said. "Nate Brothwell Bowdry." He shoved a bucket of beef fat over beside Robin and handed her a tin plate and a knife. "Cut these chunks into little pieces so as we can add 'em to the pot and melt 'em down. Can you do that?"

"Yes, suh, I can."

As she cut up the fat, she watched Leander rise and elevate the straining barrel, which had holes bored into the bottom. Nate put a bucket beneath the barrel while Cato lined the barrel with straw and shoveled cold ashes from the fire in on top.

"Awright now, back off a ways. Here we go," Cato said as he reached out and lifted a kettle from the edge of the fire. He filled the barrel with boiling water and let all the water seep through into the bucket before he added more water. "Yes, this is gonna be good strong lye. I can tell just from the smell."

When all the water had drained, Nate tipped the barrel sideways and peered down at the milky fluid in the bucket. He looked unconvinced. "Might be, but we'd best test it by floating' a raw egg on top, just to make sure. If the egg floats, it's strong enough for soapmaking. If it don't, we'll have to pour the lye from the bucket back through the ashes again."

"We'll do it," Cato said. "But I tell you that egg is gonna float. I am a expert soap-maker." He set the holey barrel aside and rustled through his haversack until he found a raw bird's egg wrapped in a pair of socks. "Now you pay attention, Nate." With elaborate ceremony, he polished the egg on his pants, then cracked it on the bucket and broke it on top of the lye.

Nate leaned forward to examine the results, but Cato's smile told Robin everything she needed to know. "See," he said. "I told you it'd float."

Nate grinned. "I wasn't name-calling, Cato. I just wanted to make sure, that was all. Otherwise we could of been wasting good grease."

"Well, that's a fact," Cato said.

Robin smiled at the satisfied looks on the old men's faces. Cato let his egg sit on top of the hot liquid until it had cooked enough that he could lift it out with a spoon. He then rinsed it with clear water, salted it, and ate it. Rubbing his hands together, he said, "Now, Essel, put all the chopped-up fat into that pot on the fire. That's it. Good. See how fast it's melting? Won't be long 'til we can mix it all up."

Leander grabbed a wooden spoon from the opposite side of the fire and handed it to her. "Always stir in the same direction, boy. It'll melt quicker that way."

Robin obediently kept her spoon going clockwise while the old men surveyed the activities of the "shout." Leander joined in the singing and Nate hummed along, but Cato bounced around the shelter in a half-hearted waltz step, using the long soap mold as his partner.

One man, a corporal, about fifty, climbed atop a stump and lifted his hands. "Stand up for Jesus, brothers! Stand up!" He held out his arms to the crowd, as if embracing the whole camp, but no one seemed to be paying attention to him. In the wan light, his narrow face reminded Robin of a fox, with its huge dark eyes and pointed nose.

"Listen up, boys," the man called. "I want you to hear this. Listen up, now!"

The singing died down as men shushed their companions. The corporal smiled. "I have something I want to say. I figure we be going into 'nother battle in a day or so, and I want you all to understand how I feel 'bout it." He paused and searched the gathering, making eye contact with every man he could. ". . . Our massas, they lived under the old flag, they got they wealth under it, and everything beautiful for they children. And under it they grinded us up, and put us in they pocket for money. But the first minute they think that old flag mean freedom for we colored people, they pull it right back down, and run up a new flag of they own. A Secesh flag. Yes, they throwed that old flag down like it was a shabby rag."

Cato cupped a hand to his mouth and shouted, "Yea, brother! The traitors did it just like you said! Go on, Ferdinand. Keep telling it like it is!"

Ferdinand wet his lips as he waited for the assenting cheers to die down, then continued in a deep voice, "But *we* will never desert this old flag, boys, not never. Not me, nor you, nor any of your own here in this camp or even our families back home in bondage. We have lived under them stars and stripes for too many years to walk away now, and we'll die under 'em. Maybe on the morrow. Maybe later, if the Lord wills, but we ready, ain't we? We ready to die for that ole flag when the time comes."

"Yes, brother! We ready right now!"

"Whenever Jesus calls! We ready!"

"More, Ferdinand. Tell us some more!"

Robin laid her spoon down and lowered her gaze to the damp ground. The speech continued, but she barely heard. The loyalty of these men always astonished her. Black soldiers were rarely allowed to fight, because many whites believed they wouldn't fight, that their poor constitutions made them natural cowards. They received less food, less ammunition, and until three months ago, less pay. They were forced to do the lowest forms of labor—

digging privies and breastworks, unloading cargo, cutting and hauling wood. White soldiers tormented and abused them. Yet each one of these men would willingly sacrifice himself on the altar of the Union tomorrow.

Robin had seen them do it. At Milliken's Bend, and Fort Wagner, and Port Hudson. Thinking of that last battle sent a shudder down her spine. It had made her sick to her stomach. May 27th, 1863. She had ridden all night along the shore of the Mississippi river and arrived just at dawn when the red ball of the sun was slipping above the horizon. The Federal infantry began their assault at sunrise, and the Southerners opened up a murderous fire of shell, canister, grape and musketry. At every pace, the black soldiers had to dodge their own falling dead and wounded. Shells from Confederate guns cut down trees three feet in diameter and at one time buried a whole company beneath their branches. The assault was doomed before it began, but the damned Yankee officers ordered charge after charge . . . six in all. Not one black soldier faltered in his duty. The only thing that had stopped them was death.

Robin swallowed down a dust-dry throat. In every case, those undaunted men had seemed happy about having the opportunity to die, which she found unfathomable. She, too, was willing to die for her cause, but she wouldn't do it happily, and she didn't consider it an honor. If you made a mistake, you got killed. There was no glory in that. No reverence. Death was just one of the rules of the game. If you wanted to play, you had to accept the fact that you might lose, and everybody on your side might lose, too. But the only people who considered dying to be a sacred act were war profiteers . . . and brave black soldiers.

Cato crouched down when the speech ended and grinned at her. "My, my, that was one mighty fine discourse, but now we are fixing to mix up the soap, so you got to use your spoon to scoop them cracklings out of the fat, Essel."

She leaned forward and did as he'd asked, placing each crispy piece on the plate she'd used to cut up the tallow.

"Now move aside just a bit, Essel. Get yourself ready to start stirring again," Cato instructed.

"I'm ready."

He lifted the bucket of hot lye water and poured a little at a time into the grease. "There you go. Stir it up quick before all the grease hops out of the pot. Good, Essel. That's the way."

Cato set his bucket down and stood with his hands on his hips scrutinizing the appearance of the soap. In the meantime, Leander and Nate lined a long wooden soap mold with an old piece of cloth.

Robin's hand stopped in mid-stir when she saw that the cloth was butternut in color: a fragment of Confederate uniform. She looked away, started stirring again.

Why did the sight hurt so much? After four years of war, Virginia was blanketed with military uniforms. If a man had the time to scrape away leaves, he could find cloth within ten paces of any camp in the state. Indeed, many Southern boys constructed "shoes" from such leavings, now that the Confederacy could no longer provide them. She ached at the thought that the cloth in that one long soap mold would be enough to warm the feet of a Southern boy through the winter.

Cato bent over with a hawk feather in his hand. "Let's test the consistency before we pour it out."

"Test the consistency? With a feather?"

"Why, sure, boy. I'm surprised at you. If we dip a plume and we can strip off the feathers, the lye is too strong and we'll have to be adding more grease. You ought to know that."

"Well, I don't."

Cato tilted his head regretfully. "Somebody ought to set down with your mama and give her what for. Boys should know such facts. Watch now."

Cato dipped his plume and brought it up dripping. He waited a moment for it to cool before he extended it to Robin. "Go on, now. Try to tear them feathers off with your fingers. Go on, don't be 'fraid."

She reached out and attempted to pull them off. The feathers wouldn't budge. "They ain't coming off, Cato."

The old man smiled as if pleased with himself. "I didn't figure they would. Two gallon of lye to two pound of grease. That's the way to make soap." He turned to the other men. "Awright, Leander, I'm coming. Hold onto that mold."

Leander grabbed one end and lifted his chin. "Nate, you take the other end. We don't want to spill none of Cato's magic concoction."

Robin watched as Cato lifted the pot and gingerly poured it into the mold. The hot liquid sent a gush of steam into the cold air. When Cato had finished, he set his pot aside and knelt down with his knife to mark off the bars of soap. "You see this one, Essel?"

Robin looked. "Yes, suh."

"This is your own piece. Tomorrow night we'll dig it out of the mold and hand it over to you, but you'll have to let it cure for 'bout two weeks before you use it. You know that, don't you?"

" 'Course, I do," she answered.

Cato gave her a look from the corner of his eye. "Well, I had to check on account of your general ignorance of soap-making. Now let's get on with more important considerations."

"What?"

Cato came over and flopped down on the ground beside her. In the firelight his dark brown skin gleamed like topaz. It took several moments before Leander and Nate took up their places across the fire from them. They all poured new cups of coffee. Cato said, "I have been pondering on your name and I have come up with several possibilities."

Nate cocked his head suspiciously. "I always worry when you get a 'clever' look in your eyes, Cato. What sort of name did you have in mind?"

"Well, I was thinking we ought to be giving Essel a name to remind him of tonight. Something like Essel Tallow, or maybe Essel Suds?"

"*Suds?*" Nate bellowed. "I knew it would be something ridiculous! Suds, for God's sake."

Leander gazed at them both with his mouth puckered in disdain. "You old nitwits," he said. "The boy can't be wandering the earth with a name like Suds! Shoot. Folks wouldn't pay no attention to him a'tall. Has to be something more dignified."

"Well, ain't nobody gonna bow to him if we call him King James neither," Cato said.

Leander cocked a brow. "Well, how 'bout Essel Rothwell or Essel Manypenny. Or even Essel Morehouse. Them names have a whole lot more distinction than Essel Suds."

Cato's smile collapsed into a frown. "May be, but they ain't got nothing to do with soap. How about Renderfat? Now that's unique."

"*Renderfat?*" Nate shook his silver head. "Well, nobody'd ever forget it, that's for sure."

"Except the boy," Leander pointed out. "And he'd be trying to forget it for the rest of his born days." He rocked back on his hindend and laced his fingers over one knee while he peered evilly at Cato.

Cato scowled back. "Well, I have been a waiting for you to come up with sumpin better."

Nate sighed and pretended to be engrossed in the new fiddle player who had just come out to join the "shout." He was playing *We Are Coming, Father Abraham.*

"Well?" Cato insisted.

"I am pondering it!" Leander announced with a flourish of his hand.

They were so serious. Over trying to find a name that went with soap! Robin laughed lightly at first, then louder when the disgruntled old men turned her way. Leander lifted a brow. Robin couldn't stop. The mirth bubbled up from the pit of her belly. It felt so good that she braced her hand on the ground and tipped her head back to let the laughter roll out.

Cato studied her for a long moment, then burst into a side-splitting roar, and when Leander growled, "Quit that! Naming's serious business!" Cato hooted, fell over backward and kicked his feet in the air.

"I do believe that old man has lost his mind," Leander remarked to Nate.

Nate propped his bearded jaw on his palm and stared out at the fiddler. Finally, he announced, "Hold up, now, I have got it."

"Got what?" Leander asked.

"Essel's name. I have figured out Essel's last name."

Cato sat up, but Robin continued to chuckle. She hadn't laughed in such a long, long time, it felt too good to stop.

Cato's gaze sharpened. "Well, what is it, Nate? It had better have something to do with soap."

Nate squared his shoulders and said, "Latherton. *Lather*ton. Don't you get it? Like lathering up to wash your hair." Eagerly, he looked back and forth between his cohorts.

"It's a heck of an improvement on Suds, I'll tell you that," Leander agreed.

Cato squinted while he thought about it. "That ain't bad, Nate. Not bad a'tall. Is it distinguished enough for your tastes, Leander?"

"I believe it is. How 'bout you, boy? How does Essel Latherton sound?"

Robin straightened up and wiped the tears from her cheeks. Each old man appeared profoundly serious. Their brows had lowered and their eyes narrowed. "Sounds plenty good to me. I guarantee that with a name like that, I ain't never gonna forget the soapmakers of the Eighteenth Corps. I 'preciate you all more'n I can say. You are mighty fine friends." She nodded. "I am Essel Latherton from this day on. Will they pay me now, Cato?"

"I am gonna make certain of it, first light tomorrow morning. I'll talk to the captain 'bout it. He'll see you get on them rolls."

A brief silence ensued where each turned to listen to the fiddler's heart-rending rendition of *Mother Kissed Me in My Dream*. Every other man at the "shout" had stopped to listen too, and in the hush, a deep baritone voice filled in the words.

Lying on my dying bed,
*   Through the dark and silent night,*
Praying for the coming day,
*   Came a vision to my sight,*
Near me stood the forms I loved,
*   In the sunlight's mellow gleam;*
Folding me unto her breast,
*   Mother kissed me in my dream.*
Comrades, tell her when you write,
*   That I did my duty well;*
Say that when the battle raged,
*   Fighting, in the van, I fell.*
Tell her, too, when on my bed
*   Slowly ebbed my being's stream*
How I knew no peace until
*   Mother kissed me in my dream.*

Nate's faded old eyes brimmed with tears when the baritone died away. He heaved a sigh and stood up, laying a hand on Robin's skirmish cap. "You take care, Essel Latherton. I am proud I could he'p with your naming. And now this old man has got to go find his bedroll." He lifted a hand to Cato and Leander. "I'll see all of you earlier than any of us wants. Good night, now."

"Hold up, Nate," Leander said as he rose. "I'll walk you back to the tent. Night, Cato. Night, Essel."

"Good night, both of you old goats," Cato said. "I'll be along directly."

As the two men walked away through the dispersing crowd Cato stretched out on his side and drew the coffee pot out of the coals. "You want more coffee, boy? There's 'bout two cups left, though it'll be strong as mud."

"I don't mind mud, Cato. I figure I have drunk a river of it in the past few months."

"Awright, better go fetch your cup where you left it over by the pole."

Cato filled his own cup while Robin retrieved hers, then he poured the last drop out for her. A soft smile lit his ancient face. "Here you go."

"Much obliged," she said. Through the tin, she could tell the brew was lukewarm, but it would do.

"Ain't too hot, is it?" Cato asked.

"Just right for me. Drinking temperature," she answered and took a sip.

Cato watched her while she drank her coffee. For fifteen or twenty minutes, neither of them said anything, they just listened to the last songs and clapped when a superior performance warranted praise. More and more men began to drift away toward the tents.

"Boy?" Cato said softly. "You been looking poorly all night. Even when you was laughing you acted like it was something new to you. What's eating at you?"

Robin bowed her head. "It's nothing. I just . . ."

"Go on. You can tell me. You said I was your friend and I am."

She hesitated, drank more coffee. "Cato? You ever wanted to run off? From the army I mean. You got to be sixty years old—and free to boot. You could hightail it up North, or out West. Why ain't you gone?"

"Oh, my dear boy," Cato said in a tender voice. His face slackened. "You just got here and already you're—"

"No, I . . . I ain't. Not really. I was just wondering. You know. Just reflecting on why more folks didn't run off. Especially the older fellas. I can't figure 'em staying on, not when the fighting is so hot."

"Well, I'll tell you sumpin," Cato said, and his wrinkles rearranged themselves into sad lines. "I felt old when I was on the plantation. My massa even put me down with the most ancient field hands and I came to believe I was like them, just a worthless old man. But since I joined up with the Yankees and been a soldier for these United States, I feel young again. I am telling you the truth, now, Essel. Sometimes I have mighty feelings in this old heart of mine, when I see these white officers leading charges into terrible enemy fire. They dying, too, you see. Yes, they dying in powerful numbers, right alongside us. And what for? For the cause of our race, Essel. They dying for you and me." He touched a gnarled finger to Robin's chest, then to his own, and nodded as if to reaffirm the words.

Her voice came out more harsh then she intended. "You figure these white boys are good as Jesus, Cato?"

Cato didn't move a muscle. He just stared at her with sadness in his eyes. "You are powerful angry, boy. Can't say I blame you much, you just escaping bondage and all, but there's a few items you got to learn and fast. First off, let me answer your question." He took a moment to smooth away the beads of moisture that had formed on the side of his tin cup. "In a way, I guess I do see these white officers as deliverers. For every one of them that dies, I expect he's saved a thousand of our people. Maybe more." The deep grooves around his mouth pulled tight. "You listen to me good, Essel. Before I would turn my back on these officers, I would be pierced through with a thousand bullets and drink my own blood."

She grimaced at the dwindling fire. Thin tongues of flame danced in mass of red coals. "I understand."

"Do you, boy?"

Cato stared out across the camp toward the officers' tents. Lamps still glowed, and against the golden canvas of one tent, a shadow moved, back and forth, back and forth. A man pacing worriedly. Cato's jaw hardened. "I have been with the Eighteenth Corps for one year, more or less, and in that time, I have seen seven, *seven* good officers killed. They died for my family back in Mississippi, Essel. Pure and simple. I wouldn't run out on any of these men. Not for no reason whatsoever."

Robin couldn't look at him. She stared down at the thick bed of coffee grounds in her cup.

"You listening to me, Essel?"

"Yes, suh. I am, but I . . . I figure you're just a good man. A brave man. I ain't, Cato. I—"

A hand, large and gentle, gripped her shoulder. "I ain't brave neither, Essel. I am just plain desperate. Way I see it, we got one chance and one chance only to free our families. It's now or never."

Robin drank down the last of her coffee and set her cup on the ground. Metal clinked against stone. Her family had owned three slaves, but she'd never viewed them as property, which resulted from the teachings of her mother. The Cherokee owned slaves, that's why many of them were fighting for the Confederacy, but they viewed slaves in a much different manner than whites. Slaves were taken, usually in warfare, then they were integrated into the family until they became family. The slaves in her family's household had been like cousins, or aunts and uncles. Ginny, Robin's mammy, had listened to her, played with her, cared for her, treated her as one of her own children. Just as Cato did now. It had never occurred to Robin back then that Ginny might be miserable and filled with hate for her. Even today, she could not believe it—none of them had run off when the war started. They had stayed until both of Robin's parents were dead. Then Robin had granted them their freedom.

Robin kicked her cup with her boot. She'd gotten letters for a while, then they'd stopped. She prayed they were all right. Perhaps that's why she always sought out Negro camps . . .

Cato leaned forward to look at her downcast face. "You ain't considering running off no more, are you?"

Robin shook her head. "No. Not now."

"Good, on account of we need you, boy. You hear me? *We need you.* We need every able-bodied man who can carry a gun."

Robin turned and met those wise old eyes and saw deep concern there. This old man who had known her for less than a day really cared about her, mostly because she was young, partly because he thought she was scared of dying and he wanted her to know the value he placed on the act.

"I'm going to fight, Cato," she said with slow deliberation. "Don't you worry none."

Cato reached over to lay a hand on Robin's back. "Good, Essel. You tired, boy? You look 'bout ready to fall over."

She inhaled and let the breath out in a gush. "I am so tired I could sleep for ten years and never get enough of it."

"Well, I can understand that. We'd be mighty glad if you'd come over and sleep in our tent tonight, Essel. So as we could keep an eye on you, and he'p you get all your paperwork straightened out after roll call tomorrow."

Robin smiled. "Much obliged, Cato."

They walked across the camp together, passing the few hangers-on who couldn't bear to let the "shout" die, then Cato stopped and lifted the canvas flap on his tent. "Inside, Essel, but watch your feet now. Leander sleeps next to the door, and he gets mighty ferocious if somebody steps on his head."

"I'll be careful," she whispered and stepped inside into the cool darkness.

"Go on to the back, Essel," Cato murmured. "Throw out your blanket next to mine."

"Will there be enough room, Cato? It looks awful—"

"Why, boy, you're so tiny you won't take up no space a'tall. Go on now."

Robin unknotted her blanket from around her shoulders and spread it out on the floor, then she lay down and rolled up in it. A faint golden gleam lit the tent wall in front of her face, and she realized the officer's tent that Cato had been looking at earlier sat just behind them. Against the gleam, she could still see the officer pacing, his shadow as pale as a ghost on the canvas.

Robin closed her eyes and fell into a restless sleep, thinking about the thousands of Union soldiers she would face tomorrow as she made her way north. Grant's fifth offensive against the Petersburg fortifications had failed only days before. Once again, Richmond had withstood the shock of Grant's great army—but how long could it last? The ground beneath her head shook with the constant comings and goings of supply trains. Yankees were never hungry or cold. They still had real coffee, and beef, and bread, and whole uniforms. Grant's coffers seemed bottomless . . .

She'd been tossing and turning for an hour when she felt Cato's hand come down and pat her head comfortingly.

"It's awright, boy," he whispered. "Get some sleep now. Ain't nobody gonna hurt you. I guarantee it. All that's over. You're safe, and with folks who understands you, so stop your worrying. Sleep, Essel. Sleep, now, boy."

Very softly, Cato started singing *When This Cruel War Is Over,* and the reverent hope in his voice stirred her own. Dear God, what she would give for the fighting to stop, for the damned Yankees to go home and leave her people alone.

She slipped into the blessed oblivion of dreamless sleep.

CHAPTER 5

"Listen to this, Garry," Mike Hathaway said to Garrison Parker as he leaned over the polished maple bar of Luke's saloon in Central City, Colorado Territory. Five crude plank tables sat in a neat row behind him, all empty. Luke stood polishing mugs with a clean towel at the opposite end of the bar. This time of the afternoon most people in Central City were at work, which left the place too quiet. Fortunately, the popping and crackling of the old wood stove in the northern corner provided a constant background of sound. A pile of split logs lay in disarray next to the stove and filled the air with the sweet tangy odor of pine sap.

Garrison squinted at Hathaway who had his eyes glued to the newspaper pages. "Well, are you going to tell me or not?" He took another sip of his beer. The mug felt cool and silken beneath his calloused fingers. "I'm still listening."

"Oh, hang on. I got caught up reading. Let me see here . . ." Hathaway adjusted the small pair of spectacles perched on the end of his flat nose before he spread out the copy of the *Rocky Mountain News,* and drew the oil lamp closer. The facets of the glass globe decorated the paper with amber triangles and made Hathaway's orange hair glitter like spun copper. "Jeff Davis was in Macon, Georgia, on the 28th of September. He—"

"On a spirit-lifting jaunt, no doubt," Garrison interrupted. "Leastways, he ought to be. Them folks down there are in sorry need of a little spiritizing." A medium-sized man with an oval face framed by a mass of curly brown hair, he had hazel eyes and a bushy beard that hung to the middle of his chest. His broad muscular shoulders bulged against the dirty fabric of an old Union army shirt. Though he'd mended the bullet hole in the right sleeve, pale blue threads had escaped to stick out like a spider's legs around the edges.

Hathaway wet his lips as he read further. "That Davis is sure a slick talker.

Listen to what he told them Georgians: 'What though misfortune has befallen our arms from Decatur to Jonesboro, our cause is not lost. Sherman cannot keep up his long line of communications; retreat sooner or later he must. And when the day comes, the fate that befell the army of the French Empire in its retreat from Moscow will be re-enacted. Our cavalry and our people will harass and destroy his army, as did the Co—coss . . .' "

"Cossacks," Garrison said.

Hathaway peered at him skeptically over the rims of his spectacles. "How would you know?"

"Kee-rist, Mike. Don't you ever read nothing but yellow journalism?" He gestured to the *Rocky Mountain News.* "The Cossacks are as famous as Job. They're right there with Samson and Delilah in the book of *Samuel.* If you'll recall they were mixed up with King David when he was warring on the Philistines."

"Oh," Hathaway responded with a contemplative frown. "I believe I do recall that."

Garrison glanced sideways at him, smiled to himself, and shifted to lean his back against the bar and stare across the narrow room. Luke's place stretched about thirty feet long, but only fifteen wide. Beyond the two small windows in the front, snowflakes pirouetted down from a cloud-strewn sky, obscuring the craggy granite peaks behind. Garrison took a deep breath. The tribes called the Rockies the Shining Mountains and said that spirits lived here. He believed it. He'd been trapped in snowstorms on the highest peaks, and when night came the mountains glowed to life, as if from some inner fire. "What else did Davis say?"

"Hmm? Oh . . ." It took him a few seconds to find his place again. "Here it is: as did the Cossacks that of Napoleon, and the Yankee general, like him, will escape with only a bodyguard.' " Hathaway rubbed his clean-shaven jaw and eyed Garrison. "Are you sure the Cossacks could have survived from the time of Job right up to that of Napoleon? That don't hardly seem—"

"That Davis, he's something, ain't he? Such vainglorious boasting. He must be scared witless, what with Sherman in Atlanta and Grant sieging Petersburg. He knows he ain't got much time left." Garrison braced his boot heel against the brass footrail that ran the length of the bar.

"You really think that's true?"

"I give the Confederacy another six months, maybe less. I heard tell that Sherman's cogitating on marching further south, wreaking havoc all the way to Savannah. If he makes it there by Christmas, then swings north again, he and Grant will have Richmond bottled up by March.

They'll smash the train tracks, cut the lines of communication a'twixt Davis and his generals, and starve the Rebel Congress to death—not to mention the loyal citizens of Richmond. If Davis don't do something unpredictable, that is. And if I were him—"

"You'd do something unpredictable. Which is perfectly predictable to any fella who knows you."

Garrison smiled. "That's just the way I like it."

"That may be, but didn't it ever occur to you that folks want friends they can count on to act given ways in given circumstances? Like knowing that when your rifle hammer strikes the cap and sends a spark into the powder the gun will go off? If it don't go off, well, it's annoying as hell." He shook his head. "That's your problem, Garry. Folks never know when you're gonna go off and when you ain't. You just ain't comfortable to be around."

Garrison held his mug up to the light to watch the bubbles rising from the bottom in little streams. They looked like they were trying to escape through the foam on the top. "I reckon I like being the only one who knows when I'm about to go off half-cocked, I—"

His voice faltered when the door to the saloon opened and a Negro woman entered. She was wearing a massive blond wig. Short and a little on the pudgy side, her dress made up for the inadequacies of her moonish face by revealing ample breasts. She tossed her head so that her silver earbobs jingled and gave both men a ravishing smile. She had to be pushing forty.

"Dang," Hathaway whispered as he leaned closer to Garrison. "She's a brave woman to come into the saloon this time of day. It's just barely past noon. Do you suppose she walked all the way through town in plain sight?"

"I reckon so. She's here, ain't she?"

"That she is." Hathaway's eyes narrowed.

"Who is she?"

"Name's Macey Runkles. She works out of Denver—with another gal by the name of Esther Wilcox. Miss Runkles has been in Central City for about a week or so. She's trying to buy that little purple house over to Tenth Street. Guess she wants a place of her own."

"The purple one, eh? So she's planning on moving her business operations here?"

"That's what I hear."

Both Garrison and Hathaway stared at her unabashedly. Five circles of black lace ringed the sleeves of her red satin dress, and when combined with the yellow sash that snugged around her waist, the getup reminded Garrison of the lethal coral snakes he'd seen swimming in the rivers down South. Sure put a damper on a man's ardor. Made him worry he might get bit in a bad place if he saddled up with her.

"Take a gander at that pile of yellow hair?" Hathaway whispered. "Must be more windy out than I thought."

"No wind could do that. Looks more like it was lightning-struck." Garrison scanned her bright red lips and cheeks. "Well, she ain't gonna put Maggie out of business, I can tell you that." Maggie Lee had a house on Pine Street and a reputation for greatness unequaled in all of Colorado Territory. He wished to Hob he could afford her prices.

"Not likely," Hathaway agreed. "But I'd wager she'll be trying pretty hard. Starting this instant. She can't take her eyes off you, Garry."

The woman's brows had lowered while she studied the whispering men.

"Hell," Garrison said. "She's looking at me like I remind her of Bloody Bill Anderson."

"Not Bloody Bill," Hathaway objected, and examined her expression more carefully. "Cochise, maybe."

They both sighed and turned back to their mugs. Down the length of the bar, Luke snickered. Garrison gave him a sidelong look. Bald and skinny, Luke had a skeletal face, as if just enough muscle sheathed the bones to keep them inside. Five teeth remained in his mouth, two on the top and three on the bottom, but their chances of sticking looked pretty iffy. Luke had a bad habit of shoving on one of the top teeth with his tongue, so that it had started to jut out at an odd angle. Half the men who frequented Luke's bar had laid bets on how long it would take that tooth to fall out. Garrison, himself, had wagered five dollars in gold that it would be less than thirty days.

"Oh, she's set her sights on you, all right, Garry," Hathaway said, nudging him with his elbow, and grinning. "Can't you tell?"

"No, I can't."

The swishing of taffeta petticoats challenged his words, thunderous in the small room. When the fragrance of lavender enfolded him, Garrison held his nearly empty mug up to Luke, "I'll have one more of these, Luke, and fast, if you don't mind."

"No, I don't mind, Garry. Not one bit." Luke went about drawing another draft of the amber ale from the keg behind the bar.

"So, Mike," Garrison pushed on, "what do you think about Hood and Bedford Forrest? You think they're gonna—"

"Excuse me, gentlemen." Macey had a deep throaty voice. Garrison turned to find her staring up at him through a heavy mask of face powder, which did little to disguise the deep wrinkles across her forehead and around her mouth. "I am Miss Macey Runkles. May I have the pleasure of your names?"

Hathaway hooked a thumb at Garrison. "This here is Garry Parker, though I ain't sure that's such a pleasure, and I'm Michael John Patrick Hathaway, the administrator of the Land Office. That stringbean down the way is Luke Foster."

"Well, I am most pleased to make your acquaintances." Macey smiled for Garrison alone, and in a low voice said, "Honey, are you sure you don't want to come over to my place and have a glass of fine whisky, instead of that poor beer?" Boldly, she pressed her hip against his thigh.

Garrison could feel her warmth through his denim pants. He felt comforted by it, rather than threatened. It had been a long, long time since he'd granted himself the luxury of a woman's closeness—and he missed it. There were times at night when he'd wake up gasping, his heart pounding so hard it terrified him, and he'd wonder if an unseen disease was marauding through his veins or if it was just the loneliness eating at him again, making it hard to breathe.

"I don't reckon I ought to, ma'am," he answered, "but I thank you just the same. One more beer, then I'd best be getting back to Main Street where my mule is tied, before she takes a notion to trample some child to death."

Macey cocked her head disbelievingly. "Oh, you're teasing me, aren't you?"

"No, ma'am."

"But why would a mule trample a child to death for no reason at all?"

"Pure entertainment, I guess, though I must admit I've never understood how she thinks."

Luke set the foaming mug down in front of Garrison and grinned toothlessly, adding, "Most folks in these parts think that Garry's mule was fathered by Satan hisself."

"But, my stars, why would anybody want to own an animal like that?" Macey asked.

Garrison took a drink from the fresh mug, then wiped the foam from his mustache onto his faded blue sleeve. "Well, first off, I got Honey when I was in the army. Owe her my life, in fact. She kicked the liver out of a Reb colonel who was going to shoot me. I been taking good care of her ever since."

"I thought that looked like a Federal uniform," Macey said, rubbing the worn fabric between her fingers. "So you fought in the war, Mr. Parker?"

He looked down at her slender dark fingers on his arm and wondered at the potent emotions they stirred: Fear and longing, but more of the former. "A while ago. I served my stint and got out."

"I'll bet you were a hero. Man as god-awful handsome as you must of been. Did you get wounded?" She seemed to be hanging on his every word.

"Well, yes, ma'am, I did," he answered. "But I'd just as soon not show you my scars, if you don't mind. They're in personal places."

"Oh, that's all right. Maybe some other time," she said and paused. Her expression grew serious. She looked him over, as if she were imagining the placement of his scars in her mind's eye.

Garrison tried not to notice.

"Did you win any medals?" Macey inquired. "I mean you must've, seeing as how you got wounded and all."

Garrison lifted a shoulder. "Everybody in the war won a medal or two. They don't mean much, ma'am."

Hathaway eagerly leaned forward. "Don't you let him feed you that, ma'am. Why, Garry was one of the great heroes of Carleton's California Column, back in '62. You ever heard of it?"

Macey's moonish face screwed up in concentration. "No. I don't guess I have. Was Carleton a general or something?"

"Dang right, he was, a brigadier general," Hathaway continued while Garrison listened. "Why, Garry Parker was decorated twice for valor, once for the battle at Picacho Pass, and again for . . ."

Garrison frowned down into his beer. The light from the oil lamp had turned the liquid a molten gold. He didn't like people talking about his war record. It brought up bad memories and made just as many enemies as it did friends. Usually it ended up starting an argument, because folks loved to bicker about the war.

Luke stood riveted at the other end of the bar, listening intently, though he'd already heard this story a half dozen times.

Damn me, anyway, for getting drunk that night and jabbering on about it.

The worst part was that Garrison knew the next time Luke repeated the story he'd have Garrison facing five hundred screaming Apache and being wounded fifteen times before he could reach his horse . . . Luke *embellished* just a mite.

"Then there was the time—" Hathaway's voice had taken on a stentorian tone, like a Shakespearian actor's at the height of his performance—"when Carleton had to get a message to General Canby in New Mexico, and he handpicked Garry and a couple of other fellers to take the message through. But they was attacked by the Apache and Garry's companions were cut to bits while he hid up in the rocks listening to the screams. Why, Garry barely escaped himself, in a running fight . . ."

Those screams echoed in the back of Garrison's mind, and he saw again—just as vividly as the day it had happened—Will Wheeling's blood tracing webs over the red sandstone in the valley below. Shrill, triumphant Indian war whoops shredded the day . . . He drank more beer to drive away the ache.

"You just can't imagine!" Hathaway blurted. "Garry rode over two hundred miles alone, terrified all the way that the Apaches would catch up with him. Then, to top it all, he was captured by the Confederates and locked in prison. Why, if Garry told you the details, it would make your hair stand right up on end."

Garrison glanced over at Macey's awed expression and said, "Listen, Mike, I think that's enough. I—"

"Now whoa up! I got a few more things to say."

Hathaway took a long drink of beer to wet his whistle and opened his mouth to continue, but Garrison stopped him short. "I'd rather you dropped my life story, if you don't mind," he said. "I came into this bar to ask you questions about mining, not to hear my worst nightmares extolled in public."

Hathaway's nose wrinkled. "Well, they're only nightmares to you, to the rest of us them stories are like legends or myths or—"

Garrison held up a clenched fist. "*Myth* on this for a while, and after you've come back to your senses, we'll talk a little business."

Hathaway grumbled under his breath and took a swig of his beer. "Damn, well, all right, what'd you want to know about mining."

"You hear all the scuttlebutt over to the Land Office. What about new ore finds? Anything hot showing up?"

Hathaway stared at him, and the nostrils of his flat nose flared when he exhaled. "Ore discoveries ain't near as interesting as Injun torture, Garry."

"Maybe not, but I reckon Miss Runkles has had her fill of the sideshow, and I—"

"Oh no, I ain't!" Macey said as she grabbed onto Garrison's arm with enough force to jerk his foot off the rail where he'd had it propped. "I would just love to hear more about you, honey."

Garrison shot a scathing glance at Hathaway, who took the hint, saying, "Hmm. Let me see here. What have I heard about new ore finds? Well, folks do come in to spill the beans about their latest finds, but they swear me to secrecy on account of repeating such thing might get 'em killed and get their claims jumped to boot. But I did hear—"

"Are you a rich *miner,* Mr. Parker?" Macey interrupted.

Garrison sighed and turned toward her. She took the opportunity to reach for his beer, downing half the glass in two swallows. His brows lifted in admiration. This woman was accustomed to drinking fast and getting on with the business at hand.

"No, ma'am. I'm not," Garrison answered as he tugged his mug away from her and held it protectively.

"But you do mine for gold, don't you? I mean with shoulders like this"— she ran her hand across his back, tracing the lines of the muscles. He suppressed a shudder—"you must do something that takes strength."

"Umm."

"What?"

"I said, 'umm,'" he repeated.

"That's what I thought you said." A frown incised her forehead. "Well, darling, if it ain't mining you do, what is it?"

Garry decided it would be best to squint at the line of glasses on the shelves behind the bar, as if he'd found something fascinating there: Macey and Mike looked, too. Mike shook his head after a few seconds and went back to his beer, but Macey kept looking, trying to see whatever it was that so intrigued her prospective client.

She dropped her hand and propped it on her hip. "You mad at me, darling? Or is it just that you don't talk much?"

"I try not to be wordy."

"Well, how come? Talking is the best way in the world to get to know folks."

Garrison shifted his boot on the brass footrail. "Well, I expect it depends on how well you want folks to know you," he answered. "I figure if a man eliminates all the foolishness from his talk, he's apt to live longer. Folks don't have as many reasons to shoot first and ask questions later."

"But it makes for mighty poor conversation," Hathaway noted. "Generally, a man's foolishness is the only interesting thing about him—that's especially true of you, Garry."

Luke piped up with, "That's a fact. You don't think riding two hundred miles through Apache territory and then straight into a Rebel ambush was smart, do you?"

Garrison scowled and Macey's red lips turned down at the corners. "You men have some peculiar notions, did you know that? Foolishness or not, I love talking almost better than anything else . . . well, not quite *anything* else." She batted her eyelids.

"My . . . goodness," Hathaway said without taking his stunned gaze from Macey, "just look at the time." Then he remembered he hadn't pulled out his pocket watch and fumbled to do so. "See there! I knew it. I must be going."

He shoved away from the bar and headed for the door, grabbing his hat from the rack before he jerked the latch up. "There's a hefty pile of work on my desk. You take care now, Garry. And you too, Miss Runkles. Good day, Luke." He hurried out the door.

Macey propped her elbows on the bar and gazed longingly up at him. Garrison glanced uneasily at her. Damn. Man couldn't even share a drink with a friend these days without having some woman interrupting. What was the world coming to?

She smiled. "Where you from, Mr. Parker? You've got an odd twang to your voice."

"That ain't an 'odd' twang. It's Texan."

"Well ain't that fascinating. But if you were born in Texas, why didn't you fight for the Confederacy?" Suspicion narrowed her eyes.

"I was born there, but I moved to California when I was thirteen to make a go at the gold fields up around Sutter's Fort. And where are you from, Miss Runkles?"

"Oh," she said, "here and there." Her brow furrowed. "I was born in St. Louis, but I moved around a lot, especially after . . . after my mama died."

Pain glistened in her dark eyes. Garrison said, "Has it been long?"

"Twenty-five years near 'bout, but it don't seem like it. Sometimes I swear I hear her moving around at night, pulling covers up over me, whispering things I can't quite make out. Soft things. Sweet. You know, like a mother does."

"My mama passed on when I was five. I don't recall much about her."

Macey's face tensed, and Garrison blinked. A crack seemed to open in her silly veneer, revealing something deeper, vulnerable, warm. She looked truly concerned about him. "But you had your daddy to take care of you, didn't you? You weren't alone?"

"My pa was there. For a time, at least. He and I didn't get along too well."

"I'm glad you had somebody. I have often thought that anybody was better than nobody. 'Specially for a child. It's hard enough being a young'un, without having to raise your own self."

"Sounds like you're talking from personal experience."

"I am. I've seen an awful lot of little girls working as 'doves.' It don't seem right. But that's just the way it is. Older women try to help them as much as they can, but it ain't never easy."

"No," he answered gently. "I don't reckon it is."

She smiled. "You almost seem like you care, Mr. Parker."

"I don't like to see nobody hurting."

"I thank you for that. It helps, just knowing there's folks out there who care. 'Specially men. That's rare."

"Well, we're a hard bunch."

She tilted her head. "You ain't got to tell me that, Mr. Parker. I know it real well."

He sipped more beer.

She watched him. "Mr. Parker, have you got any hobbies? I mean like collecting silver spurs or braided horsehair bridles? I collect paper money from all over the world."

Garrison grimaced. "I didn't know anybody 'collected' money. How come you ain't spent it?"

"Spent it?" She asked in astonishment. "Why I couldn't spend something so pretty. You should see some of them bills that come from France and England. They've got bright, beautiful colors, just like the sunset. I even got one from Germany."

"Germany?" he said, awed. "You are truly a worldly woman, Miss Runkles."

She massaged his forearm. "Oh, I ain't trying to put on airs, Mr. Parker. To tell you the truth, I ain't even certain some of the bills are real."

"Well, I'd be suspicious, too. You can't trust nobody who'd pay for honest American labor with foreign money. It's indecent."

Macey nodded. "That's true, but you know, I like those bills. I really do. I keep them all in a bundle in my lacy things drawer, and every time I open it, well, I feel just like I've died and gone to the national mint." She sighed.

Garrison looked at her from the corner of his eye. "Oh, go on."

"No, sincerely," she insisted. "I know it sounds silly, but that smell has got me through some awfully tough times."

"Well, that's all right. I feel the same way about mule manure. Every morning, first thing, I get up, throw open my door and take a deep breath."

The crow's-feet around Macey's eyes deepened. She scrutinized his blank face. "Are you making fun of me, Mr. Parker?"

"Not ever, Miss Runkles. Stories are very precious things to me," he answered.

She went quiet and he peered down at the lipstick on the rim of his mug. He'd have to drink around it.

While he drank, he thought about storytelling and the storytellers he'd known. During the war, he'd seen men who told the same story over and over, like a religious ritual. For them, stringing words together was like laying bricks; each brick laid straight and true helped to built a fortress so strong and tall it could hold out the terrors of the whole world. Garrison had his own methods for that, a little different though. He needed more than words. Sometimes, after bad nightmares, he'd get up and arrange chairs like a barricade around his bed, to keep the ghosts at bay. No, he'd never scoff at anybody's method for keeping ghosts at bay.

He took another drink of beer and smiled amiably at Macey. "I was serious about the manure. Didn't you believe me?"

"Well, no, I guess I didn't. I—I apologize. I don't know why I shouldn't, I have heard stranger stories in my time, let me tell you that."

"I wouldn't doubt that one bit. Being with foreigners must get interesting."

"Oh, that German was something, I tell you. He had so much money, he gave a little to almost anybody who came into his sight. I swear he was a philanderer." She beamed at Garry.

He grinned back. "I believe you mean a 'philanthropist,' though your first statement was probably accurate, too."

"Well, whatever, he was sure free with them pretty bills of his. And there've been other interesting men, too. I could tell you some things that would curl your toes right up over the tops of your feet. There was this one time—"

"No, don't," he pleaded. "I'd rather ponder on the possibilities for a time."

She bit her lip as though wondering why, and Garrison went back to finish his beer in silence. Luke moved in a little closer, as if expecting some sort of finale to this discussion. Garrison glared at him, but Luke just grinned.

"Oh, I get it," Macey finally said. "It took me just a minute. You mean that hearing the stories would take the fun out of 'em. I understand better than you could realize." She reached for his mug and tugged on it. He refused to let go. She gave in, but had a vengeful look in her dark eyes.

"You were saying, ma'am?"

"What? Oh . . . I was saying that I do understand you not wanting me to spoil your imaginings with factual details."

"That's good, 'cause what I would like—"

"No, honestly!" she said. Her red mouth pursed. "I was in the mercantile yesterday, listening to two old women talk about their young friend Margaret's wedding. They went on for fifteen minutes. It sounded so glorious, with lots of spring flowers and the bride wearing ivory-colored velvet—I was enthralled! Right up to the point that a third woman walked in and said, 'Cuse me, didn't you all hear that little Margaret's husband got run over by a big freight wagon three days ago? Happened in Denver." Macey shook her head. "Took *all* the fun out of it right then and there."

Garrison sagged against the bar.

Luke set a fresh mug of beer at Garrison's elbow and whispered, "It's on the house, Garry. You look like you need it."

CHAPTER 6

An irregular patchwork of pale gold and green swept past the train window, flowing outward until it mated with the wisps of cloud that painted the sky for as far as she could see. Robin had leaned so close that her breath condensed on the cool pane. The trunks of the trees became crooked blurs. She never passed through these forests, by these simple farm houses and plowed fields, that her soul did not ache with the exultation of homecoming.

Tonight, I'll see my son. I'm almost there, Jeremy . . .

She'd picked her way, often on hands and knees, along meandering game trails to get through the Union's defensive lines. One picket had fired over her head when he'd seen her, but she'd managed to vanish into the undergrowth. She'd been lucky. It had been nearly nightfall, and he'd been unwilling to follow her through the thorny brambles.

The locomotive complained when the engineer applied the brakes, shrieking and groaning in preparation for the Richmond stop. Clouds of steam rushed by the window. People reached for carpetbags and primped their children to meet loved ones. Robin had only the small satchel in her lap, which she clutched as if her very life depended upon it—and well it might—hers and many others.

The ride on the decrepit tracks had been worse than any battlefield wagon, but she forgot the discomfort when the Virginia Central Railroad depot came into view. It sat at the corner of Sixteenth and Broad, and was little more than a rickety wooden shed with peeling patches of white paint, but it proudly flew the Confederate flag from the rooftop. The red canton with blue saltire cross and thirteen stars on the white background whipped in the stiff afternoon wind. Faded from sunlight and torn to shreds around the edges, the sight of it still made her heart ache. *My Lord, not once in three years have I seen you whole.*

She'd found fragments of that flag on a dozen different battlefields, mired in the mud, or clutched in cold hands that even in death held that precious cloth near, as though it alone could save them when they stood before God and had to answer for their sins. She clamped her jaw to keep it from trembling. Sentimentality ill-suited a woman of her profession, but she couldn't help it. Sometimes she believed it was the only thing that kept her sane. If she was sane . . .

The train conductor opened the door to her car, pulled it closed with a bang and shouted, "Richmond! All out for Richmond!" before hurrying down the aisle toward the next car.

She had wired President Davis of her coming and informed him of Rose's death, but she hadn't waited for a reply. Spending another moment in Wilmington would have been too risky. Her enemies would certainly have expected her to take refuge at Fort Fisher, which was why she had avoided it. The telegraph office she'd used had been located on the outskirts of Wilmington, manned by a round-faced little man with a half-full whiskey bottle on his desk.

She hoped that President Davis had received the message and expected her this afternoon, but it didn't really matter. She would see him today if she had to fight every guard on duty in the capitol.

The shrill piping of the whistle cued Robin to grab the seat back in front of her to steady herself for the stop. Amidst screeches and hisses, car couplings crashing together, and the jubilant shouts of the people huddled on the narrow porch of the depot, the passengers prepared to leave. Skirts rustled, men put on fine silk top hats, children blurted questions. The train rocked back and forth for ten seconds or so before settling down. Robin waited until most of the other passengers had gone, then she stood and made her way down the aisle. Her legs felt rubbery from the long ride.

Warm sunshine drenched the world, but it must have rained last night, for water stood in puddles, and hooves and feet had churned the mud up badly. She stood on the last step of the car staring down morosely. The mud had to be ankle-deep. Heaven knew, she'd waded through much worse in recent months. *But I wasn't wearing a brand new lavender dress then, either.*

Adjusting her black cape, she slipped the satchel over her arm and used both hands to hitch up her skirt and petticoats before stepping down into the mud. Her bare legs were visible as she splashed through the puddles and hurried to the depot porch. A few men gave her surprised looks, and the women cast rebuking glances her way. Robin smiled in return. Social disapproval fazed her little these days. Of the past twelve hundred and twenty-five days, she'd worn a dress for exactly seven. She wasn't about to ruin this one, not after the difficulty she'd had stealing the money to buy it. She regretted only that the Yankee hadn't possessed enough greenbacks for her to purchase a pair of pantalets as well. Next time she'd pick a colonel instead of a major.

The area around the depot bustled with saddle horses and carriages, women with parasols and men waving and greeting the passengers. Robin politely shouldered through the crowd toward the door to the depot, but before she could reach for the knob, a man called, "Mrs. Heatherton? 'Cuse me, ma'am. Ain't you Mrs. Heatherton?"

A very young private in a crisp butternut uniform bounded onto the porch, his saber slapping against his boots. He swept off his slouch hat and bowed deeply. Light brown hair fell over his eyes. "You are Mrs. Heatherton, ain't you, ma'am?"

"Yes, soldier," she replied.

"I am sorely glad to see you. I been waiting here since early morn. The President didn't know for certain when you'd be coming in." He grinned. " 'Course these days even if a feller knows which train to meet he still might be waiting all day for it. If you'll come over to the edge of the porch, ma'am, I'll have the carriage brung up. You won't have to step in that awful mud no more. Then I'll escort you to the President's office. My commanding officer says Mr. Davis is mighty anxious to see you."

"Thank you, private. I'm anxious to see him, as well."

"How 'bout bags, ma'am? Do you—"

"I have none."

He blinked, then half-shouted, as though in sudden memory, "Oh, of course not! Not with you coming in straight from the field and all. I plumb forgot. Well, why don't you let me carry that satchel for you then. You'll want both hands to keep your dress out of—"

"No, thank you. I'll carry the satchel myself. But it was considerate of you to offer."

"Yes, ma'am." He put on his hat and turned away, then quickly spun around with a horrified look on his face. "I have forgotten my manners, ma'am!" he blurted. "It was the shock of seeing how pretty . . . I mean, we've all heard of the wonderful things you've done, and I guess I just figured . . . well . . . anyway, my name is Hoggins. Emory Hoggins, ma'am. I am more pleased to meet you than I can say." He bowed again in about as fine a gesture as any gentlemen she'd ever seen.

"You are very kind, private," she said and smiled for the first time in a long, long while.

His face lit up. He stammered, "Oh, no, I—I ain't, ma'am. Your fame is just a fact. Well, if you'll 'cuse me, I'll be getting that carriage. There's no justice in you standing out here in the wind." He backed up, bumped into someone, cried, "Oh, I am *so* sorry," then made his way across the porch and trotted around the corner of the depot with his brim pulled down to fend off the gale.

Robin threaded her way through the people to stand where he'd indicated. Carriages were pulling away, men and women hugging each other while children jabbered nonstop. The horses tethered to the hitching rail watched her patiently and she longed to pet them gently. There had been so many times when a horse had been her only companion, the only creature in the world who knew her for what she truly was.

"Hello, beauty," she murmured to the closest horse, and the mare whickered in return.

Across the street stood a dilapidated tavern. A soft golden glow suffused the windows and lit the faces of the men inside. Someone sang a bawdy song, and the men laughed. Robin wished she had a snifter of good brandy at this very moment, to warm her up. Despite the sunshine, her toes felt like ice. And, if she admitted the truth, she needed a brandy to chase away her fears. She'd met Jefferson Davis before, but only once, and on a grave matter of national security that still gave Robin nightmares. Rose O'Neal Greenhow, grand dame of Washington, friend of nine presidents, and the South's most renowned female spy, had been in charge of the meeting. Robin had merely attended; her real work took place in a far more invisible arena. It surprised her that Private Hoggins even knew of her role.

She had memorized the first words Davis had spoken to her: "Mrs. Greenhow has informed me of your labor in behalf of our cause. I would like to offer my sincere gratitude. I realize the terrible personal cost to the families of those involved in our secret service. You are very courageous, Mrs. Heatherton. Those of us forced to toil away from the front lines owe you, and those like you, our very lives."

A carriage with two fine white horses pulled up beside the porch. The Negro driver, an old man with snowy hair, touched the brim of his black silk hat, and nodded to her, saying, "Afternoon, madam. It's lovely weather we're having, don't you think? You take care now not to drag the hem of your pretty dress in that mud. Here, I'll pull up just a little bit more and—"

"That's fine right there, Joseph!" the private said as he threw open the door and jumped down into the mud, which then splashed his pants almost to the knees.

The driver sighed and shook his head.

Hoggins extended a hand to Robin. "Let me help you inside, ma'am, then we'll be off directly. I'm dreadful sorry 'bout the mud. I don't even remember it raining last evening."

"I hardly think it's your fault, Private Hoggins," she answered as she took his hand and in one huge step made it from the porch to the carriage.

"No, ma'am, but I apologize just the same. October can be such a damn . . . uh, forgive me, such a dang poor month for traveling.' He climbed into the carriage and his pant leg brushed her skirt, getting it muddy. He looked horrified. "Oh, my Lord! I am so sorry! I didn't even think—"

"Don't give it another thought, private. It's quite all right."

"No, it ain't ma'am! I ought to be shot for that!"

"I forgive you. Please sit down and let's go."

The stern tone seemed to bring him to his senses. "Yes, ma'am," he said and yelled, "All right, Joseph, you know the way!"

"Yassuh, I do. Giddyup there, horses."

The carriage swung around and headed up Broad Street. Hoggins seated himself across from Robin, facing the rear of the carriage, where he could see out the window and keep track of their progress. His freckled face took on an air of concentration, but it remained smooth as a baby's. She guessed his age at sixteen or seventeen.

Robin leaned back into the soft black leather cushions and watched the city pass by. Joseph turned left on Twelfth Street and the team took them through Capitol Square. The twin rows of oaks that led to the governor's mansion sported soft autumn colors. Against the acres of lush green grass they seemed too golden to be real.

The white columns of the state capitol loomed from beyond the oaks, and Robin wondered what sort of shenanigans the Confederate Congress might be considering today. Generally, she thought bitterly, they worked hard to foil the brave efforts of the soldiers starving on the front lines.

"Have you heard the latest news, ma'am? I mean 'bout Hood in Georgia?"

"I am not certain I care to hear any news of the glorious General Hood, Private, not after his failure to keep Sherman out of Atlanta."

Robin had met quite a number of Texans during the war and liked very few. She'd assessed them all as boastful blackguards at heart.

Hoggins frowned. "Well, Hood is long on effrontery, that's a fact, but he's got them Northern boys running 'round like chickens with their heads twisted off."

"Indeed?"

"Yes, ma'am. Four days ago the Army of the Tennessee broke up the Western and Atlantic Railroad something terrible. They cut the Federal link between Atlanta and Chattanooga. Sherman's supply line is gone. I do mean *gone*. I'd like to see how he's gonna stick in Atlanta without ammunition and food for his bluebellies. Just you wait. Hood'll have him out of Georgia faster than you can say licketysplit! Oh, this war ain't over yet. No sirree, not by a long shot."

Robin stared at the young man in disbelief. He talked like a civilian, like a man who could not, would not, realize the gravity of their country's situation. Weary anger warmed her veins. How had Davis managed to shield the people of Richmond so? Did none of them understand what was happening out there? That over 100,000 men were absent-without-leave? Men who had waited years for a furlough, begged for one, all the while getting desperate letters from loved ones, "When are you coming back, John? The children and I are doing poorly. I have tried plowing, but in this old rocky ground, I can't get much done," or "We've had nothing but dried peas to eat for almost a year now. We need you home, Raymond. Cain't you come home for just a short spell? You could help with the planting, then you could go right back . . ."

The army called such desertions "plow furloughs." Everybody knew that these men were not cowards. Many returned as soon as they'd seen to it that their wives and children had enough food to carry them through the winter. But their absences crippled the army just as badly as any desertions.

Yet from all across the South courageous men rose to fill the ranks. The injured and sick transferred from offices, commissariats, or the home guard to rejoin their old fighting units. She could not count the men she had seen on the front lines who had arms or legs missing, a patch over one eye, or worse—those who had risen from hospital beds with still bleeding wounds so they could take up their muskets again.

Her anger metamorphosed into despair. Robin stared down at her hands. Against the black wool gabardine of her cape they looked very much like a man's, callused, nails broken, cuticles chewed to nothingness.

Private Hoggins leaned forward. "I'm sorry, ma'am. Did I say something to—"

"No. No, Private," she lied, not wanting to hurt the boy's feelings. "I sincerely wish that more of our people had your undaunted good cheer. The fight would be nowhere near as difficult."

"If my commanding officer would just let me go fight, I swear I could lick the whole Yankee nation by myself. I have asked and asked for a transfer to the front lines, but he won't hear of it. Says he needs me here."

"I'm sure he does, Private. Be glad you are home."

"Yes, ma'am," he answered.

But in his lowered eyes she could see that for him the splendor had not faded. He still considered the war a noble, sacred enterprise. *Dear God, how can You be so cruel?*

Robin sighed and turned to the outside world again. The three-story building that housed the Department of State filled her view. An ugly concrete and steel monstrosity, it covered an entire city block. Only the flowers in the garden and the tall Italianate windows with arched tops provided any visual pleasure.

As the carriage pulled up to the front door, the private leaped out, and helped Robin down. The mud proved to be almost nonexistent here. Her boot heels sank into the moist ground, and she lifted her skirt and cautiously selected the best path to the door.

"Right this way, ma'am," Private Hoggins said as they passed the first-floor Treasury Department, then climbed the stairs to the third floor. Two military guards stood at ease outside a great mahogany door.

Hoggins saluted the guards and announced, "This here is Mrs. Heatherton. The President is expecting her, so I 'spect you ought to let him know she's waiting."

One of the guards raised a gloved fist to knock on the door. "Mr. President, sir, Mrs. Heatherton is here to see you. Shall I show her in?"

The sound of a chair scraping on a wood floor came from within the room. Then a voice, as dignified as it was weary, answered, "Yes, of course, Lieutenant. Thank you."

The lieutenant opened the door and gestured for Robin to enter. She sucked in a breath and walked forward. The door closed behind her.

Jefferson Davis met her halfway across the room and took both of her hands in his. His lean face had a waxy ivory sheen that accentuated the gauntness of his cheeks and sharpness of his pointed nose. Twin bruises encircled his pale eyes. Yet he carried himself with an aristocratic grace that could not be mistaken. Clearly he had been reared as a planter's son before he trained as a military tactician. He had attended West Point, she knew, graduating a year before General Lee. "I was deeply saddened by your wire, Mrs. Heatherton. I share your grief and was consoled to learn that Mrs. Greenhow was buried with full military honors. You were there, I take it?" Concern filled his eyes.

"Yes, Mr. President. I watched from afar. The cortege moved from St. Thomas's Church to Oakdale Cemetery with an honor guard. Her coffin was draped in a Confederate flag."

Davis squeezed her hands and stepped away. He wore a gray waistcoat and matching trousers with a white pleated shirt. Lace cuffs protruded from his coat sleeves. When he spoke again, pain tinged his voice. "As well it should have been. She was a very great lady, indeed. Without her there would have been no victory at Bull Run."

Slowly, like a frail old man, he walked back toward his desk beneath the open window on the far side of the room. Wind blew the emerald velvet curtains and set them to thudding against the wall; it reminded Robin of the hollow sound of dirt being shoveled into a fresh grave. But the president took no notice of the sound. In fact, he seemed to notice very little.

"Please be seated, Mrs. Heatherton. I fear that I am too weary to keep standing much longer myself, and I know your journey could not have been more comfortable than mine. You will be as exhausted as I."

Robin crossed to one of the chairs and sank into its plush depths. While she unbuttoned her black cape, Davis pulled another armchair close, sat down heavily, and eyed the satchel on her lap.

"I had heard that you'd been away, Mr. President," she said. "We get only tidbits of news in the field, but I was aware that you delivered speeches in Macon, Montgomery, and Augusta. When did you return to Richmond?"

"Just this morning. I came in from Columbia, South Carolina. I must, consequently, beg your patience if I ask you to repeat things for me. I've managed scant sleep in the past fifteen days, and my concentration is not what it ought to be. I am certain that riding a train throughout the night is far worse torture than the racks criminals were subjected to in medieval Europe."

Robin smiled. "I concur with that."

"I knew you would. Well, shall we get on with the business at hand then? I know you will be anxious to spend time with your family here in Richmond. How long is it that you have been absent from them?"

"Seven months, sir."

"Much too long a time."

"Yes, I'm afraid I miss my son very badly, Mr. President."

"I quite understand."

She opened her satchel and drew out the letters. "These were in Mrs. Greenhow's bag." She handed them across to him. Davis took them and frowned down at the water-smeared ink. "As you can see, they are marked 'absolutely confidential.' Ordinarily I would have read any and all such dispatches, just in case the letters themselves had to be destroyed rather than allowing their capture. But I did not read these, sir."

"I see."

While he opened each letter and read the contents, Robin studied the room. She'd never been here before, and the opulence stunned her, from the satin-brocaded chairs and rose-strewn carpet to the Chinese silk embroidery that adorned the tables. "Rich man's war, and poor man's fight," the privates had started calling it.

Jefferson Davis rose from his chair, tossed the letters on his desk, and went to stand before the window. He pulled contemplatively at the beard under his chin.

"Is there anything I might be able to clarify, Mr. President?" Robin asked.

He gave a vague shake of the head, then sighed aloud, "No, it is just that I find the information hard to credit, that's all."

Robin leaned forward, sitting on the edge of her chair. He wasn't questioning Rose's reliability, was he? "Mr. President, those letters were given to Mrs. Greenhow by Admiral Hobart-Hampden, but they came from Ambassador Mason, who received them from Commander James Bulloch in Liverpool. I can think of few more reliable sources, sir. What do you find hard to credit? If I may ask?"

Davis gazed at her for a long moment before speaking. "I am aware of your abilities to safeguard dangerous information, Mrs. Heatherton, but I do not wish to burden you with so heavy a load as this. If any hint of this story were to reach the world beyond these doors, I dare say our future would be very grim, indeed. More grim, even, than it is already."

"I understand."

Davis' dark brows drew together. "Let me tell you that despite my bold words of encouragement to our dear citizenry, I fear the worst, though I cannot yet admit the possibility."

She nodded. "Mr. President, I do not mean to put pressure upon you, but I may be able to help you interpret the information in those letters, if you will allow me to know their contents. After years of working with Mrs. Greenhow I have developed the ability to decipher even very subtle nuances of meaning in her writing. If you will forgive me for speaking frankly, sir—"

"Having heard of your reputation for exactly that, Mrs. Heatherton, I assure you I will not be offended." Davis gestured with a pale hand. "Pray continue."

"There may be details that you are missing, Mr. President. Critical details. Please, let me help you."

Davis folded his arms and appeared to be contemplating her words. Then he came over to stand in front of her, looking down gravely. "I am certain that I owe you at least that much. Please forgive my hesitation." Yet he paused again, as though deciding how much to reveal. "What do you know of our Torpedo Bureau, Mrs. Heatherton?"

"I—I'm sorry, sir," she said, embarrassed. "Very little, I'm afraid."

"Then perhaps you are more familiar with the activities of our secret agents abroad. We have for some time been engaged in attempts to persuade various European scientists of the viability of our cause. Were you aware of this?"

Robin's throat went dry. She had considered those reports to be rumors of the worst sort, malicious, vain attempts to engender hope where none existed. The stories had been fantastic, of engineers working day and night constructing a glorious new weapon in a shed on the shores of the James River, of soldiers assigned to dig a deep hole in the riverbank, and of dismembered barrels of naval guns being fitted into the hole to create a long tube. She had even heard that the famed navigator Matthew Fontaine Maury was involved in the project.

She laced her fingers in her lap. "I know that one of our agents in England has been working with Lord Kelvin, sir, but I do not know the nature of his efforts."

"I myself understand only the most basic elements of the concept, but Lord Kelvin claims he knows the proper means to liquefy oxygen." Seeing Robin's eyes narrow, he continued, "In addition, another of our agents has been working with Ernst Mach—"

"The great German physicist? What might he contribute to our Torpedo Bureau, sir?"

"What, indeed." A faint smile touched his lips. "Our agents tell me he has the ability to provide us with a turbine and a gyroscopic stabilizer mechanism."

"To what effect?"

He cocked his head and his brows lifted, as though he couldn't believe it himself. "To power and guide a revolutionary new missile, Mrs. Heatherton. The Tredegar Iron Works is, at this very moment, in the process of constructing the basic device. By all accounts, we should be able to fire this missile at Washington within a few short months."

Robin sank back into the overstuffed chair. "Rose said that the information in those letters could turn the tide of the war . . . I didn't believe her."

"Nor do I, altogether. You see now why I hesitated to discuss these details." Davis went to his chair and sat down again, crossing his legs. His pale eyes bored into Robin. "But what I must seek to do now is to convince my men in the Torpedo Bureau that indeed it can be done. They must work round the clock to assure it is done."

"How may I help you?"

His patrician mouth tightened. "I must confess that you can best help me by allowing me to discuss another matter with you."

"And what is this other matter?"

"If I may so dare, I would like to ask a very great favor of you."

"A favor?"

"Yes. It is true, is it not, that your husband is serving as a cavalry officer with General Forrest in Tennessee?"

"Yes."

"Good. Please allow me to make this as clear as possible. Though I am accused of the opposite, I attempt to save as many of my troops as is possible while still accomplishing our goals. I believe you may be able to assist me here. You and your husband. But the mission will require that you be away from Richmond for several months."

I won't be home for Christmas. Oh, Jeremy. . . . A tight band constricted around Robin's heart. She nodded. "I understand. Please go on."

"General Hood is devising a method for driving that devil Sherman from Georgia. To accomplish this task, he will require every possible scrap of intelligence. I am convinced of the effectiveness of your talents for information gathering, Mrs. Heatherton."

"I am, of course, willing to do whatever you ask of me, but—"

Davis interrupted, "In fairness, there is something else you must know before you agree to this. Let me provide you with information of a more personal nature."

"I'm listening, sir."

"Do you know of a man named Thomas Corley, Mrs. Heatherton?"

Robin shook her head, but her shoulder muscles knotted at the forbidding tone of his voice. "No. At least I can't place the name."

"I feared as much," Davis said. "I, too, have only recently become aware of his existence. Indeed, I was informed just four days ago, while in Augusta. He is a provost marshal for the Federal Bureau of Military Information. Ah, yes, I see that you understand. But you may incorrectly assume his mission to be of a standard nature, rooting out and prosecuting spies, or those who have given aid and comfort to us."

Robin frowned. "You are saying that is not the case?"

"I am. Dependable sources report that he is quite deranged and blames you for the death of his brother at the battle of Ball's Bluff. Apparently Major Corley will stop at nothing to achieve revenge. He has offered one thousand dollars in gold for your capture, Mrs. Heatherton, and I have, through sources of my own, discovered that this money does not come from the Federal Treasury. These are the Major's personal funds."

"So this 'mission' is in reality a vendetta against me?"

Davis vented a tired breath. "It would seem so. Upon receiving this disturbing information, I dispatched agents to monitor the house where your son is staying—circumspectly, of course. I felt certain that any who might have been enticed by Major Corley's handsome reward would seek you there. So far our agents have observed no activity, but—"

"But," Robin said. With that sort of reward, she would never be safe again. Nor would any member of her family. Her gaze sought the window and the direction of her son. Was Corley so insane that he would harm a little boy to get back at her? "Corley's bounty hunters will come looking for me here."

"I am glad that you grasp this situation, Mrs. Heatherton. After the remarkable work you have accomplished for our country, I felt it my personal duty to apprise you of this latest development. The mission with Hood's forces would at least provide you with some distance from this Major Corley."

Robin looked up. "I am honored by your concern, Mr. President, but I assure you—"

"You may, of course, refuse to accept the mission. But my advice is that you first allow me to wire General Forrest so that he might arrange a time and place for you to speak privately with your husband about it. I am in hopes that General Forrest will be willing to release your husband from his current duties so that the two of you may work in concert on this project." Davis touched his chin with the first two fingers of his right hand and sat very still. His face seemed to lengthen and narrow as he waited for her response.

"How much time do I have, Mr. President? I would like to see my son before I leave Richmond, especially since neither my husband nor I will be home for the holidays."

"We must move quickly on this, but take what time you need. When I have received the answering transmittal from General Forrest, I will contact you at your mother-in-law's home. Will that be appropriate?"

"Yes, sir."

"Very well then." Davis nodded. "By the way, before it slips my mind, General Lee asked me to convey his fond regards. He has not forgotten your tireless efforts at Fredericksburg."

"Please return my heartfelt wishes when you next speak with him, sir. My confidence in the General has never dwindled."

"Nor has mine. Though I fear he too often feels himself unappreciated, what with the dire predicaments in Petersburg and Atlanta."

"That shall change come spring, Mr. President," she added with false hope. "I have no doubt—"

"Yes," Jefferson Davis said, "it shall change." But his voice wavered, like a man looking through the present to a frightening, uncertain future. "If I can keep my engineers scurrying like ants, and if Lord Kelvin and Mr. Mach can meet their promises. Or," he added "if Divine Providence should see fit to aid General Hood's efforts. And should you decide to accept this mission, you will know that far sooner than I."

He stood. "Now, allow me to reveal the General's plan to you. Though I confess I dislike it, under the circumstances, I believe it is our only hope should the Torpedo project fail."

"Not our only hope, Mr. President. There is still Sarah Slater."

Memories swirled. The meeting where Rose had presented Sarah's plan had taken place over a year ago, yet the grave tones of voice, the tight facial expression remained crystal clear in Robin's mind.

"Yes," Davis sighed. "There is still Mrs. Slater. Though I do hope we can discern a path other than the one she offers. I loathe conspiracies, particularly when they involve such . . . final . . . remedies."

"So do I, sir. Truly. Forgive me for interrupting you. What were you saying about the General's plan?"

CHAPTER 7

The storm clouds parted, leaving a peephole for the moon to spill silver light down upon the rolling forested hills. All around Robin a magnificent net of diamonds sparkled to life as every raindrop that trembled on the autumn leaves gleamed and glittered. The muddy Tennessee River below metamorphosed into a half-mile wide shining serpent. She glanced back over her shoulder. Her crawl across the bluff had left a clear, dark swath through the wet grass. If a Yankee sentry should happen to stumble upon it in the moonlight, it would mean swift death, but it couldn't be helped.

She turned back. On the highest hilltop to the north, the stockaded fort occupied a commanding position, overlooking the massive Union depot and storage facility on the riverbank. Silently, she counted the artillery pieces that bristled from the fort's parapet. Twelve in all.

Taking a deep breath, she eased forward on her belly and peered down at the river. The haversack on her back was light, containing only a small ration of food and her blue cape. Johnsonville, Tennessee, sparkled with hundreds of bivouac fires. Secret reports warned that about two thousand soldiers manned this fort, and she believed it. The wharves swarmed with men. Three gunboats, eleven transports, and eighteen barges were moored at the landing. Negroes unloaded the barges, heaping the supplies into the cars of two freight trains waiting to make the run to Nashville. Officers and white soldiers came and went, and despite the hour a few civilian passengers strolled along the wharves, visiting the jumble of army stores that crowded around the immense warehouse. Bottles glinted in front of one store, while another sported new silk top hats—just what every battle-weary soldier needed—and still another displayed boxes of ammunition and gunpowder.

The animated scene wore an air of complete security, which amazed

Robin. Had the recent naval victory lulled the Federals into believing themselves safe?

General Forrest had related the major events to her last night. Several days before, he'd captured two Federal vessels, the *Venus* and the *Undine*. He'd tried to move both upriver, but the *Venus* had been so overpowered by the Federals that the Confederate commander had been forced to ram the bow into the riverbank and scuttle the vessel. Then, just that morning, Robin had witnessed the fate of the other vessel. The *Undine* had fallen under heavy attack, trapped between Union gunboats. Captain Gracey had ordered his men to soak the mattresses in oil, then set them afire before they abandoned ship. When the fires reached the magazine, the horrific explosions had ripped the *Undine* apart.

But if the Yankees imagined that General Forrest had fled to lick his wounds, they had a grisly surprise in store. For twenty-four hours Robin had been watching the Confederates reconnoiter, deciding where to place their batteries. After nightfall the cannoneers manhandled their guns through the mud, gouged embrasures into embankments, and concealed the batteries with brush. At least three stood at the ready: Thrall's in the north, Morton's across the river, and Walton's to the south.

Come tomorrow, all hell would break loose. Despite the fact that the three Union boats had twenty-eight guns among them, they had almost no chance of escaping. She'd heard stories of Forrest's legendary temper, but after having witnessed that hard-eyed glare, she knew he'd do whatever was necessary to kill every man in Johnsonville.

By next nightfall, this camp and its surroundings for miles up and down the river are going to be a solid sheet of flame. Forrest will be moving his troops by the glare.

The jaunty music of fiddles and harmonicas carried up the bluff to her.

Fifty feet below, four soldiers stood silhouetted before a large fire, talking, laughing. One of them broke into a jig and began singing *We Are Coming, Father Abraham* at the top of his lungs. He had a healthy Irish brogue. A bottle of popskull must have made the rounds, because the soldier didn't bother to start at the beginning:

> *You have called us, and we're coming, by*
> *Richmond's bloody tide*
> *To lay us down, for Freedom's sake, our*
> *brothers' bones beside;*

Or from foul treason's savage grasp to
wrench the murderous blade,
And in the face of foreign foes its
fragments to parade.
Six hundred thousand loyal men and true
have gone before;
We are coming, Father Abraham, three
hundred thousand more!

The other men clapped and laughed while Robin worked her way through a thicket of chickasaw plum, propelling herself over the wet grass by pushing with her toes and pulling with her elbows. Leaves brushed her blue shirt, but the fabric had absorbed so much moisture that only faint hisses resulted. The agonizing slowness was almost unbearable. *Charles should be waiting just ahead . . .*

The message she'd received at Paris Landing had surprised her—not that posing as a Yankee soldier would be new for Charles. At large encampments where the men barely recognized their commanding officers, the imposture required little skill, and Charles had done it many times, but given the recent military antics along the river, it seemed very risky.

She inched forward another foot; a sour smell, like homemade wine, scented the air. Clusters of small withered fruits dangled from reddish twigs in the heart of the plum thicket. She must have bruised them. She started to smile, then froze. Through the tangle of stems, something moved.

He lay on the ground like a lean snake. A skirmish cap covered most of his blond hair, but his patrician profile was unmistakable. She whispered, *"Charles."*

In the silvered gleam, she saw a look of relief slacken his face. "Oh, Robin, thank God. I've been worried sick."

She crawled to meet him and he wrapped his arms around her, hugging her so hard it drove the air from her lungs. For a moment, he just held her, saying nothing, kissing her hair and face, and Robin let herself drown in the comfort he offered. How desperately she wished they could just run away, tonight, run away and head for Colorado Territory to start a new life. She hugged him back.

"Are you really here, Robin? I can't believe this isn't a dream, like all the other times I've held you in the past year."

She stroked his back tenderly. "I'm here, Charles. We may even be able to stay together for a while. President Davis—"

"Wait—please. I . . . I don't want to talk about the war yet." He shifted so he could look down at her, and his eyes traced every line of her face, as if comparing each with his memory, seeing how much she'd changed. "I haven't much time. I promised Private Geller I'd supervise the barge unloading at nine o'clock. But I must hear news of home, even if only for a minute or two. You were in Richmond, you must have seen Jeremy and my mother. How are they?"

"Both are well, Charles. Your mother is working at the hospital. She has shredded almost every dress she owns to use as bandages. I was amazed. She dresses in homespun and is proud of it." Robin had never really gotten along with Mrs. Heatherton, but the war seemed to have changed the old woman, draining the animosity from her heart.

"And Jeremy?" Charles removed her hat to touch her hair, as though feeling its black wealth for the first time. "How is our son?"

"He's . . ." Robin's throat constricted. Images of that tormented little face would not leave her alone. "He's . . . lonely. When I told him neither of us would be home for Christmas he ran up to his room and refused to come out. I found him hiding under his bed, crying."

"I felt like crying myself," Charles said with a deep sigh. "I only heard the news yesterday. If General Forrest's messenger had not also told me you were just across the river, I think I'd have shot myself. Did you have time to explain to Jeremy why we couldn't come home?"

"I tried, Charles." In the branches above them, an owl hooted, and both Robin and Charles swiveled to see its eyes glinting in the darkness as it sailed between the trees. She twined her fingers in Charles' damp blue sleeve and continued: "I lay down on the floor beside Jeremy's bed and talked to him until he fell asleep. But . . . You must understand, you've seen him for a total of six weeks in the past three years, and I'm not much better. We've been away for so long he barely remembers us, but he loves us more than he ever has. Your mother said he's been pre-paring for Christmas for months, talking about what he would tell us when we came home, about school, and the siege, and how his pony was killed by a shell. He . . . he has a new toy . . . he made it himself . . ." Her voice shook and she stopped, unable to continue.

That toy had broken her heart.

Charles laid his hand warmly against her cheek. In the pale moon gleam his blue eyes looked sad and colorless. "What toy, Robin?"

"It's a . . . a little white horse named Traveller."

Charles smiled, and she knew that had they not been so close to enemy forces, he would have laughed aloud. "Why would that disturb you so? It sounds charming. General Lee would be delighted."

"General Lee is the cause of it, Charles. It happened several months ago when the General was in Richmond. We were invited to attend a dinner in his honor. Jeremy and I went . . ."

"And?"

Robin inhaled a deep breath of the wet, green scents of the river. "Your son has changed a great deal, Charles. He's more grown-up than any five-year-old has a right to be, and more—"

"What happened when you introduced him to the General?"

"He acted as though he'd been waiting his entire life to talk to Lee. He walked right up and said, 'General, sir, do you ever have trouble going to sleep?' "

Charles' brows lifted. "I can well imagine what Lee said to that, especially after Gettysburg."

"Lee answered, 'I admit that I am often wakeful, Jeremy. Why do you ask?'

"And Jeremy looked up at him, stammering, 'I—I can't sleep a lot, sir. My stomach hurts. I guess it's because I'm scared. Are you ever scared, sir, I mean in battle?' "

Robin rolled to her side to face Charles. His forehead furrowed. Behind him, oak leaves shivered in the faint breeze that swept up the river.

"And what did Lee say?" Charles pressed.

"Oh, he was very kind. He knelt down and put a hand on Jeremy's shoulder and said, 'No, Jeremy, not in battle. You see, I have Traveller with me and I know that Traveller won't let anything hurt me, at least not if he's able.' "

"And that's where the toy comes from?"

"Yes." Robin nodded, remembering her son's face. Illumination had blazed in his eyes, as if God had just come down from heaven and revealed the secret of salvation to him.

Charles smoothed her hair. "So what's wrong with that, Robin? Children need such toys. They drive away the terrors that lurk in the darkness. When I was a boy, I had a toy sword that I carried everywhere. I even slept with it in my hands." He chuckled. "Just in case some creature formed out of the darkness and tried to jump me while I was asleep."

"Jeremy doesn't just sleep with Traveller, Charles. He eats with it, takes it with him to the privy. Your mother said she tried to take it away from him a few months ago and he screamed as if she'd threatened to cut off his leg."

Charles frowned at the blades of grass that thrust up between them. Absently, he began mashing them flat with the palm of his hand, as if to eliminate even that small barrier. "That is a little extreme, but he's only five, Robin. He'll outgrow it. Once the war is over and he is with us again, he won't need the toy anymore. I don't even remember what happened to my sword. Somewhere along the way, it became unimportant and got lost. You'll see, that will happen with Jeremy's toy horse, too."

"I pray you're right. But he . . . he didn't seem well when I saw him, Charles." She searched his face. "I didn't want to tell you, but—"

She shook her head, reluctant to admit even to herself how strange, how disconnected from reality, their son had seemed. "Never mind. Don't pay any attention to me. It was probably my imagination and not Jeremy at all. I was under a great deal of pressure."

Charles' face darkened. "Tell me."

"Let's discuss the war instead."

He nodded. "Yes, we'd better. I only have about fifteen minutes left and I'll need five to get down to the wharf. Go ahead. What did President Davis say? I'm very curious about this new mission of ours."

Robin reached out and gripped Charles' hand. The fingers felt large and strong in her grasp. It bothered her that she would have to omit the most interesting part of the story, but such was the case. Davis had sworn her to secrecy.

"First, he has already written General Forrest requesting that you be released from your regular duties here, so that we may both be reassigned to intelligence work with General Hood. The President has spoken with both Hood and Beauregard and devised a new strategy for winning the war."

"What strategy?"

"Hood plans on crossing the Tennessee River at Guntersville, smashing Sherman's rail supply line in the Stevenson–Bridgeport area, and then moving on Nashville. He hopes to resupply his own forces there, as well as gather more recruits, so that he may head northward into Kentucky and Ohio. Everyone knows that the Bluegrass region is filled with Southern sympathizers, so even more men should flock to our cause and swell Hood's ranks. Hood expects to wreak enough havoc to force Sherman to pursue him and believes he should be strong enough by the time he reaches Cincinnati to whip Sherman. After that he will cross the Cumberland and come up in the rear of Grant's blue host outside of Petersburg. This shift should allow Hood and Forrest to defeat Grant, or at least keep him busy long enough for General Lee to march on Washington."

Clouds had covered the face of the moon again, leaving them only the dim wavering light of the Union's bivouac fires. Charles' jaw moved as he ground his teeth in thought. "Do you believe it?"

"I believe it's possible, yes. Even if Old Wooden Head Hood cannot defeat Sherman, or if Sherman refuses to pursue him, and heads south toward the Gulf, as is rumored, Hood and Lee would be in position to annihilate Grant at least two weeks before Sherman could arrive to assist him. Winter is coming. You know how infernal the roads in Georgia and the Carolinas become. Hood will have a far easier time moving caissons along the frozen routes of the North than Sherman will in the gumbo of the South."

Charles didn't seem to be breathing. "And what of Mrs. Slater? I don't understand why all this is necessary. Hasn't President Davis authorized her to—"

"Only as a last resort, Charles. He hates the idea as much as I do."

Charles sat up suddenly and peered over the edge of the bluff to the wharf below. Robin rose and followed his gaze. A short, fat soldier paced arrogantly in front of the laborers, hands propped on his hips. "That's Geller down there shouting at the Negroes. He's a perfect little bully. And I'm late relieving him. I haven't much more time. What else, Robin?"

"Just one thing."

She ran a hand through her hair and tilted her head to meet his gaze. "I don't want you to dwell on it, but I'm being pursued by a provost marshal."

"A provost marshal? But isn't every spy hunted—"

"Not like this. He's offered a thousand dollars in gold for my capture. Apparently I provided information that led to the death of his brother at the battle of Ball's Bluff and he's vowed to kill me for it."

Charles' voice came out low and strained. "For God's sake, Robin . . . with that kind of reward—"

"I know."

Charles pulled her to him and kissed her forehead. "I want you to listen to me. Don't argue, just listen. If anything happens to me, I want you to forget the war. Go home, grab Jeremy, and get the hell out of the South. Disappear. You know how to do that. Change your name, your appearance, go some place that this man would never think to look. A place as far from the war as you can find. Do you understand me?" He reached down and tipped up her chin to pin her eyes with his own.

"Yes, I understand. I will."

"Good. Now, please Robin, I want to love you," he said, and laid a gentle hand on her breast. "For a few blessed minutes, let me love you."

In answer, she began unbuttoning his uniform coat. He kissed her and hastily worked at her buttons.

They loved each other in a sudden thunder shower with lightning slashing the sky above and a soft mat of autumn leaves and uniforms beneath them. When he began moving quickly, they stared into each other's eyes. The rainy world faded to nothingness. Only the sweet friction between them mattered. The sudden tide of sensation overwhelmed first her, then him.

Afterward, Charles kissed her hair and held her tightly.

But it lasted only a minute.

He backed away, dressed. "I'll meet you here just before dawn. Don't panic if I'm a bit late, and if you have to move from this spot, wait for me near Morton's artillery battery, on the other side of the river. You know where it is?"

"Of course, but don't be late, Charles. We need the darkness to—"

He smiled. "I am aware of that. Thank you. . . . I love you, Robin. I love you so much. Don't take any unnecessary chances."

"I never do."

"I know." He grinned warmly at her, lifted a hand in farewell and trotted away, weaving through the trees to get to the trail beneath the fort that led down to the river. She watched him until he vanished behind a rise—then she dressed.

The raucous activities below seemed to have intensified. In at least four camps soldiers were clapping and singing. Three men played fiddles now, all different tunes. Robin closed her eyes for a time and concentrated on the sweet notes that rode the night wind.

When she opened her eyes, Charles had reappeared on the wharf, walking toward Geller. The little man shouted curses at Charles. She could hear *"sonofabitch,"* but Charles just smiled and gestured calmly. Finally, Geller laughed and left the wharf, marching toward the makeshift saloon north of the depot where a crowd of men had gathered before a plank bar propped on two whisky barrels.

Robin crawled forward on her hands and knees until she could stretch out on her stomach behind a clump of winged sumac. Below her, Charles moved about with perfect ease, monitoring the Negro laborers, saluting the officers who passed, joking with the privates who came to loaf on the wharf and watch the black men work.

Yes, Robin, look at him. He's really there. He's breathing. His heart is beating. . . . Soon, you'll be together.

Bits of conversation drifted up to her, and Robin cocked her head to hear better. The Irishman who had been dancing the jig earlier now squatted before the fire, shaking his head, while he told of Fredericksburg. Several of the youngest men opposite him listened with their eyes glowing. Coffee cups had stopped midway to their lips. The Irishman's voice rose and fell as he described window blinds flapping like huge bat wings in destroyed houses, being trapped so near the stone wall that marked the Confederate line that he could see the men in gray cook breakfast and clean their muskets, "no more than eighty yards distant!" The young privates—new recruits, Robin suspected—seemed to stop breathing when the veteran lifted both hands and drew wavy lines in the air. She caught only the word, "lights," and knew what he was speaking about.

Across the canvas of her imagination the glorious *aurora borealis* that had spanned the heavens that night at Fredricksburg flared to life. Fiery lances had shot through a wavering pearlescent haze and spawned garlands of golden flame that stretched into infinity. They had buried their dead by that eerie glow.

Robin rested her chin on her hands. Rain had started falling again. Protected by the thicket, she couldn't feel it, but it speckled the surface of the muddy river below and pattered on the tree leaves, making them dip and sway. The rich scent of soaked earth encircled her. She inhaled and held the fragrance in her lungs for as long as she could.

Charles had knelt down to help one of the laborers lift a heavy crate. They walked toward the train car, carrying their load, and she studied the way his hard muscles showed through his shirt.

A warm sensation flooded out along her limbs: just being able to see him again made her feel safe. With the warmth came numbing tendrils of exhaustion. Robin yawned. She could not risk napping, but while she waited for him, she could daydream. She rolled onto her back, propped her revolver on her chest, and stared up at the stars. Her thoughts drifted to lazy summers long ago, when bumblebees flitted through the grass, and the sweet scent of magnolias wafted on afternoon breezes . . .

Soaked to the bone, cold and tired, Charles paced the dock anxiously. It was after one o'clock in the afternoon! What had happened to the man who was supposed to relieve him? With the relentless rain had come bitter wind. He shoved his hands into his pockets and shivered. The dim gray light glistened from the river. On the southern horizon, the wall of storm clouds had begun to disperse and shade golden.

Damn it! What happened to Calhoun? . . . Robin, I'm coming. I'm coming!

Black men marched back and forth before him, carrying the last of the crates from the boats to the waiting train, but he barely noticed. He could *feel* General Forrest's cannoneers readying their artillery, checking their aims, but he could not walk away from his post, not without arousing suspicion.

Up and down the river a low hum of conversation, punctuated by coughs, competed with the soft patter of the drizzle on the wooden dock. Men moved all around him, most nothing more than soaked wraiths in the mist.

"Private Jonesborough?"

"Yes," Charles said and turned so fast, he skidded on the slick dock. When he'd regained his balance, he saw a sergeant standing before him, short and stocky, with hard green eyes. Black hair hung over his ears, but his hat had shielded his broad flat nose and high forehead. Charles' heart started to pound. He snapped a salute. "The unloading is almost completed, sergeant."

"That's fine, private." He surveyed the loaded train cars with a critical eye and nodded. "You've done a good job. Now, come with me. I have another task—"

"But, sir," Charles objected. "I was supposed to be off duty hours ago! My relief hasn't showed up. I was hoping you'd come down to tell me I could go find my tent."

"This won't take long. I know you've been standing out here all night. Follow me, soldier."

"Yes, sir."

Charles had to lock his eyes on the sergeant's back to keep from glancing up to where Robin waited for him. Was she watching? He dared not endanger her by looking.

Charles bowed his head against the rain as they strode through the ankle-deep mud near the railroad track and started up the rain-speckled river, away from the tents and men. Puddles filled every hollow, and the sergeant made no attempt to veer around them. He bulled his way through, splashing and cursing, as though in a hurry . . .

When they stepped over the tracks and rounded the end of the last railroad car, Charles looked up, and for a moment he could not believe his eyes.

Six privates stood in front of him. Rifles lay cradled in their arms, the barrels pointed downward to keep them dry. Behind the six stood five officers, including Colonel Charles R. Thompson, in command of Johnsonville.

Charles stopped dead in his muddy tracks; several soldiers emerged from hiding places behind buildings, between railroad cars . . . hemming him in.

"Sergeant, what the hell—"

"Put your hands up, son." The man pulled his pistol from its holster and aimed at Charles' stomach. "They just want to talk to you, ask you a few questions, that's all."

"Who are they?"

"Officers from Washington City."

Charles did as he'd been told and lifted his hands high over his head while the sergeant searched him and removed his weapons.

A red-haired man broke from the group of officers and strode toward Charles . . .

Robin crawled forward to peer over the edge of the bluff at the docks and train cars below. She'd seen Charles walk away with the sergeant, but with the drenching rain, she'd lost them as they angled away from the encampment and men.

Pulling her telescope from her haversack, she got down on her belly and braced her elbows. The lens panned group after group of men sitting around campfires, breakfasting, as if nothing were amiss, before she found the group, a quarter mile away, where Charles stood. A cry lodged in her throat when she saw the six riflemen line out and kneel down, taking aim.

The soldiers fired and a billowing cloud of black smoke roiled upward into the silvery mist. Charles fell, twisting around, collapsing like a rag doll.

"Jesus Christ!" someone shouted. "What the hell's going on?"

The telescope fell from Robin's numb fingers. It landed in the rain-soaked grass without a sound.

She stumbled to her feet and ran, taking a route through the dense trees, slipping in the mud, falling and rising, sliding down a deer trail toward the shore. *Charles? Charles!*

She pushed by a burly soldier who stood riveted, staring in the direction of the firing squad and found herself caught up in the crowd of ten or twelve men that rushed toward the distant site. The scent of gunpowder made her heart jam sickeningly against her ribs. Desperately, she lashed out with her fists.

"Get out of my way! Damn you! My husband. They shot my husband!"

A lieutenant dressed in a worn great coat grabbed her arm and stared at her Union uniform. "Who are you, miss? What are you doing here?"

"Let me go! Damn you!" she screamed, wrenching her arm free and brutally shoving through the mob. *Charles needs me!*

"My husband. Where is he?"

In the dark recesses of Robin's soul, a small pathetic voice kept whispering, *"No, no, he can't be dead! God, no, no . . . !"*

Pulling her pistol, she shoved it into the back of the man in front of her. "Move, *goddamn you*, or I'll kill you right now!"

The soldier cast feverish eyes on her and backpedaled. "What the—"

"My husband!" she screamed. "Where is he? I have to get to him!"

The rest of the camp had wakened to the disturbance. A hush fell as men stood up, murmuring to each other, squinting through the rain in the direction of the commotion. In a few moments, curiosity would get the better of them. They'd begin ambling over to see what had happened . . .

Robin shouldered forward.

She started to shake. He lay so still, so very still on the muddy ground. Rain beaded on his face.

Blood . . . blood-soaked blond hair . . . bullet-shredded shirt. The wedding ring she'd given him gleamed in the brightening light of dawn.

Like a machine, Robin's soul froze this instant. She couldn't blink, couldn't allow time to move, knowing if it did, the truth would sink in and she wouldn't be able to stand it. *"No, it can't be . . . "* Her soul kept repeating the words over and over, like a prayer.

A man's hand, large and tender, brushed away the lock of hair that had fallen over her eyes, then reached down and closed around her gun hand with the power of an iron shackle. He wrenched the pistol from her grip.

"Mrs. Heatherton," he said.

Robin turned and looked up dumbly into the face of a very tall, red-haired man. A big man. He had odd, pale blue eyes. A cruel smile twisted his lips.

The entire world died around Robin. Her heart slowed, jolting her with each thunderous beat, and the lavender hue that penetrated the rain shaded to gray at the edges of her vision. Only his eyes existed in all of creation. "Major Corley."

"Ah," he said with a nod, "so you know who I am."

In answer, she threw herself backward, ripped free, and lunged for the pistol on the hip of the closest man. She tore it from its holster, swung around and fired.

The bullet took Corley in the left shoulder, the force slamming him to the ground, where he rolled, cried out, and scrambled to his knees, gasping, *"Don't just stand there! Shoot her, damn you! She's a spy!"*

Robin lurched forward, her pistol aimed straight ahead.

Veering away from the camps that lined the shore, she picked up her feet and ran hard. Waist-length black hair streamed out around her. She hadn't gone more than a hundred feet before she collided head-on with two soldiers. They gaped in surprise. One had the sense to unsling the rifle from his shoulder. Robin didn't break stride. She aimed for his heart, killing him quickly, cleanly.

As though her shot had been a signal, all ten pieces of Morton's artillery went off. The deafening roar of cannon fired almost simultaneously shook the ground beneath her feet. From everywhere a cacophony of shouts erupted. Feet splashed in the mud as men ran for cover. Confederate artillerists concentrated their fire on the gunboats, and the crews scrambled to abandon ship. Vessels exploded, setting the wharves aflame, sending up a blinding wall of black smoke that not even the rain could penetrate. Union cannoneers replied wildly, firing and screaming as they watched sparks alight on the landward installations. Soon all the stores blazed.

"Stop her!" Corley shouted. "Don't let her get away! Shoot her! Shoot her!"

But with the holocaust around them, no one cared about Robin anymore. She ran freely.

The warehouse, situated on high ground, collapsed under fire and a river of blue flame poured down the hillside, crackling as it scorched trees and earth. What a stench! Bourbon. There must have hundreds of barrels stored in that warehouse.

Robin shrugged out of her pack, gulped air, and dove headfirst into the water, going deep, as deep as she could.

CHAPTER 8

Garrison Parker turned up the collar of his buffalo coat and picked his way over the icy rocks toward the water that cascaded down Russell Gulch. Wind had been howling for the past hour, sweeping the tall pines clean of snow and piling it in ten-foot drifts against the slopes. A solid sheet of leaden clouds filled the sky. It would snow again soon. He could taste it in the air, that biting earthy flavor. Up the hill, his mule brayed a stern reprimand.

"I'll be there in a minute, Honey!" he shouted back.

She snorted and pawed the ground.

If Honey could have talked, he knew, those snorts would have been curses. The temperature had plummeted to around zero, and she was stamping her hooves to keep warm. But he couldn't give up now. The rusty gold pan hanging from a thong on his belt clanged as it hit his pocket watch chain. He'd work just one more section of the creek, then he'd fetch Honey and head for home.

"You got nobody to blame but yourself," he muttered. "You knew this storm would be rolling down 'round noon time."

Some people had big toes that heralded rain, others had prophetic corns or calluses, and Garrison had his nose. Broken in too many brawls to count, the frail bones had healed into a perfect, if slightly crooked, weather vane. Just before a bad snow storm, his nose ached like nobody's business. This morning he'd awakened in such pain that he'd lain in bed for an extra ten minutes trying to remember who'd hit him last night and wondering if he'd won or lost. When he realized the rest of him didn't hurt at all, he'd determined that it couldn't have been a fight, least not a good one. That could mean just one thing: Today was not the day to go hunting gold. His better judgment told him to stay inside close to a roaring fire.

So, naturally, he got up, threw the packs on Honey and headed for the high country. Life had convinced him that people who listened to their better judgments rarely had full stomachs. And never got rich.

Garrison knelt to dip his pan in the creek. His hands tingled in the frigid water, but he swished his pan around and around. Small amounts of sand and water poured over the edge with each circle, leaving the heaviest stream gravels lying in the bottom where he could scrutinize them.

Nothing!

He tossed the gravel back into the creek and stood up. Clouds blew by above his head, sliding down toward the distant city of Denver. A fine mist of snow crystals had started to fall, and he'd left his hat over his saddlehorn, which meant his mop of brown curls drooped more by the second, sheathing his ears like cold rags.

Miserably, he peered at the sky and said, "Well, hell, it's time I was going home anyhow."

Rising, he tied his pan back on his belt and trudged up the hill, his boots squealing as they crunched the snow. Honey, a splotch of mottled gray against the white, watched his approach through half-lidded eyes. Garrison stopped and studied her for a long moment. She had that glare that boded ill for all concerned.

"Damn it, Honey, I know it's cold. But it ain't like I forced you to stand something I wasn't standing myself."

He continued toward her at a slower pace, sang a few verses of the *Battle Hymn of the Republic*, sprinkled with curses, and smiled at Honey. She laid one of her ears back in response. But just one. That was a good sign. A cautious smile twisted his lips.

When he got to within six or seven paces, he gingerly lifted his hand, hoping she'd let him get close enough to lunge for her lead rope. All the while, he spoke in a calm voice, "Good mule. That's a girl, whoa, now. Be a good mule. Oh, you are *such* a pretty mule, Honey."

Just as he leaped forward, Honey sidestepped, laid back both ears, and tore free from the small aspen tree she'd been tethered to. Dancing around like a Mexican jumping bean, she managed to stay two steps beyond of his reach when he lunged and lunged again for her rope.

"Now, Honey, don't go getting all het up over nothing! We're going home. I swear to God! Whoa. Whoa up there. See me? I'm standing still. I ain't doing nothing!" He looked up at the mountainside, taking in the clouds, pretending to be paying attention to anything but her, while he edged forward.

She cocked her head and peered at him through one eye, giving him that wicked look that told him she knew him for what he was: A liar. With a snort and a kick, she trotted up the hill. The packs on her back, which held all of his mining tools, as well as a brand new unopened bottle of whiskey, swayed and shifted. His hat fell off the saddlehorn into the snow.

"Honey!" he shouted. "Goddamn it, whoa! *Whoa!*"

Honey broke into a run, mane and tail flying as she scaled the steepest slope in sight. Her dapple-gray coloring blended so well with the low scudding clouds she almost disappeared.

Garrison squinted after her so long that flakes of snow crusted up on his lashes. He batted them off. "Folks are right. Mules are evil creatures. Straight out of hell."

As he struggled along in her tracks, the snow intensified, falling in huge fluffy flakes, filling in his footprints almost as quickly as he made them. He shoved his bare hands in the pockets of his buffalo coat. In the valley below, the gale sucked up white lances and hurled them at the peaks. His toes had begun to ache.

"Danm. I can't believe this. Here I am in the middle of a blizzard on my birthday. It figures. God's own justice for imbecility."

He had to fight his way through a knee-deep drift. The wind shrieked by his ears like an enraged banshee, tugging at his collar and sleeves. Several rock overhangs thrust through the mantle of snow ahead. Garrison glared at the slope where Honey had vanished and headed for the closest overhang to take shelter.

"I ought to just walk home by myself. It'd take a few hours, but it ain't like I got any other pressing engagements this afternoon. Not like celebrating or nothing." He grumbled curses to himself. He'd planned a gala evening at Luke's bar.

The first overhang extended about four feet back; the roof hung too low to allow him to sit up straight, but it would be enough. He duck-walked inside and flopped kittywampus against the rear wall. Through the shrilling of the gale he thought he heard hee-hawing.

"I hope you get ate by a grizzly!" he shouted. "A big one!" He picked up a chunk of rock the size of an orange and threw it as hard as he could in Honey's general direction. "Why did humans ever take up with animals in the first place? Should have stuck to slitting their throats and roasting 'em slow over the coals. World would've been a better place."

He twisted around so he could straighten his legs, but his boots ended up out in the snow. Pulling them back in, he brought his knees up, and winced when they scraped the ceiling. Dirt cascaded over his face. He spit it out, "Blast it all." He leaned sideways to peer around his long legs. Outside, the wind hurled sticks and gravel by.

He felt depressed. "Hell, what am I doing here? I been grubbing around these mountains for a year, and haven't seen a single fleck of color. Before that I wasted two years in the army. Thirty years old today, and I ain't never had nothing. And at this rate I ain't never gonna have nothing."

Irritated with himself, he watched the storm. After a while, the snow eased off to intermittent flurries, but bitter cold replaced it. The air started to shimmer. *Must be ten below now. I had damned well better get home.*

Sliding out from under the overhang, he rose and stretched. Blue patches shone in the northern sky, but the wind was still vicious. Around him, the slopes glistened with two inches of new snow.

He started trudging uphill, toward Central City. No more than fifteen minutes had passed before he heard a clopping behind him.

"Don't you come up here!" he yelled. "I'm gonna sell you to a starving Indian tomorrow morning and watch him while he blows your brains out. I don't want to have nothing more to do with you!"

Honey trotted up beside him and matched his pace. When he looked over at her, she thrust her hairy gray chin out and shook her head, flapping her ears back and forth as if to say, "the hell you are."

"Oh, yes, I am. You just think I won't on account of I owe you my life, but my gratitude went south with the birds about half hour ago. Go on, get out of here! Don't you try to make up with me!"

Honey blew softly, swiveling an ear his direction, and he reached out and grabbed her trailing lead rope. She didn't seem to have any objections.

He glared at her. "Damn, a fella could tell you're a female without even looking. You're about as fickle as the wind. *And you lost my hat!* Blast you. There's no finding it now, not with winter just setting in. I'll have to wait till it melts out come spring. By then it'll be mouse-chewed to beat hell, too."

Honey blinked as though she hadn't the slightest idea what had perturbed him. She had adopted the Superior Mule expression.

"You think it's me, huh? 'Cause I made you stand out in the cold all morning? Well, I got bad news. It ain't snowing no more and I think we've got the time to go check one more place before nightfall. Up around Banta Hill. I been wanting to go up there. May as well be today. It's on the way. 'Sides. if I take you home right now, you'll figure you won the battle of wills, and I can't never let that happen. You'd get the notion that you can push me around."

She affectionately nudged his shoulder. "Oh, it's all right. I know why you were mad at me." He reached up and patted her jaw, then tilted his head sideways to rest his cheek warmly against her gray neck. "Glad I got you, old girl. Even if you ain't the best mule in the world. Hell, you're damn near as old as I am."

They'd been climbing for about two hours when Honey stopped dead in her tracks and pawed at the ground to expose the grass in the Elkhorn Drainage. Garrison tugged on her lead rope, but she planted her feet and refused to budge. "This is as far as you're going, huh, girl? Well, all right, it ought to do." His breath fogged before him, indicating how much the temperature had really dropped. Only a fool would be out today, but knowing such things didn't dissuade him one bit.

Garrison tied Honey to an old pine stump, and unlaced his pan from his belt. Twenty paces down hill, the creek gurgled beneath a crust of ice, overlain with fresh snow. As he walked, he gazed at the mountains. Clouds hugged the slopes in fluffy ephemeral tufts, obscuring the pines, and casting shadows that roamed the valleys with the slow stealth of hunting ghosts. In the frigid air, the peaks seemed even taller, looming over him like monstrous blue giants, alive and as powerful as thunder. High places did that, filled up the soul with wonder—or at least his soul. He couldn't speak for anybody else. It was only at moments like this that he truly believed in God.

Using the heel of his boot, he bashed on the thick ice covering the creek, shattering it with a sharp noise like breaking glass, and bent down to dip his pan. The water was cold beyond belief, turning his hands into one undifferentiated ache. When he'd sloshed enough water out to get a clear view of the leavings in the bottom of the pan, he stared unblinking.

Color? Disbelief crowded his excitement. He fumbled for the magnifying glass in his pocket and studied the dark flakes. They were ragged as a saw blade.

With patience forged of constant disappointment, Garrison sat down in the snow and took a deep breath. "Stay calm, old boy," he commanded as he rubbed a numb hand over his bearded face. "One thing for sure, gold that's washed very far is smoothed by rubbing against the sand."

Fingers trembling, he tucked his glass away and pulled out his plug of tobacco and knife to shave off a good chew. The few scrubby pines growing in this drainage creaked around him, their branches flailing in the wind. The source of the flakes had to be within spitting distance, but with all the snow, could he find it? His eyes moved over the boulders. In their blankets of white, they resembled hunched monsters that had been frozen in place for a thousand years. On some of them, he swore he could make out the hollows of cheeks and eyes and the humps of noses and ears.

"Close, old man, so close you could reach out and touch it."

Closing his eyes, he juiced up his tobacco, then spat out a brown streak. "All right now, easy does it. Don't get excited. Not yet."

He had to get down on all fours to follow the brown streak, which led up a small hill. When he'd gotten to the end of the streak, he used his buffalo sleeve to brush away the snow. His eyes jerked wide before he clamped them shut.

It couldn't be.

He opened one eye a slit, then reached out and picked up the gold-veined rock. It was as big as his fist. He held it close to his thundering heart, and murmured, "Lord God amighty."

Before the fact even sank in, he'd thrown the rock down and was scrambling uphill on hands and knees, sweeping snow away with both hands as he went. Snow packed his sleeves and started melting, running down his wrists, so cold it felt like burning fire. But the vein before his eyes was wide and long—and cobwebbed with pure gold.

He hadn't seen any claim stakes.

He ran around like a lunatic, stumbling from pine to pine, rock to rock, but snow obscured so much of the ground he couldn't be sure he hadn't missed the stakes. "It's all right," he gasped, out of breath. "I'll check in town to—to see if a claim's been registered. But just in case this ground is open..."

He raced up, boots slipping on ice, to reach Honey. She studied him with utter disdain, as though she knew he'd gone over the edge this time. He ignored her and went about staking his own claim. As he hammered the stakes in, his heart thumped its way higher and higher into his throat until it lodged there like a big rock. He could barely swallow.

Whirling around, he yelled, "Honey! Kick up your heels, girl! We're going to town!"

By the time the false-fronted buildings of Central City rose over the hill, Garrison had dreamed himself into a millionaire. It took all of his concentration to avoid the muddy ruts on Main Street. Wagon and horse traffic had churned the road into a freezing chocolate wallow. People scurried by, hats pulled low to shield their faces from the wind. Some waved to him, but most feared the bitter cold too much to take their hands out of their pockets, so they just nodded. Passing a dozen shops, he picketed Honey to a post in front of the Land Office, brushed snow from his coat, and headed for the door.

He could hear voices from within, so he knew Mike must be working late. Stamping mud off his boots, he lifted the latch and entered the room. The warmth hit him like a fist in the face, leaving his skin tingling.

Mike Hathaway, who sat behind a small desk in the rear of the room, looked up, nodded to him, and went back to talking with his customer. The nattily dressed man wasn't a miner; he looked more like the governor or something, with his fine silk hat, black string tie, and new boots. Garrison took the opportunity to cuddle next to the potbellied wood stove that stood near the door. The Land Office was a cubicle no more than twelve by fifteen feet, but it felt large because it had almost no furniture, just a desk, two chairs, and a file chest where Mike kept important documents. The white walls were papered with maps of all sizes and shapes.

By the time Silk Hat left, Garrison's dripping clothes had spawned a lake on the wood floor.

Mike leaned over his desk and peered at it. "I see you decided to leave me enough water to mop my floor."

Garrison smiled crookedly. "How you been, Mike?"

"I been better." He thrust a hand toward the door, then began shoving the papers on his desk into the semblance of an organized pile. "You see the sort who want to start businesses in Central City? Why, I'd just as soon live with snakes. I couldn't understand half of what he said. That eastern accent was as thick as Satan's."

Garrison stepped around the pool at his feet and moved closer to Hathaway's desk. "I thought Satan was from Kansas."

"Well, I reckon each of us hears him different, who knows. Now, I am just about ready to close up and go home for dinner. What can I help you with, Garry?"

"Claim records, Mike. Up around Banta Hill?"

Hathaway scowled. "There's a million claims up there."

"Well, pull out the damn map and look for me anyway, will you?"

Hathaway exhaled in disgust, but reached behind him and riffled through several rolled up papers until he reached the right one. Unrolling it, he put his cup of coffee on one curled end and his left hand on the other. "All right, where?"

Garrison leaned over and studied the map, then tapped it with his finger. "Right about here." He straightened up, holding his breath as Hathaway walked to the file chest and searched one after another. Garry's heart sank when Mike pulled out a file.

"Oh, hell," he said, jamming his hands in his pockets. The big lump of ice that had been floating around his chest settled like lead in his stomach. "I knew it couldn't happen, not to me. Who owns it?"

Hathaway returned and sat down at his desk. He had to put on his spectacles before he could answer. "Feller by the name of Terrence Collier. Filed on it in '59."

Garrison's heart ached. He closed his eyes to stifle the welling emotion. "Damn."

"Well, now, hold up a minute." Hathaway shuffled a few sheets. "Says here he didn't file proving he did the required work last year. You want to challenge his claim? It'll be tricky. If Collier's got receipts or verification showing he worked it, it's still his. And he probably does. Anybody who'd let a claim in that area go out of sheer forgetfulness is a half-wit."

"I hope that's exactly what he is."

"You can hope, but more likely he's dead. Only somebody dead would be *that* forgetful."

Hopefully, Garrison asked, "You think he might be? If he is, what do I have to do?"

"First off, get out there and sink some stakes. Next—"

"Already done that, Mike."

"All right, then, you just need to fill out these papers and get 'em back to me as soon as you can." He reached below his desk and handed three white sheets across the plank top. Garrison took them.

"I'll have these back first thing in the morning, Mike."

"All right, I'll expect you. Have a good evening now."

"I will, Mike. You, too." Garrison headed for the door.

Outside, snow had begun to fall again, glazing the windows of the buildings with scallops of white. People hurried by, their scarves pulled up over their noses, while they maneuvered down the slippery wooden sidewalks. Honey flapped her ears at him and pawed the snowy ground. Ice rimmed her nostrils.

"Damn, I'm sorry, Honey. Truly, I am." He untied her and swung up in the saddle.

A mixture of ecstasy and anxiety burned in his chest as he reined her up Main Street. She broke into a trot, trying to get warm, and Garrison let her go.

"Please, God," he whispered. "Let ole Collier's soul be resting in peace."

CHAPTER 9

Emma Bradford Heatherton leaned against the doorframe of her grand-son's cold bedroom, watching her half-breed daughter-in-law pull things from the old cherry chest of drawers, the shiny mahogany armoire, race to pack only the most essential items: A coat for Jeremy, wool socks, under-clothing, a few rare and precious jewels that had been in the family for a century . . . Charles' prized knife that had belonged to his grandfather. Robin had always been an outsider in this house, Emma thought. She had pleaded with Charles not to soil the family name by marrying Robin, but he'd refused to listen. The only good thing that had come of that union was a child. Her beloved grandson. Dear Lord, what would happen to Jeremy without Emma's tutelage? She shuddered to think. He would probably grow up to be a wild Indian, just like his mother.

Jeremy trotted at Robin's heels, as silent as death, pale-faced, his eyes enormous with terror. One of his hands held tight to Robin's flying skirt, while he clutched Traveller to his chest with the other.

Emma pulled her black shawl about her narrow shoulders and listened to the wind howl through the house. Sleet had begun falling an hour ago and now pattered steadily at the windowpanes. That icy cadence frightened Emma, made her feel as cold inside as outside.

Her dim old eyes drifted over the treasured objects in the room, and a sudden dryness stuck her tongue to the roof of her mouth. The long rectangle of cold white light that stretched from the window across the floor to the foot of Jeremy's bed framed the mementos of Charles' life. Beneath the window sat the cedar chest he had crafted with his own hands at the age of twelve. Once a month for fifteen years, Emma had oiled and polished it. The wall between the bed and cedar chest was covered with medals and ribbons. She'd been so proud of her son. A faint smile touched her lips. He'd won every spelling bee in grammar school, and later, at the University, he'd headed the debating team. Blue and red ribbons, bronze and silver medals . . . and the old four-poster bed where Charles' father had first made love to her. She'd conceived her son in the warmth of that ancient refuge.

Once she had looked upon these things and gained strength from them. But now . . . now they brought unbearable pain.

Emma crushed and recrushed her soaked handkerchief in nervous hands. It would be Christmas in five days and she would be alone . . . alone for the first time in sixty-seven years. She pushed away a straggling gray lock that had escaped her hair net and dabbed at her eyes. Alone, and all because her vile daughter-in-law had not one shred of kindness in her hard heart.

"Robin," Emma said sharply. "Must you go now? Can you not wait for just a few days, until after—"

"No, Mother," Robin answered. "I'm sorry." Her eyes had not stopped blazing since she'd burst through the back door last night, and this morning they seemed to hold some infernal fire raging in her soul.

If only Emma had the courage to slap Robin for her insensitive ways. That's what she needed. A good sound thrashing. Emma had once mentioned this fact to Charles, and he'd laughed so hard it had made Emma's cheeks go crimson. He'd finally responded that only a suicidal madman would dare strike Robin Walkingstick Heatherton.

Emma's mouth tightened. Robin rushed around like a damned soul trying to slip away before the jaws of hell clamped shut forever. Emma realized guiltily that Robin, too, must be hearing the sound of Charles' voice, his soft laughter, and seeing his warm blue eyes, and was perhaps experiencing these things with an agony even more intense than Emma's own. Robin wanted to get out of this house and away from all those things that tore her heart. But . . . but . . . Emma needed her! She couldn't stay here alone!

"Oh, Robin, please. I am not asking that you—"

"Mother, I'm being hunted. I told you that. I must take Jeremy and go as quickly as possible. I'm endangering you by being here at all. I know this is very difficult for you. I . . . I'm sorry," she repeated. "But you must be brave."

Emma shrank back, folding in upon herself. She had never been brave in her life. Even after her husband had died five years ago, she'd had loyal servants to soothe and take care of her. But now . . . there was no one. Except Robin. "Robin, don't leave me, dear. How can I—"

"I have no choice, Mother!"

"But where will you go? This is your home."

"I—I don't know. Even if I did, I wouldn't tell you. That knowledge alone could bring you pain."

Emma's jaw trembled. God damn the Yankees! They crept up like circling wolves, cut supply lines, and left women and children to starve slowly, without wood for heat or candles to shed light in the terrible darkness, and now she couldn't even know where her precious grandson was going? She could have cared less about Robin, but Jeremy, oh Jeremy! Charles had often spoken of the West . . . perhaps that's where Robin would take Jeremy. Emma's empty stomach cramped with grief and hunger.

"But Jeremy wants to stay for Christmas, Robin," she pleaded. She'd scrimped and hoarded to make this Christmas special. "Don't you, Jeremy? Don't you want to stay with Grandmama for the holidays? There will be a present under the tree for you and . . . and . . ." *For Charles, too.*

"Please," Robin said. "Please, don't do this to me, Mother. I—I'm not thinking well as it is. I can't shoulder your burdens as well as my own. Not right now. Try to understand."

Jeremy stared at Emma as he followed his mother around the room. His mouth opened and he tried to speak, but his lips worked silently. He looked like a terrified baby fox with his leg caught in a trap, knowing something was going to eat him at any moment. Emma's heart went out to him. Oh, how she loved that boy. He looked so much like his father.

Emma took a small step into the room and shouted, "Robin, listen to me! You'll be safer here in Richmond than out in the winter storms! I know that we are losing battles elsewhere but our great army has stopped General Grant. He will never be able to penetrate the defenses—"

In a sudden, violent move, Robin straightened from where she'd been stuffing clothing into a small bag and thrust an arm toward the window where sleet poured down in a blinding white sheet. "Mother, how many hundred-gun salutes have you heard? Every time the Union wins a battle they celebrate by firing their cannons up and down the Petersburg lines. Richmond cannot last! She will fall—*and soon*! You must leave here. This afternoon, I will speak to President Davis about an escort to assist you out of town. But you must decide where you want the men to take you."

Emma's tears began to flow. She stared at Robin. Robin was such a tall woman, and so thin, she seemed to have no flesh left at all. Her red-flowered white dress, which had once fit so prettily, now hung loose, as though encasing a jumble of old bones. She had braided her hair, then coiled it into a bun on top her head, leaving her oval face exposed to the cold winter light. Except for her straight patrician nose, she looked very Indian, her high cheekbones rouged, her eyes dark and flashing.

Emma choked out: "Why are you abandoning me? Do you hate me so much?"

"Mother. Stop this. Where do you want to go?"

"But, but . . . I don't know! This is my home! And you and Jeremy are all I have left! If you leave me—"

"That's not true, Mother. You have a sister in Augusta."

Emma made a sound of angry dismay. "I suppose if you really are going to abandon me then that's my only choice. Isn't it?" Her throat constricted. She tried to swallow the tears, but they started deep in her chest. She buried her lined face in her hands and wept.

Robin's quick steps crossed the wood floor and Emma felt her daughter-in-law's young arms go tightly around her shoulders. In a second or two, Jeremy had grabbed Emma's leg, holding on tight, and Robin began stroking Emma's hair gently.

"Oh, Mother, forgive me. I'm so sorry. I know you're missing Charles as much as I am. I'm just so frightened that I . . . There, there, don't cry. I love you, Mother. I'm so sorry I've been harsh. Charles would have wanted me to be so gentle with you and I . . ."

Emma rested her forehead against Robin's shoulder. "Robin, please, don't leave me! This is my home, and I can't bear to be alone!"

"You won't be alone if you go to live with your sister."

"Oh, you are so cruel to me! You know I've always hated Eleanor! How can you—"

Robin released her suddenly and stared down through eyes as hard and dark as obsidian. "I'm sorry, Mother. We must leave now. Forgive me. We'll write the first chance we get."

"No, no, Robin! Not yet." Emma clutched at her flowered sleeve. "Please! At least stay for lunch? I took down a jar of blueberries yesterday and made a pie. A pie! I got some flour! And you know how expensive flour is! It's been going for two hundred and fifty dollars a barrel. Please, Robin, stay and share it with me—just the three of us. One last time. We can open your presents early. . . . *Please*, dear."

Robin hesitated, then answered, "All right. We'll stay . . . but just for an hour. Then we must be going. You understand, don't you?"

"No. No, not really, but . . ." The reprieve would give her another hour to work on Robin, to convince her to stay. Hope buoyed, she ordered, "Stop packing now and come with me to the kitchen. I'll make some coffee. It's the same old chicory-and-scorched-grain mixture, but it will at least be hot. And it will taste so good with the pie. Just you wait and see."

Robin followed Emma, but Emma could see how stiffly her daughter-in-law walked, how frightened she looked. Every time they approached a window, Robin stopped to look out before she would pass it . . . and behind her Jeremy trotted on silent feet, quiet, so quiet that Emma wondered if the boy would ever speak, or play, or laugh like a white child again. Already he was turning into a stealthy little Indian.

Rain.

It dripped from the trees. Sent silver veins trickling through the dead grass. Beaded on Jeremy's eyelashes.

He shook wet black hair away from his face and crawled through thick underbrush to get inside an old berry bramble. The inner vines had died and broken off, leaving a dark hollow where he could stretch out on his stomach atop dry dirt. Outside, his mother was walking through a field of dead soldiers, jerking haversacks off their backs, undoing the laces, pulling out food and stuffing it into her own haversack. The air tasted bitter, like putting your tongue to copper.

Jeremy propped his chin on his shaking fists and lowered his eyes to stare at the ground. Rabbits lived in this bramble. He saw their footprints under his nose. Pulling Traveller from his coat pocket, he let his horse run free, galloping through the dry dirt, trampling the rabbit's tracks to dust. Traveller liked to run. He *needed* to run. Far away. Far, far away . . .

Jeremy listened. Traveller was neighing inside his head again. Neighing and neighing as if being hunted by a bear. It had started at dawn. Faint, like whispers of wind blowing across Jeremy's soul. He looked down, and Traveller stared up at him with huge tormented eyes.

"It's all right," Jeremy whispered. "Don't worry. It's all right. They're just dead men. They can't hurt you. See? They're not moving."

But . . . but they *seemed* to move.

Flapping wings filled the field. A huge crow landed on the body of a man no more than fifty feet away and begin plucking at his bloody chest.

"*No! No!*" Jeremy screamed, but his mother did not hear, because the cry just flew through his soul. His teeth were clamped so tight his head was trembling. No sound could make it past that barricade.

Only Traveller heard. The horse had started breathing hard. Gently, he patted Traveller's side.

"Soon. We're leaving soon. As soon as Mama gets us enough food. Don't be scared."

Jeremy could feel Traveller's fear.

His mouth went dry. He grabbed Traveller and tucked him inside his shirt so the horse could crawl through his ribs and into his heart. Jeremy's blood always felt warmer when Traveller slept in his heart.

Jeremy's mother had told him that someday he would forget about Traveller and find other toys to play with. This didn't make any sense.

Traveller lived inside Jeremy. Breathing, running.

And sometimes Jeremy lived inside Traveller. He would crawl into Traveller's stomach, curl into a ball, and sleep safe and warm.

No one screamed in there.

It never smelled like gunpowder, or anger, or—

"Jeremy?" his mother called. She sounded worried. "Jeremy! Where are you? Hurry!"

He scrambled out of the bramble and stood in the cold rain. A big drop fell out of the tree and splatted on his nose. He lifted a hand. "Here! I'm here, Mama."

She lifted a hand in response, and started toward him with the bulging haversack slung over her left shoulder. She looked so tired. She walked like each step hurt. They hadn't eaten at all yesterday. Jeremy's stomach growled in anticipation, even though he knew the rations would taste woody, like crumbly old paper.

"Hungry?" his mother asked as she knelt before him. Her gray cape and hat were soaked. Strands of black hair straggled around her face.

"Yes, Mama."

She reached up and tenderly touched Jeremy's cheek, then she smiled. "Let's eat then, before—"

"Mama?" he said anxiously. "Mama, could we go away . . . from here? I don't want to have those men watching me while I eat their food."

His mother's face tightened and, for a long moment, she just stared at him. "Oh, God," she choked out. "I can't believe I almost made you . . ." Then she grabbed Jeremy and hugged him tightly. "Forgive me, Jeremy. I'm sorry. Mama's sorry. I'm so used to—"

"It's all right, Mama. But let's go. Let's go now."

She took a deep breath, stood up, and reached for Jeremy's hand. "We'll walk until we find a dry place to sit and eat. A dry place far from here."

CHAPTER 10

March 1865

While the dealer tossed cards across the shiny wooden table top, Owen Fontaine puffed his cigar and lazily watched the haze of fragrant blue smoke spin and billow near the ceiling. A half-empty bottle of brandy stood near his ashtray on the table and beside it sat a crystal snifter. Roulette wheels clicked in the background, accompanied by the rhythmic thudding of dice at the craps tables. He smiled as he glanced around the sternwheeler's sprawling casino. Among the soiled doves dressed in butter-yellow satins, forest-green silks and deep purple velvets, he spotted seven truly attractive women, all hanging onto the arms of men, including several Union officers. The room bustled for this early in the evening, but they'd make St. Louis tomorrow, and people were taking advantage of this final night aboard.

Owen lifted his brandy glass and took a swallow. Through the window to his right, he could see the fiery ball of the sun melting into the river, turning the water a glimmering brassy hue, and closer, he caught his own reflection in the soot-streaked glass. Large brown eyes stared back at him. A woman had once told him they had a wistful, translucent quality, like the eyes of an angel. He'd laughed at the time and found her comment even more amusing now. His black string tie stood out against his white pleated shirt and gray broadcloth jacket. Tall, with striking white-blond hair, he was still a handsome man, if thirty-five. His thin aquiline nose and pointed chin gave his face a noble haughtiness.

"Place your bets, gentlemen," the dealer said. He wore a ruffled green shirt with a black garter on the sleeve. He couldn't have been more than twenty.

Owen picked up his cards and studied them. The gray-headed man to his right was a new opponent, named Collier. He'd come aboard at the last stop.

His seamed brown face and fringed leather jacket marked him as a frontiers-man of one sort or another. It would take a few hands before Owen could read Collier, but George Santford was quite another thing. He knew every facial expression of the bald heavyset man who sat directly across the table from him. And, at this moment, Santford appeared unhappy with his cards. Of course, he'd been drinking whisky for three hours, which made the read-ing much easier. Santford only became difficult to read when he was twitching due to the discomfort of his clothing, rather than his cards. He had a poor habit of dressing in suits too tight. The gold button that secured his white coat over his ample belly strained to stay closed.

"I'll bid fifty," Santford said and threw the necessary chips into the center of the table.

Everybody matched and chose the cards they wished to discard. "I'll take two," Owen said.

The dealer proceeded around the table, but Owen was distracted when a beautiful woman walked through the casino's double doors. The red-jacketed guard stopped her. Owen could hear the big man explaining that "no unescorted women" were permitted in the room. The woman smiled. Owen didn't catch her words, but the tilt of her head, the shine in her eyes, left him—and the guard—stunned. Clearly, this was a lady. Indeed, she looked like royalty in exile. Her blue watered-silk gown cascaded with white lace, and between her creamy breasts she wore a sapphire pendant worth enough to ransom a small country. Black ringlets framed her oval face, ac-centuating her high cheekbones and huge dark brown eyes. He checked her hand. No wedding ring.

"Mr. Fontaine? . . . Sir?" the dealer called. "Are you playing, sir?"

"Oh, forgive me, William." He turned back to the table. "Where are we?"

"Mr. Santford has just raised his ante by another one hundred dollars, sir. Will you match?"

Owen scrutinized his cards. Full house. Three jacks and a pair of fours. Straightening in his chair, he tossed first two, then three, chips into the center. "I'll match the one hundred and raise another fifty." He smiled and sat back to puff his cigar. Tendrils of smoke curled up around his face.

Santford fidgeted, rearranging his cards. Collier didn't move a muscle, but he stared at Owen through the hard unblinking eyes of an old wolf.

Owen turned his attention back to the woman. She'd made it past the guard and was strolling elegantly around the room. Owen knew a good deal about people—had begun learning the day his father kicked him out of the house at fourteen—and this lady had an air of deliberation, as if she were searching for something. Was that how she'd gotten past the guard, told him she was meeting someone here? Nothing escaped her notice, especially not the size of the wagers on the tables. First her eyes appraised the stacks of chips, then the men. Then she moved on. She smiled whenever she caught the eye of a Union officer. But something else touched her gaze at those moments, as well, a strange glitter that Owen could not assess. Distaste? Excitement? Both? Or even, perhaps, neither.

"I'm out," Collier said and laid his cards down.

Santford grinned like an alley cat at Owen. "Well, Fontaine. Seems it's you and me. I'll raise you another hundred." His chips clacked against the pile.

"Oh, not me, George," he answered with a firm shake of his head. "It's all yours." He threw his hand down.

Santford laughed and raked in the pile of chips. "Well, well, Mister Fontaine, bad luck already? And you were so high and mighty last night!"

Owen deferentially dipped his head and sighed. Santford had lost well over two thousand dollars to him last night. He could afford a little generosity this early in the evening.

While the other men studied the dealer's shuffling of the cards, Owen glanced over his shoulder. What a magnificent woman. She had stopped at the roulette wheel fifteen feet away, watching as it clicked to a stop.

"Seventeen black!" the wheel operator said and began raking chips away.

A silver-bearded old man reeled to his feet and bellowed, "Blast you! Goddamn it! This table is crooked as a hickory stick!" To emphasize his words, he lifted his cane and swung it menacingly at the operator, who ducked just in time. Gasps and shouts rang out as people rushed to escape. The old man was dead drunk.

Owen shoved his chair back, preparing to rise and intervene if necessary.

"You are offensive, sir!" the operator shouted. "This table is strictly—"

"The hell it is! You cheated me!" The old man staggered forward, swinging his cane, but the momentum caused him to sway, stumble sideways and twist around.

The beautiful woman sidestepped with the decorum of a dancer as the sot tumbled face-first at her feet, his cane flying across the room. Gold coins spilled from his pockets and rolled around the floor in little circles. The roulette players shook their heads and cursed, as they moved back to the table, but the woman knelt down beside the old man, examining him tenderly. She put a slender hand against his forehead.

"Operator?" she called in a cultured Boston accent. "Please find someone to escort this gentleman back to his room. I believe he's finished gaming for the evening."

While the operator scurried to comply, the woman gathered the hem of her silk gown and pulled it away from the sot's face. Owen blinked. He surveyed the room. No one else seemed to have noticed that with that feminine gesture she had deftly collected five twenty-dollar gold pieces.

When she rose, she turned in Owen's direction and he greeted her with an admiring nod of his head. That regal smile returned to her face. She walked toward him.

Owen stood up and bowed. "Good evening," he said. "I hope you won't mind if I say that your kindness to that poor gentleman just now enriched my soul," and in a much softer voice, he added, "and yours, too, I noticed."

Her smile remained perfect. She matched his soft tone. "I doubt then, sir, that you have much of a soul to be enriched. You are certainly no gentleman."

He suppressed a laugh, bowed again, and said, "You're right. It was tactless of me to have noticed. I apologize sincerely. Please let me give you a glass of brandy as a peace offering." He pulled out the empty chair beside him and held it for her.

She scrutinized the chair as though she might refuse, but instead seated herself, saying, "Thank you."

"You honor me by your presence."

He signaled the waiter, then pulled up his own chair. Santford, he saw, was studying the woman with a lecherous eye, while Collier paid her no attention whatsoever. The dealer gave her a nod, assessing her with the practiced ease of one used to "ladies" at the table. Owen gave her a sidelong glance. Had he misjudged her? Was she nothing more than a gloriously clad prostitute?

"Allow me to introduce myself," he said. "I'm Owen Fontaine. And I am addressing . . . ?"

"Mrs. Ro—Rose Chamberlain."

The waiter appeared and said, "What may I get you, sir?"

"Mrs. Chamberlain? What would you like?"

She turned to the waiter. "Please bring another snifter. I'll have just a taste of Mr. Fontaine's brandy."

The waiter returned almost immediately and Owen poured her snifter half-full. As he handed the glass to her, he said, "Missus? So you're married, then?"

"Widowed, I'm afraid."

"I'm so sorry. Did your husband die in the war?"

She nodded, and Owen regretted asking. Pain glinted in those brown depths. Had the loss been recent? Or had she been so devoted to the man that it would always hurt this badly?

"Again," he said. "I am sorry."

The dealer had waited politely. "Are we ready to begin again, gentlemen?"

"Yes, go on, please," Owen said and turned to face the table while William dealt.

As the cards went around, she asked. "Did you fight in the war, Mr. Fontaine?"

"No, Mrs. Chamberlain. I bought my way out. Paid a crazy Irishman three hundred dollars to fight in my place, and I've never regretted it." He noticed that Mrs. Chamberlain was appraising him anew, and that distaste had crept into the set of her mouth. He was too glad to be alive to care much what she, or anyone else, thought about his courage.

Collier was focused on the dealer, verifying that each card came from the top of the deck, while Santford arranged his hand into some semblance of order. Possible straight? Bluffing?

Owen let his own cards lie, waiting until the deal was done. Mrs. Chamberlain drank her brandy in a distinctly unladylike fashion—it was . . . *practiced.* He sighed to himself. Well, it made sense. No decent woman would be seen in a such a place.

He picked up his cards. Not much there. A pair of sevens. When he turned back to Mrs. Chamberlain, he found her studying his cards. He smiled, threw two chips into the ante pile and picked up his brandy. "Well, what do you think?" he asked.

"I'm afraid I don't know much about this game, Mr. Fontaine. Though I've always thought it fascinating to watch."

He accepted the statement at face value. After all, anyone who did know anything about poker knew that staring at another player's cards was a crime worthy of a bullet between the eyes. "I think I'll keep these," he said, indicating the pair.

"That seems wise."

Collier had caught at least part of their discussion. He pursed his lips disdainfully, disturbed by a woman giving advice about a man's game.

"How many cards, Mr. Fontaine?" the dealer asked.

"Three," he replied, discarding the useless ones and pulling the new into his hand. Pathetic. Another pair. Deuces. Owen leaned forward. "It's my turn to start, isn't it, William?"

"Yes, sir."

"Thank you." Owen collected ten fifty-dollar chips and pushed them into the center of the table. "I'll raise five hundred."

Collier's eyes narrowed, but Santford laughed out loud. "You've got a good one, eh, Fontaine?"

"I think so, George," he replied.

"Well, I'll match your five. What do you think of that?"

Owen just smiled.

William said, "Are you in, Mr. Collier?"

The grizzled frontiersman grumbled, *"Damn,"* under his breath and threw his cards down again. "No, I ain't in." He flopped back against his chair and folded his arms tightly over the leather fringes on his chest, glaring across the table at Mrs. Chamberlain, as though his bad luck were her fault. She met his hostility with an inscrutable expression.

"All right, Fontaine," Santford said. "Let's see this wonderful hand of yours."

Owen displayed his two pair, to which Santford blurted, *"That's it?"* and spread his three of a kind out with a flourish. Then he guffawed as he raked in his winnings. Collier observed the finish suspiciously, his wolf eyes narrowing to slits.

Owen shrugged and placed his arm over the back of Mrs. Chamberlain's chair as he refilled her brandy glass. "Easy come, easy go," he said.

"Really?" she asked in a friendly voice. "I just thought you weren't any good at this."

He chuckled and looked up. And his smile faded. A knowing gleam filled her eyes. This woman understood that he'd deliberately lost the hand. So . . . he'd underestimated her. Interesting. He smiled again and whispered, "Be careful. I don't know what you're planning, but I've seen more innocent eyes over the fuse of a howitzer."

"I'm always careful, Mr. Fontaine," she replied and smiled so warmly it melted even his forewarned heart.

She held his gaze a few more seconds, then shifted to look across the table at Santford, and Owen saw his opponent turn giddy. George grinned like a lunatic.

Owen set his brandy bottle down and waited until Santford guzzled more whisky, then whispered, "You should know now that I expect a cut if you win."

She bestowed a look of such adoration upon him that he pulled his arm from the back of her chair in self-defense. "Oh, Mr. Fontaine," she said, just loud enough for the other men to hear. "How kind of you to offer to teach me the game. But are you certain these other gentlemen won't mind?"

"Mind?" he said, giving her look for look. "Why, I don't think so. These seem like very patient men to me. But allow me to ask their permission." He turned to the table and said, "Gentlemen, Mrs. Chamberlain, would like to learn to play poker. Would it—"

"I ain't playing with no woman!" Collier announced and thrust out his chin. "What do you take me for?"

"Now, don't be upset, Mr. Collier," Owen said. "She's not playing for fun, she'll be using real money. And I'll help her along with the hands. That way you won't feel bad about taking her hard-earned cash." He looked at Santford. "You don't mind, do you George?"

"Me? Not at all. Why, I'd be delighted to let the little lady play a few hands." He winked at her, and Mrs. Chamberlain smiled.

"Well, Collier?" Owen insisted. "What do you say?"

"I *ain't* playing with no woman!" he repeated stubbornly, and accented his words by slamming a fist into the table, which sent Owen's neat stacks of chips tumbling into one large disordered pile. "I refuse, by God!"

"But why?" Owen insisted. "For heaven's sake, I told you I'll watch out for her so you don't feel bad—"

"I ain't worried about taking *her* money!"

"Oh," Owen said and paused for effect. He lifted a hand and waved it about negligently, as though searching for the proper words. "Sorry. I didn't realize you were worried about her taking *your* money. If that's the problem then I suppose—"

George Santford exclaimed, "Scared, eh! Of a little woman like that?" He burst out laughing, and slapped Collier on the back. The old man lurched from his chair and roared, "Keep your damn hands to yourself! You drunken fool!"

"*Gentlemen,*" William called, "Gentlemen! *Please.* Shall I call the bouncer?"

Collier glared as he eased down to his chair again. Santford's laughter dropped to a series of undignified snorts.

William proceeded, "Are we playing poker, gentlemen, or not?"

Owen answered, "I certainly am. That is, providing Mrs. Chamberlain and I have challengers."

"I'm playing!" Santford affirmed.

Collier's mouth puckered as though he'd eaten rotten meat. "I'll play," he said grudgingly, but pointed an accusing finger at Owen. "But *you,* mister, had better be on the up-and-up, or I'll shoot you dead as a 'possum. You understand me?"

Owen gave Collier a hard stare. "Oh, I think I do, yes. And because I do, I've changed my mind, William," he said without taking his eyes from the frontiersman. "I will not be helping Mrs. Chamberlain. She'll be playing her own hands. Does that ease your mind, Mr. Collier?"

Collier ground his teeth before he nodded. "Some."

Owen turned to Mrs. Chamberlain. "I most humbly apologize for offering to teach you, madam. It seems I am the subject of distrust at this table, so you must play for yourself. If you would like to back out of the game, I'm sure no one will object."

"I would like to try," Mrs. Chamberlain said. "I believe I understand the basic principles well enough to proceed. Thank you for allowing me the privilege—especially you, Mr. Collier. I did not intend to cause you any discomfort. Please forgive me." She moved her chair closer to the table.

Collier's stony face softened a little, but he watched Mrs. Chamberlain rather than William while the cards were being shuffled.

Owen, however watched William. The dealer had squared his shoulders, adopting a stern expression, and it obviously had nothing to do with the previous argument. William kept glancing unpleasantly at Mrs. Chamberlain. Being a whore, his eyes said, was all right, interfering in a man's game was not.

William announced, "We've got a fifty-dollar minimum, Mrs. Chamberlain—"

"May I purchase the necessary chips from you? Or . . . or can I use greenbacks?"

"Chips are preferable, ma'am. How many would you like?"

"Two thousand dollars' worth?"

William delivered the amount in two stacks, red fifties and blue hundreds. Mrs. Chamberlain opened her dainty purse and extracted a roll of bills, which, if Owen were a guessing man, approached perhaps ten thousand. Or had she wrapped a few fifties around a wad of ones? George Santford tossed off another whisky and filled his glass again from his bottle, smiling like a knave the entire time.

William dealt, and Mrs. Chamberlain retrieved her cards awkwardly, turning the face cards right-side up, to the open chuckles of George.

"I'm sorry," she said. "Did I do something wrong?"

"Not yet," Owen replied.

"May I have two cards, please?"

"Ain't your turn," Collier pointed out. "Give me three." He picked up the new cards and glowered at Mrs. Chamberlain.

Owen said, "I'll take one, William. Thank you."

"Now . . ." Mrs. Chamberlain glanced timidly around the table, "Now may I have two cards?"

"Yes, ma'am," William said. "Now it's your turn."

"Thank you. And may I bid four hundred . . . is that all right?" She asked the question in such a frightened voice that even Collier lowered his stern eyes. "Is it?"

With a drunken laugh, Santford said, "Let me get my cards first, honey. Then after Collier plays you can outbid him all you want." He elbowed Collier in the side, and the old man gritted his teeth so hard it set his jaw askew. "I'll take three, William."

"Yes, sir." William dealt them out.

Owen studied Mrs. Chamberlain from the corner of his eye. The lamplight accented the smooth curves of her beautiful face and lent a bluish fire to her jet black hair. She noticed his attention and turned to face him. Why did her eyes affect him so? It was as though some hidden vulnerability lurked there and she had decided to let him, and him alone, see it. Her fragility drew him powerfully. Every masculine bone in his body *longed* to protect her, to help her, indeed, to do whatever was necessary to keep her looking at him in that intimate way.

Collier said, "I bid another two hundred."

Owen anted up without a comment.

Mrs. Chamberlain wet her lips nervously and said, "I would like to match Mr. Collier's ante and raise him another two hundred." She separated her chips and laid them in the growing pile in the center of the table.

Santford matched and so did Collier. Owen shook his head and said, "I'm out, William." He sat back and sipped his brandy, relishing the fire it stirred in his veins.

Mrs. Chamberlain looked up at William and said, "Do I need to show my cards now, dealer?"

"Yes, ma'am. That's correct."

She spread out a pair of fives, queen high, and Collier's grim face brightened. Santford had another three of a kind, eights, which meant that Collier's three jacks took the game. He pulled in the winnings with a faint smile.

Mrs. Chamberlain folded her hands in her lap and shrugged serenely. "I need more practice, I think," she said.

Owen smiled. In a very low voice, he answered, "Really? I just thought you weren't any good at this."

At around one o'clock in the morning, Owen retired from the game and concentrated on drinking instead. Collier and Mrs. Chamberlain stared at each other across the table, each winning with enough regularity to keep the other playing. Most of the casino's patrons, as well as a very disgruntled George Santford, had left about midnight. Those who remained had gathered around their table to watch the gorgeous woman who played so skillfully. William yawned often, and he'd dragged up a chair to sit in while he dealt. He would, of course, expect a huge tip for his services. And Mrs. Chamberlain could afford it. She'd cleaned out Santford, stripped about two thousand from Collier, and even managed to glean a thousand from Owen.

Odd that it didn't rankle. Instead, he felt amused by the entire affair.

He lifted the latest brandy bottle, more than half empty, and gestured to Mrs. Chamberlain's glass. "Another?"

"Yes, thank you."

He poured and wondered. This was her third glass, and her accent had become slightly more pronounced—almost as though she had to remember to enunciate her "r's." That puzzled him. Because he knew about accents. He'd been born in a Cockney slum outside of London, and it had taken him almost ten years after arriving in America to lose that accent. People now often asked whether he were from Illinois or Indiana, but it hadn't been easy. And she was very young. Twenty-three? Maybe twenty-four. What accent came naturally to her? He pondered that question as he watched her accept her latest cards. She was not from Boston, of that he felt certain. Her mystery delighted him.

Collier anted a hundred, the new minimum, and Mrs. Chamberlain matched. Collier took two cards. She took one.

"I'll raise you another hundred," Collier said gruffly.

"I'll see that and raise you two, Mr. Collier." Mrs. Chamberlain extended her hand and placed her chips with the others.

Collier wiped away the sweat that trickled down the deep creases in his cheeks, then shoved in the chips, and called, "Let's see your cards, woman."

Mrs. Chamberlain's heart flush gleamed red in the dim lamplight. Collier threw his cards facedown. He slumped back in his chair as though he'd just heard the trumpets of Judgment Day.

The people around the table whispered wildly. Estimates of Mrs. Chamberlain's winnings ranged as high as ten thousand. It was really closer to five, Owen knew. Because he'd been keeping a rough count.

William stood up, no doubt needing a break badly, and Collier yelled, "Sit down, damn it! Deal!"

"Mr. Collier, if you don't mind, I need to—"

"I *do* mind, boy! Deal!"

With great dignity for a man so exhausted, William took his chair and sighed, "Shall we start again with a hundred-dollar ante, Mr. Collier? Or are you nearing your limit?"

The old man slammed a fist into the table and the eight remaining chips in front of him scattered across maple top. "Here's my answer!" He retrieved a chip and slapped it down in the center.

William dealt. "How many cards, Mrs. Chamberlain?"

"Two, please."

"And you, Mr. Collier?"

"Three, boy."

William turned to Mrs. Chamberlain. Waiting.

She tipped her head back and sighed, using one hand to massage her neck. With gentlemanly grace, Owen set his glass down and said, "May I?"

She yielded with a nod. His fingers tingled at first touch. The silken texture of her skin excited him. He massaged the tight muscles, and for just a moment, she closed her eyes and trusted him. Did she have any idea what that did to him?

She opened her eyes. "I'll wager five hundred, Mr. Collier."

Owen went back to his brandy.

The cards in Collier's hand trembled, but he matched, and laid out his three aces, queen and jack.

She wasted no time in exposing her own four-of-a-kind—lucky sevens.

Collier sank back without a sound, staring at his two remaining chips.

William dealt another hand with a wide, long yawn, and after both players had taken cards, he asked, "Well, Mr. Collier?"

"Give me one card."

"And you, Mrs. Chamberlain?"

"Two, William. Thank you."

Collier wet his lips and said, "I'll wager you a hundred more."

"I'll see that and raise you five," Mrs. Chamberlain said, placing the necessary chips in the center. With aplomb she asked, "Are you able to match me, Mr. Collier?"

Collier leaned back and pulled his cards down to his lap. She couldn't see how his hands shook, but Owen could. The old man stared hard at his cards. After several moments he said, "What will you take to cover me?"

"What are you offering?"

A cool breeze blew through the casino, and the lamps wavered and spat. The chandeliers tinkled softly. Faces in the crowd were predatory, eager for the kill.

Collier closed his eyes and pulled some folded papers out of his breast pocket. He caressed them before placing them in the center of the table. "I got a mining claim in Colorado Territory. It's—"

"*Colorado?*" Mrs. Chamberlain murmured. Her face slackened as though she couldn't believe she had heard him right. Holding her cards to her chest, she leaned across the table toward him. "Did you say Colorado Territory?"

"That's right." Collier stared at her. The acrid smell of his sweat overpowered Owen, but Mrs. Chamberlain seemed unaffected. The entire room hushed. "That claim is smack in the center of the richest square mile on earth. It's worth a thousand times your damned bet, missy."

Owen straightened in his chair, gazing at the yellowed papers. "Mrs. Chamberlain," he said. "I know something about such matters. If you will permit me, I would like to verify the authenticity of Mr. Collier's mining claim."

"Yes, please, Mr. Fontaine. I would be very grateful for your expertise."

Owen turned to Collier. "Would you mind, sir, if I—"

"Not a'tall. Go." Collier gestured to the papers.

Owen unfolded them. It was indeed a gold claim and registered in Central City, Colorado Territory. Blood surged in his ears. Collier hadn't been joking when he'd boasted it was in the richest square mile on earth. Owen refolded the papers and replaced them on the table. He turned to Mrs. Chamberlain, saying, "They are genuine."

She hesitated, filled her lungs with air, and through a halting exhalation, said "That will be fine, Mr. Collier. What do you have?"

The miner ran a weathered hand through his gray hair and laid his cards down. "Full house. Eights over tens."

As she laid out her cards, Owen jerked forward.

"Full house!" he read out, since she seemed to have lost her voice. "Queens over sevens!"

Collier's old eyes filled with tears. "My God almighty," he whispered. "Beat by a woman. I'm dead broke."

Mrs. Chamberlain bowed her head soberly.

She made no move to collect her winnings, so Owen took the initiative and pulled them over into her enormous pile of chips. He picked up the claim papers. After several moments, he opened them and said, "I believe you need to sign these over to Mrs. Chamberlain, don't you, Mr. Collier?"

The old man nodded gravely, and waved for one of the waiters. "Bring me a . . . a quill, son."

While the young man raced across the room, Collier stared at Mrs. Chamberlain. The disbelief in the old man's eyes made Owen ache. Losing that claim must have been like hearing of the unexpected death of a loved one. Mrs. Chamberlain did not lift her head. She kept gazing at the hands folded in her lap.

The boy raced back with a quill and a bottle of ink. He set them down before Collier, who signed the papers in a few swift strokes.

Collier pushed his chair back. He appeared far more lean and stoop-shouldered when he stood up, as though the game had taken away some of his strength. "I ain't happy, Mrs. Chamberlain. But you played fair and square," he said with dignity. "I want you to know that *I* know that, and that I don't hold what you did against you. Good night."

"Thank you, Mr. Collier." She looked up at him, and he nodded and strode across the dim room toward the door.

Whispering people filed out behind him.

When Mrs. Chamberlain did not immediately rise from the table, Owen signaled the boy who'd brought the quill. "Mrs. Chamberlain is very tired. Will you please take her winnings and deliver the appropriate number of greenbacks to her cabin."

The boy licked his lips and stared open-mouthed at the mountain of chips. "Yes, sir." He took a bag from a nearby table and raked it full, saying, "Would you like to count it first sir, or will you trust me to—"

"There's exactly four-thousand-six-hundred dollars there, porter," she said, "but thank you for you asking."

Owen smiled and took her arm, helping her to her feet. As though in a daze, she opened her purse, pulled out a hundred-dollar Treasury Bill and handed it to William.

"Thank you, William. Good night."

"Good night, Mrs. Chamberlain," he said with a broad smile.

Owen escorted her out onto the deck where stars glittered like frost crystals against the black velvet sky. The night's coolness enveloped them. Removing his coat, he draped it over her shoulders, and placed a hand against her back, guiding her toward the bow, away from the noise of the paddle-wheel, the glow of the lamps, and anyone who might want to ask her silly questions. The powerful scents of damp earth and flowers surrounded them.

When they reached the bow, he braced his arms on the railing and lifted his face to the silver wash of starlight.

She stood quietly beside him.

"Are you all right?" he asked.

She nodded.

"You're a gracious winner. Or perhaps a better description is a 'morose' winner. I thought that was why you wanted to enter the game. To win."

She pulled his coat closed over her breasts and shivered as she leaned back against the railing. When she looked up at him, her brown eyes glinted gray. "Thank you for helping me. How much do I owe you for that?"

"Oh, I don't know." Wind billowed his white sleeves and flattened his shirt against his chest. It felt good after the casino's heat. "How much do you think my help was worth?"

A smile touched her lips and sent a flush of warmth through him. "Quite a lot, Mr. Fontaine. How shall I repay you?"

He straightened. She probably didn't mean that the way it sounded, but he was just drunk enough to hope she might. And if the truth be told, no *lady* played poker with her skill. "What did you have in mind?"

"Well, I'm not sure what's proper. And, after all, money is not something you need. Is it, Mr. Fontaine?"

He frowned, caught off balance by her pointed comment. "I beg your pardon? I'm afraid I don't get your meaning."

"Do forgive me," she replied. Her voice had changed, grown deeper and more precise. "It's just that I saw you talking with General Smith earlier, and I assumed he would be rewarding you very handsomely for your services."

Owen didn't move a muscle, but he felt as though God Himself had taken a huge hammer and bashed him in the head to bring him to his senses. "You . . . saw me . . . You couldn't have. There was *no one* around. I . . . Mrs. Chamberlain, just how much of my conversation with the General did you overhear?"

"Quite enough."

He stared at her, dumbfounded. Even worse than overhearing the details of his business transaction, she seemed well aware of the illegalities and was not the slightest bit unnerved by the fact that most men in his position would murder her outright for her eavesdropping.

"My Lord, I am very embarrassed," he said in a sudden rush. "This makes twice that I've underestimated you. What a fool I am." He couldn't help it. He laughed. "But this is *blackmail,* Mrs. Chamberlain! Pure and simple."

She studied the stars with a serene face. "Blackmail is never simple, Mr. Fontaine."

He felt himself pale. "And I thought I'd been so careful this afternoon. Well . . . let me see. If I say I only want twenty percent of your winnings, will you promise to be careful where you mention my conversations with Union officers?"

"Men in your profession are very vulnerable, Mr. Fontaine. Far more so than they like to believe. I've no desire to see you dead. I'll give you five percent."

"Five?" he shouted indignantly. She had not even looked at him when she'd said it. Did she take him so lightly? Why, he could break her slender neck . . . "Tell me something," he said. "Is it just the fact that I run guns that bothers you, or the fact that I run guns to the Confederacy? These are surplus Union weapons, Mrs. Chamberlain. Is it my fault that a few unscrupulous Yankee generals want to make some personal profit before the war ends? *I'm a businessman!* I can't—"

"Ten percent, Mr. Fontaine. Take it or leave it."

He managed to calm himself enough to close his mouth. "I—I appreciate your generosity," he stammered, aware that perhaps he really ought to. He shook his head to clear it of any lingering notions of her frailty. "Excuse me, madam. May I be so bold as to ask, who *are* you?"

She gazed out at the river where branches twisted and bobbed in the swift current. Starlight dappling through the trees sent shadows flickering over her beautiful face. Sadness tinged her voice when she said, "I'll send your ten percent to your cabin in the morning. Does that meet with your approval?"

He crossed his arms, half angry now, though still drawn to her like a man who'd been locked in prison since puberty. No, since *before* puberty. She maddened him. "No, *Rose.* It does not meet my approval. Ten percent of a mining claim is not so easily delivered."

"Of a mining . . ."

Her voice trailed off, and Owen smiled with satisfaction. It had not occurred to her that ten percent of her winnings included more than just the paper money. "Don't tell me you'd planned on welshing on my percentage of the gold claim? Did you, *partner?*"

She removed his coat and held it out to him. He took it. "I am very tired," she said. "May we finish this discussion tomorrow, Mr. Fontaine? Over breakfast?"

"After watching you in action tonight, I'm not sure I can trust you for that long."

She gave him that magnetic smile. "Really, Mr. Fontaine. I am quite reliable. Besides, even if I didn't meet you for breakfast, you wouldn't have much trouble finding me on this boat. Or do you think that I will dive overboard tonight to avoid you?"

He ran a hand through his damp blond hair and smiled. Goddamn, she was magical. Even the calculating glint in her eyes attracted him. "Probably not in that elegant dress, but—"

"Shall we meet at ten, then?"

"Well, I . . ." He sighed. "Yes. Yes, that will be fine, Mrs. Chamberlain."

"You were very kind tonight, Mr. Fontaine. I'm grateful. Good night." She turned her back on him and started to walk away.

Boldly, he grabbed her wrist, spun her around, wrapped his arms around her, and kissed her. It was better than he'd even imagined. She struggled, but it didn't take long for her to change her mind in his expert embrace. Like a leaf unfurling in warm sunshine, her body melted against his. Adrenalin washed his veins. He kissed her softly at first, but grew more aggressive as the seconds swept by, his lips hard on her mouth, shoulders and neck. How long had it been since a woman had fired his blood so powerfully? Especially one who was blackmailing him? It intrigued him to think that perhaps that's *why* he coveted her. She was daring and clever, with more sheer audacity than any woman had a right to.

"Are you certain you wouldn't like to finish our discussion tonight—in my cabin?" he whispered. "I might be willing to forget my ten percent of the claim."

"Might you?"

"Very possibly."

He could feel her smile against his lips, and he smiled too. When she tried to push away from him, he refused to release her. Instead, he forced her back against the railing, and parted her lips with his own. "Not yet, Rose, I'm not . . ."

He felt something that at first he didn't recognize—which certified the depths of his intoxication. The pressure against his ribs grew painful.

Owen stopped kissing her. "That's not a gun, is it, darling?"

"Very possibly," she answered.

CHAPTER 11

Jeremy kicked off his quilts and shoved them onto the floor with his bare toes. The breeze that blew through his open porthole felt cool and silken against his sweaty skin. He rolled over and went back to dreaming of his mother . . .

They sat together on the floor of his bedroom in Richmond and she told him stories about his father, of ironclads and running the blockade, stories filled with danger and honor.

His lips quivered. He wished he and Traveller could go and find his father. They'd been trying . . . but heaven was very hard to find.

The soft fluttering of lace curtains brought him fully out of his dreams, and he found himself blinking at the patterns of starlight that lay like silver petals on the wood floor. Tears burned his eyes. He pounded his pillow with a fury.

"No! I don't want to be awake. I have to sleep!"

Traveller, tucked inside his nightshirt, woke and whickered softly.

"Sorry," Jeremy whispered, and patted Traveller. "I—I'm sorry."

He squeezed his eyes closed, blocking everything out so he could dream about his mother some more. It happened every time she left him alone in a strange place. Being with her had turned out to be harder than he had ever imagined. Since she had come to get him, he had not spent more than two nights in the same bed—when he'd had a bed, and that had not been often. Despite the winter cold, they had slept in the forests rolled up together in a single blanket. The strange sounds, scents and frequent gunfire always made his heart pound so hard he thought it was coming right out through his ribs.

In Richmond, his grandmother had always been there if he called out. But he and Traveller had been alone a good deal since his mother had taken them. Jeremy didn't even know for sure where she had gone tonight. "To make money," she'd said. That was all.

Her absences terrified him.

His grandmother had told him that gambling was very wicked, and he knew that's what his mother was doing. Their first week away from home, he'd watched in horror while his mother bet on horse races, cock fights, louse races, and anything else she could find, to win money to buy food for them. She'd learned to gamble in the army, she said, where men bet on anything, just to keep away the boredom of camp life. Jeremy had told her that he didn't like her gambling, and she'd promised not to—once they were safe.

"*Mama?*" he whispered. "Where are you? Me and Traveller are afraid here by ourselves."

He buried his sniffing face against his feather pillow, and concentrated on the rhythmic patting of the waves against the boat.

A soft thud sounded. He rolled over. The door opened and a rectangle of golden lamplight grew across the floor.

Pain twisted Jeremy's stomach. He swallowed his tears, not wanting to cry in front of his mother. It might embarrass her that Jeremy wasn't as brave as his father. He grabbed Traveller and held him against his heart. "Mama?"

"I'm here, sweetheart."

Her blue dress *shished* as she came across the floor and knelt by his bed to pull the sheet up over him. "Can't sleep again?" She smelled of liquor, which frightened Jeremy even more.

"I—I keep waking up."

She tucked the sheet around his sides and beneath his toes, and her cool hands felt good. "Well, maybe I'll lie down beside you for a while and we'll both sleep better. How does that sound?"

He smiled, and slid over, leaving her space.

She took off her dress, folded it, then pulled their small bag from beneath the bed. Jeremy's chest hurt. He clutched Traveller more tightly, watching her take out a pair of man's pants and an old Union army shirt. She put them on over her shimmy and pantalets.

"Mom . . . Mama? Are we getting off the boat?"

"Not for a couple of hours, Jeremy," she said as she climbed into bed beside him and hugged him. Up close, she smelled more like pipe smoke and flowers than liquor. He let out a breath and snuggled against her. "Let's sleep for as long as we can."

"Then we'll go?" He looked up into her face, but she'd already closed her eyes. Starlight streaming through the porthole gleamed from the silver hair-pins in her black ringlets.

"Yes," she answered through a deep yawn. "Then we'll go."

"Do we have to swim this time, Mama? The water was so cold last time."

"I know, sweetheart, but we won't be in it for long. The boat's staying close to the west side of the river. Ten minutes. That's all. You're a big boy, I'll bet you can stand it for that long."

"Yes, Mama . . . I—I can. I will." He clutched Traveller with one hand and laid the other on her warm neck. His father would have been able to stand it. "But, Mama? Where are we? Are we close to a city this time?"

"Pretty close. St. Louis isn't far."

He pondered that information. "Will I have to memorize another new name?"

She answered sleepily, "Yes, we'd better."

"What name?"

"Oh, I don't know. You think up one this time. We'll use whatever name you choose."

Jeremy thought about it. He needed something closer to his real name. He'd had trouble remembering Chamberlain. After trailing the possibilities around his head for a minute, he said, "How about Herton, mama? Instead of Heatherton?"

"That's a little too close. How about Townsend?"

"How about Heathe?" he countered, knowing he'd never remember Townsend.

"All right, that will work." She hugged him and kissed the top of his head. "Sleep now, Jeremy Heathe. I love you. Try to sleep, son."

Jeremy closed his eyes . . . and soon, very soon, he and Traveller were flying, galloping across clouds, getting closer and closer to the brilliant stars of heaven where his daddy lived.

Robin knelt on the dark deck with Jeremy standing before her, his eyes wide as he gazed down into the black water. She'd dressed them both warmly in wool pants and shirts. Jeremy wore a coat, and the small haversack on his back was filled with a few critical items, including Traveller, the precious family jewels, Charles' antique knife. A heavy money belt snugged Robin's waist. She had abandoned the rest of their meager belongings in their cabin; they could afford to buy new clothing at the first town. A single lamp gleamed in the pilot house, and Robin could see two men silhouetted against the golden glow.

"It's almost time. Are you ready, Jeremy?"

He shifted nervously. "I guess so."

She adjusted his pack one last time. Majestic piles of cloud blotted the stars as they drifted across the endless indigo sky. Robin frowned. Once they had entered the water, she would have to use the boat to shove off hard or the current would suck them into the thrashing paddlewheel. The utter blackness would make it very difficult to plot a quick course to shore, but if she just kept swimming, they would make it.

Robin exhaled unsteadily. Rose had probably believed the same thing . . .

The trees along the bank creaked and moaned as the paddlewheel approached a sharp bend. To stay in the main channel, the boat had to hug the shore—which is what Robin had been waiting for.

She leaned against the rope she had tied off on the deck railing, testing the strength of the knot, then turned to her son and smiled. "All right, Jeremy, curtain time. Are you ready?"

"Yes."

His hands gripped her shoulders, and he clamped his little legs around her belly. The thick money belt provided a secure seat for his bottom. His breath warmed her ear. "Hold on tight, now," she said.

"I will, mama."

Robin lowered herself over the side and rapelled down the hull of the sternwheeler until she reached the water. She eased in and heard Jeremy gasp. The current dragged at them.

"Cold, Mama!"

"I know, sweetheart, but look over there. See how close the shore is? A hundred feet, that's all. Just hold on and we'll be on dry land soon. Then we'll build a fire and warm up."

His head nodded against her neck.

Robin used the rope to steady herself in the powerful current while she braced her feet against the boat, getting ready to spring out and away.

The sternwheeler swung westward as they rounded the bend and Robin felt the tug of the current die as the boat momentarily shielded them from the brunt of the river.

"All right, Jeremy, we're going in."

He tightened his hold and she shoved away from the boat, lunging out into the black waters of the Mississippi. The icy liquid ate into Robin's flesh.

In only moments, the sternwheeler's backwash struck them and Robin had to paddle hard to stay afloat in the swells. For a few breathless instants, they soared upward on a crest, then plunged down into a dark valley, up and down, up and down. The boat sailed forward, pulling away from them so fast that it vanished from sight around the bend before Robin had made it halfway to shore.

"Are you all right, Jeremy?" she asked as she breaststroked for the bank. Her hands had begun to ache from the frigid water.

"I'm cold, Mama. And scared. I'm more scared than cold, though."

"Well, don't be. We're all right."

A smudge of clouds drifted over their heads and blotted out the stars, leaving them in darkness so complete, Robin could no longer be certain where the water ended and the shore began. She trained her ears on the sounds of the river, hoping a change in pitch would signal her when she was getting close. Owls hooted in the trees and she heard the unmistakable trill of crickets. And something else . . . a rhythmic shishing like . . .

The sudden rush of water made her jerk around.

Somewhere upriver the floodwaters had undercut the tree's roots and sucked it whole into the current where it now tumbled over and over, its branches churning the water, thrashing up a white froth.

Jeremy screamed. Robin reached around, grabbed his coat sleeve and flung him away from her, toward shore. The first cartwheeling limb struck her in the back so hard it knocked her breath out. Robin flailed, gasping for air.

Jeremy shrieked, *"Mama! Mama!"*

The second limb crashed into Robin's chest and dragged her under. Panic blinded her. Her shirt had become entangled in the branch. She fought to tear it off.

As the limb swung her up and brought her to the surface again, she ripped free of her shirt and plunged into the water. Every stroke of her arms sent a jagged pain through her chest, a pain so stunning she could barely breathe.

"Jeremy?" she called. "Jeremy? Where are you?"

"I'm here! I'm over here, Mama! I'm up on shore!"

The tree cartwheeled its way downstream. Jeremy began to cry. She let that sound guide her.

CHAPTER 12

L oud knocking woke Owen. He turned onto his stomach, pressed the pillow over his ears and pretended he didn't hear it. But when it persisted, he rolled to his side and squinted one eye at his pocket watch on the bedside table. Almost noon! And he'd been supposed to meet Mrs. Chamberlain at ten . . .

He cursed himself and glared at the walnut paneling of his cabin. His bed sat on the starboard side, just beyond the footboard a small chest of drawers stood below a high porthole. The blankets lay on the floor where he'd abandoned them in the night. By God, he had one outrageous headache.

The knock came again.

"Who is it?" he shouted and instantly regretted it.

"Porter, sir! We have arrived at St. Louis. Also, sir, I have a letter for you. It's marked 'urgent.' "

"Just a moment, please." Owen reached for his trousers that hung on the chair a few feet away, slipped them on, and rubbed his unshaven face. "I'm coming. Don't go away."

"I won't, sir."

He walked to the door and flung it wide. The morning was cool and damned bright. The sunlight speared his brain like a bayonet. He scowled at the young man in the black suit who extended a thick envelope.

Owen took it. Woman's handwriting. That could only be one person. He sighed in relief. When he hadn't shown up for breakfast, she had probably written to arrange a new time and place to meet. "Thank you, Porter." He searched his pockets and tipped the boy two bits.

"Thank you, sir."

Closing the door, Owen threw the letter on his rumpled bed, then went to open the porthole. A gust of wind washed over his bare chest, coming from between the red brick buildings on the waterfront. The gangplank was down. People were disembarking! Couples walked past on the deck outside, laughing and talking as they worked their way toward the levee. A group of women with colored parasols leaned over the railing, watching the mob that had come to meet the boat. On the levee, geese quacked.

"Damn it," he muttered. "She could already be off the ship and in town somewhere."

Owen took several deep breaths and went to his bedside and picked up his bag. Throwing out a pale green linen suit, he dug deeper. "Something with flair," he murmured, selecting a white ruffled shirt, tan waistcoat and trousers.

When he was ready to leave, he retrieved the envelope and opened it. The scent of money struck him first, then the sight made his sour stomach cramp threateningly. Thousands of dollars nestled inside. Startled by the amount, he pulled out the note.

March 4, 1865

Dear Mr. Fontaine,

I regret that I will be unable to keep our breakfast engagement this morning, but I wanted to offer you my sincere gratitude for your aid last night.

You will find two-thousand-three-hundred dollars enclosed, which constitutes fifty percent of my cash winnings last evening. I do hope this generous amount will discourage you from seeking to collect any further monies from me. It would truly grieve me to be placed in a position where I was forced to contact Federal authorities in regard to your business activities.

I do not begrudge your purchase of guns from scurrilous Union officers to sell to the belabored Confederacy. Jefferson Davis can assuredly use them—but I doubt President Lincoln will see it that way. Our glorious Union has judged treason to be a hanging offense.

Again, I trust I am no longer in your debt.

Yours sincerely,
Mrs. Rose Chamberlain

He laughed in sheer disbelief. What nerve! " 'Cover my share?' What kind of fool do you take me for? That claim is in Central City! My God, Rosie, miners have taken over a hundred million dollars in gold and silver out of that area in the past five years." Or so he'd read—and if half of the stories about The Richest Square Mile on Earth were true, that claim ought to bring a cool million. Which meant she owed Owen at least another hundred thousand dollars!

Retrieving his brown slouch hat, bag, and small satchel, he walked out the door into the brilliant sun. People crowded the deck, moving slowly for the gangplank. He melted into the herd and was nudged inexorably forward.

Owen craned his neck looking for Rosie. Yes, *Rosie*. It gave him a perverse delight to call her by that affectionate nickname, especially since he figured she would hate it.

When his boots thudded on the wooden gangplank, his tension lessened. On the levee, another porter with a notebook stood, taking the names of everyone who passed by, insuring that all of those who were supposed to leave the vessel had done so. The tall youth wore a dusty black uniform and had thin blond hair and a mustache, which he'd sculpted to curve around the edges of his mouth.

"Excuse me, Porter? . . . Young man? Uh, excuse me!" he shouted over the din of greetings from the levee.

"Yes, sir?" The porter turned.

"Has Mrs. Rose Chamberlain left the boat, yet?"

He scanned his list of names and shook his head. "No, sir. She must still be aboard."

"I see. Thank you. Perhaps I'll just stand to the side, then, and wait for her."

"As you wish, sir."

Owen broke away from the stream of humanity and went to the edge of the levee where he had a clear view of the gangplank.

For over an hour, Owen waited, growing more pensive by the minute. Tangles of families trudged down, toting bags. Next a long series of businessmen wearing fine suits and smoking cigars sauntered out, along with several army officers. Finally, the crew began to leave.

Owen paced anxiously. The crowd had dispersed, leaving only a few of the typical riverboat parasites—pickpockets, soiled doves, and drunkards—loitering around the levee. At last, the captain descended the ramp.

Owen walked over and asked, "Captain, I'm sorry, sir, but could you help me?" The man in the blue uniform stopped. "I'm waiting for a lady. I haven't seen her leave yet. Is it possible she's still aboard?"

The captain shook his head. An elderly man with short gray hair and a beard, he had honest eyes. "My crew has checked every cabin. Everyone who was on board has left. I'm sorry you missed your friend. Perhaps she left when we first landed. Now, if you'll excuse me—"

"Of course, Captain." Owen stepped aside. "Thank you."

The captain walked by, and Owen removed his hat to run his coat sleeve over his sweating forehead. Blond hair stuck to his temples in tiny wet curls. Even the porter with the list had gone on to other duties. The steamboat sat quiet, almost empty, rocking on the river's current. He frowned angrily at the windows of the casino.

Was it possible that the porter had missed her? *Not likely, you idiot.*

"She jumped ship. That's what she did! And to think that you joked about it last night."

He'd been hooked—and badly. The hide-out pistol in his jacket pocket pressed warmly against his chest. If he didn't get control of the killing rage that had swept over him, he was liable to shoot some innocent bystander just because.

He swung around to survey the bluff. Among several red brick buildings, one bore the sign "Saloon" in big black letters. Wooden steps led up to it.

Owen pulled his hat down to shield his eyes against the sun. His stomach objected to the very idea of whisky, but his rage demanded it. Laughter leaked out of the saloon and wafted down to him. Despite the time of day, the place sounded crowded. His boot heels thudded on the wooden plank stairs.

As Owen neared the top, the stench of the privies that emptied into the river rose around him, nearly gagging him. He shoved his satchel under his arm and drew a clean handkerchief from his jacket pocket, tenting it over his nose. A sign was posted on the rear door of the saloon: "Enter through the front!"

Owen cursed and began walking down the narrow alley between the saloon and a hotel. Urine stained the walls and piles of trash blocked his path; he kicked through the bottles, tin cans, and bits of paper, all the while breathing through his handkerchief.

Just as he neared the mid-point of the alley, a deep voice came from behind him. "Mr. Fontaine?" the man called. "No, don't turn around. Drop your bags and put up your hands. *Slowly.*"

Owen did as he'd been told, easing his bags down and raising his hands over his head. "Who are you? What do you want?"

The sound of boots behind him made Owen shift his eyes to the right. He could sense the man standing there, but didn't dare turn to get a look at him.

"Where is she?" the man asked.

Owen shook his head. "Who?"

The thrust of the pistol against his spine sent a white hot pain through him. He stumbled forward, then regained his balance. "I don't know who you're talking about!"

"Oh, I think you do," the man said. "Several of the ship's crew reported that you operated as Mrs. Chamberlain's partner at the poker table last night. Now, I want to know where she is. Tell me, and this will end very quickly. I don't want to have to hurt you."

Owen went numb when, this time, the gun barrel pressed into the back of his head. "Good God, what's she done?"

This isn't another of your discontented partners, is it, Rosie?

Impatiently, the man answered, "She is an enemy of the Union! If you are found to have given her aid in any way, it will be viewed as treason, Mr. Fontaine. Please think about that. The dealer last night said she'd won a mining claim in Colorado Territory. Where in Colorado? What city?"

Owen's brows went up. That made twice today he'd been threatened with charges of treason. He sighed. "Let me assure you, sir, that I am just as curious about her whereabouts as you are. She ran out on me—and took my share of the winnings with her. I would very much like to—"

"I don't give a damn about your petty problems! Where *is* she?"

"I don't know for certain!" *Why the hell am I protecting her?* "She may have—"

The gun butt thudded against his skull. He spun weakly, but it seemed an eternity before his knees hit the ground. He sprawled face-first into the trash. A bottle shattered, and fragments of glass pierced his right leg. Blood. Warm blood, soaked his pants.

Someone was going through his pockets, taking his gun, removing Rose's note from his pocket, unfolding it . . . then he blacked out.

Susan Jacoby braced her right foot on the velvet chair seat and leaned forward to unhook her garters. She performed the act with theatrical expertise. Men appreciated such things, and she knew it. Slowly, sensually, she pushed the black silk stocking down, then pulled it off to reveal a shapely leg. In the full-length mirror, she could see her client watching her with a hot gleam in his blue eyes—but he appeared insecure. As if this might be his first time in the house of a soiled dove. He kept shifting positions on the edge of the bed, naked, muscular. A thick mat of reddish-brown hair covered his chest and groin. But nothing could obscure the terrible scar on his shoulder—it looked to be a bullet wound. His eyes darted around the room, taking in the mahogany dresser and chair, the elegant oil paintings on the walls. Nervously, he lay back on the bed, his head on the red satin pillow.

Susan's brow furrowed as she removed her left stocking. He'd stopped looking at her to stare wide-eyed at the ceiling. And he'd seemed so eager a few minutes ago! He had picked her from a crowd of a dozen other doves, cornered her in the saloon, pushed her against the wall, and told her he liked women with long black hair. Tall women. He'd asked, "I can't tell in this light. Do you have brown eyes? Or are they blue?"

"What difference would it make, honey?" she'd countered. "I've got everything else you'll need."

"You *must* have brown eyes."

She'd frowned and nodded. He'd tucked a ten-dollar gold piece into her hand, and they'd headed upstairs.

And now he wasn't even looking at her! He'd begun clenching and unclenching his hands.

Susan turned and smiled seductively. "Don't fret about this," she said. "I know all the right—"

"Then let's get on with it!"

"Well, all right, honey, I'm on my way."

She slipped her ivory chemise over her head, removed her garter belt, and strolled to the bed where she stretched out beside him and lifted a hand to stroke his manhood.

He jerked away, rolled over on top of her, and pinned her arms over her head. "Don't touch me! Don't you touch me, do you hear me?"

"I hear you," she answered, confused. The hot glow in his eyes had changed to something wild, almost hateful. "But if you don't want me to touch you, then why the hell are you here?"

"Just—just lie here. Don't move until I tell you to! Spread your legs!"

Susan obeyed. He wet his thin lips and began kissing her hard, like an unschooled boy. Good Lord, he had to be around forty and he'd never learned to kiss a woman. She turned her face away. "Listen, honey, if you'll just let me—"

"Don't talk! *Not until I tell you to.*"

"Then stop manhandling me! I don't take kindly to rough . . ."

His fingers wrapped around her throat, terrifying her so badly that she barely felt him force his way between her legs. He moved feverishly, his thrusts violent, and with each one his grip around her throat grew tighter.

"Don't talk!" he kept repeating. "Don't talk! Don't talk!"

Susan fought to scream, but no sound came out.

The instant he ejaculated, he withdrew and scrambled to his feet. He looked stunned. Blinking sweat from his eyes, he stared down at her as though he didn't recognize her, or could not believe what he'd just done.

"Shh," he said, extending a hand as if ordering her to stay put. To stay quiet. His blue eyes were huge. He backed toward his clothes.

Susan reached over to her bedside table, pulled open the drawer, and removed her two-shot derringer. She cocked it. "Get . . . out!" she gasped, and started choking. "Or—or I'll kill you!"

CHAPTER 13

*H*arsh white light streams in through the stagecoach window. It began snowing an hour ago, and the ride has become almost too jarring to endure. Each time the coach hits a bump I feel as though a knife blade has been plunged into my heart.

My son still sleeps, stretched out across the long leather seat, his dark head pillowed in my lap. Blessed God, what will happen to him if I let down my guard and Corley moves in for the kill?

Outside the window, snowflakes whirl from a bruised sky. They cloak the vast plains with an undulating blanket of white. The brightness aches. I close my eyes, and lean my head against the seat back.

How many days have we been riding the stage. Four? Or is it five? Maybe more.

This agony . . .

Keeping my mind clear is my only real defense against my enemy, yet I've been blanking out for long periods, then awakening in terror. The pain feeds off my mind, like a ravening wolf, eating away my strength. And this cold . . .

I gave up praying three years ago, after the battle of Shiloh. I helped Union soldiers dump the bloated bodies of over seven hundred Confederate boys into a single mass grave, and something inside me cried that there could be no God. This was proof.

But I've found myself praying for the past few days, as I drift in and out of consciousness—praying that this broken rib hasn't punctured my lungs or heart, praying that I'm not bleeding too badly inside . . .

I have been wounded before, but nothing like this. This pain has made me a stranger to myself. It is as though the intensity of it has

*crowded "me" from my mind, and left someone I do not know staring
down into my soul with hollow eyes.*

*I stare back, but I do not recognize that woman. She is too weak,
too frightened to be me. I am not that coward.*

I am not . . . I am not . . .

The words have become a plea.

"Fort Scott, Kansas Territory!"

The stage driver's disembodied voice startled Robin from a sound sleep
and into the agony. Gingerly, she straightened up. Dust coated the varnished
oak interior of the coach and lay thickly on Jeremy and the brown leather
seats. So much had accumulated on her black cloak that the garment seemed
to have sprouted tan fur. She had neither the desire nor the strength to brush
it away. Already, she was shaking.

Jeremy rubbed his eyes and sat up. He had tucked Traveller inside his
gray coat to keep the horse warm, but the toy's white head stuck out between two buttons. The black dots of eyes seemed to be watching Robin,
studying her. "Where are we, Mama?"

"The driver said . . . Fort Scott." When had her voice become so hoarse?

Jeremy jumped down to stand before the window as the stagecoach rolled
into a huge square lined with white two-story buildings. Broad porches
fronted many of the structures, shaded by carefully pruned trees. Spring had
just touched the tips of the branches. Smoke rose from every chimney.

"Whoa! Whoa, now!" the driver shouted, and the stage rocked to a stop.

Robin eased forward to look at the fort while the driver climbed down.
An ocean of blue uniforms met her gaze. Robin's skin crawled. The post was
manned beyond its capacity, for tents covered the parade ground, canvas
billowing and flapping in the stiff wind.

She counted tents, officers' and enlisted men's quarters, then shook her
head. There had to be fifteen or sixteen hundred men stationed here. She
recalled that William Clark Quantrill and his Raiders had attacked Lawrence,
Kansas, in August of 1863, specifically to force the Union to waste soldiers
by posting them in the middle of nowhere. Apparently, it had worked.

"All right, folks." The driver, Frank Root, put down the step. Long and
lean, he wore a broad-brimmed felt hat tied down over his ears with a red
handkerchief that was knotted under his chin. When he flung open the coach
door, the icy dust-scented wind swept in. It fluttered the hem of Robin's long
cloak. Her arm trembled as she pulled up her hood to shield her face. "We'll

be here for about two hours, ma'am, delivering the army payroll and gathering a few supplies. There's a sutler's shop over there and Ole Drake has always got a hot pot of coffee on the fire." He smiled around a wad of chewing tobacco. "Why don't you go inside and get warmed up. Then we'll—"

From the driver's seat, the man riding shotgun yelled, *"Frank? Quelle heure est-il?"*

Root pulled out his pocket watch and answered, *"I'll est midi et quart."*

The little Frenchman jumped down and spread his arms in exasperation. *"Les bagages, je—"*

"J'ai le temps de le faire, Henri. Est-elle jolie?" The little Frenchman smiled, and Root waved a hand. "Go on, Henri, get out of here. Go see your girlfriend. I'll take care of unloading our cargo." He turned back to Robin. "Sorry, ma'am. Let me help you out."

How strange it was to hear French words spoken in the far West. It made Robin homesick for the soft gentle tones of the South.

Jeremy leaped down to the step, then to the ground, and turned to wait for Robin. Frank Root extended his gloved hand and seemed to be pondering what was taking her so long. Robin slipped the chain of her small purse over her arm and braced her hands on the seat. She had to take a deep breath before she could even attempt rising. Her legs almost refused to hold her, but she stood and put her hand in the driver's. Scanning her face, he gripped her hand as he helped her to the ground. Worry lined his forehead.

"Ma'am? Are you all right?"

"No," she answered. "I—I'm ill, Mr. Root."

Fort Scott's sounds and scents accosted Robin. Gruff laughter and soldiers' conversation filled the day, and she could smell eggs frying, bread rising, and the pungent blend of tobacco and wood smoke. Despite the wind, the distinct metallic odor of gunpowder clung to everything. "I . . . I seem to be a little dizzy, Mr. Root. Could you, perhaps, point me in the direction of the post surgeon's office?"

"Oh, yes, ma'am," he said and supported her arm as he led her around the rear of the stagecoach. Jeremy grabbed a handful of her cloak and followed. "I've heard he's a right good doctor, too," Root said as he pointed to a beautiful building with a piazza encircling the principal, or second, story. "That's the hospital, ma'am. I'm sure the doctor can ease your complaints."

"Thank you, Mr. Root."

He let go of her arm and touched the brim of his hat. "Well, I'll be getting to my duties. You and the boy be back here by two o'clock, now, you hear?"

"We will. *I promise you that.*"

He walked away, and Robin stood with Jeremy in the buffeting wind. The fifty paces to the hospital seemed a hundred miles. She wasn't sure she could make it. Already nausea had begun sending foul messages to her brain, and she hurt so badly her vision went black around the edges every time she inhaled.

"Come along, Jeremy."

He looked up through wide frightened eyes. "Will he give you medicine to make you feel better?"

"I'm sure he'll try," she answered and concentrated on placing one foot in front of the other.

Narcotics were the common prescription for pain, but badly as she needed something, she could not risk anything that would numb her wits. Corley was still out there. Robin could not, would not, underestimate his information-gathering capabilities. Especially not now. She knew that, from the moment of her injury, she'd been growing increasingly careless, wearing the same dress, speaking in the same accent, using the same handwriting— because such things required no thought. But any one of those traits might lead him to her.

The wind whipped her cloak around her legs with such force she had trouble keeping her balance.

Soldiers stared at her as she passed, and she knew that her weaving, shuffling gait must be like a frail old woman's. Jeremy walked along beside her with Traveller clutched in both hands, his eyes on the men.

"Mama," he whispered. "There's sure a lot of damned Yankees here."

"Yes, but aren't you glad they're here, Jeremy, and not in Virginia?"

He nodded, and Robin smiled down into his eyes—Charles' gentle eyes. He looked like a little vagabond. His hair and clothing bore a thick coat of dirt from the stage, and he kept grinding his teeth. Probably to rid them of the grit.

When they reached the piazza that overhung the hospital's front door, Robin stopped a moment to lean against the column while she caught her breath. The pungent odors almost made her retch. Though they blended into one overwhelming scent, she could identify each element: Chloroform, paregoric, camphor, quinine, spirit of nitrous either . . . She stopped her memory from proceeding with the list. Every soldier knew by heart the contents of the army's medicine pannier—regardless of the side he or she fought for. As memories rose and tied themselves to each of those scents, sweat began to soak the armpits of her black basque.

A tall, blond orderly opened the door, and peered out with a frown. He wore a white shirt. "Excuse me," he said. "Are you ill, ma'am?"

"Yes, I—I need to see the physician."

"Come in, please." He held the door open for her.

Robin forced her feet to cross the ten paces between them and stood shaking in the middle of the wood floor.

His brows drew together. "I'll show you to the examination room and notify the doctor that you're here."

"You're very kind."

She followed him into the small room and eased down into a wooden chair as the orderly pulled the door closed. "Jeremy?" she said. "Come over and sit by me . . . so I know where you are."

"Yes, Mama." She heard his swift steps, then felt his hand groping through the layers of petticoats to find her leg; he patted it. Robin breathed a little easier. So long as her son was nearby, she could protect him.

"No matter what happens, Jeremy, I want you to *stay close* to me. Don't let anyone tell you to go away. Do you understand? Stay right beside me, no matter what."

"I will, Mama."

The frigid light streaming through the window on the opposite wall seemed to drain the life from everything in the room—the examination table to her left, the line of shiny glass bottles, rolls of bandages, and surgical instruments laid out on the long counter to her right, the polished fir floor. Each fixture had faded to a pale gray. That same light fell upon Robin and her soul seemed to leak from her body, leaving a dried out husk. *Dust. I feel like dust.*

Steps echoed in the hallway, and the door opened and closed after the doctor and nurse. He had brown hair, wore spectacles, and stood about five and a half feet tall. His long sideburns connected up with a full beard. He carried an open book in which he jotted notes with a quill. The woman was overweight with netted gray hair, and wore a pale green dress.

"Good day. I'm Doctor Bloomfield, and this is Nurse Hambly. What is your name?"

"Mrs. Anna . . . He . . . Heathe." Had she used that name? She couldn't recall. Is that what Root had called her?

"And how may we help you, Mrs. Heathe?"

He stared down at her through cold blue eyes, antiseptic eyes that saw only the body, not the human being inside. She'd seen many such eyes during the war, but they had never ceased to anger her—or make her feel lonely.

How could anyone grow so accustomed to misery that they disconnected the pain from the person? Dead was dead, no matter how horrifying the corpse looked, but living and hurting was quite another thing. The nurse, at least, looked worried.

With effort, Robin managed to get to her feet. Her knees shook. "I have at least one broken rib, doctor. Maybe more. I don't—don't think so, though. Just . . . one."

He looked her up and down, taking in her silver earbobs, and expensive clothing, obviously wondering how a woman of her means could come to have such an injury. "Please, disrobe. Let me have a look."

She unbuttoned her cloak and let it drop to the floor, because she did not have the energy to turn and drape it over the chair. Jeremy gathered it up in his arms and held it like a dutiful servant. Robin reached down to stroke his hair before she began unbuttoning her black wool basque.

"Madam," the doctor said indignantly, "surely you want your son to leave while I am examining you." His eyes narrowed.

"No, I do not," she answered. "I want my son to stay right where he is. But, Jeremy, I—"

"But Mrs. Heathe, it is inappropriate!" Nurse Hambly said. "He can sit in the hall. I assure you, he will be quite safe."

Robin glanced at the nurse's stern face. "Jeremy, I would like you to turn the chair around, sit down, and face the wall while I'm examined. Will you do that for me?"

"Yes, Mama," he said and rearranged the chair. He threw her cloak over the back, turned it around, then climbed up into the seat. Taking Traveller from his pocket, he petted the horse while he stared at the wall.

She smiled at her own foolishness. When they'd been out in the forest, running, hiding, Jeremy had never been more than five paces from her. Even when she'd gone into the brush to take care of "necessities," she'd known that Jeremy's eyes were glued to whatever portion of her anatomy he could see. He had *had* to be able to see her, especially on those long terrible days when they'd been surrounded by the sounds of cannon and mortar fire.

Robin removed her basque and walked painfully to the examination table. When she sat on the edge and unfastened her white corset, pain struck her like a fiery lance. The corset had been supporting her ribs, and without it, she felt her lungs and heart might spill right out onto the floor. She hunched forward, breathing hard. It took a minute before she had the strength to remove her chemise.

The nurse gasped. Doctor Bloomfield laid his notebook and quill on the counter and came across the floor. His cold eyes jerked wide when he saw the black bruise that spread from her collarbone to the bottom of her rib cage. "How did this happen?" he demanded.

Nurse Hambly said, "Did you take a fall from a horse?"

Robin didn't answer. The doctor moved forward. As he poked at the bruise, her vision blurred. The room transformed itself into a concave pit of darkness where only Bloomfield's hands existed; they moved in black nothingness, swaying, disappearing, then plunging toward her like white bolts of lightning. She could not make a sound—could not frighten Jeremy. He had already endured so much.

But those hands . . . those hands caused so much pain that they seemed to reach beyond her aching flesh, going deep into her body to the place where her soul lived. With each prod, her very being split, yawned wide, and slapped back together again. Rage vied with the urge to weep.

He's not trying to break you, Robin. This man doesn't even see *you. All he sees is wounded flesh. You are not a human being in pain to him, you are just bruised meat.*

But she wondered why doctors always seemed to look through their female patients, rather than at them—as though a woman didn't really require their full attention.

"You are correct," he said after a few moments. "You have one broken rib. Fortunately, the bone has already realigned itself so I won't be forced to set it."

Robin nodded.

Doctor Bloomfield adjusted his spectacles and walked to the counter where his book and quill lay. He unstoppered a bottle of ink, dipped his pen and began to write. "I am authorizing your admission to the hospital here. We will need to monitor—"

"I'm not going to your hospital, Doctor. Bandage my rib so it's immobilized and I will be on my way."

He swung around. "Don't be ridiculous, Mrs. Heathe! You are running a very high temperature. Just from the feel of your skin, I can guess that it's around one hundred and four degrees. Unless you receive proper attention, and soon, I fear greatly—"

"And I fear greatly that you had better hurry, Doctor." Robin lifted her head and glared at him. "I have one hour left to eat lunch and make my stage."

She should be in hospital. She knew it. Battlefield hospitals were little more than graveyards, places people went to die, but fort hospitals were completely different. Renowned for maintaining a good stock of medicines and other supplies, and for actually saving lives.

"Mrs. Heathe, perhaps I have failed to make myself clear. I—"

"On the contrary, you have been perfectly clear." Putting a hand to her broken rib, she held it while she inhaled. Nurse Hambly's nostrils flared as she watched. "The worst pain comes when the broken ends of bone grate against each other. You *can* stabilize them to keep them from shifting, can't you?"

Bloomfield's prim mouth pressed into a bloodless line. "Why can't you spend a few days in the hospital? There will be another stage."

"Because I can't, that's why."

"I do not understand—"

"I don't *require* that you understand, Doctor," she shouted, "only that you do as I ask!"

He squared his shoulders, turned and strode to the bandages, which lay on the counter. "Well, if you insist on killing yourself," he said as he reached for a roll. "I suppose I—"

"Please use the sturdy linen bandages, Doctor. The lint bandages never work as well for injuries such as this."

He gave her a sidelong look, then drew his hand back, walked a short distance down the counter, and reached for a new roll. "You seem to know something about wounds, Mrs. Heathe. Did you serve as a nurse back East?" As he walked back, he unrolled the length of linen bandage.

Gathering her strength, Robin managed to lift her arms enough that he could wrap the bandage around and around her chest. "Yes," she lied. "A hospital in Boston."

When he'd finished, she felt so bitterly tired, she longed to lie back on the table and sleep forever. It took an act of courage to button up her corset and slip on her basque. She concentrated on the soft sound of Jeremy's voice; he was talking to Traveller, telling the toy how scared he was that his mama might die like his father had. Robin went cold inside. She struggled to find some bastion against the tide of despair that swept over her. Oh, how she'd love to believe a sanctuary existed, a place where she and Jeremy would be safe, where they could play together in sunny meadows—a place where she could allow herself to think about Charles, and come to terms with the grief and guilt.

She watched Jeremy's hand. Under its guidance, Traveller had begun to gallop through the air, back and forth, back and forth, anxious to be away from this place. She bowed her head. She hadn't realized when she began working as a spy that the price she would pay for serving her country was eternal banishment from it. Nor had she understood the price her family would pay.

As she slid off the table, she said. "Thank you, Doctor. How much do I owe you?"

"Three dollars, madam. But before you go, let me give you something for the pain."

"That won't be necessary."

"It *will* if you're riding a stage, Mrs. Heathe. The journey might well cause you enough misery to send you into shock!"

He went to the line of glass bottles, picked one labeled 'laudanum,' and came back to hand it to her. A tincture of opium. She had no doubt that it would strip her of her vigilance.

"No, thank you."

He shoved it at her. "You *will* need this, Mrs. Heathe. I can assure you—"

"I don't want it, Doctor."

"Don't be foolish! How can you ever hope to take care of your son when you're so weak you can't even—"

Without thinking, Robin slapped the bottle from his hand. It hit the counter and showered glass fragments across the floor. The nurse let out a sharp cry and Jeremy whirled around.

Bloomfield stepped back. Red crept into his pale cheeks. "You are not in your right mind, Mrs. Heathe. Please, listen to me. Do you know what will happen if you take a fall, or even just a bad step, and that broken rib should slice through the chest wall? The infection—"

"I believe you call it 'osteomyelitis,' don't you, doctor? A suppurative inflammation of the bone and bone marrow that results in a lingering, and very painful, death?" She said the words calmly, but blood surged in her ears. More than once, she'd helped a medic set a simple broken finger, and come back a week later to find the patient dead. When a bone had been exposed to air, it filled with pus and began a process of eating itself alive.

Bloomfield exhaled. "Well, at least you understand the gravity of your situation." He extended a hand. "I'll have to charge you an extra two dollars, Mrs. Heathe, for the laudanum. Five dollars total."

Step by cautious step, Robin made her way past Nurse Hambly to her cloak, took a five-dollar gold piece from the pocket and laid it on the seat of the chair. "Thank you for your help, Doctor. Let's go, Jeremy."

* * *

Garrison Parker pulled his blanket up around his throat and breathed in the fragrance of the night. The warm temperatures had coaxed the sweet vanilla scent from the ponderosa pines and set it loose on the wind. All around him, melting snow banks hissed and groaned. Garrison stared at the sky. Shooting stars streaked the heavens, each one alone in its journey.

Like him.

He slipped his arm under his head and chased that thought around for a time.

Honey stood down slope, cropping grass at the edge of the trees. The vista behind her was magnificent. A fresh dusting of snow gleamed on the highest peaks, and in the starlight they seemed to burn with a cold white fire.

He rubbed his tired eyes. "Damn it. Go to sleep."

But he knew he'd be awake until dawn drove the demons back.

Almost three years had passed since that hot June day of 1862, yet his nightmares had lost none of their potency. With each recurrence the screams of his friends seemed to grow louder and louder—as if those long dead men might still be able to convince him to come down out of the rocks and help them.

The Apache would have just killed you, too.

He'd never forgiven himself. Will Wheeling had screamed Garry's name over and over . . .

And he'd done nothing. Apache bullets had kept him pinned down, unable to shoot, or move, or do anything except lie up there and sob like a damned baby while he watched his friends die.

Even after he woke from the nightmares, he had trouble pulling himself back to this world. His soul was always certain that the frantic thumping came from war drums, not his heart, and that the pressure against his spine was sandstone, not soft blankets.

Worse, when he did manage to rouse himself, he fell into thoughts about Lottie. As thought the horrors of war naturally led to the horrors of women. Strange, the way the mind connected things.

Had it really been a year and a half since she'd left? Hurt like a week ago. He'd met her in a gold camp in northern California. They'd moved in together, and for six months her idea of a relationship had been to cook for him, to wash his clothes, to keep his cabin clean. On weekends, she'd swept the floor, stood over the stove, baking bread, roasting meat, cutting up vegetables—or anything else she could think of to avoid being with him.

He'd loved her anyway, with a desperation she'd never understood. She'd had long blond hair, bright blue eyes, and a face like an angel's. Lottie had made him laugh. She'd also made him forget.

Despite the agony at the end, he'd never blamed her for leaving him. He *was* hellfire crazy sometimes. He'd get into a fight at the drop of a hat, or take off on an adventure any dimwit suggested. If anybody dared to criticize, his hot temper burst forth like a volcanic eruption. Lottie had dared, and after his rage seeped away, he always felt as if he was freezing to death from the inside out.

Garrison gripped a handful of his curly brown hair and tugged, reminding himself he was alive.

"A goddamned bank teller," Garrison said and grunted. "A man with regular hours and fine clothes. Duane, that was his name—the man who never had dirt under his fingernails. Or so Lottie said."

Garrison laughed, darkly amused with himself. It amazed him that he remembered the name of the man Lottie had left him for.

Toward the end, every time he'd tried to touch her, she'd broken into tears and shouted at him. He hadn't understood at the time. If she had wanted to leave, why didn't she just sit him down, gently tell him so, and go? It would have killed him, but in the long run, the death would have been quicker.

Instead, he'd come home one day to find a note on the kitchen table: *"I have decided to marry Duane Kurtz. I hope you ain't got no hard feelings. Your friend, Lottie Jameson."*

The fact that she'd added her last name to the note hurt him more than note itself, like he might not know who she was otherwise.

A prickling sensation started in his belly.

"Hell, I may as well get up. I ain't going back to sleep now."

Garrison threw off his blankets and rose, stretching in the starlight. The fragrant breeze chilled his face, but he felt warm inside his buffalo coat. He shoved his hands into his pockets.

His half-built log cabin stood ten feet away. An array of saws, adzes, a cant hook for rolling heavy trunks, and a pair of log tongs lay in a neat row on a bed of sawdust along the northern wall. After four days of peeling bark from pines, even his bones ached. But today he'd start laying the roof timbers. If the warm weather held out, he'd be done by nightfall. The cabin wasn't going to be big, only twelve by sixteen feet, but it overlooked Russell Gulch and Clear Creek. When darkness fell, the lights of a dozen mining camps glittered like jewels in the valley bottom.

He asked himself, not for the first time, why he was rushing to build on the claim? What the hell was he doing? Mr. Terrence Collier could ride up tomorrow and tell Garrison to hightail it before he called the sheriff. And he would have to.

But it was so beautiful up here. Above him in the silvered blackness, a

bat flitted, twisting, squealing. Garrison could barely keep sight of it as it
proceeded on its hunt.

Strips of bark covered the ground around the cabin, whiskering the snow
with golden curlicues. Sawdust was everywhere. Including under his bedroll.
It made a fine soft layer of insulation against the icy ground. He looked back
at his tumbled blankets. Two of them. Thin. Cotton. No woman would be
warm enough with just two thin cotton blankets, not in this cold climate, not
sleeping out in the open. And he wondered if there were other men walking
around tonight resenting their blankets.

He ambled to the edge of Banta Hill where Honey stood grazing. She
looked at him curiously, wondering why he wasn't asleep.

"Dreams," he murmured in answer. "I keep having dreams, Honey. Bad
ones. About the war. About Lottie."

Honey blew and swiveled her head his direction. Her brown eyes shone
like still lakes in the reflected gleam from the mountains. Garrison scratched
her jaw. "I know. You hated Lottie. Maybe that's the real reason she left. She
got tired of your teeth marks festering on her butt. Maybe if you'd been a
little easier on her . . ."

Somewhere up in the peaks, a lone wolf barked and broke into a solitary
serenade of the night: A signal to the pack, the wolf had spotted prey and
needed help to bring it down. Both males and females hunted, but he recognized that clear high voice. He'd seen this female trotting across the slopes
many times over the past year and heard her give similar calls.

Her lonesome voice echoed off the peaks.

Garrison listened for the responding yip. Listening hard. Wolves mated
for life. Where was the male?

"Come on, man," he whispered. "Answer her. She needs you."

Honey used her nose to nudge Garrison's shoulder, as though worried
about him, and he realized his voice had gone hoarse. He petted her velvet
nose. "Oh, I'm all right, Honey. I was just thinking about needing . . . and
being needed. And, yes, goddamn it, about Lottie."

When the male finally yipped and broke loose with an ecstatic howl,
Garrison jerked up his head. "Good man. I knew you wouldn't let her down."

He envied the wolves. Hunting together, well, no matter what the quarry,
there was nothing more important than that.

Sighing to himself, he walked over to the tools and picked up his log
tongs. If he got to work now, he could have the roof timbers laid by dawn.

CHAPTER 14

Every time the stage jostled, the leather curtain over the window puffed out, letting in icy air, and allowing Owen a view of the countryside. Huge herds of buffalo grazed in the distance, little more than endless black dots against a background of snow-covered plains. Sagebrush thrust up gnarly turquoise branches through the white, and occasionally a cottonwood tree nestled in a drainage. Otherwise, Colorado appeared to be a Godforsaken wasteland. He shook his head. The reflected sunlight was so bright that it bludgeoned his eyes. He tugged his black hat down and concentrated on the hiss of wind whistling around the door to his right. The tangs of sage and wet earth scented the cold air. He inhaled deeply of those fragrances, hoping they would take his mind off how much he hated stage travel. No one had ever figured a way of heating the coach or cushioning the jolts, and it was impossible to truly rest, though he'd been trying hard.

He'd boarded the stage three days after he'd reached St. Louis, which meant Rose was ahead of him on the trail, and since he was almost in Denver, she had probably already reached Central City. At least, he hoped she was still there. Given her nefarious nature she might have . . .

"Mr. Fontaine?" a honeyed voice said. "Mr. Fontaine, are you awake?"

He debated on whether to answer. Beneath the brim of his hat, he saw Sally Sanger straightening her pink dress. A skinny woman with bright red hair and glinting green eyes, she'd been talking his ear off for over two hundred miles. The instant she'd boarded the stage at the Lillian Springs station, she had appraised the worth of his expensive black overcoat, boots and hat, and decided to throw herself at him. Owen had slept most of the trip out of self-defense. The two other men in the coach, Frank Root and Andre Guillard, seemed glad she'd decided to shower her attention on Owen.

Root, the alternate driver, was a tall, thin man; he lounged on the long seat beside Sally, his eyes closed. Around fifty, he wore a grimy leather jacket and scuffed boots. The fourth passenger, Mr. Guillard, sat beside Owen, dressed in a tan silk suit. Brown hair stuck out beneath the brim of his ivory felt hat. The big Creole had barely spoken since he'd boarded at Fort Wicked. Despite a heavy muffler coiled around his throat, he spent much of his time coughing, sneezing, and generally sounding contagious. When he did speak, his hoarse whisper carried a French accent.

"Mr. Fontaine?" Sally called again, extending a foot to kick him in the ankle.

Owen pushed his hat up. "Oh, I'm sorry. Were you addressing me, Miss Sanger?"

She smiled and leaned forward so that he was forced to stare down the front of her low-cut dress. "Yes, I was. I saw you move and thought perhaps you could tell me something about this new country we've entered." She lifted the window curtain with a finger. "Just look at those mountains! They are so breathtaking. Do you know what range that is?"

"I suspect, Miss Sanger, that Mr. Root is far better qualified to answer that question than I. After all, I've never been to Colorado Territory before." He dipped a hand toward Root, who grunted. "Hmm?"

Owen took the opportunity to reach down on the floor, open his satchel, and remove a St. Louis newspaper that he'd purchased just before he'd left. He unfolded it. The colorful headlines proclaimed, "LEWD WOMAN MURDERED AT HOUSE OF ILL FAME! KILLER BEING SOUGHT!" Owen scanned the article. Intriguing. The murderer had used the dead woman's pot of rouge to paint red feathers over her naked body . . .

"I was wondering," Sally said sharply to Root, "what mountains those are?"

"The Rocky Mountains," Root answered and closed his eyes again.

"That's where the gold towns are, isn't it?" She redirected her question to Owen.

He kept reading. Eyewitnesses claimed that on the night of the murder they'd seen an army officer courting the dead woman. Owen hoped it hadn't been any of his nefarious associates. If the man were captured and convicted, it could severely curtail his business operations. "I certainly hope so, Miss Sanger."

Her smile broadened. "Are you heading to one of those towns, Mr. Fontaine?"

Cautiously, he answered, "I'm probably heading to *all* of those towns, Miss Sanger."

"Well, isn't that a coincidence. I reckon I am, too."

"Uh . . . I see." And he feared he did.

"Maybe we can arrange to ride together? It would just make me so happy to have the company." She winked in anticipation.

Owen glanced at her, then brusquely refolded his newspaper and stuffed it back into his satchel. Women weren't ordinarily so forward with him and, while he'd originally found Miss Sanger's manner amusing, now it irritated him. None of the multitude of doves he'd patronized in the past had tried to corner him like this.

"I'm very sorry, Miss Sanger, but my schedule is so uncertain, I can't make such plans."

As the stage crested the hill, the chunky buildings of Denver came into view, nestled against a backdrop of snow-clad peaks. Several tent camps clustered around the edges of the buildings. He'd heard that Denver and Central City each had a population of around 2,700, making them the largest "cities" in the Territory. He shook his head, amused by the western standard for what constituted a "city." Back East, this pitiful combination of lean-tos and tents would not even qualify for a shantytown.

"Oh, I wouldn't mind being on an irregular schedule, Mr. Fontaine," Sally Sanger pressed. She'd started flipping the ends of her white sash in frustration. "I am accustomed to such uncertainties. And I'm sure we can find something to do in the in between times."

Frank Root had pulled his dusty felt hat down to cover half his face, pretending sleep, but Owen glimpsed a sudden wide spread of white teeth beneath the brim.

Owen smiled, too. "Why, Miss Sanger, I have the perfect solution to your problem. Mr. Root rides this line from town to town constantly. I'm sure he'd be happy to escort you on your journey."

Root jerked upright, staring at Owen, then turned to meet Sally's hostile gaze. "I—I'd be happy to—to see you . . . so long as you're on one of my routes."

Sally looked him up and down with distaste. "No. Thanks."

Root exhaled a relieved breath and lounged back against the seat, but he gave Owen a spiteful look before slipping his hat down over his face again.

"What business did you say you were in, Mr. Fontaine?" Sally asked, fluttering her eyelids in interest.

"War."

"War?"

"Yes, I act as weapons consultant to the War Department," he lied.

"Oh—you mean you sell guns to the Union?"

He noted that Guillard's pale blue eyes were still focused on the leather window curtain, but he had turned his head ever so slightly toward Owen. He was paying close attention to the conversation.

"Not exactly. My expertise is in the efficiency of weaponry. I recommend ways of increasing the effectiveness of cannons, for example, to assure more men are killed or maimed with each shot."

Sally's smile waned. "That's—interesting."

Pleased with himself, he said, "Yes, I think so."

She seemed to be working on what to say next. Her eyes narrowed in contemplation. "Well, at least you're helping defeat those vile traitors. I've never been so mistreated in my life as when I was trying to do a little business in Atlanta."

"I can well imagine," he said as he watched her pull a fan from her dainty black purse.

"Oh, you have no idea." With a flick of the wrist, she snapped the fan open and began briskly recirculating the air in the coach. "Why, the sonsofbit—well, they wouldn't even let me get a decent hotel room!"

"The barbarians."

"It was just terrible. I'm glad you're helping kill more of them. The fewer that live the better."

Frank Root opened one eye and tilted his head to peer at her. "A might bloodthirsty, don't you think? Until a few short years ago, them people down South were an important part of this nation. I continue to pray they will come to terms with Mr. Lincoln and rejoin the Union."

Mr. Guillard broke out in a coughing fit that ended all conversation. His massive shoulders shook with the effort. When the fit had subsided, Guillard pulled a handkerchief from his breast pocket, blew his nose, and hoarsely whispered, "My apologies."

Sally frowned at Root. "What!" she said. "You want the damned Rebs back? Well, personally, I hope all Southerners die before Lincoln gives in. They don't deserve the blessings of the Union." Smiling at Owen, she continued, "I think your crusade to improve our weapons is wonderful. The Union needs more brave men like you."

"Oh, bravery is a characteristic I lack completely," Owen confessed. "I think it's far better to desert and take a chance on a bullet in the back than meet the enemy face-to-face and certainly take one in the heart."

"But you're helping win the war!"

"That is an accident of nature. It's immaterial to me which side wins."

She looked confused. "Then why are you working for the Union side?"

"I make more money putting howitzers in the hands of the boys in blue. You see, the South is flat broke. They couldn't afford my prices." It pleased him that he could be so creative when the situation demanded.

Patriotic fires sprang to life in Sally's green eyes; she set her jaw as though preparing for a fight. "You mean you'd work for the rotten Secesh if they could pay you?"

"Unquestionably."

"Why, that's dishonorable, sir. And . . . and probably treasonous!"

Owen smiled. "My dear Miss Sanger, do you want to know the truth about warfare?"

"I doubt that you could tell me, sir."

"Well, I think I could tell you a few things," he answered. "But perhaps you would rather not be informed of such realities."

"Are you trying to insult me?"

"Trying?"

"Go on! I'm listening." She had begun to fan herself so energetically that red strands of hair created a writhing halo around her face.

"All right. I will. War, Miss Sanger, is nothing more than economic sleight-of-hand. It—"

"What does that mean, 'sleight-of-hand?' "

"A feat of magic. The power of illusion. A hoax. Let me give you an example. If you are a manufacturer of minie balls, you must do everything you can to keep men killing each other, or demand for your product will drop to zero and you'll wind up bankrupt. So, how do you maintain the demand? Why, you whip up the public's fervor for battle."

"I hardly think—"

"You don't have to think—at least not much. If you just listen, Miss Sanger, you will discover that pretty words like glory and duty and honor are shouted the loudest by men who have never even seen a battlefield. Men who will do anything to protect their own hides because they have substantial investments in the war, and what's the use of a good war if you get killed before you can collect your winnings?"

Angrily, Sally responded, "The greatest investment possible, Mr. Fontaine, is a man's life. Surely you won't deny that."

Owen flopped back against his seat. "You have curious notions, Miss Sanger. I know many men whose lives are not worth one-tenth of my war investments."

Sally's pale brows lowered. "Is money the only thing you find valuable, Mr. Fontaine?"

Owen had to think about that for a moment. "I must admit, I cannot think of one single thing that is beyond the power of money. After all," he said with a knowing smile, "even love can be bought and sold. Don't you agree?"

"That may be." She glanced around the coach at the other men, obviously upset with them for not having taken her side. "But you can't buy your way into heaven, Mr. Fontaine. I will guarantee you that!"

"Really?" Owen laced his fingers over his stomach and watched the country go by beyond the flapping window curtain. In the distance, a large herd of antelope flowed like water, down into a drainage, shooting up again to flood out across the plains. "Well, Miss Sanger, maybe God has just never had the right offer."

Frank Root's chest vibrated with soundless mirth, but when Owen glanced sideways at Guillard, he found cold eyes upon him. There was something . . . savage . . . about that gaze. Was Guillard some sort of religious fanatic or just another silly patriot? Owen said, "I do hope I have not disturbed you, Mr. Guillard. I meant no offense."

Guillard did not move a muscle. He just stared at Owen, as if imagining what it would feel like to slit his throat and let the blood run down over his huge hands.

"What are you doing out here," Sally began, and Owen gratefully turned away from Guillard, "if you're trying to make money off the war? The fighting is almost all back East."

"I'm searching for a friend. She has a mining claim somewhere in this vicinity."

"Oh. A woman!"

Owen's brows arched. "You object?"

"No, I do *not* object," Sally said. "What's her name? Maybe I know her."

Owen laughed. "I am quite certain, Miss Sanger, that you do not know Rose. She is hardly your type of—"

"Rose?" Root asked. He straightened up and shoved his hat back. "Rose Heathe? Tall woman with coal black hair?"

Owen's heart pounded. The last name was different, but that was not surprising. "You know her?"

"She rode this very stage to Denver just about a week ago. She was right sick, too. Did you know that?"

"Sick?"

"Very sick. She visited the hospital at Fort Scott, to see the doctor there."

Owen's breathing went shallow. Had she been attacked by the same foot-pad who had knocked him senseless in St. Louis? He'd been mulling over that event since it had happened, but had been unable to connect the puzzle pieces: His assailant said she was a traitor, which probably meant she was born in the South, but no one would hunt her because of her birthplace. Owen was fairly certain her pursuer was a man she'd swindled somewhere along the way. "What was wrong with her, did she say?"

"No. But that boy said she'd broke a rib when she got tangled up with a tree in the floodwaters—"

"Ah," Owen said, "the floodwaters." He took off his hat and slapped it hard against his knee. Dust puffed and drifted around the inside of the coach. He crossed and recrossed his legs, before saying, "Pray, go on, Mr. Root. I'm sorry."

"Well, there ain't much more. Her son—"

"Son?" Owen interrupted. "What *son?"*

"His name was Jeremy."

Owen flipped his black hat back on his head, and rubbed his temples. "My God. She has a son."

"Five or six years old, I'd guess," Root said. "You didn't know?"

"It was a fact she failed to mention."

The stage rolled into Denver, passing crude cabins and a few brick build-ings. A half mile ahead, a sign proclaiming "THE OVERLAND STAGE COMPANY" glistened with yellow paint. A dozen or more people milled around outside, waiting for the stage.

"Don't you like children?" Sally demanded.

"I didn't say that." Owen folded his arms across his chest. "They're all right if you lock them in the barn and slip food to them under the door until they're eighteen."

"Not only are you seriously lacking in honor, Mr. Fontaine," Sally pointed out. "You're not even human."

"Is that relevant—"

The driver called, "Get ready, folks! Denver!"

Sally Sanger collected her small bag and grabbed the door latch. As soon as the stage rolled to a stop, she leaped down without even a goodbye. Owen sighed, very glad this leg of his journey was over.

He gestured to Mr. Guillard. "Please, go ahead, sir. I still have things to collect."

Guillard passed by with a cool glare and followed Sally into the clapboard stage office to await his luggage. Owen watched him go and turned to smile at Root while he retrieved his satchel. Root was beating the dust from his leather sleeves.

"That Guillard," Owen said. "He's a strange one. Did you catch where he was from?"

"He said New Orleans, but that was a lie."

"A lie? How do you know?"

Root buttoned up his coat. "Despite his accent, he doesn't speak French. My mother was born in New Orleans and when Guillard told me that's where he was from, I tried talking to him in my rusty French. He didn't understand a word."

"Are you sure he just didn't answer because of his sore throat?"

"I'm sure. None of the words registered in his *eyes*, Mr. Fontaine." Root stepped down to the dusty street and went about helping the driver unload the luggage.

Owen sat quietly wondering as he looked at the stage office. Through the open door, he could see Guillard pacing back and forth like a caged tiger. The man moved with military precision.

But not like a soldier exactly, more like . . . like a West Point graduate who had been hitched to a desk for too long.

Owen opened his satchel, removed his new Army Colt revolver and tucked it into the big slant pocket of his black overcoat. Only then did he step out of the stagecoach and onto the cold crude streets of Denver.

CHAPTER 15

Robin's long blue cape billowed around her as she walked through Central City holding Jeremy's hand. He used his other to hold his hat on while he gawked at the brick, stone and clapboard buildings, then at the buckboard that rattled by, pulled by six mules. The narrowness of the street made it seem as if the tall false-fronts leaned over them. Their stage had arrived two hours earlier, and Robin had had time to find a hotel room, put Jeremy down for a nap, and hang up her clothes while he slept. They both felt better.

On the mountain slopes around town sat enormous yellow piles of dirt. Tailings from the mines. There had to be over a hundred such piles. Despite its name, "The Richest Square Mile on Earth," she had not expected to see so many openings in the ground. The slopes resembled great prairie dog towns, like those she'd seen from the stage.

"Mama?" Jeremy said and tilted his head back to gaze up at her. Spikes of dark hair stuck out around the brim of his hat. He'd been acting strangely all morning, riding with his eyes glued to her face, whispering to Traveller. His round cheeks glowed pink from cold.

"What is it, sweetheart?"

"Mama, may I have a new pony? Once we find a house to live in?"

"Of course, you may. What kind of pony do you want?"

He lowered his eyes to watch his feet move on the wooden sidewalk. The toes of his brown boots bore a coating of yellow dust. "I want a pony just like Traveller."

Robin squeezed his hand. "You mean a white one?"

He nodded.

"If we can find one, Jeremy, you can have him."

He gave her that little boy smile that always broke her heart, and Robin bent down to kiss his tiny fingers. "You may have anything you want, Jeremy. If it's available out here in these wild regions."

"Thank you, Mama."

The street crested a hill and snaked downward steeply. Because of the angle of the sun, they walked the rest of the way to the Land Office in cold gray shadows. When they reached it, Robin peered in the window, and saw a red-haired man sitting behind a desk. Two chairs sat in front of the desk, and near the door stood an old potbellied stove with a stack of split pine logs piled beside it.

Robin knocked, and when the man looked up and waved her in, she opened the door and pushed Jeremy through before her. The man stood up.

"How can I help you, ma'am?" He wore a red and black plaid shirt with tan pants. His nose was flat beneath dark blue eyes.

"You are the administrator of the Land Office?" Robin asked as she closed the door and walked forward.

"Yes, ma'am. I'm Mike Hathaway. And you are?" He extended a hand to her.

She reached out to shake it. "I'm Mrs. Rose Hale. I'm pleased to make your acquaintance, sir. I am the new owner of a mining claim here and am hoping you can—"

"Which mining claim, Mrs. Hale?" Hathaway's eyes had narrowed.

Robin lifted her black handbag and removed the claim papers that Terrence Collier had signed over to her. She handed them to Mr. Hathaway. "This claim, sir." While he unfolded them and put on his spectacles to read, Robin explained, "Mr. Collier was my uncle. He left me the claim in his will. I hope everything is in order."

"So Collier's dead, eh?" Hathaway asked and lifted his gaze to pin Robin's.

"Yes, I'm afraid so."

Hathaway didn't look as though he believed her. Robin tried to appear at least a little sorry about her 'uncle's' demise, but Hathaway's suspicious expression didn't change a bit.

"Please have a seat, Mrs. Hale." He gestured to the chairs before his desk. She sat down and pulled Jeremy up onto her lap, where he leaned back against her, and tucked a hand in his coat pocket to finger Traveller. "I am very sorry to tell you this, Mrs. Hale," Mr. Hathaway said. "But everything is not in order. In fact, you have a big problem."

"What sort of problem?"

Hathaway flopped back into his chair and ran a hand through his bright red hair. "Well, your uncle failed to 'prove up' on this claim last year and another fella—"

"What does that mean? 'Prove up?' "

"It means he did not provide me with documentation showing that the mine was worked last year. According to law, you have to do that. Since your uncle didn't, another fella filed on the claim."

Hathaway handed the claim papers back to Robin, and she folded them and tucked them into her handbag again.

"I see," Robin said. Had all of her hopes been for nothing? All of her dreams? Anger stirred in her veins. "Let me see if I understand this, Mr. Hathaway. Along with my claim papers, I should also have some sort of 'proving up' papers, is that right?"

"Yes, ma'am. They ain't got to be fancy or nothing, just a statement from Collier saying he produced gold from that claim during the year of our Lord, 1864." He leaned back in his chair and examined her. He looked worried, and Robin wondered what stake he had in this.

"Mr. Hathaway, what is the name of the gentleman who has filed on my claim?"

"Garrison Parker. He's a fine fella, ma'am. Really. Hard worker. Honest. If a might peculiar. But, heck, who ain't?"

Jeremy twisted in Robin's lap to lay his head against her breasts, and she patted his back while she thought about this new development. Jeremy's warm breath penetrated her basque and touched her skin, comforting her. "Do you know this Parker well, Mr. Hathaway?"

"Yes, ma'am. He's my friend." Hathaway put his arms on his desk and laced his fingers. He'd said the words simply, with respect and genuine affection.

"Would it be possible for you to find him? I would like to talk with Mr. Parker about this problem."

"Well, I think I can. Do you want me to set up a meeting?"

"I'd be very grateful if you could."

Hathaway nodded, but his brows drew together. Anxiously, he tapped his desk with his clasped hands. The woodstove cracked and popped and the sweet scent of pine sap filled the air. "There's one other thing you should know, ma'am. Garry Parker has built a cabin on that claim. It means a lot to him. I . . . well, I think it's the first real home he's ever had. You understand what I'm saying?" His florid face tensed.

"Yes, Mr. Hathaway, I do," she replied. He didn't want Robin to hurt his friend. "I'll decide what to do with Mr. Parker once I've met him."

Hathaway inclined his head. Sincerely, he said, "If you'll work with him, ma'am, I don't think you'll regret it. When and where would you like to meet with Garry?"

"I'm staying at Mrs. Wirth's hotel. Would seven o'clock this evening be acceptable?"

"I'll see what I can do."

Robin set Jeremy on the floor and rose from her chair to reach for Mr. Hathaway's hand again. He had a firm handshake. "You are very kind to help me, Mr. Hathaway. Thank you. I'll be waiting at my hotel—"

"I'll send word just as soon as I know, ma'am."

Robin smiled. "Thank you. I'll be talking to you soon, then. Good day, Mr. Hathaway."

"Good day, ma'am."

Garrison stared across the table at Mike Hathaway. Second shift at the mines had just let out, and Luke's saloon bustled with laughing, talking men. The smoke had grown so thick Garrison's eyes were watering. One Irish miner stood propped against the bar, singing at the top of his lungs. He did not, however, have a voice like a canary's—more like a mating vulture's. Every time he hit a high note, Garrison's teeth ached.

He smoothed his fingers down the sides of his mug and frowned at the window. The fires of sunset had set the drifting clouds ablaze and blushed pink into the false-fronted downtown buildings. Horses and wagons clattered by with their traces jingling.

"Well," Garrison said. "Has she got it, Mike? What's your gut tell you?"

Hathaway shrugged. "How should I know? She came strolling in 'bout two this afternoon and handed me the claim papers. When I told her that you had filed a challenge to the claim, and that I needed to see proof of it having been worked last year, she just folded up her papers and asked me to find you."

Garrison closed his eyes. "Damn it, Mike. I knew something was wrong. I been having bad nightmares."

"Now don't get crazy yet. She's still got to show me the proof."

Mike drank in silence, and Garrison's eyes drifted over the cold blue mountains beyond the thin pane of window glass; his heart clutched up. When he'd risen that morning, he'd counted seventeen different mountain peaks shimmering in the crisp clear air. It would kill him to have to leave his cabin.

"One thing bothered me about her story," Hathaway said. "The part about

Collier being her uncle and leaving her the claim as an inheritance . . . it just didn't ring sterling to me."

"Don't to me neither. I expect I'll ask her about that when I see her tonight."

Hathaway's orange hair had a bluish glint through the smoky haze. "Now, listen, Garry, I think you ought to fight her, too, but go at it gently, will you? The way she was dressed, she might be some kind of princess or heiress or something, and if you get that arrogant tone in your voice—"

"You saying I got a way with women, Mike?"

"—she might just hire Ben Veldman—he don't like you anyway—or one of his thugs, to ride up to your cabin and shove a rifle up your—"

"Princess, eh? Good looking?"

Hathaway drained his beer and set the mug aside. "You'll see." It sounded like a threat. "And since you have no intention of taking any of my good advice, I had best be getting home. I just wanted you to know that she agreed to the seven o'clock meeting."

"Thanks, Mike," Garrison said. He looked up to meet his friend's concerned eyes. "For acting as a go-between. I know you got better things to do. Thank Ginny for that dried apple pie she sent up. It sure was tasty. Made my cabin feel like a real home. I . . ." his voice faltered. He shut his mouth.

Hathaway gripped Garrison's wrist hard. "I know you're sick about this, Garry, but just this once, *listen to me*. Take it slow and easy with Mrs. Hale. Even if she proves the claim was worked last year, there's got to be a way for you to keep your cabin. She seemed reasonable. If you don't make her mad, maybe she'll let you work for her part time, and eventually pay your cabin off, or you could take out a bank loan and buy it outright. Think on it."

"I am thinking, Mike." He shifted uncomfortably in his chair. "I really am."

Hathaway stood up. "Good. Will I see you tomorrow morning in my office? Mrs. Hale said she'd be there around 8:30."

"I reckon so."

Hathaway touched his hat and left.

Garrison massaged the back of his neck. The muscles had knotted up. All around him, good cheer filled the air, and he felt like hell. Well, he'd known it was too good to be true.

Up to now, he'd feared rational things, bullets, starvation, freezing to death in the snow, having some horse kick his brains out. But the possibility of losing that little log cabin on the hill made him plain desperate. Which was silly. He'd still have Honey, his health, and plenty of mining tools. He could start over again anywhere he wanted to. But . . . he didn't want to. Damn, he didn't. That cabin had given him a sense of home and hearth, and the thought of leaving it turned him inside out. He'd had so many things taken away from him—his mother had died when he was five, his father had thrown him out when he turned fourteen, and he hadn't seen the old villain since. The Apache had taken his best friends . . . and finally he'd lost Lottie.

He felt like a little boy again, cold inside, and running, running hard to reach a sanctuary that always vanished the moment he found it.

Angry with himself, he whispered, "You're a Goddamned fool, Garrison Parker. You should have never built that cabin."

Rising from his chair, he shouldered his way through the crowd to the bar, where he lifted his empty mug so Luke would see him.

"Another beer, Garry?" Luke shouted above the din. The Irishman had begun to shriek the *Lament for Robert Emmet*.

Garrison squinted one eye to fend the noise off and yelled, "Reckon I'll have something stronger, Luke. How 'bout a double shot of whisky?"

"Coming right up."

When Luke set the glass in front of him, Garrison held it up to the light, watching the amber liquid gleam, then downed it with one quick throw of his hand.

"I'll have another one, Luke."

"Another double?"

"That's right."

Luke's thin face went serious. Sweat glistened on top of his bald head. "You sure, Garry?"

"I said so, didn't I?"

"Well, I was just . . . I talked to Mike earlier and . . . Garry? You ain't going to bully that woman, are you? I mean I know you're upset—"

"Damn, Luke, does everybody think I'm so charming?"

"Just asking, Garry. That's all. I'll get you that drink."

Luke hurried away to fetch the whisky, and Garrison let out a deep breath. He propped his boot on the brass footrail. Half the patrons had taken up the Irishman's tune, singing so loudly it reminded Garrison of a herd of rampaging buffalo. He could barely hear himself think.

If Mrs. Hale had the proof, it was all over. His only course of action would be to plead for mercy. But if she didn't have it, and tried to toy with him, to trick him into letting her keep the claim . . . By God, he'd put up one hell of a fight.

He shook his head. He could fight any man on earth, but a woman? He'd have to work himself up to it. The very idea had already started eating at him, moving through his body, gnawing every nerve, melting into one solid ache.

"Here you go, Garry," Luke said as he set the new whisky down.

"Much obliged, Luke."

Luke gave him a backward glance as he walked down the bar to deliver another drink. Garrison just pushed the glass around with his finger. After a few more of these, he ought to have enough false courage to do battle with Satan himself—but Satan had testicles. Which would make fighting him a good sight easier. . . . At least he thought Satan had testicles. Everybody said so. Garrison contemplated their probable size and dimensions.

"Garry?" Luke said, appearing out of nowhere. He was using a clean towel to polish the bar. His hand moved in practiced circles.

"What?"

Luke leaned over the bar and lowered his voice. "You want me to go down there with you to meet that woman? I'll let Elijah tend bar and—"

"Well, now, that would make her take me seriously, wouldn't it? 'Cuse me, Mrs. Hale, this here is my bartender, Luke Foster. He came along to see that I don't make a jackass out of myself. Kee-rist, Luke! I will be fine. I promise."

Luke nodded, but dubiously. "So you ain't going to bully her? Not like you usually do after you been drinking and—"

Garrison bellowed, "I ain't gonna bully the woman! Shall I write it in blood on the bar?"

CHAPTER 16

Robin paced the hotel room in her shimmy, trying not to wake Jeremy. A dazed sensation had possessed her. The room was small, barely eight by ten feet, but a bed, chest of drawers, armoire, and a stand for the flowered water pitcher and bowl crowded the space. The *Rocky Mountain News* lay on the chest of drawers. She had not been able to take her eyes from the headline since Mrs. Wirth brought up the week-old paper an hour ago:

UNION TROOPS OCCUPY RICHMOND
AND PETERSBURG, VIRGINIA!!
A.P. HILL KILLED IN FINAL ASSAULT!

The news had stunned her. She had not seen Hill in over a year, but his ironic smile had pulled her through so many horrifying nights that his loss made her physically ill. And what of President Davis? The paper said only that the Confederate Congress had fled Richmond before the fall. Where would Davis be now? And Lee? Was General Lee still fighting? *Of course he is. He'll fight to the last breath. He must.*

Robin walked to stand over the bed. Amidst the swells of sheets and blankets, Jeremy lay, curled on his side. He looked so peaceful. His mouth was open slightly and his face glowed with a tawny brilliance in the lamplight. One of his hands clutched Traveller, whose head peeked over the collar of Jeremy's white nightshirt. It comforted Robin to look at him. To know that at least he was safe. Dear God, what would have happened if Jeremy had been in Richmond when Grant broke through the lines? And Charles' mother? Was she safe? Had Augusta been spared? Sudden guilt ravaged her. She had been so harsh, so terrified the last time she'd seen the Old Miss. How could she have . . .

Stop this! You'll drive yourself crazy. You knew the Cause was lost . . . You must think about your life here, now.

She closed her eyes for a long minute, steadying her nerves.

Quietly, she went to the armoire, opened the double doors, and pulled out a silver velvet gown trimmed with black crocheted lace. The heart-shaped neckline would accentuate her bosom, and she'd add a magenta sash to show off her waist. A diamond necklace and matching earrings would complete the outfit.

As she dressed, she shoved her grief away and forced herself to think about Garrison Parker. Garrison Parker, not the war. Not A. P. Hill's death. Not the dreadful possibilities that now faced President Davis. Had the Tredegar Iron Works failed to produce the new missile? And what of Sarah Slater and her terrifying plan?

Garrison Parker. Robin slipped her dress over her head and smoothed it down over her hoops. *Parker. Parker.*

Mr. Hathaway had told her very little about Parker. That spoke well for the man. He had loyal friends, and loyalty was something that had to be earned. So, she expected Parker to be a man worthy of respect. She hoped so—especially given the fact that she did not have the proof papers that Mr. Hathaway said were required for her to keep the claim. Not that such papers posed any particular problem. She could fabricate them before breakfast. No, what really worried her was finding a competent, knowledgeable man to run her mining operation. She knew nothing about gold. She had to find someone who did.

From what little she knew, Mr. Parker might be that man. He was bold. After all, he'd filed a challenge to the claim and built a cabin on the land long before he'd had any real evidence of Terrence Collier's failure to "prove up." It would simplify her life a great deal if this Parker was trustworthy.

Robin adjusted her corset so that it supported her bandaged rib, and buttoned her dress front. She still could not pull her shoulders all the way back, but the fiery pain had subsided to a constant dull ache.

It took her half an hour to braid her waist-length hair and pin it up. When she'd finished, wispy black ringlets spiraled down from her temples while an interlocking weave of tiny braids encircled the crown of her head. She slipped a few diamond hairpins into the braids. Her reflection in the mirror bespoke courtly elegance.

Robin retrieved her evening bag, kissed Jeremy on the cheek and closed the door behind her.

She descended the stairs to the dining room and looked around. The tables were set beautifully. Oil lamps sat in the middle of emerald green tablecloths. A low hum of conversation greeted her. Half of the twelve tables were full, but she saw no man sitting alone.

Mrs. Mabel Wirth, the proprietor, came across the floor. A small, heavy-set woman with gray hair, she wore a red and black checked dress. Her rosy cheeks jiggled with the impact of her stride. "Where may I seat you, Mrs. Hale?" she asked.

Robin gestured at a table in the corner by the window, where she'd be able to watch the sidewalk and keep her back to the wall. "If that one is not reserved, Mrs. Wirth—"

"Heavens, no. On a week night? I could only wish. Please follow me."

She led the way. Robin sat down and looked out the window at the snow-glazed mountain peaks. Even at night, they gleamed. "Thank you, Mrs. Wirth. I am expecting a gentleman, but while I wait, may I have a cup of coffee?"

"Of course, and if you'll tell me your friend's name, I'll bring him over when he comes in."

"Thank you. His name is Garrison—"

"*Parker?*" Mrs. Wirth said sharply.

Robin eased back into the chair. "Why, yes. Do you know him?"

Mrs. Wirth's prominent nose quivered with what could only be fury. "I do, ma'am. He owns a dapple-gray mule with a bad temper. That creature . . ." She halted and curtsied halfheartedly. "Oh, let me bring your coffee. I shouldn't have said anything." She spun and headed for the kitchen.

Robin eagerly awaited her return, hoping to ask her more questions, but a young blond boy of about ten brought the coffee instead, setting it down and scurrying away.

The huge clock in the corner bonged seven times . . .

Robin sipped her coffee and watched the moonlight play through the clouds that drifted over the town. From the moment the stage had rolled in this morning, she'd been awestruck by this country. She'd wandered over the eastern half of the continent, but none of the mountain peaks back there had left her feeling as . . . haunted, as these did. They seemed to have eyes that saw everything and cared about nothing. A little like God.

Bits of conversation from the other tables made their way to her. The man sitting two tables away, wearing a black jacket and white pleated shirt, was speaking to another gentleman in a blue suit. "... *under heavy bombardment at Sayler's Creek ... Federal flanks closed around Ewell ... forced to give up. They say over 8,000 Confederates surrendered. I hope they shoot every last one ...*"

Robin gulped down her first cup of coffee and ordered another. The longer she waited for Parker and listened, the more difficult it became to remain calm. Scenes kept flashing ... mutilated men screamed, caissons rattled, artillery thundered ...

The man in the blue suit pounded on the table, half-shouting, *"Lee is an old fool! What does he think he's doing? Grant has him surrounded on three sides near Appomattox Station ... useless ... killing his men!*

Robin clenched her cup of coffee so hard it trembled, almost sloshing the contents onto the green tablecloth. Grant had Lee surrounded? Dear God, could it be true? Why had she heard nothing of this?

Marse Robert would be desperate. She tried to picture what was going on. Knowing Lee, he would have called in his generals to confer. Rain, or maybe even snow, would be falling this time of year. Longstreet would be sitting calmly, smoking his pipe, while Gordon and Fitz Lee, the General's nephew, would be hunched over a crackling fire. Lee would be pacing, explaining the tactical situation. His voice would be steady, strong, but all of their hearts would be breaking ...

By eight o'clock, Robin had drunk three cups of coffee and was on the verge of pulling her derringer from her evening bag and killing someone— anyone would do—just to relieve her anxiety. Where the hell was Parker? Grizzled miners, who saw her sitting alone in the window, had begun to walk in off the streets just to wink suggestively at her. At first, she'd forced polite but cool smiles, but now she glared murderously.

The hotel door creaked open and another gruff looking character in a buffalo coat stumbled inside. He wove drunkenly from table to table, staring every woman in the eye and mumbling incoherently. Robin's brows lowered. Like every other male in this part of the country, he had an unkempt mop of curly hair and villainous whiskers that obscured two-thirds of his face.

The sot bumped an empty table and sent a glass lamp toppling over the edge to shatter on the floor. When the kerosene burst into flame, he whooped—a healthy imitation of a Rebel yell—and tried to stamp out the fire. The man in the black suit and his scurrilous friend leaped from their table and cursed as they backed away. Mrs. Wirth ran through the kitchen doors with her mouth open.

"Jesus Kee-rist, Mabel!" the sot shouted, stumbling sideways. "You put lamps in the damnedest places!"

Mrs. Wirth swung around, and pointed at Robin. "Get over there right now, Garry!"

Robin squeezed her eyes closed, then opened one a slit. *My God. He's a Texan.*

The fire was out, but Parker's pant legs still smoked. The two damned Yankees grabbed their coats and left. Robin felt so grateful she could almost forgive Parker for his birthplace.

Mrs. Wirth glared at Parker. "If Mrs. Hale wasn't waiting for you, Garry, I'd throw you out just like last time!"

Parker made a vain attempt to straighten up, but couldn't keep his feet in one place. "Now, Mabel, you know I didn't mean no harm last week. Honey just wanted a little something to eat, but when I rode her in, folks scared her, and—"

"And she turned my tables into piles of kindling! I been using them to heat the hotel!"

"Oh, come on, Mabel," he whispered loudly. "You thought it was funny. I know you did."

Mrs. Wirth gave him a potent shove in Robin's direction. "Mrs. Hale is *waiting,* Garry."

"Is she?" He turned, stumbled, and blinked as though trying to focus his eyes. "Which one is she? There's a lot of women in here tonight."

Mrs. Wirth gripped him by his coat sleeve and manhandled him until he faced Robin. *"That* is Mrs. Hale."

Parker spread his feet to brace himself up, while he squinted at Robin. "You can't possibly be . . . Are you? Mrs. Hale? The claim-jumping female from back East?"

Robin lifted a brow. "I assume you are Mr. Parker?"

"I am." He zigzagged to her table and braced his hands on the back of the chair across from her. He smelled like a distillery. Brown curls drooped around his bearded face. "Wondered why Hathaway wouldn't describe you. Just said, 'you'll see,' like maybe you was Lord Grizzly or something."

"Obviously," she responded. "I am not."

"That ain't so obvious, ma'am. Not yet anyway." He fell into the chair beside her, and his hazel eyes took her in from head to toe. He had a penetrating gaze. "I reckon you're pretty all right. And you know it, too. So I guess we'd better get down to business before you start trying some of them fancy feminine airs on me."

Robin didn't answer. She was watching him try to take off his buffalo coat. He was having trouble getting out of the sleeves. Finally, he bent over, stepped on the right cuff with his boot, and tugged hard. The effort sent him and his chair plunging backward.

When his head cracked the wood floor, Robin picked up her coffee, and took a fortifying sip.

"Damn it," he said, shaking his head. While he was flailing on his back, he managed to swim out of his coat. Beneath it, he wore a green and white plaid shirt and denim pants. Broad muscular shoulders slimmed to a narrow waist, but over half of his body seemed to be legs.

Three more people threw money on their tables, gathered their hats, and left. Mrs. Wirth ran alongside them to the door, apologizing the entire way. "I'm so sorry! Please come back. He's almost never here!"

Robin sighed. Parker had managed to sit up. "You are not at all what I expected, Mr. Parker."

"Well, that's all right," he said. "I generally ain't what I expect neither." With great deliberation, he managed to right his chair and climb back into it. He left his buffalo coat sprawled limply on the floor.

Cautiously, Parker extended his long legs and crossed them at the ankles. He let out a breath, as though relieved to finally be stable.

"May I offer you a . . . a cup of coffee, Mr. Parker?" Robin offered.

"I ain't never let a woman buy me a drink in my life, Mrs. Hale. You see, it would make me beholden to her and that's a mighty scary place for a man to be. Thanks just the same."

"Suit yourself."

"Frankly, I'd rather get down to business."

"All right." Robin nodded, but hesitated. He looked as if he were holding his breath. His shaggy eyebrows had drawn together into a single unbroken line across his forehead, and he'd clenched his jaw. What was he preparing himself for? The end of the world? Robin said, "After talking with Mr. Hathaway, I understand there's some question as to whether you own the Banta Hill claim or I do."

Parker shook his head. "No, ma'am. There ain't no question. I own that claim."

Robin smiled. "I hardly think so, Mr. Parker. My uncle left me that claim and I have the papers to prove it."

"Your uncle, eh?"

"That's right."

Parker examined her for a few seconds, then leaned forward, braced one elbow on the table, and pointed a finger at her. "Ma'am, do you know that every time you lie your eyes get an eerie glow? Just like you was real proud of yourself for making it come out sounding right."

Robin laughed. "Well, if it's that easy for you to spot, Mr. Parker, you've obviously been exposed to a large number of liars. What part of Texas are you from?"

He scowled and sank back into his chair. "Down around Laredo, Mrs. Hale. And which pompous eastern enclave are you from?"

Robin swirled her coffee, watching the black liquid wash the sides of the cup. "I was born in Boston, but I have spent the past five years in Virginia. When you meet my son, you'll notice that he has a Southern accent."

"You've got a son?"

"Yes," she answered. "He'll be six next month."

Parker's stony face softened momentarily, then turned hard again, as though he was angry with himself for letting his facade slip.

"Mr. Parker," she said. "I understand you have built a cabin on my land?"

"That cabin's on *my* land . . .'less you got proof otherwise."

"But I do, Mr. Parker."

"Let's see it."

"I'll submit it to Mr. Hathaway in the morning. But tonight I'd like to discuss another matter—"

He reached across the table and gripped her hand hard. "You'll show it to me, now." His voice had gone deep and threatening.

Pain shot up her arm. "No, Mr. Parker, I won't. And if you continue hurting me—"

He tightened his grip. "I ain't leaving my cabin 'til you come up with them proof papers."

"I *told* you to let me go, you —" Robin wrenched her hand free, and held it high, preparing to slap the drunken fool out of his chair. He watched her with wide unconcerned eyes and she figured he probably got slapped often, so the threat didn't bother him much. She lowered her hand and gripped her coffee cup again.

Parker turned and yelled, "Mabel!" She'd gone back to the kitchen. He pounded the table, and Robin held tight to her reeling coffee. "Mabel!"

The older woman cracked the door a slit, poking out just her gray head. "What do you want, Garry?"

"Bring me a bottle of your best whisky. And bring Mrs. Hale another cup of coffee."

Mrs. Wirth shuffled her feet. "You ain't paid me for the last time, Garry. I can't be giving away—"

He leaned his head back against his chair, and groaned, "Ah, Mabel, you know I'm good for it. I ain't never yet—"

"Put it on my bill," Robin instructed.

Parker shook his head. "No, ma'am. I won't be taking anything from you. I can't—"

"Oh, all right, Garry!" Mrs. Wirth said. "But this is the last time!"

He grinned and shouted, "You are a sterling woman, Mabel."

Mrs. Wirth disappeared into the kitchen and returned with a bottle of whisky and another cup of coffee. A shot glass rested upside down over the cork of the bottle. Mrs. Wirth slammed the whisky bottle down in front of Parker, making him jump, then gently set Robin's coffee down. "I hope he ain't bothering you, Mrs. Hale. If he is, you just let me know—"

"He's not, Mrs. Wirth, but thank you for asking."

Mrs. Wirth nodded, gave Parker a warning glance, and trotted away.

Parker sloshed himself a glassful of whisky and downed it in a single gulp, then turned glassy eyes on Robin.

"You ain't gonna show me your proof?"

"Not tonight, Mr. Parker."

"Suppose we get to the truth. You ain't got no proof. That's it, ain't it?"

She didn't answer.

He laughed impertinently. "That fact didn't take much figuring, Mrs. Hale. You see, I may not know much else, but I do know miners and mining. If Collier was dead, them proof papers would be in your hands. He'd have made sure of it, 'cause he knows the way the game's played. The fact that you don't have them means Ol' Collier wanted to cause you problems." Parker ignored his shot glass, reached for the bottle and tipped it to his lips. Whisky dribbled down his chin. He wiped it away with his green plaid sleeve. "Which means he wasn't happy when he signed them papers over to you. What did you do? Win 'em in a horse race?"

"You're repetitive, Mr. Parker. You've already called me a liar once, twice doesn't make it any truer than the first time." But Robin was watching him closely now. He wasn't nearly as stupid as he looked.

"The fact is, Mrs. Hale, I don't give a damn how you got that claim, but I do care whether you keep it or not." Emotion tinged his voice. He lounged across the table until his face was only inches from hers. "Because I'm gonna start mining that land on Monday, and nobody's gonna stop me . . . 'less, of course, the law says I can't. What do you think of that?"

There, the gauntlet had been thrown down. Now they both knew where they stood. He wanted that gold and badly. She'd never be able to trust him as her mine manager. He'd be stealing her blind behind her back. Robin gave him a ravishing smile. "Why, Mr. Parker, I think you've just done me a great favor. Thank you for your time." She reached down for her evening bag and slipped the gold chain over her wrist, preparing to leave.

The grin faded from his face. "Didn't you hear what I said? I'm going to start mining that land on Monday! Any gold I find is mine!"

"I heard you quite clearly," Robin answered. "But I have no intention of giving you so much time. I want this settled tomorrow morning, in Mr. Hathaway's office. Then, if you're not gone from my claim by sunset, I'll have the sheriff remove you."

A frightening glitter filled his eyes. He picked up his bottle of whisky and smashed it into the wall behind her. Flying glass and liquor spattered her dress. Robin cried out as she sprang to her feet.

"Damn you!" she cursed, shaking glass from her silver velvet dress. "You'll regret—"

"You'll get the worst of it! I'll . . ." Parker grabbed her arm and whirled her around to face him. She could *feel* her broken rib pulling apart. The sudden pain was so stunning, she stumbled into Parker, and her evening bag dropped to the floor. He wrapped his arms around her to keep her from falling. "Ma'am? Oh, ma'am, I'm sorry. Are you—"

"Get away from me, Goddamn you!" She slapped him with all the force she could muster.

He released her so suddenly, she staggered, and arched forward, trying to breathe. Men rose from their dinners around the room and ran to help her, asking questions, calling Parker insulting names.

He didn't even seem to hear them. Since she was bent over, he had to get down on his knees in front of Robin to peer up at her miserable face. He looked very frightened and regretful. His voice had changed, becoming soft and anxious. "Oh, ma'am, I . . . Did I hurt you? I didn't mean to. I—"

"Mr. Parker," she hissed through clenched teeth. "You are lucky I do not have a pistol on my person." Her derringer was in her purse a forsaken three feet away.

"Well, ma'am, I expect I'd let you shoot me if I thought it'd make up for—"

"Garry!" Mrs. Wirth yelled. "Dear God, what have you done this time?"

"Now, Mabel—"

"I don't want to hear it!" Mrs. Wirth raced out of the kitchen. On her way past the woodstove she grabbed a poker. "Get out of here! Now, Garry!"

The crowd parted as Parker reached for his buffalo coat and reeled to his feet. His expression was one of cold defeat. "Mabel! At least let me explain before you kill me."

"If I kill you, I'll never have to hear your excuses again!"

Parker stumbled backward toward the door while Mrs. Wirth swung her poker at him. It made a strange whistling sound as it cut the air, like a minie ball.

Robin managed to pick up her bag, then made her way through the murmuring crowd, and climbed the stairs that led to her room.

When I am asleep he comes to me as a lion, a big golden-maned lion. He curls his body around mine and his breath is warm on my cheek. I am always a little afraid, because in the dream I only half recognize him. I am trembling when I twine my hands in his fur and pull his big body tightly against mine. My arms shake from the effort.

I bury my face in his warm fur and cry. I never look up. I can't let myself. What would I do if I saw blue eyes instead of brown?

Two nights ago, one of his paws turned into the gentle right hand that I remember and I woke screaming.

I cannot believe the change he's undergone. Man to lion . . .

Or it is life to death?

CHAPTER 17

Garrison groaned at the insistent tugging on his hand and opened his eyes to peer up at the steep slopes. The snow-encrusted ground sparkled as the moon wavered like a silver coin through the pine branches.

Honey tugged again, whinnying as she dragged him over a series of sharp rocks. "Oh! . . . Ouch! Goddamn it, Honey! Whoa!" He jerked back.

Honey pawed the ground, throwing dirt and snow in his face.

"All right! I'm awake!"

Damn. He looked around, wondering where in the hell he was.

"Blast it all," he muttered, as he sat up. The act took nerve.

He must have passed out halfway to his cabin and fallen off Honey with the reins still wrapped around his hand. He was lucky she hadn't trampled him to death in punishment.

Unwrapping the reins, he spread his cramped fingers. Hurt like Hades—but not near as fiercely as his head did.

"Oh, Honey. This is bad. Feels like I got fellas double-jacking in the middle of my skull."

She snorted disdainfully.

A pale lavender glow had just begun to creep over the eastern peaks. He swallowed hard.

"Morning . . . already?" *And I didn't even make it back* . . . His eyes drifted up the slope to Banta Hill, knowing his cabin stood cold now, the woodstove down to ashes—just like his damnable soul.

With painstaking care, he rolled to his knees and got to his feet, gripping Honey's mane for support. She watched him with condemning eyes. Her warm breath condensed into a white cloud before him. "We got to be at Mike's by half past eight, old girl, to fight for our cabin." He patted her neck and lifted his boot to try and slip it into the stirrup.

Honey shied, dancing sideways, which made him leap on one foot to stay within stirrup range. "Damn it, Honey! Quit it!"

She still had her ears up. He was all right. Without another word, he gripped the saddlehorn, tucked his boot in the stirrup and swung up into the saddle. Honey started downhill, as though in a hurry.

He didn't try to stop her, but, by God, the pace was agonizing. Every step the mule took boomed inside his brain like an explosion, making his stomach churn. He just hung on and let her go.

By the time they trotted into Central City, misty rain blanketed the mountains. Wind drove the needle-like drops into Garrison's face. He had turned up the collar of his buffalo coat, but water continued to trickle down his neck.

Garrison dismounted and tied Honey to the hitching post in front of the Land Office. Shops were still dark. "Closed" signs hung in the windows.

"Reckon we got half an hour yet," he said as he stepped onto the wooden sidewalk and slumped down beside Mike's door.

The second-story balcony protected him from most of the rain, and he figured it was a good a place as any to catch a nap. He bowed his head and closed his eyes.

. . . The sound of voices woke Garrison. He squinted up through the drizzle at the ashen sky. Gauzy tufts of cloud blew over the town, with the sweet pungency of drenched pines. Shop owners had begun drawing back curtains, lighting lamps, taking the "CLOSED" signs out of the front windows. In the gray morning, those orange glows made Garrison feel warm inside. Despite the fact that he was freezing and soaked. His underclothing clung to his skin like pine tar.

Mike Hathaway's voice called, "I'll be right with you, Mrs. Hale."

The name made him jump. He stumbled to his feet. What time was it? It couldn't be much past eight.

He braced his hands against the door to peer in through the window. Two men sat in chairs before Mike's desk, engaged in an animated conversation about stopes, double-jacking and chute tappers filling skips—and Mrs. Hale stood by the woodstove, looking confused, her hands extended to the warmth. She wore a long royal blue cape. Her hair was piled on top of her head, and held with tortoiseshell combs. From this side view, he could see the straightness of her nose and the fine high arch of her cheekbone. A little boy stood at her side, clutching a toy horse to his chest and staring around as though he feared monsters in every corner. The horse was crudely carved. Looked to be the boy's work. That stirred Garrison's heart.

He opened the door, a sheepish expression on his face. When Mrs. Hale turned, he said, "Mornin'."

"Why, Mr. Parker," she said. "How good of you to get up off the sidewalk to grace us with your company. I trust you didn't sleep there all night."

"No, ma'am, I did not," he answered, but refused to elaborate.

Mrs. Hale watched him shrug out of his buffalo coat and hang it on a nail on the wall. He walked toward the stove and extended his hands to the old potbelly. As the heat penetrated his shirt and pants, it steamed out the smells of wet leather, sweat, and mule. For several seconds neither of them spoke. They listened to Mike's voice drone on about mining. Then Garrison cleared his throat.

"Uh—ma'am, I'd like to apologize for my poor behav—"

"*Poor* behavior, Mr. Parker?"

The little boy edged closer to his mother and tucked himself into the folds of her cape, peering out at Garrison with curious eyes.

"Well, maybe it was a bit worse than poor," he admitted. "But I am truly sorry."

Mrs. Hale lifted one graceful brow. "I'm not interested in your apologies, Mr. Parker. It's obvious you're an uncivilized savage who has no respect for women."

Garrison hung his head and scuffed his toe against the leg of the stove. Mud fell off his boot onto the wood floor. "Well, at least half of that's true, ma'am, and I admit it, but still—"

"*Which* half, Mr. Parker?"

He rubbed his hands together to get the circulation going. "Did I tell you that you're looking mighty pretty this morning, ma'am? I hope you slept well. Mabel has a fine place, leastways that's what I've—"

The men talking to Mike laughed, causing both of them to turn. Hathaway glanced up briefly at Garrison, then went back to the map spread across his desk. Only one lamp illuminated the office, and its light was barely enough to encompass Hathaway's desk. Outside the drizzle had thickened to rain and gray shadows held the rest of the small room.

Garrison gazed down at the frightened little boy hiding in his mother's cape. He winked.

The boy just stared.

Garrison knelt down. "What's your name?"

"Jeremy H—Hale," the boy said with a clear Southern accent.

"That's a nice toy horse you got there. What's his name?"

"Traveller."

Garrison grinned. "By jiggers, he does look like Traveller. I had a toy horse when I was a boy, too. But mine was a mare. Her name was Mary."

Jeremy frowned. "What color was Mary?"

"Coal black. Except she had a white blaze on her forehead." He reached over and drew the design on Jeremy's forehead. A fleeting smile crossed the boy's face before he backed away and pulled his mother's cape more securely around him—like a suit of armor.

Garrison tilted his head toward Mrs. Hale. In a whisper, he said, "I don't think your mama likes me, do you?"

Jeremy shook his head, and Garrison saw Mrs. Hale look down, but he didn't meet her gaze.

"Well," Garrison said. "Can't much blame her. I dove a mite too deep in the bottle last night and wasn't much of a gentleman when I met her."

Mrs. Hale explained, "He means the whisky bottle, Jeremy. You know, like the one Mr. Hornbuckle carried around in his coat pocket? Remember how we used to see Mr. Hornbuckle *lying around on the streets in the rain* with that bottle sticking out of his pocket?"

Jeremy nodded, and Garrison's mouth quirked. He stood up. "Your son seems like a nice boy. Where's his father?"

Mrs. Hale held his gaze for a long moment, then looked past him, out to the rain that poured off the balcony. Across the street, the Assayer's Office opened for business as its lamps went on. The warm wavering light reflected in the puddles of the rutted road. Mrs. Hale said, "My husband is dead, Mr. Parker. He was killed in the war a few months ago."

Garrison glanced down and saw tears trace lines down Jeremy's pink cheeks. Mrs. Hale put a gentle hand on the boy's dark hair, and whispered, "It's all right, Jeremy. Don't cry, sweetheart."

Jeremy looked up at her. "Is it raining in heaven, Mama? Like it is here?"

"No," she smiled at her son. "It's sunny, and warm, and all the flowers are blooming. There are wild canaries singing in the trees."

"Daddy's there with Grandpa?"

She nodded, but the motion appeared to take great effort. "Yes. They're probably drinking sassafras tea and laughing. Doesn't that sound wonderful, Jeremy?"

The boy leaned his head against her leg and she stroked his hair tenderly. "Daddy's doing just fine," she murmured. "Don't you worry about him."

Jeremy mouthed the words, *But I miss him.*

The exchange had sounded like a ritual, as though each had repeated those same words many times. A familiar ache started in Garrison's breast. He'd lost his mother when he was about the same age as Jeremy, and he remembered very well the terror that had possessed him. Mrs. Hale probably wasn't feeling much better. She had narrowed her eyes against the hurt.

Garrison turned and walked to the window, giving them privacy, while he surveyed the twists and turns of the storm clouds. Dark gray wisps tumbled by, just over the tops of the buildings, so close he could almost reach out and touch them. If the clouds kept getting lower, Central City would soon be enshrouded in fog. . . . *Killed a few months ago. God Almighty.* Cold air seeped in around the window panes. He shivered.

The two men sitting in front of Hathaway's desk shoved their chairs back with loud screeches, and stood up. Garrison heard their "thanks" and "goodbyes," and noticed that they tipped their hats to Mrs. Hale as they left. She nodded politely in return.

Once the door swung closed, Hathaway glanced first at Mrs. Hale, then at Garrison. "Why don't you both come over and take seats so we can talk this out."

Mrs. Hale removed a sheaf of folded papers from her cape pocket. Shepherding Jeremy with her free hand, she gave the papers to Hathaway before she sat down.

"I believe that's the documentation you needed, Mr. Hathaway," she said as she lifted Jeremy onto her lap. The boy held Traveller against his stomach. "I'm sorry it took me so long to find it, but I wasn't certain what I was looking for."

Hathaway frowned at Garrison, who still stood by the window. "Garry—"

"I'm coming, Mike. Don't rush me."

Hathaway gave him a reproachful look, then reached for his spectacles and put them on. Lamplight glinted golden off the small lenses as he unfolded the pages.

Garrison could tell the content of those papers from the dour expression on Mike's face. In defense, he crossed his arms over his damp shirt and hugged himself as he walked forward. The wooden floor boards creaked beneath his weight. "Has she got it, Mike?" he asked in a surprisingly calm voice.

"Yes, she does, Garry." Hathaway glanced at him over his spectacles. "You want to see it?"

"No." He shook his head. "No, that's not necessary. Not if you're certain it's Collier's signature."

Hathaway stared him in the eyes. "I'd swear to it in court. It's got all the right flourishes."

Garrison forced a swallow down his dry throat and nodded.

Mrs. Hale set Jeremy on the floor and rose from her chair. "If that's all you require from me, Mr. Hathaway, I think I'll go."

"Yes, ma'am," Hathaway said. He stood and extended his hand to her. She shook it. "Thank you for being so cooperative, Mrs. Hale. I wish you the best of luck. If I can ever be of service—"

"Well, actually, Mr. Hathaway, you can," she said, and glanced at Garrison.

"How's that?"

Mrs. Hale deliberately turned her back to Garrison, and said, "Mr. Hathaway, honestly, I know nothing about mining. I have to find someone *reliable* who can teach me the things I need to know. Could you, perhaps, recommend someone?"

Garrison shook his head when Hathaway looked his direction. "No, Mike. She won't listen to a word I say. We . . . uh . . . got off on a bad foot last evening."

"Uh-huh," Hathaway said without opening his mouth. He shoved the maps around his desk for a few seconds. "Well, Mrs. Hale, Garry Parker knows more about that claim than anybody, but if you are dead set against—"

"Mr. Hathaway," she said through a weary exhalation. "Would you trust a besotted brigand to tell you the truth about anything?"

Hathaway answered, "If the brigand was Garry Parker, I would. Especially if he was talking about mining."

She studied Hathaway's face, as if judging whether he meant what he said, then turned to Garrison. Her dark eyes met his like a saber thrust.

He straightened up and dropped his hands to his sides, meeting her scrutiny with aplomb. After what seemed an eternity, she said, "Your friends believe in you, Mr. Parker. Mrs. Wirth aside, that is. I—"

He shifted from one foot to the other. "Mabel's a fine woman and all, but she don't really know me very well."

"I don't think she wants to either, Mr. Parker."

"Yes, ma'am, I got that same impression." He hung his head and looked as miserable about the fact as he could.

Her grimace intensified. "Well, despite your charming personality, perhaps we can do business. I need to know as much as I can about mining, and I am more than willing to pay for your time."

"I'd be happy to tell you about the claim without any pay, ma'am. Matter of fact, after last night, I figure I owe you at least—"

Shouts and cheers erupted in the rainy streets outside. Men ran by the window, waving papers over their heads. Rifle shots cracked. Just a few at first, sporadic, then a staccato that rivaled the volleys of the battlefield.

"What the *hell* is going on?" Hathaway asked. He ran for the door and threw it open. Cold, rain-scented wind rushed in.

Garrison took three long steps to stand beside Mike. Carriages barreled down the muddy streets, filled with cheering people. Blaine Harding, the city assayer, burst from the office across the street, and started running down the wet sidewalk, clutching a copy of the *Rocky Mountain News* in his hands.

"It's over!" he shouted. *"The war's over!* It's over at last! The paper just got here!"

Garrison leaped out the door and ran, splashing through the mud to cross the street. "Blaine? Blaine! Let me see that paper!"

Harding shoved it into Garrison's hands and continued racing down the street, shouting into every shop. People rushed around outside, standing in the downpour, shouting, chanting, hugging each other.

Garrison read the headline and swung around to look back at Mike and Mrs. Hale, who now stood outside beneath the balcony. *"Lee has surrendered! It happened yesterday, at Appomattox Court House in Virginia!"*

Mrs. Hale grabbed Jeremy by the hand and dodged two careening buggies to get across the street. She strode up to Garrison, her face as hard as stone, and said, "Please. I must see that paper."

Garrison handed it to her and read over her shoulder as she scanned the article on the front page that detailed Lee's surrender of the Army of Northern Virginia. Shouts of "Glory Hallelujah!" and "Praise God!" erupted down the street. Someone started singing *Cheer, Boys, Cheer*. By the time Mrs. Hale neared the end of the article, the paper in her hands was shaking so badly she could barely hold it. Garrison reached down to help her steady the page and looked into her desolate, disbelieving face. He frowned.

"Ma'am? Are you all right?"

She stood very still. Jeremy started crying, a soft muffled series of sounds, but she didn't seem to hear him. The boy sat down on the sidewalk and started whispering into Traveller's white ear.

"Ma'am?"

Garrison studied her expression. Last night, she had said she had spent the past five years in Virginia. Were her sympathies with the Confederacy? Did she still have family there? Maybe even relatives in Lee's army?

A man came out of Luke's saloon with a pair of cymbals and began striking them together like a crazed fool. The clangs blended with the rattling of racing wagons and shouts of joy. Six men in tattered blue uniforms marched in a line behind the musician. Laughter rose, but beneath it was a timbre of tears. Fragments of their conversation carried. The place names seemed to spread wings as they were spoken: Gettysburg . . . Chancellorsville . . . Shiloh . . . the Wilderness.

Mrs. Hale closed her eyes. She looked so pale, like pure sculpted marble.

Garrison gathered his courage. "Mrs. Hale," he said gently. "You read the article. Those men . . . Lee's Army, are going to be paroled. They won't be sent to prison camp. They'll be going home. Tomorrow, probably. And . . . and I'll wager that food is already getting back into Richmond after the siege. You know how the profiteers are. They'd be back with supplies the instant they thought they could make a dollar."

She lifted her eyes to look at him, obviously wondering why he'd used the tender tone he had, and he saw the pain that lay in every line of her face. She opened her mouth, as if to speak, but her lips trembled and she closed it.

There was a long silence, filled with rain, and singing, and the smell of mud and wet horses.

Without thinking, Garrison enfolded her in his arms and pulled her against him. "It's all right," he said. "Don't you see? This means men can go home and take up their lives again. The dying will stop."

She put a hand in the middle of his chest and pushed herself away from him. But it didn't look as though she meant it personally, rather she seemed to be fighting with herself, trying to calm down. She was struggling to keep from crying, or to keep from killing something.

A savage glow lit her eyes. It frightened him a little. He said, "Ma'am? . . . Ma'am, is there something I can do? I mean to help?"

"Yes. There is, Mr. Parker," she answered. "Would you accompany me back to my hotel . . . to . . . to talk to me about mining? I could use a glass of whisky just now, and I—I don't want to drink alone. Please, I would appreciate it if you would allow me to buy you a whisky."

It sounded like the plea of a battle-weary soldier. Hoarse. Passionate. He found himself nodding. "Just this once, ma'am. Yes, I will."

Garrison stood before the window in Mabel's hotel. All of the tables were set with emerald green tablecloths and oil lamps and sparkling silverware. The wood floor shone like glass. He felt guilty for tracking mud in but it couldn't be helped. Not on a day like today. He clasped his hands behind his back and watched the rain fall. Clouds obscured the mountains, but now and then, a gap would open in the storm and a peak would appear, shining with fresh snow. The filthy streets had cleared of people. Everybody had gone back to work.

He unclasped his hands and brought them around in front to reclasp them. Then he unclasped them altogether and shoved them in his pants pockets. After that, he started pacing.

He'd never had a woman invite him to share a whisky before. He wasn't quite sure how to act. He'd never known a decent woman who drank whisky. Though he thought the idea was interesting enough.

While he pondered the fact, Mrs. Hale descended the stairs, and he turned to face her. She had changed into a black dress. Her silver earbobs were gone, and she'd removed the tortoiseshell combs from her hair, leaving her face framed in a mass of loose damp black curls. A fringe of tiny curls stuck to her forehead and cheeks. He smiled. She looked softer, more feminine. But pale and drawn.

Garrison balled up the hands in his pockets and tried to smile. "Jeremy asleep?"

"Yes. Finally. I'm sorry to keep you waiting. I had to tell him a lot of stories."

She came across the room and Garrison pulled out a chair for her.

"If you don't mind, Mr. Parker, I'd like to sit in this chair."

"Don't mind at all," he said and pulled out the chair she'd indicated. Just as she had last night, she sat with her back to the wall. Did she have so many enemies?

"I hope you were telling Jeremy happy stories about flying horses and such," he said as he took the chair beside her. They both faced the window and the storm. The rain had turned slushy, as though it might change to snow before long. Icy drops splatted on the wooden sidewalk. He watched them. She watched them.

"No," she said, "about his father."

Garrison absorbed the statement. "He must be mighty proud of his father."

"Yes, he is. Did you fight in the war, Mr. Parker?"

"Yes, ma'am. I did. Though I think I fought for a different side. Not that it matters."

"You don't think it matters?"

He shook his head. "No. I don't. We all fought for what we believed in, and I ain't never been one to condemn a man for his beliefs—even if I disagreed with him."

She looked him over, then lowered her gaze.

"Where was your husband killed. Can I ask?"

"In Tennessee."

Her voice carried no weakness, as he'd imagined it would, but rather a strong wrathful timbre. She gazed out the window at the muddy street, where puddles lay in the hoofprints and buggy tracks. Rain drops dappled the surfaces, sending out colliding silver rings. But Garrison could tell that she saw none of that. Her full lips were pressed together, her jaw clenched. He suspected she was not with him at all, but in Tennessee with a rifle in her hands, killing everyone who'd ever dared to fire a shot at her husband.

Contemplatively, he smoothed the wrinkles in his damp shirtsleeve. He knew how she felt. Over and over in his dreams, he'd refought the battle of Pichaco Pass—and killed every Apache alive. He was never pinned in the rocks, or low on ammunition, never so thirsty that his sobs came dry as dust because his body had no tears to spare. His hands never shook so badly that he couldn't aim his rifle. No, not in those dreams. Wrath, soul-deep and deadly, gave him the ability to change history . . . And allowed him to go on living with the memories of what had really happened.

"Was your husband fighting with General Forrest?"

"Yes. He was."

There. She had said it. Her husband had fought for the Confederacy. Garrison respected her for that. Admitting such a thing in this part of the country was tantamount to asking for people to insult you in public, banish you from decent society, and hound you until you left town.

"Your husband was lucky to have had the chance to fight with Forrest. When all is said and done, I believe Nathan Bedford Forrest will be recognized as one of the most brilliant military tacticians in history. General Lee was a hell of a commander, but Forrest . . ." He cocked his head and lifted his brows appreciatively. "Forrest scared the hell out of more men than Napoleon, Ghengis Khan, and Sam Grant put together."

She smiled, a small fleeting smile. "Yes. And he was a gentleman. In the finest sense of the word—though he had no formal education."

It was the first time Garrison had heard Forrest spoken of with something other than loathing and terror. "Did you know him?"

"Oh, not . . . not well," she answered, but Garrison had the feeling that wasn't quite true. Her warmth and fondness could have not have been impersonal. "I met him once or twice. That's all."

After an interval of silence, he said, "Well, I don't know where Mabel is, but I do know where the whisky is. I think we ought to help ourselves 'til Mabel gets back. What do you think?"

"Yes. Thank you, Mr. Parker."

He rose and headed for the kitchen. Mabel kept her bottles on a shelf just inside the kitchen door. He pushed the door open and looked around. The fire in the wood cookstove burned, but not a soul was visible. He surveyed the bottles and took down a good one. He figured Mrs. Hale would appreciate that. All he could find were wine glasses, but they'd do.

When he emerged from the kitchen, Mrs. Hale was sitting with her elbows on the table, her hands clasped beneath her chin in an almost prayerful position, watching the twisting clouds.

He walked slowly, giving her time to finish her thoughts, then set the glasses down, uncorked the bottle, and poured each nearly full.

"Is that too much?" he asked.

"No. That's fine. Thank you."

He seated himself again and picked up his whisky, waiting for her to do the same. As he clinked his glass to hers, he said, "To the end of the war. May peace last forever."

Mrs. Hale closed her eyes when she drank and finished the glass in six swallows.

"Feeling better?" Garrison asked.

"Not yet." She extended her glass.

"Well, shouldn't take long at this rate," he observed as he refilled it.

He sipped his whisky slowly. Despite the fact that his mouth had agreed to drink with her, neither his stomach nor his head thought much of the idea. "Is there anything else you'd like to discuss? About the war, I mean."

She ran a hand through her tousled black hair and shook her head. "No. Frankly, I'd rather change the subject."

"You're sure?"

"Yes, Mr. Parker. But I thank you for asking. And for joining me here." She sounded embarrassed, as if half-apologizing. "I needed . . . company."

"I understand, Mrs. Hale. When the war demons are on me bad, I always have to find company, too."

"The war demons?"

"Ghosts. Sometimes I can't even keep 'em at bay by setting up a barricade of chairs around my bed. That's when I need to find company in the worst way. On occasion, I have saddled my mule at three o'clock in the morning and ridden to town just to see who might still be up."

"And if no one was?"

He ran his finger around the rim of his glass. "I found somebody to wake up."

She laughed, apparently genuinely amused. "You must not have many friends."

"Do you know you're the second person in the recent past to tell me that?" He leaned back against his chair and crossed his legs. " 'Course, the first person to say it is the man I wake up most often—which is probably why."

"Is that Mr. Hathaway? You seemed to be very good friends."

"Yes, ma'am." He indulged in another small sip of whisky.

Her smile lingered a few moments, then began to fade. As it did, her smooth forehead furrowed, and her eyes went hollow. It didn't take a genius to know that her mind had started drifting back to unpleasant times and places.

"Ma'am?" he said. "Earlier, you asked about mining. I'd like to tell you about it, if you're ready to hear what I have to say."

"Yes. Yes, please," she answered, and sounded eager. "Tell me as much as you want to. I'd be very grateful."

She moved her chair around to look at him, and the gray light streaming through the window penetrated her black curls and cast spiderweb shadows across her face. A pink flush had returned to her cheeks. What a beautiful woman. But she looked exhausted. He could tell by the slump in her shoulders.

He braced one arm on the table. "Well, let me tell you, the Banta Hill claim's gonna be one hell of a mine." A sad note entered his voice, and he had to force it away before he could continue. "I ain't never seen a vein of gold like she's got, and I been looking a long time. But you've got to mine her right."

"And how should I do that?"

"You have to understand about the lode first. Lodes are mostly telluritic—carried by pyrites of iron, copper, or arsenic. Colorado's different from other places. Out here lodes crop out radially from the peaks in every which way." He spread his fingers across the table. "Sort of like tree roots, winding and twisting through the mountains."

"I see." She nodded. "Please, go on."

"Banta Hill has a major vein on the surface. So the first thing your miners will need to do is sink a hoist shaft alongside the ore body. Then they'll take a level heading and run the tunnel the entire length of the deposit."

"Why?"

"To expose the extent of the ore, ma'am. They have to know what they're working with to start off, or they'll end up sinking shafts randomly and waste a lot of time. Plus," with his fingernail he drew a line on the table. "Later that same shaft can serve for hauling out wastes."

"That makes sense. What next?"

"Well, it gets a little more complicated. Watch this." He sketched lines on the green tablecloth, showing where the ore body might run. "After they've drifted out the length . . . uh, sorry . . . tunneled out the extent of the deposit, then they'll have to find out how wide it is so they can lay their strategy for getting it out of the ground." He took a deep breath. "Next they'll extend the drift laterally. You see?"

"Yes, I think so. What you're saying is that first I need to know the way the lodes wind and twist before I'll know how to 'drift' out the rest of the claim. Is that right?"

"Yes, ma'am," he said. "You're catching on quick. After they know the extent of the deposit, then they'll stope—dig out—the rock. Drifting's only when they're trying to figure what they've got."

"All right, Mr. Parker. Let's say I've determined the length and width of one vein, then what will I do?"

"Build a headstock, set up a boiler, and rig a steam-powered windlass. After that, they'll lay out a series of winzes, chutes and transfer raises where the ore can be dumped at the lowest levels into buckets or a skip. I'd go for the skip method myself—"

"Mr. Parker, I did not understand a single word—"

"I'm sorry, ma'am. I didn't mean to throw so many strange terms at you all at once. What I meant is that the miners will have to work the mine from the bottom to the top with levels interconnected through a series of tunnels."

"But won't that be dangerous? What happens if I tunnel—stope—out hundreds of passageways. Doesn't the mountain become unstable?"

Garrison smiled his admiration. "That can happen, yes. I have seen more than one 'glory hole.' That's what's it's called when the mine collapses in on itself."

"How will I safeguard against that?"

"Your miners will have to crib, which means they'll pile up logs in the back of the stope. And, more important, when they've worked out an area, they'll need to take all of the wastes and backfill it. Both methods will help support the overlying rock."

"I see." Turning, she frowned as she gazed down at the window casement and seemed to be concentrating on the color. The white paint had absorbed the azure depths of the storm. It gleamed with a reflected blue light.

Garrison looked at her. From this side view, she looked all the more slender and frail. He lifted the whisky bottle and refilled her glass. She'd had the equivalent of about eight shots, but seemed stone-cold sober. The only change he noticed was the vulnerability in her eyes. She had stopped trying to hide it.

It affected him oddly. Before he knew it, an old ache had knotted up his belly. What was it about the male mind that made a man want to jump in with both feet to pet and protect any female that looked hurt? Some unhealthy defect. He wondered if Mr. Darwin had considered that when writing *Origin of Species?*

Probably means Man is doomed. Especially those males who jump in to protect females who damn well don't want to be protected.

He took a healthy swig of whisky and squinted at the buggy that rolled by outside. Mud covered the horse all the way up to his belly, and ice crystals glittered on his back. Temperature must have dropped. The high mountains were like that. Only fools and newcomers tried to predict the weather.

"Well," she said, "I had better be going. Jeremy will be waking from his nap soon, and I want to be there when he does."

"I understand."

"Thank you. You've been very kind." She extended her hand for him to shake.

"My pleasure, ma'am."

He took her hand. Her fingers felt cold and small in his palm. She smiled and shook his hand. He returned the pressure. And for no apparent reason, his damnable lungs seemed to stop working. He was looking into her eyes, those deep dark eyes, when a tingle of warmth began in his hand and spread through his whole body. It felt like a strengthening current of electricity. The faint fragrance of lemon verbena she wore became incredibly clear. As did other things—the rain outside, the pine burning in the woodstove in the kitchen, the scents of mule and leather that clung to his own clothing. Garrison sat so still that the pearl button on his left sleeve caught the light and projected a tiny, gleaming star on the window pane.

The physical contact could not have lasted more than four or five seconds, but when she released his hand, he felt numb all over.

"Thank you again, Mr. Parker," she said. "One last thing. I would like to see the claim. Would you be willing to show it to me?"

"Yes, ma'am. Be glad to."

She stood up and he managed to get to his feet beside her. The softness of her expression, the new warmth in her eyes, made his heart pound.

"You've been more than kind. I don't know how to thank you—"

"You already have, Mrs. Hale. I'm the one who ought to be thanking you. And I do. For pardoning me for being a jackass last night. When would you like to see the claim?"

She thought about it a moment. "There are things I must do for next two or three days, find a house, hire servants, set up bank accounts. Would three days from now be all right?"

"Fine. Do you own a horse, ma'am? There's a road up there, but if it keeps storming, I don't think a buggy—"

"I'll have a horse by then, Mr. Parker. What time will I see you?"

"I'd like to get an early start. There's a lot to see. Collier even sank one shaft—in the wrong place, I might add. If it sets well with you, I'd like to meet you around six in the morning."

"Fine." She nodded. "Until then. Good day."

"Good day, ma'am."

She headed for the stairs and he picked up his hat from where he'd thrown it on the floor by his chair. Unconsciously, he rotated the brim, sliding it through his fingers, until she disappeared.

Then he walked out into the snow and took his time getting down the street.

CHAPTER 18

"Macey? Darling, could you help me straighten up? I'm so nervous I'm afraid to lift anything for fear I'll drop it and smash it all over the floor."

"Of course, I'll help," Macey said and shook her head. "But I don't know why you're so worried, gal. He's just another damned man."

Dressed in a pink satin chemise and black stockings, Esther Wilcox rushed around the front parlor of the house they shared in Denver. He might be just another damned man, but he would be Esther's first client in four days. Macey smiled as she straightened and fluffed the yellow pillows on the white sofa, which sat before the rock fireplace, then made certain two brandy snifters sat beside the decanter on the coffee table. As an afterthought, she slipped a lace doily under the crystal decanter. The white frills looked mighty fancy against the deep dark walnut. When she stood back and surveyed the tiny room, she nodded approvingly. The gold lettering on the leather spines of the books in the small bookcase shone, free of dust, because she took pains to keep them that way. She loved the writings of Hawthorne, Frederick Douglass, and Shakespeare, and she loved this little house with its lavender curtains and flower-strewn rugs.

How different it was from that hovel Macey and Esther had first lived in when they'd moved to Denver! Just remembering made Macey's knees go weak. In the space of an ordinary pantry, two beds had been shoved together, then separated by a sheet hung over a line. They hadn't even had enough leeway to wedge nightstands in by the beds. They'd called it the "hoosegow," though so many flies had buzzed around their heads, they'd often joked that it was more like a butcher shop.

The odors, the filth, the unclean men had finally become unbearable. But it took more than filth and poverty to drive Macey and Esther out—it had taken three murders in three months. It was an unholy sight when men got to fighting each other betwixt that sheet. They'd get all twisted up and start shouting and cursing and finally one of them would reach for his gun . . .

Well, I don't know why it bothered you so much. You were raised with such doings.

Macey's own mother had been murdered. Poor, black, and a convert to Judaism, in a city that believed all Jews were next of kin to Judas Iscariot, Maimie Runkles had been trusted by no one. She couldn't even get a job as a laundress or cook. Naturally, she'd turned to prostitution. The men had unkindly named her "Moose Maimie," because of her prominent nose. Macey had been born just before her mother's fifteenth birthday. She knew nothing about her father and didn't want to. She figured if her mother didn't want to talk about him, she had good reason.

When Macey turned twelve, her mother had taken sick. It was a wasting sickness that left Maimie unable to walk without grabbing on to things to keep herself upright. Men had stopped coming.

Macey knew what to do. Nobody had to tell her. She fixed her hair, rouged her cheeks and lips, started to work, and kept her mother alive. She bought food and medicine—and even, on occasion, pretty dresses for them both. At first, she'd been overwhelmed by the number of men who wanted such a young girl. Why, her breasts had just budded. But they came in droves.

The Kansas City marshal had spent less than a minute studying Maimie's body. Obviously she'd been shot. Obviously she was dead. And obviously she was a black whore. "No use wasting time on sech cases as these," he'd said, "could a been any one of hundreds that done it."

For years after that, Macey had drifted. Traveling from town to town. She'd tried her hand at many different professions, including dressmaker, domestic servant and nanny, but she'd found that "respectable" was just another word for dirt poor. Lone women, especially black women, couldn't get jobs that paid real wages; life was that simple. As a dove, she made about sixty dollars a month. "Decent" jobs for women paid half that.

But she'd be forced to quit someday soon. Her forty-two years had begun to show, badly. Though she'd miss Esther, she longed to move to Central City. In a mining boom town, she could make a last killing before the business killed her. The crow's-feet at the corners of her eyes looked as deep as canyons. Fortunately, she'd found ways of fixing her hair to hide the gray, until lately. Now that it still showed, she added a garnet-studded hair comb to draw men's attention. When all that failed, she would don a wig.

"Oh, what time is it?" Esther said, and hurried into the bedroom to check the old grandfather clock in the corner. "Landsakes, Macey! It's darned near 2:00 P.M. He'll be here any minute."

Esther came back out of the bedroom dabbing perfume between her big white breasts.

"What is the matter with you, girl?" Macey asked. "You're acting like this was the first time you'd seen the elephant, and I know for a fact that ain't true." She grinned at Esther.

Esther pushed her long black hair over her shoulder and straightened to her full five-feet-nine inches. "Oh, Macey, you ain't met Andre. He's . . . well, I'm sure he's rich."

"Well, you ain't gonna see any of it, except for two dollars, so what difference does it make?"

"I don't know." She shrugged. "Last night, at the Apollo Hall, he acted, well, kind and thoughtful. You seen that bottle of French perfume he give me. I got the feeling that maybe he really liked me."

Macey smiled at the sweet hopeful expression on Esther's pink face. Hell, every line girl dreamed of meeting a millionaire and having him fall head-over-heels in love with her. She *had* to. It was the only thing that made life bearable. "Honey," Macey said gently, "you go right ahead and believe anything you want. I hope like all get out that he does really like you. In fact, I hope he gets down on his knees . . ."

The knock came. Heavy. Made with a fist.

"Oh, Macey, he's here! You run upstairs now and when I'm finished—"

"I'm going! See you later."

Macey rushed up the stairs.

Esther watched her go and took a deep breath. Once she'd collected herself, she walked to the door, draped one arm on the frame and turned the glass knob. A giant of a man stood outside with a fine white hat in his hands. Tall, with broad shoulders, he had brown hair and a thin mustache. Around thirty-five, she guessed. Pale blue eyes studied her. He bowed and gave her a lopsided grin.

"*Bonjour*, Esther," he said in a cultured French accent.

"Well, good day, Andre. I been waiting for you. Come on in."

She opened the door wider, to admit him, then shut it. When she turned, he grabbed her in a bear hug and kissed her so hard it almost brought blood.

Esther twisted away and laughed to cover the pain. "Why, you're eager, ain't you, honey?" she said, touching her lip to make certain it wasn't bleeding. Hurt like Hades, but he was so handsome, she wanted to please him.

"I don't have much time," he answered as he headed for the sofa. "Give us a drink, will you?"

"Sure. Sure . . . you just get yourself comfortable and I'll pour two brandies."

He lounged on the sofa and watched her fill the snifters half full. His brown coat and tan canvas pants bore stiff creases, like he'd just picked them up from a Chinese laundry. His black string tie draped down over his white shirt. Esther tossed her waist-length black hair over her shoulder and handed him his glass. She did it with a queenly flair, chin up, her jade earbobs dancing as she smiled.

"How have you been, Andre? Is the Apollo a good hotel?"

He took a healthy drink of his brandy before he answered. "Good enough." Patting the sofa beside him, he said, "Come sit. Like I said, I haven't much time."

Esther hurried to snuggle up next to him. She slipped an arm behind his head and ran her fingers through his freshly washed hair. It smelled of soap. "You must be rich, Andre, to buy soaps that smell so sweet."

"Of course, I'm rich. How could you tell?"

"Well, it warn't just the soap. No, sir. I knew right off from the lordly way you carry yourself. Like a man with a million dollars in his pocket."

His eyes drifted over the room, lingering on the curtains, rugs and fireplace, and a cruel smile twisted his lips. "And I'll bet that you've seen a lot of millionaires, haven't you, Esther?" He looked at her and she could see the derision in his eyes.

Esther couldn't pull away. She really liked him—a lot. Gaily, she said, "Oh, I've seen a few in my time, Andre. Why there was this German one time. He was mighty odd, believe you me. I—"

"Is that right?" Andre asked. "Why if I'd known of your sophistication, I assure you I would have gone elsewhere." He sounded half-angry and Esther hadn't the slightest idea why. Andre continued, "And to think that I came over here on a recommendation from a man I met on Ferry Street." He took another drink.

"Did you? What . . . what was his name?"

"I didn't catch it." Andre finished his brandy and set the glass on the table. "He died shortly thereafter. I didn't have time to chat with him."

"What do you mean, he died?" Esther asked. "What did he die from?"

With one hand, Andre unbuttoned his pants. "A bullet to the head," he said. "But he was a traitor to the Union. He deserved killing."

Esther pasted a rigid smile on her face. Why would a Frenchman be so all-fired patriotic? "Well . . . maybe we should be getting on with . . . things . . . since you're short on time. And I got some other appointments this afterno—"

Andre reached out and gripped her shoulders hard. His blue eyes went cold. He shook her until her head snapped back and forth. The brandy fell from her hand and smashed on the floor.

"Stop! Stop it, Andre! What are you—"

"That man said you liked it *rough,* Esther. That's why I courted you last night and came here today."

Esther tried to stand up, but he pulled her down again. "Let me go! That fella lied!" she said, and struggled to get away. "I don't like nothing rough! He lied, I tell you!"

He shoved Esther down on the floor and her hands landed in the broken glass. Trembling, she stared at the tendrils of red that crept between the roses in the rug. Before she could move, he reached down and ripped off her pink chemise with his huge hand, then he fell on top of her. As he spread her legs with his knee, his hands tightened around her throat. She gasped for air.

"Now," he whispered seductively. "Fight me. *Fight me, goddamn you!*"

Macey stood upstairs, listening, her heart in her throat. When she heard Esther choking, she flung open her bedroom door and took the steps down three at a time. The sight that met her eyes terrified her.

Esther struggled, writhing and gasping. Her eyes had begun to protrude. She managed to choke out, *"Macey . . . help!"*

"Oh, my God!" Macey screamed.

She rounded the foot of the staircase and threw herself on Andre, jerking his huge shoulders back with all her might. "Let her go! *Let her go, Goddamn you!"*

CHAPTER 19

The night is moonless.

I stand in my bedroom, wearing my ivory chemise and delicate convent-made panties, gazing into the mirror. Curious. A breath of wind stirs the flame of my oil lamp and sends light leaping over my face . . . no, over her face. I recognize that woman, but only because I see her Cherokee mother there, in the shape of the face, the dark eyes and long straight hair.

It is a strange sensation. That face used to belong to someone I cared about . . . but she died.

She died in a rainy forest in Tennessee.

Why does her body continue to walk and smile and eat when it has no soul?

I have asked Charles about this. He lays his furry golden paw against my cheek, and murmurs soothingly that guilt keeps her body alive.

Charles tells me that women often live in bodies without souls. Because women are supposed to be ever faithful to their husbands and families, supposed to take care of them no matter the personal cost, are never supposed to fail them . . .

I look into my mother's eyes.

She stares back hollowly.

And I know, finally, what she meant about being hunted by dead voices and mirrors.

Robin's black skirt stirred dust motes to life as she walked toward the bay window. Slanting rays of amber light cascaded around her, but the new two-story house was so empty and quiet. She could hear mice scurrying in the walls, and every step she took brought a creak or groan from the shiny wooden floor. Only the tiny red and blue flowers on the wallpaper provided visual cheer.

Through the bay window, she could see the single blue spruce tree near the front gate—it cast wavering shadows over the veranda where Jeremy crawled with Traveller galloping before him. His little face had reddened in the cold, but he seemed oblivious to anything other than his toy horse. He played like a wind-up child going through the motions of imitating a real boy, his face expressionless, eyes vacant.

Robin frowned. How strange that he would accept no other toy. She had bought him several on the long trip, but he had just bitten his lip and stared at her as if the very thought of playing with something else was treacherous. This attachment seemed . . . unnatural. Yet she could not convince herself to take it away from him. Traveller never yelled at him, never left him alone, never frightened him. Traveller was the only true friend Jeremy had.

Robin folded her arms over her chest. *He'll be all right. He just needs to get used to being in one place. After he gets used to being safe and secure, and he's made some friends his own age, he'll gradually forget about Traveller. Just as Charles said.*

Her eyes drifted over the dining room. It faced south, gleaning the warmth of the winter sun, and the door to the kitchen stood in the north wall. It would be cool in the summertime. A staircase ascended next to the kitchen door, leading to the three bedrooms upstairs, and another small bedroom hid beneath the staircase. The former owner had allowed Robin to purchase some of his furniture, to give her something to sit on until she could hire a man to build her more. Back East, furniture makers abounded, but not here. Central City had exactly one and he was overwhelmed with work. Despite her offer of twice his usual wages, he'd informed her it would take at least two weeks before he could even begin on her order.

A table and two chairs nestled in the curve of the dining room's bay window. A bed and dresser filled the master bedroom upstairs. A carved walnut sofa stretched before the enormous river-rock fireplace in the parlor, adjacent to the dining room. Its blue velvet fabric contrasted warmly with the grays and tans of the stones. Despite her substantial bank accounts, clothing and a few other precious things, Robin found that this house and its meager furnishings stoked a longing for the grandness of her life before the war—for rich mahogany and cherry woodwork, crimson brocaded drapes, fine crystal stemware that shimmered in candlelight . . . for the leisurely elegance of a world now gone forever.

Robin leaned backward, stretching her tired muscles. She had barely slept last night. When the first whispers of dawn penetrated her bedroom, she rose from her tumbled quilts and, standing in her thin nightgown before the window, gazed out over the mountains. Everything was silent and blue, and Central City at sunrise looked like a fairytale town. The winding dirt streets snaked along slopes so steep that sometimes they seemed to cling to the rocky foundation like slender vines. Rows of plank houses splashed the brightening vista with shades of butter yellow, pale green, brick red. Most yards were weeded and fenced with pine poles. The daylight picked out the mountain wildflowers that dotted the snowy panorama and flashed in the wings of diving hawks and eagles. All around lay the ethereal peaks, quiet and glistening in the gold of the newborn sun.

It was all so beautiful, but in a way it also struck her as . . . too peaceful. In the world where she had been reared, people waged a constant war against the wilderness. They dug up tons of rocks and cleared fields, then they chopped and slashed and burned all the tenacious seedlings that refused to give up. Even then, green shoots took root in hidden places beneath porches and under houses and shoved and probed until they split brick and stone and wood, and managed to poke their heads out to reach for the sun.

Here, people seemed to live in harmony with the wilderness. Unlike the fertile South, this wilderness never tried to crowd them out; it just watched and listened, and pondered the future, while human beings went about their trifling affairs.

Outside, Traveller's hooves thumped the veranda while Jeremy sang *Dixie* in a high childish voice: "For faith betrayed, and pledges broken, wrongs inflicted, insults spoken . . ."

Robin stood quiet and still. She continued the words in a whisper, "Swear upon your country's altar, Never to submit or falter, Till the spoilers are defeated, Till the Lord's work is completed. Halt not till our Federation secures among earth's powers its station. Then at peace, and crowned with glory, Hear your children tell the story . . ."

With the sound of his young voice dying away, Robin felt the glory of the old days dying. Jeremy was five. He would not remember the serene dignity of the life she and Charles had so loved. Virginia would mean only the rattling of sabers and the terrifying roar of artillery—his pony being killed by an exploding shell.

And next to that thought, close on its heels, came the certain knowledge that if Jeremy remembered his father at all, it would be from the stories she told him.

Robin gathered the hem of her black skirt and made her way to the other bay window in the parlor. Light refracting through the glass cast long amber rectangles over the wood floor and shadowed every scratch and pit. She clenched a fist. Jeremy *would* know his father. He would hear all the details of Charles' heroism, of the sacrifices he'd made to protect his way of life. Jeremy would come to understand and respect not just his father's courage, but his father's gentleness, his profound tenderheartedness.

Yes, and just as she vowed these things, she vowed as strongly that her son would never know of the times when his father had been impatient, or unkind, or scared half to death. No, Jeremy would never know that his father had hated the war—would never hear from her lips that his father had wept for two days straight after the battle of Shiloh, or that he had broken three bones in his right hand the day Vicksburg fell. She had fought Charles, trying to keep him from slamming his fist into a gnarled old oak. He had shouted at her, then used all the strength in his body to shove her to the ground. It had knocked the wind out of her. Robin had rolled to her side, gasping ... and the sight had shocked Charles back to his senses. He'd fallen beside her and buried his face in her hair, blurting wild apologies, making desperate promises. She had held him, just held him, until he'd cried himself out and fallen into a dead sleep.

No, those things were hers, and hers alone.

The memory of Charles that she would shape in her son's mind would be of a noble Southern gentleman who had never faltered in his duty to his country or to his family.

She owed Charles that.

The tea kettle whistled, and Robin went to the kitchen. Oak cupboards covered the walls. The cast-iron woodstove squatted in the rear, near the doorway that led to the back yard. Steam gushing from the kettle had already clouded up every window in the kitchen.

She grabbed a potholder, lifted the kettle, and poured the water into the white porcelain teapot she had prepared earlier. The fragrance of Souchong tea swirled around her head. After replacing the lid, she took two cups and the teapot and used her shoulder to push open the door to the dining room. The white porcelain gleamed with an unearthly brilliance as she set the pot and cups on the polished oak table in the bay window.

Ten minutes remained before her next interview. Robin seated herself and poured a cup of tea. For that small amount of time, she wanted to sit and think about Charles. She hadn't really been able to since—since his death. She needed to.

*　*　*

Macey opened the squeaky front gate and entered the yard of the big two-story house. A little boy sat on the veranda, watching her. He had large blue eyes and hair so dark it almost looked blue-black in the glaring sunlight. She smiled at him. He didn't smile back. He just stared. She swallowed hard and strode up the dirt path to the veranda. A beautiful woman sat in the window, wearing a black dress. Her black hair was piled high and sparkled with diamond hairpins. Macey nodded to her as she climbed the steps and went directly to the door.

Before she knocked, she fumbled with the pearl buttons on her white collar to make sure they were buttoned all the way to her chin, hiding her bruised and swollen throat. Then she smoothed out her gray skirt, and checked her hair, which she had oiled and combed back into a bun. Her attire was matronly and modest—at least she hoped it was. It had been so long since she'd donned anything so unflattering that she couldn't be certain how she appeared to other people, particularly women. It had been years since she cared how she looked to a woman.

But she cared today. She cared very much.

This woman was new in town, and if God had not abandoned Macey, Mrs. Hale would not have had time to research her background—at least beyond the resume Macey had sent over. That piece of paper told the truth, as far as it went. Macey prayed it was far enough. At least Mrs. Hale had asked to interview her, so God hadn't turned His face away yet.

After Andre Guillard, she had wondered. She had endured much abuse in her time, but had never felt like a man intended to kill her. The horror had been black and suffocating, like falling off a cliff and plunging down, down . . . and never hitting bottom. When he had gone, she had lain on the floor next to Esther and they'd sobbed in terror. But it hadn't taken long for her intrinsic common sense to rouse itself and slap her into action. Her career as a soiled dove had ended in a heartbeat. Macey didn't care if she was penniless from now on, so long as she had a warm bed, food in her belly, and never had to open her bedroom door to a man again.

When she overheard two women in the mercantile gossiping about the mysterious Mrs. Hale, the new owner of the Banta Hill Gold Mine, and mentioned in passing that Mrs. Hale had posted an advertisement in the market for a housekeeper, Macey knew that God had been listening to her prayers and was offering her a way out. If she had the courage to take it.

Sucking in a deep breath, she lifted her gloved hand and knocked.

The door opened, and Macey gazed up into the face of a tall, slender lady. A beautiful lady, in an exotic sort of way. Deeply set dark eyes rode over high delicate cheekbones, which accentuated the straightness of her nose and fullness of her lips. The lady's only arguable flaw was her complexion—it was not that pasty white that women of status preferred. Instead, it was light brown and smooth as silk. It intrigued Macey that Mrs. Hale took no pains to cover up her natural coloring with pale powders or rouge.

Macey curtsied as best as she could. The muscles in her legs and lower back still hurt. "Mrs. Hale? I'm Miss Macey Runkles. I am pleased to make your acquaintance."

"How do you do, Miss Runkles?" Mrs. Hale said warmly. "Please, come in."

Macey entered and stood awkwardly looking around. Why the place didn't even have curtains!

"This way, Miss Runkles," Mrs. Hale said and led her across the nearly empty sitting room to a table where a teapot and two cups steamed. Macey's resume lay at an angle beside the teapot. She recognized her own flowing scrawl.

Mrs. Hale sat down and gestured for Macey to take the other chair, which she did. Sunlight spilled over the table and glinted off the fine china. "Please, make yourself comfortable, Miss Runkles. I took the liberty of pouring a cup of tea for you when I saw you coming up the path. I hope Souchong is to your liking."

"Oh, I'll drink pretty near anything. Except milk, that is. It just don't set well with me. Never has. Even when I was a little girl." She lifted her cup and sipped it. It tasted bitter, but she smiled politely. "That's mighty good, ma'am."

"I'm glad." Mrs. Hale looked Macey over carefully.

Macey pretended not to notice the way Mrs. Hale's sharp eyes surveyed each bump and bruise that Macey had tried so hard to disguise with makeup. But she couldn't help seeing the way Mrs. Hale's eyes tightened and her jaw set. If the lady had been a man, Macey would have sworn it was well-hidden rage.

"So," Mrs. Hale said in a soothing voice. "I see that you worked as a nanny in St. Louis, is that right?"

"Yes, ma'am."

"You took care of four children?"

"Oh, yes, they were awfully good kids, too. Three girls and one little boy. He was six, about the age of your son."

Mrs. Hale used a finger to go down the list of jobs on Macey's resume. Two upright lines etched the skin between her eyebrows. "And you worked as a laundress at Fort Riley, in Kansas?"

"Yes, ma'am. I washed, starched, and ironed uniforms for the officers. And I did a little mending, when it was needed."

"I see." Mrs. Hale smiled and looked up. "Your resume shows wide gaps in your employment history, though, Miss Runkles. Could you tell me—"

"Yes . . . yes, I could, ma'am . . . I just. Well . . ."

"Please do, Miss Runkles."

Macey wet her lips and put both hands on the oak table. She caressed the smoothness with her gloved fingertips. It felt warm from the sunlight, which melted a little of the ice that had formed in the pit of her stomach. "I didn't fill in some spots, ma'am, because—" she inhaled a fortifying breath— "Mrs. Hale I ain't always had what you'd call 'respectable' positions. But all that's over now, and I want you to know that I can do just about anything, and I mean that. Really. I am an expert dressmaker. I'm good at hairstyling and needlepoint. I can cook up a storm. I can even sing pretty good if I've got accompaniment, and . . . and I love children, Mrs. Hale." She leaned toward the lady. "I love children so much. I would be a good nanny for your little boy. I'd take care of him just like he was my own."

Mrs. Hale's face softened. She lifted her cup and sipped her tea. "May I be frank with you, Miss Runkles?"

Macey's stomach clutched up. She managed to nod. "Yes, ma'am. I would take that as a kindness."

Mrs. Hale set her cup down and laced her fingers in her lap. Her elegant face had gone serious. "A friend of mine came by yesterday afternoon, and I told him you had applied for the position as my housekeeper. I asked if he knew anything about you—"

"Oh." Macey's spine went weak, she eased back in her chair. "I—I know what he must have told you, ma'am, but I—"

"Do you?" Mrs. Hale said with a tilt of her head. "Well, let me repeat what he said, so we're both certain we know the same things."

"Yes, ma'am." Macey's voice sounded small and hopeless, even to herself.

Mrs. Hale said, "He told me he thought you were a fine caring woman, despite your unfortunate circumstances. He said he'd heard you could read and write, and even kept books in your house."

"Oh, yes, ma'am!" Macey responded with an eager nod. "I couldn't live without my books. Sometimes they . . . well, they've been my only company. I can always count on the people in my books to be there when I need them. Other folks ain't so dependable."

Mrs. Hale smiled. "I understand." She paused and relaced her fingers. Her smile faded to an almost mournful expression. "Miss Runkles, I would like to give you the chance to change your life, but I must tell you something before I offer you the position as my housekeeper."

Macey sat up straighter. "What is it, ma'am?"

"I may be forced to ask things of you that no other employer has. I may—though I hope not—have to leave town abruptly, for days or . . . or even weeks. On business. During that time, I will need someone to be both mother to my son and guardian of my home. It is a lot to ask of a housekeeper. But I will pay you well for your loyalty. Are you willing to accept such responsibilities?"

Macey bit her lip. Despite the fact that Mrs. Hale's voice came out strong and steady, a fear seeped through the words that Macey recognized. She'd heard it in too many women's voices to miss it. This refined, wealthy lady was scared silly of a man. Yes, indeed, that's exactly what it was. Anger began to simmer in Macey's chest. She was starting to believe that the only good man was a dead one.

Macey leaned forward and put her hand over Mrs. Hale's and squeezed gently. "I'll be here if you need me. You don't have to bother about that. I won't let Satan hisself come through that door if I think he means harm to your boy, and you don't have to worry 'bout me learning to use a gun neither," she added, "because I'm already right practiced at it. And to tell you the truth, I wouldn't mind shooting a man. No, ma'am, I wouldn't mind it at all."

Mrs. Hale lifted her chin and studied Macey with those dark intent eyes. "Will you answer one more question for me, then?"

"Anything, ma'am. What is it?"

"Why didn't you kill the man who hurt you?"

Macey swallowed hard and drew her hand back into her lap, placing it palm up on her knee. Though she'd cleaned and salved her cuts, dots of blood had permeated the cotton glove. Mrs. Hale saw them, too, before Macey clenched her fingers into a fist.

"I just . . ." Macey sat for a moment, collecting herself. "I have never been through something like that, Mrs. Hale. I truly believed he was going to kill me, and when he got up off me and left . . . I—I was so grateful to have him gone that I couldn't think of nothing else." Tears welled in her eyes. She used the back of her glove to wipe away the few that ran down her heavily made-up cheeks. "At one point, I looked over at the drawer where I keep my pistol, but I felt too weak to get up and pull it out. I just couldn't find the strength."

Very calmly, Mrs. Hale said, "You are lucky to be alive. If the necessity ever arises again, I will accept no excuses. I will expect you to kill any intruder before he has a chance to hurt either my son or you. Do you understand?"

"Oh, yes, ma'am," Macey said, and felt a little like a soldier receiving orders from a superior officer. "Like I said, you don't have to worry none about that. I'll never let such a thing happen again. That Andre Guillard just caught me off guard, that was all. I guarantee—"

"Good." Mrs. Hale reached over, lifted Macey's right hand, and shook it gently, so as not to hurt her. "When can you start?"

Macey's mouth hung open. "Today! I'll need to go fetch my things, but—"

"I'll hire a man with a wagon to help you." Mrs. Hale stood up and the morning light bathed her in a golden aura. Her diamond hairpins glittered. She looked regal. "Now, let me show you your room."

Macey stood up, a little unsteady on her feet. She still could not quite believe she had the job. "Oh, I'd like that. Thank you."

Mrs. Hale led her to the door beneath the staircase and opened it. Macey followed her inside. The wood floor gleamed. A tiny stone fireplace stood in the northeast corner beside a built-in bookshelf, and the back wall had a long window. Beyond the pane, a big yard spread to a fence, and then the rocky mountain slope rose steeply. On the other side of the fireplace, a door opened into the kitchen. Through it, Macey saw a beautiful wood cookstove. Delicate pink flowers painted the green enamel of the oven door.

Macey smiled, and Mrs. Hale said, "I hope this will be satisfactory. I know it's small, but—"

"Oh, it will be fine!" Macey insisted. "I can already see my books on those shelves by the fireplace. Why, I almost feel at home and I haven't been here for more than a minute."

"Good. I'm looking forward to getting to know you."

As she walked down the path toward the iron gate, happiness swelled Macey's heart. She felt as if she had just been adopted into a family. It warmed her deep down. It wasn't until Macey started running down the street that she realized she hadn't even asked what her pay would be.

But it didn't really matter.

She was free! *Free . . .*

CHAPTER 20

Dusk settled over the city of Denver in a deep purple haze. A few yellow gleams of lamplight dotted the windows of the false-fronted buildings. Owen hurried. He still had time to reach the Black Diamond Saloon and get out before full dark, and he figured he had to, if he wanted to make it back to his hotel alive.

Owen kept his hand on the hide-out derringer in his waistcoat pocket as he continued down Ferry Street. The road was lined with shanty bars and bordellos, some leaning so precariously they looked like they might collapse at any moment. Squint-eyed cutthroats loitered on the sidewalks, appraising his gold-trimmed tan suit with eager eyes. Women winked from front doors. He scowled at them all. The odious scents of heavy perfume, vomit, and urine made him want to run.

But he couldn't. A tobacco-spitting soldier in a worn blue uniform had told him that if he wanted hard-to-find information he could most likely get it at the Black Diamond Saloon. Owen understood what that meant: It would be a place that no decent human being would be caught dead in.

"Aye, now there's a pickin' for ye." A squalid miner jabbed his partner in the side and pointed at Owen. He glared in return. They both laughed, beating their empty rum bottles on the railing in front of the saloon.

Owen gritted his teeth.

How long has it been since you were in a place so cheaply revolting?

His thoughts soured, remembering bad times when he'd lurked around places like this pawning bonds for nonexistent railroads. It might not have been an upstanding job, but it was a hell of a lot more profitable than grubbing for gold, busting sod, or laying track.

"Hey, pretty boy! Hey! You!" A pudgy brunette on an upstairs balcony yelled. She waved a soiled red handkerchief to get his attention, and when he looked up she shouted, "Come on up! My whisky's cold and my hands are warm, *very* warm, honey."

Ordinarily he would have made light of it by giving her a jaunty bow, but today he just pulled the brim of his hat lower and bulled forward.

He waited for a clattering wagon to jounce by before crossing Third Street. Then, heaving a disgusted sigh, he shoved through the swinging doors of The Black Diamond saloon—a pathetic hole with two booths and three tables. Crude posters of nude women covered the rough-hewn walls. The bar was a bare board tilted on two mismatched whisky barrels. Eight men lounged around tables. Their conversations halted as he entered, hostile eyes turning his direction. Now he understood why the soldier had directed him here. Every man in the place wore at least one garment of military issue: A pair of sky blue cavalry trousers, a skirmish cap, battered black boots.

Owen took a booth and knew the instant he put his elbows on the table that it had been a mistake. His right sleeve stuck. He pulled it off and glared at the fuzz of tan wool that remained glued to the table. Disgusted, he waved over the barmaid.

"What can I get you, honey?" the short blond cooed. She wore a red dress cut so low her nipples were visible beneath the lace inset.

"First of all, you can clean this damned table. Second, I'll take a whisky."

She gave him a look that would have wilted stone. "Anything to eat? Rube makes a fine—"

"No."

"How 'bout some—"

"I said, no! Just bring a wet rag and a glass of whisky!"

Her lips pursed and she strutted away. When she returned, she took a single swipe at the table, making one clean swath, then sat his whisky down hard. "Anything else?"

"Yes," he answered and held a ten-dollar gold piece up to the lamplight, twisting it so it glinted. "I'm looking for information."

She smiled, and grew courteous. "Why I'd be glad to help you, mister. Information about what?"

"A man. When I met him he was going by the name of Andre Guillard. You want to ask around?"

She nodded, grasping for the money. Owen pulled it back and said, "Open your palm and don't move it." She frowned, but did it, and he dropped the coin in her hand from three inches above. The last thing in the world that he wanted was to touch a woman of her quality.

He watched as she went from table to table, putting enticing hands on burly shoulders and whispering. Curious looks were cast his way, but men kept shaking their heads.

Owen glared at the clean swath on the table. All around it, splotches and rings created a grisly mosaic. Lord, what he would give to be out of Denver forever! But he needed information first. Guillard was a dangerous man, of that Owen had no doubt. He had been dogging Owen's steps for days. Every time Owen turned around, he saw Guillard, smiling in crowds, laughing in bars, talking in hotel lobbies. And Owen knew that despite his own nefarious dealings, Guillard was not really interested in him. *The man wanted Rose.* He was following Owen in the hopes Owen would lead him to her. Just for that reason, Owen had remained in Denver. He couldn't proceed to Central City until he had lost Guillard, and he didn't want to lose the man until he knew who the hell he was and what he wanted.

Owen took a sip of his whisky and almost gagged. "Rot gut! Good God."

He shoved the full glass to the opposite side of the table—far enough that he didn't even have to smell the vile aroma.

He shook his head. Already he'd wasted almost two hundred dollars trying to find out Guillard's identity and the only real lead he'd gotten came from a mealymouthed sot who'd spilled beer on his best suit while hissing, "He's a *Pinkerton.* I heard tell he's running down a war criminal." But there'd been other suggestions as well. One glassy-eyed bartender had even claimed that Guillard was on General Grant's staff—sent west to scout out the Indian wars situation on the plains.

Owen's nerves had been humming all day.

A chair screeched, and Owen looked up. A tall man in a sergeant's uniform rose from his table and started across the room. Icy blond hair capped his square head.

"Why do you want to know about Guillard?" he asked as he braced a hand on the table and peered down menacingly at Owen. His bulbous nose gleamed redly in the dim light.

"He's been following me. I want to know why. Who is he, and why is he in Colorado Territory? Do you know? I'll pay you well."

"How well?"

Fontaine pulled a twenty-dollar bill from his pocket and laid it on the table. "This is to start. For each *good* piece of information, I'll give you another twenty. Now, what's Guillard's real name?"

The sergeant's blue eyes narrowed. "I ain't telling you that 'til the last. And it will cost you a pretty penny."

Owen grumbled an obscenity to himself, but nodded. "All right. Go on. Why is he in Colorado?"

The sergeant slid in on the opposite side of the booth and leaned across the table to whisper, "He's looking for a woman."

"Why?"

"Don't you want to know her name?"

"No, but I do want to know why he's after her. Do you know?"

The sergeant shrugged. "I ain't heard that part, but he's been asking around town about a Robin Walkingstick Heatherton. I guess she's a half-breed Cherokee. Got in some kind of trouble back East."

"Is Guillard a Pinkerton agent?"

The sergeant shook his head and grinned. He had only two yellow teeth left in his mouth, both on top.

"Well?" Owen demanded.

The man squinted one eye and tapped the table with dirty fingers. "You already owe me another forty dollars, mister. I'd better see it, or you ain't getting no more information."

Owen dug his wallet from his coat pocket and threw the bills on the grimy table. The sergeant scooped them up and stuffed them in his pants pocket. Owen said, "If Guillard isn't working for Allen Pinkerton, who *is* he working for?"

The sergeant whispered. "The deputy provost-marshal-general."

"The deputy . . ." Owen felt himself flush. His spine started to tingle. He leaned forward. "Are you telling me that Guillard works for Colonel George Sharpe?"

"I am," the sergeant said and chuckled. It sounded like a rusty hinge. "He's an agent, I hear. High up in the Bureau, too. *A major.*"

Owen's gaze drifted around the dank room, lingering on the spiderwebs in the corners and the vomit stains on the walls. With this much information he could find out Guillard's real identity himself. But it would take time. He'd have to telegraph a cryptic message to his contacts in the Bureau of Military Information, hope they understood what he wanted, then wait for a reply. He couldn't spare the days. Nor did he want to risk exposing those precious sources of information.

Owen tossed a hundred-dollar bill on the table, leaned back, and crossed his legs. "I see. Well, let's get to the final question. What's Guillard's real name?"

The sergeant reached for the money, but Owen slammed a hand down atop the man's grimy fingers. *"What's his name?"*

The sergeant's jaw muscles bunched. "There's a man in town who met him once in Washington City. Says his name's Corley. Major Thomas Corley."

Owen lifted his hand, allowing the informant to grab the bill. "Thank you for your time, sergeant."

The big man stuffed the money in his pocket. "I wouldn't cross Corley if'n I was you, mister. From what I hear, he ain't got a human bone in his whole body." He slid out of the booth and went back to the table on the far side of the saloon where three men greeted him with hushed questions.

Owen strolled out onto the dirty sidewalk. Twilight had settled over the city, bringing with it a cold breeze. Gusts flattened his silk shirt across his chest and waffled the brim of his brown slouched hat as he hurried down the street. In the distance, clouds obscured the high peaks of the Rockies. He pulled his hat low and followed Ferry Street until he hit Fifth, then crossed the bridge and headed for the Apollo Hall.

A plain-looking two-story building with a balcony and carved turnposts, the Apollo bore only a slight resemblance to most western buildings. It was not false-fronted, but had a gabled roof, and inside, fine crystal chandeliers caught the light and threw a flickering kaleidoscope of colors over the walls and high ceilings.

Owen could hear the clicking whir of the roulette wheels as he jarred the door open. He proceeded straight to the long oak bar and lifted a hand for the bartender. The squat, bushy-faced man strode over. He had little pig eyes and a pointed nose. He wore a white pleated shirt that was miraculously still clean.

"What'll you have, mister?"

"A bottle of your best whisky."

"Coming up." He turned and pulled a faceted bottle and glass from a mirrored shelf behind him. Brusquely, he set them on the bar. "That'll be seventy-two dollars."

"Lord above!" Owen blurted. "This city's a damned expensive place, do you know that? For what I've spent on five days in Denver I could have lived in Boston a month!"

"Well, ain't that interesting." The bartender looked bored.

Owen sighed and tossed the money on the counter, deciding he deserved the best tonight. Fine whisky always salved a sore ego—and trolling through the bawdy side of town had definitely bruised his. It had brought up too many painful memories.

Retrieving his bottle and glass, he found an empty table against the back wall. Men swarmed around the gambling tables. Poker and faro were going strong. Though it was only seven o'clock, half the crowd already reeled drunkenly. Male laughter mixed with the lusty female voices of doves.

Owen took a red velvet chair and set his bottle and glass on the beautiful oak table. He poured himself a glass and sipped, savoring the smooth rich flavor while he stroked the bottle lovingly. *Ah, darling, I needed you tonight. All day long I've been feeling like I was eighteen and trying to steal enough to buy supper.*

He'd run away from home at the age of sixteen after losing a fist fight with his father. Jacob Fontaine had bullied everyone he'd ever met, his wife and children included. "Yer just like rats in a feed store!" he'd say. "Good fer nothings who eat me out of house and home!" The night Owen had left, he'd jumped into a brawl between his mother and father and unleashed years of his own hatred. He'd beaten his father to the kitchen floor and grabbed a butcher knife to slit his throat. His mother had screamed and leaped on Owen's back to drag him off his father.

It was too damn bad, too. The old man deserved killing.

With a hair-trigger temper, hard fists, and a chip on his shoulder big enough to weigh down the greatest of men, Owen had made his own way, and he'd celebrated to beat hell when, at the age of twenty-three, he'd heard of his father's death.

Owen refilled his glass and studied the facets of his whisky bottle. What a life he'd led. By the time he'd turned twenty, he'd swindled, seduced, and—yes—murdered enough people to fill this hall. Well, he hadn't actually murdered those men himself, he'd hired out the work, but it amounted to the same thing.

And he regretted none of it.

He lifted his eyes and surveyed the room. The Apollo buzzed with arriving dinner guests. Women entered on the arms of men, their gowns showered with velvet ribbons and yards of lace. Bosoms were exposed. Bustles and bows adorned derrieres. He took it all in, letting the sights and sensations of wealth comfort him. All he'd ever wanted was enough money to do as he pleased, regardless of what the rest of the world wanted. It had taken years, but he'd achieved that goal—and then some. He prided himself on the fact that he had enough cold hard cash to bribe his way into almost any circle.

A tall Army officer entered the front door, a colonel with red hair and a lean weasel-like face. After careful study, Owen decided he didn't know him. Still, the man looked familiar, and the officer glanced his way often enough to make Owen uncomfortable. As a diversion, he reached into his coat pocket and removed the map that Gest Hattan at the Land Office had sold him. He used his finger to trace a line from Golden to Idaho Springs, then over the mountain to Gregory Diggings, which, he discovered, was a locale not a town. Black Hawk, Central City, and Russell Gulch were all located in the Gregory Diggings district. He wished to hell he was there now, but he couldn't risk—

"Pardon me."

Startled, Owen jerked his head up and stared at the colonel. He had pale blue eyes and freckles. "Yes?"

"May I sit at your table?" The man waved a hand to the crowded room. "It seems there aren't any other seats left."

"Please, Colonel. I'll be going soon anyway." Damn right, he would. Sitting with an unknown army officer didn't tickle his fancy. Owen folded his map and tucked it back into his pocket.

The man removed his blue woolen cape and swirled it over the back of a chair. "I'm Thomas Corley," he introduced, extending a hand.

"Owen Fontaine." He shook the man's hand, while his stomach plummeted through the floor. No wonder he looked familiar . . . *A chameleon. Of course. I would have never recognized him.* He'd promoted himself, but why would he decide to drop the rest of his disguise? Did he imagine that his uniform and new rank would intimidate Owen? Though Owen felt a little ill, he wasn't so easily unnerved. He smiled broadly. "What brings you to this godforsaken Territory, Colonel? The army started roughing up argonauts?"

Corley laughed, but it sounded forced. "No, I'm conducting an investigation for the Department." He sat down and folded his arms over his massive chest.

What is it about his voice that strikes a chord? It sounds nothing like Guillard's voice, but . . . **Have** *I met Corley? When? Where?*

"Which department are you with, Colonel Corley?" Owen asked as he searched his memory. The voice left a bitter taste in his mouth, so it must have been an unpleasant meeting.

"Military Information."

"Indeed? What could possibly bring you to Colorado? Especially now that the war's over?" Owen lifted the whisky bottle. "You like good whisky?"

"I like nothing better."

"If you could find a glass, I'd be happy to—"

"You're very kind." Corley stood and made his way to the bar, eying the women he passed like fine pieces of horseflesh.

Owen scrutinized his map again, making certain he knew the names of all the towns within about three hundred and fifty miles of Denver, and when

Corley started back with his glass, Owen, once again, tucked the map into his breast pocket.

Corley sat down and extended his glass. "Thank you, Mr. Fontaine."

Owen filled it for him. "Well, nothing's too good for our glorious army. We won the war, didn't we?"

"Yes," Corley answered as he lifted his glass and sipped. "We won the war." A smile curled his thin lips, but it was not a pretty sight. "Your clothing bears the mark of eastern civility, Mr. Fontaine. Surely you're not a regular inhabitant of this part of the country."

"No, not at all. I'm here on business."

"What sort? Commerce? The railroad?"

"Gold."

"Really? The person I'm searching for is involved in gold mining. Perhaps you know her? Robin Walkingstick Heatherton. Sometimes she uses the names Harmon, Katton or Chamberlain?"

Owen stared as though shocked, then he straightened in his chair. "As a matter of fact, I'm looking for a woman as well. When I met her she was going by the name of Mrs. Rose Chamberlain. I'd be very interested to know her whereabouts. We have—er—a slight misunderstanding regarding a business arrangement."

Corley lifted a brow and laughed sourly. "Yes, well, she's famous for disappearing with the goods before her partners collect their shares, and unfortunately many of those partners have been military officers."

"Is that so?"

Corley nodded. "I assume you haven't found her yet?"

"No."

Corley lifted his glass in a toast. "Too bad. Let's hope one of us finds her before her other pursuers do. Otherwise, she might not live long enough to go to trial. She's being charged with treason, as well as several other crimes."

"What do you mean 'other pursuers?' "

Corley drank his whisky, obviously relishing the flavor, and spent a few moments watching the rainbow lights that swirled on the ceiling, cast by the swaying crystal chandeliers. "Well, Mr. Fontaine, let me just say that she has *many* enemies, ranging from esteemed senators in Washington to riverboat gamblers. Frankly, I'm surprised she's not already dead."

"Hmm. Interesting. But regardless of her other pursuers, Colonel, I wager I'll find her first. You can lay bets on that."

"Well, if you do," Corley said. "You should be aware that the Department is offering a reward for information leading to her capture."

"Really? How much?"

"One thousand dollars."

The sum would have persuaded most men to try passing their sisters off as Rose. *Sweetheart, what have you done?*

"My, my. That's an impressive amount," Owen said. "I will, of course, be more than happy to turn her over to you when I find her, Colonel. Will you be headquartered in Denver?"

Corley crossed his legs. "Yes, at least for a time."

"Good."

Corley pretended to have developed a sudden fascination with men's fashions. He scrutinized every silk hat, cravat, and pair of boots in the place. Owen observed with a mild fascination of his own. Corley's expression had gone grim, as if he were contemplating his next words. Finally, in a casual voice, he asked, "So you don't have any idea where she might have gone?"

"Well . . . yes. Actually, I do." Owen drank more whisky.

When Owen made no further efforts to explain, Corley gave him a hard look and inquired, "And what would you require to share that information with me, Mr. Fontaine?"

Owen pulled the map from his pocket and held it close to his chest, like a prized poker hand—which was a Goddamned apt analogy. "Two things, Colonel. First, I expect to receive the thousand-dollar reward. Second, I expect that if my nefarious business partner is convicted of the crimes you claim, I will receive title to her entire gold claim. Surely the Department can be of assistance in such arrangements?"

Corley's lips moved in a faint smile. "Of course, Mr. Fontaine. In fact, I can guarantee that you will receive full title *before* she goes to trial. I'm sure she swindled you—just as she has everybody else." He leaned forward, his jaw hard, hands clenched. He looked as if he would burst if Owen didn't hurry. "Those terms are perfectly acceptable, Mr. Fontaine. So, please. Go on."

Owen pretended to be reluctant, gazing around the room, drumming his fingers on the table. "All right, even if the title falls through, at least the reward will help me recoup my expenses."

Owen unfolded his map and spread it out across the oak tabletop. He used his finger to trace the winding dirt roads that led to the far southeastern corner of the territory, showing Corley the fastest route to Fort Lyon. Then he began to speak.

When he'd finished, Corley nodded and smiled. "Very good, Mr. Fontaine. When will you be ready to leave?"

"Me?"

"Of course. I'm sure you'll want to accompany me on the journey south, to witnesss her capture and assure you get your reward. Isn't that right?"

The question held a hidden threat. Either Owen went or . . . or what? Did Corley know about his arms dealing? Is that why he refused to let Owen out of his sight? No matter, Corley's tone of voice left Owen with a pretty clear idea of what the "or" might mean.

"Why, of course, Colonel. I'll be ready to leave at dawn tomorrow, if that's satisfactory."

CHAPTER 21

The sun had not yet risen when they reached the steep trail that led up the mountainside to Banta Hill. Black spears of pines lined the way, moaning and creaking in the freezing wind. Robin gripped her reins hard. Her bay gelding chomped at the bit and swiveled his head to see why she had tugged.

She whispered, "Sorry, boy. I'm sorry."

Stop this. You must let the nightmare go. Let it go.

For two nights in a row, the old dream had come back. Over and over, all night long, she had run through flaming forests filled with mutilated men. The nightmare had begun to change, in small, terrible details—last night she had sensed that Charles ran ahead of her through the wilderness, and she ran harder, trying to find him, never able to. Twice the forest had shifted from Virginia to Tennessee, where even the river burned with an eerie brilliance. Images of the carnage blotted out all other thoughts and would not leave her alone . . . even now. If she did not concentrate on the cold and mountains, she saw a body without legs lying half-hidden in the snow . . . a head and legs without a trunk tucked into the shadows. Over there, amidst the rocks, a head. Just a head. Bullet holes riddled swollen flesh. The groans and cries of the wounded mixed with the wind in the pines.

Robin couldn't draw a breath without feeling a fist in her windpipe.

She pulled up the hood of her blue cape and forced herself to be here, now, guiding her gelding along the trail behind Garrison Parker and his mule, Honey. Parker wore his long buffalo coat and had his gray felt hat tied down over his ears with a long piece of blue woolen cloth. Ice caked his mustache and beard. Every time he turned to speak to her, he looked more like a silver-bearded old man.

The trail wound up the mountain through rocks and across snowbanks. As they rounded another bend, Robin peered down at Central City. A cloud of blue wood smoke hung over the buildings. The lamplit houses dotting the streets resembled a slithering strand of amber beads. Beyond town, fog clothed the bases of the highest peaks and left them looking disembodied, like hovering rotten-toothed monsters. The summits glistened, backlit by the first rays of dawn, but beneath those orange caps, inky shadows blanketed the world.

"You see that?" Garrison pointed to the tall snow-clad pinnacle that dominated the area.

"Yes."

"That's Black Hawk Mountain. Remember what it looks like. From the top of Banta Hill she's just about due east. That way you can't get lost. But if you ever do, take out your pistol and fire three shots in a row. In this part of the country that means you're down and hurt. Anybody in hearing range will come running."

Robin nodded, but said nothing.

Garrison swiveled in his saddle to look at her. His worn felt hat glimmered with frost, and in the ghostly gleam, she saw the concern that lined his face. "Mrs. Hale? Did you hear—"

"Yes, I—I'm sorry. Thank you for telling me. Black Hawk Mountain. Fire three shots. I won't forget."

She caught his worried expression before he turned back around.

Had she been acting too strangely? She had no way of knowing, because she hadn't really been in Colorado for hours. Her soul had been wading streams, crawling through mud, marching down endless dusty roads . . . and scaling mountains: *Kennesaw. Lookout Mountain. Little Round Top.*

After all the sweat and terror, heart pounding, feet slipping on rain-slick rocks, acrid black smoke filling her lungs, each place faded into a mirage of memory . . .

Leaving her sick and disoriented.

Garrison maneuvered his mule around an upthrust rock and dismounted. He walked forward, studying the stone. Against the golden aura that swelled on the horizon, he looked very tall and dark, and not quite real.

Robin drew her gelding up beside him. In a strained voice, she asked, "What are you looking for?"

"Something that ought to cheer you up. But I don't know if you can see it in this light."

"I don't need cheering up. I'm fine, thank you."

"Is that right?"

"Yes."

"Uh-huh."

He started kicking a rock with the heel of his boot. Robin watched him curiously. Ice cracked and broke off, then went sliding downhill, clunking and clinking, shattering into dozens of tiny sparkling fragments. "Here it is. If you'd like to come over here, Mrs. Hale, I'll show you what gold looks like."

She dismounted and walked forward, pulling her horse by the reins. "Gold? Where?"

"Right here," he said, tapping a spot on the outcrop. "I reckon you'll have to kneel to see it though."

Robin bent over. Tiny hairs of gold laced the rock. She exhaled and her warm breath spun out in a silver wreath and spiraled away in the wind.

"Is your heart racing?" Garrison asked.

She tried to sound eager. "A little, yes."

"Only a little? We'd best come back in good light, then. Your heart ought to be beating its way out of your chest. And when gold fever's really got you by the throat you can't hardly breathe."

Robin straightened.

Garrison's bushy brows drew together and his gaze went over her face in detail, noting every line. "Come on," he said gently. "Let's get you some place warm where we can talk."

"I don't need to talk, Mr. Parker. I'm quite well. Let's proceed as planned."

They mounted their horses in silence and wound uphill, passing groves of young conifers and enormous boulders. Snow grew deeper as they climbed. Massive drifts huddled like slumbering beasts in every shaded hollow, and in the lee of one drift, wolf tracks dimpled the white. It created a curious mosaic—black rocks, the deep blue of the drift and the tracks shining wells of dark purple. The colors of this country filled her with a sense of the alien.

The trail widened and Garrison dropped back to ride side-by-side with her. He had his hands propped on his saddlehorn. But he appeared to be thinking hard. "How's Macey Runkles working out as your housekeeper?" he asked, obviously trying to engage her in conversation.

Making an effort, Robin answered, "Very well, Mr. Parker."

"So she's been pretty good to you and the boy?"

"Oh, yes. The first night she stayed in the house, I went to bed late and found a glass of wine waiting on my bedside table. Then, when I crawled under the quilts, there was a hot brick rolled in a towel at the foot of my bed. It's been a long time since I slept so warmly." Indeed, Robin had been so grateful, she'd crept downstairs and gently knocked at Macey's door just to thank her. Every time she looked at Macey, she thought of Cato, Leander

Brushy, and Nate, probably because they had taken care of her too. Kindness was so rare. It carved a permanent place in the heart. "I want you to know how much I appreciate you recommending her. She's a hard worker, and she seems to love Jeremy."

"Well, good," he said. "I figured she just needed somebody to give her a hand up. Anybody with as many books as she's got can't be dumb as a post. Did she fill up them bookshelves in her room?"

Garrison had been there when Macey first began unpacking her books; he'd looked on in awe. Robin guided her horse around a rock, swinging wide, and when she came back within conversation range, she said, "Yes, and when she ran out of room on the shelves, she lined the remaining volumes up along the wall at her bedside."

"I ain't really surprised. But I ought to be. A Negro woman, and one who's had a mighty hard time of it, yet she reads like a professor."

"She says the characters in the books are her best friends. They're always there for her when she needs them. I think she reads a few chapters every night. I see lamplight shining beneath her door for some time after she retires."

"I'm glad, Mrs. Hale, that you were generous enough to give her a chance. Ain't many folks would have risked it. Not with the predilection of small towns to jabber and condemn. I hope she don't have no trouble when she goes out shopping for the house."

A smile touched Robin's lips. "I dare say that anyone with enough courage to insult Macey publicly would regret it. I don't know what she was like before I hired her, and I don't care," she added so that Garrison would not feel obliged to tell her. Because, in truth, Robin did not care. Over the past four years she had gained a keen ability to judge people based upon a few minutes of conversation, and she knew Macey to be a good, decent human being, regardless of what others might think of her. "But I can tell you this: Macey is downright committed to being respectable—for my sake, she says—and I wouldn't like to be the person who told her she wasn't. I've never experienced the rough side of her tongue, but . . ."

Robin's horse balked at a patch of ice so glazed it shone like a mirror. "Stop that!" she ordered as she kicked the big bay. He whinnied, eyes rolling with fear, and stumbled around it. She envied Garrison's mule. Over the past two hours, Honey had plodded along steadily, apparently unafraid of anything.

"You all right?" Garrison called over his shoulder.

"Yes. But I don't understand why Honey never stumbles or shies like Fullhouse."

"Because Honey's a mule. Ain't no animal on earth more surefooted than a mule. 'Course, mules only come in two kinds: The good and the dead. Dead mules are the ones that were smarter than their masters and felt obligated to prove it."

As they came up over the ridge, a small log cabin appeared on the very crest of the hill. It had two small windows in the front, facing east, and a stovepipe sticking out of the middle of the roof. A hitching rail stood in front. Behind the cabin, a panorama of blue and lavender peaks stretched into infinity.

Garrison trotted Honey to the front door, dismounted and slapped her on the haunches. She sauntered off with bit jingling and began to paw at the snow to find grass. After Garrison had batted ice from the sleeves of his buffalo coat, he walked over and grabbed the reins of Robin's horse, holding them while she dismounted.

"I think we'd best tie your horse to the hitching post, Mrs. Hale," Garrison said. "He don't know this place yet and he might just hightail it for home if we let him graze."

"Thank you, Mr. Parker . . . but I thought we were heading directly to Collier's old mine shaft?"

"In a bit, Mrs. Hale. In a bit."

She glared at him as he led her horse away, but he never looked back.

When she turned to follow him, the sun peeked over the mountains and sent a flood of light rolling across the slopes in a vast yellow wave. Peaks changed from disembodied monsters to jagged granite pinnacles, while pines cast off their black cloaks and glittered with the palest of greens. Snowbanks hissed and groaned. It was like watching the land undergo the ritual of transubstantiation—where the very earth itself mutated into the glorious body of God. Boulders seemed to preen, showing off their orange and green lichen-mottled surfaces. At their bases, wildflowers appeared, tiny, and so white their purity rivaled the snow.

Garrison opened the front door to his cabin and made a sweeping gesture with his arm. "Come on inside, Mrs. Hale. It's still pretty warm."

She stamped her boots to knock off the snow. It wasn't proper for an unescorted woman to enter a single man's house, but she hadn't been "proper" in a long time, and warmth trickled from the door. She entered. Garrison came in behind her.

A bed stood along the left wall, covered with a Hudson's Bay blanket. The red, yellow, and black stripes at head and foot lay evenly aligned. On the right wall, cast-iron pots and pans hung in irregular order, and below them stood a rough-hewn kitchen table with two chairs. The woodstove squatted in the back against the long western wall, opposite the front door.

"Grab a chair," he instructed. "I'll build up the fire."

While he went about shoving split logs into the firebox, Robin sat down and folded her gloved hands in her lap. The place smelled sweetly of pine sap and woodsmoke.

"I'll get this fire going good," Garrison said, "then I'll warm the coffee and we'll talk before we go take a look at that shaft of Collier's."

"I told you I didn't need to talk."

"I heard you."

He lifted his battered coffee pot from the left side of the stove and moved it to the right, over the firebox. Then he prodded the fire with a poker. Robin scowled at him. Did he pay attention to what anyone told him? Probably not. Which she found enlightening. That sort of sheer impudence required practice.

Robin said, "What was your rank in the army, Mr. Parker? Major or colonel?"

"Major. How did you know?"

"Just a wild guess."

Garrison squinted at her, then took off his buffalo coat and his hat, and laid them on the foot of his bed. When he turned back, he eyed Robin for a moment and sat down in the chair opposite her. His brown hair lay in a hundred curls. He ruffed them up with his hand, which only succeeded in heightening his barbaric appearance. "Coffee'll be hot in a couple of minutes."

She continued to scowl at him.

He leaned his chair back on two legs and braced his shoulders against the log wall. "You been acting like a soldier cut off from his company all morning. What's wrong?"

"Nothing is wrong. I told you that." She enunciated each word. "I've been having trouble sleeping. I'm tired. That's all. You know—"

"Yes, ma'am, I damned well do know. I know that *look,* and it's a whole lot more than going without sleep."

She peered angrily down at her gloves. The warmth of the woodstove had penetrated the black leather and touched her hands. Her fingers tingled. She flexed them to help the action along.

"Well?" he insisted. "You going to tell me what's got you stirred up, or not?"

"I hardly think—"

"I have nightmares about the war, too, Mrs. Hale. Bad ones. I'll put mine up against yours any day."

He was offering to match her, story for story. It was a good tactic. Exchanging one vulnerability for another. Some day, she hoped she could actually do that. It would be a relief to talk with a man who had also witnessed the horrors—but today was not the day.

"No, thank you," she responded. "Your nightmares might be worse than mine and, in that case, I don't want to hear them."

"They might not be, too, which could be a relief to you."

"It's not worth—"

"If you'd just talk through them, you might feel better. Did that ever occur to you?"

Robin shoved her blue hood back irritably and her long riding braid flopped over her shoulder. Undoubtedly he thought her dreams entailed hunger, and fear, sieges and the roar of artillery—and all in the relative safety of a house somewhere in Virginia. "It has occurred," she replied.

"Well?"

"All right, Mr. Parker. Listen. I'm lonely. I miss my husband. I miss my home. I miss my . . . my *life*. There. Do you feel better knowing that?"

His curly head moved in a bare nod. "Yes, ma'am. I do." Then he nodded again, fervently this time. "That's the worst, I think. The loneliness. Folks can talk about death, and dying, and losing anything else they want to, but behind every one of 'em is the fear of loneliness. Dying alone. Being alone."

The fist swelled up in her throat again. *Yes, alone with the memories.*

His voice grew gentle, as if he could tell. "Well, Mrs. Hale," he said, "you ain't the only person who's ever been lonely. So at least you ain't alone in that. I been living with loneliness for so long, it's taken on a life of its own. Hell, I hear it moving around the cabin in stocking feet, making coffee, frying bacon. I've even gotten to the stage that I can ignore it most of the time."

"Nobody can ignore loneliness," she answered. "I don't care how tough you are."

Their eyes met and held, and a slow smile came to his face.

"You ought to try it before you condemn it. You might be surprised. Set the loneliness free, and let it walk around for a while on its own two feet. When you can see it up close in its altogethers, it ain't near as frightening."

"Let it walk around. You mean, turn it into a person? A *naked* person?"

"That's right. Mine even has a name."

Her brows lifted. "A name?"

"Mary."

Robin grabbed the fingertips of her left glove and jerked it off, watching Parker. The lunatic looked deadly earnest, despite the wry twist to his lips. "And, why, pray tell, would you give your loneliness a *woman's* name?"

"That ought to be obvious."

Robin chased his answer around for a time. Did he mean that "naked" and "woman" just naturally went together? Or was the match "hurt" and "woman"? More than likely all of them. A naked woman had hurt him somewhere along the line, and badly. He'd never gotten over it. She wondered who that intimate friend had been. And why the woman had left him when he'd cared about her so much.

Robin pulled off her right glove. "The coffee's perking, Mr. Parker. If you don't take it off the stove it will soon be strong enough to walk off by itself."

"So it will."

He rose, pulled his sleeve down over his hand, and dragged the pot to a cooler spot on the far side of the stove. Setting two cups down, he began filling them, working from one to the other, evening out the contents. "Well, this ain't too bad. We each got a full cup out of it."

He suppressed a smile as he carefully walked back, set a cup in front of Robin, then slid into his chair again. He sat facing her this time, his elbows on either side of his tin cup. Misty spirals of steam rose and melted the remaining clumps of ice in his beard. Drips began to splat on the table.

She sipped her coffee.

"Mrs. Hale," he said, his voice low, "you can't expect to move halfway across the country and fit right in. You've got to give Colorado a chance. You'll have a life here, too. And I reckon it'll be fine one." He took a moment to blow down into his coffee to cool it. More steam gushed up around his face. "I think I know some of what you're feeling. My first week in Central City, I felt like somebody had cut my heart out. I'd been raised in the desert and took comfort in things like slow-moving rivers, rolling hills that went on forever, and scraggly palo verde trees that wouldn't give shade to an ant 'less he crawled up the trunk and skittered under a branch. Texas, for all its emptiness, was warm and friendly. The Rockies ain't. They're about as cold and aloof as a place can be. Now don't go getting crazy when I say this, but this mountain range is a lot like a woman. She don't give a man nothing for free. He's got to earn it, and she's gonna make it as goddamned hard as she can, 'cause she wants to know what he's made of before she'll open her arms and snuggle up to him."

"That cold woman must have hurt you very badly, Mr. Parker. I'm sorry she did. She ruined your opinion of women."

He straightened in his chair as if stung by her perceptivity. "Well, I didn't have much of one to begin with."

"What was her name?"

A triangular pucker of skin formed between Garrison's bushy brows. He grimaced at his coffee. Outside, wind whistled around the cabin's eaves, soft, mournful, and flurries of snow crystals gusted by. The sun's warmth had dissolved the fog, liquefying it into white stringers of cloud that curled around the highest peaks.

"Just in case it matters," Robin said, and he looked up at her. "I didn't expect an answer to that question."

"No?"

"No."

A faint smile tugged at his mouth, as if he were grateful.

Robin drank more coffee. That look warmed her deep down. Though war was pure hell, she missed the camaraderie of men. The unselfish tenderness of one soldier to another could not be compared to any other kind of relationship. In many ways, bonds established during combat possessed more power than those of wedlock. They involved no sexual bargaining, no pleading for affection, or bantering to establish dominance. At least, not at the front lines. You covered your friend's back and knew without looking that he was covering yours. Unlike marriage, that kind of trust could not be broken by a harsh word, or look, or even by failing in your duty. No, not even death could break the bond of one soldier to another. At Gettysburg, she had watched four soldiers grab their dead friends and try to drag them to safety. One of those soldiers had been a woman. Each had known perfectly well that he was risking his life for a corpse, but the need to pull his friend out of the line of fire overwhelmed all other considerations.

In the final analysis, terror reduced men and women to the single most basic human need—to protect and to be protected. . . . All else was contrived.

Garrison finished his coffee and set the cup down, waiting for Robin to do the same. He twined his fingers and watched her.

"You make a good pot of coffee, Mr. Parker." She drank her last few swallows. "Thank you. I guess I needed this time to talk more than I thought." She put her cup down and gazed around the cabin. "You love this place, don't you?"

He nodded. "I do. More than I can tell you. That's why I was such a jackass the first night we met. I was just scared silly about losing my cabin." He shifted uncomfortably in his chair. "I am still hoping we can work something out so I—"

"We will, Mr. Parker. I don't want to kill you near as badly now as I did then."

He smiled. "I appreciate that. Well, you ready to go see that shaft?"

"Whenever you are."

He shoved his chair back and fetched his buffalo coat and hat from the foot of his bed. While Robin put her gloves on, he slipped his arms through his coat sleeves. Muscles strained against the faded blue fabric of his army shirt.

"Come on," he said. "It ain't far. We can walk."

Her boots crunched on ice as she followed him up a narrow, winding game trail, then angled down over the crest of the hill. Dusty morning sunlight reflected blindingly from the haze of blowing snow. Robin held her hood closed at her throat and squinted against the glare. In the distance, the orb of the sun had turned to molten copper. It wavered in illusory glory through the remaining wisps of fog.

Robin shoved her hands in her cape pockets and walked down a steep incline behind him. The trail swerved right around the face of the hill. She stopped when she saw the gaping hole in the mountainside. It yawned about six feet in diameter, yellow tailings had fallen from it to roll down the hillside.

"It's larger than I'd imagined," she said. "When you said a tunnel I thought you meant—"

"Looks wide out here," Garrison said, "but inside you'll have to duck. Ceiling's awfully uneven. Be careful."

The maw faced east, allowing the sun to stream in. It lit the opening with a torchlike brilliance, but faded to obscurity the further she went into the belly of the mountain. Jagged rocks protruded from the roof and spiked from the floor and walls. Robin took her time, so she didn't trip. She paused to pick up a strange looking metal object. It resembled a railroad spike, but had a hook on one side and circlet of iron on the other. "Mr. Parker? What is this?"

He turned. "Candlespike. You hammer 'em into the solid rock, then set a candle into that round circle and it gives you light to work by."

"I see." She put it back on the floor. "How far does this shaft go back?"

"Not near far enough. About another hundred feet." Garrison had one hand braced on the right wall. He walked bent over, taking small steps in the growing darkness. "If your dear uncle, may God rest his damnable soul, had possessed the sense of a gopher, he would have opened this tunnel a hundred yards closer to where my cabin sets."

"Why?"

" 'Cause that's where the main ore body breaks the surface. Didn't make no sense whatsoever to sink the discovery tunnel here."

Down the center of the tunnel a smooth path had been carved, as if Collier had leveled this route deliberately. Perhaps as a road to haul ore?

"Now, Mrs. Hale," Garrison said. "There's a steep drop-off up ahead. Watch your step."

"I will," she said absently. Her eyes had just caught the glitters of the gold in the ceiling. Nuggets the size of her fist stuck out of the rock. Excitement raced through her veins, leaving her feeling lightheaded. Dear God, the worth of this claim must approach a million dollars! Perhaps more. Her heart started to pound, in a fine imitation of Garrison's description of "gold fever."

"Mr. Parker?" she called. "I think I finally understand what you meant by . . ."

When she placed her foot atop dark nothingness, she knew instantly what she had done. She made a frantic grasp for solid rock, missed, and fell. It seemed to take an eternity before she struck bottom. Black shapes rose up before her eyes like lunging monsters. One hit her in the chest, and she rolled over and over through the swirling darkness, her arms flailing, until she slammed against something cold and dark at the bottom of the shaft. She lay on her face, gasping.

"Mrs. Hale? Mrs. Hale!"

Garrison's frantic voice sounded so very far away, like cannon fire from a distant battlefield.

She heard rocks falling, feet slipping on gravel.

Vaguely, she felt him turn her over. Her vision pitched and swayed, and through a reeling sea of disconnected images she saw the hideous fear on his face and knew he was asking her questions, but she could not quite hear him.

The agony in her chest brought instant understanding.

My rib . . . Oh, God.

His hands felt warm when they unbuttoned the front of her dress, pulled apart the hooks on her basque, and touched her breasts . . .

Arms slid beneath her shoulders and knees, and she smelled fragrances of woodsmoke and coffee, and knew her cheek pressed against his shoulder. Her next memory was of sunlight striking her face with agonizing brilliance. His long running steps affected her like hammer blows to her chest, ripping her apart.

Her stomach pumped . . . and pumped again . . . Darkness crept in with the stealth of an assassin and annihilated the light. Amidst the blackness, a shattered face formed.

Like a puzzle.

Relentlessly, she put it together, drawing the eyes from the upper right corner, the mouth from the bottom left, a lock of red hair from the very center.

Thomas Corley.

Jeremy!

Terror forced a name from her lips, a name almost too difficult to remember, but vital, and it brought immediate reply:

"Macey ain't here, Mrs. Hale. But I am. I'm right here. Don't be scared. I'm here."

Honey snorted and leaped sideways when Garrison ran past and kicked his front door open. It struck the log wall with a resounding crack as he lunged inside.

Mrs. Hale's face had gone white and bloodless, and though he had covered her injury with her blue cape, in his mind he could still see the rib thrusting up, slicing through her chest wall. With the toe of his boot, he tore the Hudson's Bay blanket from his bed and eased her tall body down onto clean white sheets.

For a moment, he stood looking down at her, breathing hard.

Her beautiful pale face had sunk into his feather pillow, and her long braid snaked out across his bed like a midnight rope. Blood soaked her clothing. He tore back her cape and dress and pressed both palms around the rib to try to quell the flow.

"It's all right, Mrs. Hale," he whispered. "Just sleep. I'll take care of things. Everything's going to be all right."

War had forced him to learn many things, including makeshift field surgery, but he'd never dealt with an injury so severe. He'd set arms and legs . . . but ribs . . . He didn't even know where to begin. Did he have to slit a hole big enough that he could see the connecting part of the rib, to make sure he could fit the ends back together?

Mrs. Hale moaned. It came as a soft, anguished sound. She struggled, trying to get up.

"Lay still, damn it."

She seemed to hear. Her taut muscles relaxed and her head lolled to the side again.

When the blood flow slowed a little, Garrison threaded her arms through her vomit-soiled clothing and undressed her completely. In the gut-wrenching terror, he barely noticed her nakedness.

But . . . but he did notice other things. With his right hand, he touched each old bullet wound, four in all, and the place where shrapnel had lacerated her left thigh. Finally he moved his fingers to the puckered burns on her calves. When had she run through a fire?

He wet his dry lips, wondering.

Garrison rose, poured water into the wash basin, then pulled a clean rag from the small drawer in the basin stand, and carried the basin to the side of the bed, where he set it on the wood floor.

Kneeling, he dipped the cloth in the water and tenderly washed the co-agulated blood from her side. The sight made him sick. The jagged end of bone protruded just beneath her left breast. Splinters of rib glistened in the wound. He'd have to pick each one out.

"For God's sake, Mrs. Hale," he said as he washed her beautiful face and neck. *"Didn't you hear me?* I told you about that drop! I told you!"

Riding for the doctor was out of the question. She could go into shock, or start vomiting again and choke and die. He'd have to try to set the bone by himself.

It had to be done.

Quickly. To get it closed up before infection set in.

Garrison stroked her pale cheek with unthinking intimacy, letting his fingers trace the line of her jaw. "Shouldn't take long, Mrs. Hale. Just sleep. Sleep as deep as you can."

Garrison slumped into the chair he'd pulled up by Mrs. Hale's bedside and rubbed his aching eyes. Outside, the constellation Orion wavered through patchy clouds. What time did that mean it was? Two o'clock in the morning? Three? Snowflakes pirouetted from the sky, mounding up on the window sill, scalloping the edges with a thin ruffle of white. The oil lamp on the kitchen table flickered and spat, bringing shadows to life; the old cast-iron pots hanging on the wall transformed themselves into birds and fluttered around the room, while the woodstove waddled back and forth across the floor in a poor imitation of a fat goose.

Garrison lifted his cup of coffee from where he'd held it on his knee and took a drink. Cold, hours old, it tasted scorched.

He drank it anyway and listened to Mrs. Hale.

She'd been delirious for two or three hours. The fever had begun in early evening, just after he'd finished setting her rib. He'd plucked bone chips from her wound, pushed the ends of rib back together, cleaned the gash, then torn a sheet into strips and securely wrapped her chest. She'd slept soundly until the fever got too high.

". . . Sarah," Mrs. Hale whispered urgently, "Sarah Slater, Mr. President." Garrison rested his bearded chin on his chest and sighed.

"No. No, sir. Only if Richmond falls . . . conspiracy has asked . . ."

In the throes of the fever, her outbursts ranged from coherent remarks to complete gibberish, but Garrison had pieced some of the story together. Sarah Slater, it seemed, worked as a spy for the Confederacy. Mrs. Hale had detailed much of Mrs. Slater's life to "the President" as if part of a report. Sarah had been born in Connecticut of French parents and moved to North Carolina in 1858. She had married Rowen Slater in June of 1861, and when he'd enlisted in Company A of the 20th North Carolina Infantry, Sarah had begun her covert activities. On one occasion, if Garrison had understood, Sarah had assumed the role of a French woman and carried important papers and money from Richmond to Canada to be used for the defense of Confederate agents being held for the St. Albans, Vermont, bank raid where over $200,000 had been stolen. The papers supported the fact that the agents were not thieves, but were on a secret mission for the Confederacy. As a result, the Canadian judge had refused to extradite the agents to the United States for trial. On her way back to Richmond, Sarah Slater had met a man named John Harrison Surratt in New York and he had escorted her through Maryland, helping her make her way safely across the Potomac, and back to the Confederacy.

"I . . . I don't know, Mr. President," Mrs. Hale struggled weakly, her head moving from side to side. Her facial muscles worked as if in distaste. Sweat beaded on her nose and ran down her smooth cheeks, soaking the black hair that framed her face. "If necessary . . . but . . . I can arrange the naval connection . . . steamer *Harriet De Ford* . . . if we capture and run her down Chesapeake Bay . . . Sarah has already met with Booth . . . he'll send his theatrical costumes, prompt books, other belongings to the Bahamas . . . after . . . he'll hide on shores of Potomac . . . then the steamer will pick him up . . . run the blockade . . ."

Garrison walked to the stove to refill his cup with hot coffee. The floorboards creaked when he picked up the pot, and Mrs. Hale stopped murmuring. She lay still, as if frightened. Her long braid had fallen over the side of the bed and looked very black against the tumbled blankets she had thrown off in her fever. Garrison poured, and the coffee came out like tar, thick and black. To make it drinkable, he added a third cup of water from the battered tea kettle that sat above the stove on the warming shelf. Tiny tornadoes of steam lifted from the surface.

Mrs. Hale maintained her silence.

Clutching his cup in both hands, Garrison walked to the window to watch the snow fall. The flakes had turned fluffy. A patchwork quilt of black and gray clouds covered the sky. Every so often a star would pop out, flare, then vanish beneath the storm's billowing onslaught. At dusk, he'd turned Mrs. Hale's horse loose, and the gelding now wandered along behind Honey, his back glittering white, grazing on whatever he could paw free from the frozen ground.

Mrs. Hale moaned, "Yes, I . . . if *Harriet De Ford* can't . . . Canadian yacht . . . maybe the *Octavia* . . . owner . . . he . . . might be willing . . . Oh, I'm . . . hot . . . so hot . . ." In an effort to kick off her blanket, she tried to roll over.

Garrison bounded back, put his coffee in the seat of the chair, and sat on the edge of the bed. "No, Mrs. Hale, don't do that. *Don't move.* You've already lost a lot of blood. If you tear open that wound again, you're liable to feel a whole lot worse. Can you hear me?"

He reached down for the rag in the washbasin on the floor and wrung it out. The clean water felt icy cold. No matter how hot the cabin became, the area near the floor always remained frigid. Gently, he mopped her face and throat, then lifted each of her arms and wet them down. She sank back into the bed, yielding to the coolness.

"Better?" he asked. He hadn't expected an answer, so when her dark eyes fluttered open and fixed on him, he asked, "You awake?"

She stared up with glassy eyes. Her voice sounded almost reverent. "You're very kind to—to do this."

He eyed her speculatively. Did she know him? Or was she still lost in another time? "Well, it ain't no trouble."

"I—I don't know how to thank you . . . Mother . . . she . . . she's been so frightened. The siege . . . she had to get out of Richmond."

"I understand," he answered as if he did. "I'll get her out. Don't you worry none."

"Augusta is the only place she can go . . . she has a sister . . ." A sudden stricken expression tensed her face. Her head rolled sideways and she peered at him. "He . . . he won't find her there, will he?"

"No. I don't think so."

"But . . . do you think he'll seek her out? I mean, to try to get a clue as to where I've gone?"

"I doubt it, but can she tell him?"

Mrs. Hale shook her head, or maybe she shuddered. Her whole body seemed to pick up the motion, and it occurred to Garrison that it might be fear—of "him?" "No. No, I . . . I'd never endanger her by telling her anything about my . . ."

Her voice dropped to an unintelligible whisper. Garrison continued the dialogue. "Then don't fret about it. If she don't know where you've gone, he can't find out. You're safe. You understand me? You're safe now. Stop worrying about him."

"But he might . . . might hurt her."

"Even if she can't tell him nothing?"

"Yes. I fear for her."

Mrs. Hale clenched her teeth, and a sudden sweat made her skin shimmer in the orange gleam of lamplight. Garrison bent over and brought up the blanket again, tucking it around her sides, drawing it to her chin.

"Then he's a Goddamned sonofabitch," Garrison whispered tenderly, "and somebody's sure to shoot him pretty quick, if he ain't already dead. Try to get some sleep now, Mrs. Hale. There's nothing more you can do. Least not 'til you get yourself well."

She blinked at the shadows dancing on the ceiling, and appeared to drift from one memory to another. Her expressions changed by the second, hatred, happiness, sheer terror . . . "I—I hate this place," she said.

"You still have to try to get some rest."

"Why do they keep us here. Can't we go back to Old Capitol?"

"Not right now."

"Carroll is nothing but a typhoid factory."

Tears filled her eyes, and they touched something vulnerable inside Garrison. He wrung out his rag and wiped the sweat from her forehead again. She leaned into his hand and closed her eyes.

"They—sent Belle home last week. And I feel so hot."

Garrison frowned. Belle . . . Boyd? The famed Confederate spy? Was Carroll, then, Carroll prison? If he remembered right, that's where Boyd had been held.

"Well, you ain't got the typhoid, and I can tell you that for a fact, so calm down. You're going to be fine, if you'll just try—"

"No, no, it's all right. The doctor told me yesterday. But . . . why won't they send me home? Why would they . . . why would they send Belle home and make me stay? I want to go home. I want to go so badly. My son needs me."

She turned her face away from him to the log wall. Tears ran silently down her cheeks.

It could just be the fever. Pure imagination. But if she had known the people she claimed, and had been incarcerated in Old Capitol and Carroll prisons . . . somebody thought her dangerous. Damned dangerous. "Him?" Had she been one of Jefferson Davis' own couriers? It sounded like it.

"I want to go home," she pleaded. "I want to go home. Please. I just want to go homeIwanttogohome . . ."

She kept repeating it over and over as she sobbed.

He reached out and stroked her dark hair. "You are home, R—Rose," he said, trying an old trick that he'd seen work more than once during the war. "Look around. You're sick. Things may not look exactly right, but they seem familiar don't they? Jeremy's asleep in his bed over there. Safe and sound. See your . . ." *What?* He tried to think. "See your mirror and your hairbrush? You threw your favorite dress over the back of the chair when you got back from supper. Your boots are by the door." Her face calmed as her eyes moved about the room. "You're home. You're home, and you're safe, and you've got to get some rest because you're sick. Now try, darlin'. Close your eyes and don't worry about nothing. Just dream of being home. Jeremy's fine. You're fine. I'm fine. Everybody's . . ."

She reached up, gripped his hand, and pulled it down to kiss his calloused palm. Her lips felt soft and hot, so very hot. "Oh, Charles," she whispered forlornly. "I've been so afraid. I've been having nightmares, about lions and flaming rivers, and I—"

"Well, that's all they were. Nightmares. Now, I . . ." He debated on whether or not to say it, then decided to. "I'm right here, and I ain't leaving your side. So for God's sake, get some sleep. Will you listen to me for once?"

A faint trembling smile touched her lips, and she closed her eyes like a dutiful soldier. In only a few minutes, her breathing changed to the deep rhythms of sleep. Garrison eased his hand from her grip and tucked her arm beneath the blanket.

Charles. Her husband.

Garrison went to the stove and fed it more wood, keeping the cabin hot, as hot as he could stand it, hoping to break her fever. He used his iron poker to get the logs to lie flat over the bed of red coals, then hung it back on the peg on the wall. Pine sap crackled as it boiled away into a fine sweet fragrance.

Damn, he was tired.

Yawning, he stretched his tired back muscles and went to put a hand very lightly on her forehead. Still burning up. If the fever didn't break soon, he'd have to carry her out and pack her in a snowbank. Once, a very long time ago, he'd done that to a wounded friend in California's Sierra Nevada mountains. Jake's fever had gone down all right, and when he'd come to, he'd shown his gratitude by thinking up some mighty useful curse words to call Garrison.

But Jake had not been anywhere near as sick as Mrs. Hale. Garrison scrutinized her worriedly.

He had to get her a doctor. Tomorrow. No matter what.

CHAPTER 22

Outside, horse hooves squealed on ice. Garrison lifted his head and listened. Wind shrieked, rattling the loose windowpanes, sending silver veils of ice crystals gusting by. Between obscuring blasts, the wolfish gray-brown bulk of the mountains appeared and disappeared with unearthly grace. Had he heard the hooves in his dreams?

He had slept in a cramped position, his upper torso bent across the table, and all night long one dream after another had plagued him, keeping him suspended in that hazy realm between real sleep and wakefulness. All of his dreams had been about war.

Scenes of the Fort Fillmore guardhouse where he'd been incarcerated for six months continued to linger in his mind. He'd spent hours pulling straw out of the adobe walls, just to have something to do. Fillmore had been overcrowded, with underfed men too weak from the New Mexico heat, and the killing thirst, to do more than lie in their own filth and listen to the Mexican bandits calling taunts from the other side of the Rio Grande. More than once, he'd thought he was going to die in that stinking hole—but, finally, he'd been exchanged.

Garrison squinted out the window. Dawn had broken cold, sunless, and gray. Pallid light shimmered from six inches of new snow. By the crisp scent of the wind, he knew there would be more snow before the day ended.

Garrison got to his feet and stretched his arms while he yawned. The last log he'd added to the fire had been damp, and the pungent smell of creosote filled the cabin. Forcing his tired legs to work, he crossed to the stove and shoved more wood into the firebox. Then he refilled his empty coffee pot with water and grounds and set it over the hottest spot to boil. Water trickled down the sides of the old pot and sizzled on the stove.

Across the room, Mrs. Hale lay on her back, the smooth sculpted curves of her body evident beneath the blanket. Her long braid had grown frizzy from the heat and sweat, and her eyes had sunken into dark blue bruises. Garrison's throat tightened. She looked damned bad. Her chest moved with swift shallow breaths.

He had started across to check her temperature when a familiar voice called: "Hello, the cabin!"

Garrison bounded for the door and opened it a crack. Mike Hathaway stood silhouetted against the dove-colored gleam of dawn. He finished tying his horse to the hitching rail, tugged his hat down, and trudged through the snow for the door.

"Mike, I am so glad to see you that I could kiss you."

"You ought to. I wouldn't get up at three in the morning to ride through a blizzard for just anybody. Where the hell have you been? You all right?"

"I'm fine, but—well, come in. I'll tell you about it while you warm up."

He opened the door wider, and in a billowing cloud of frigid air Hathaway entered. Snow crusted the red hair that stuck out beneath the medium brim of his brown hat. As Hathaway batted the frost from his sleeves, his blue eyes landed on Mrs. Hale and widened.

"What the *hell* happened?"

"Sit down, Mike. I'll pour you a cup of coffee. It's a long story."

The pot had just started to perk. While Mike took off his coat, draped it over the back of his chair, and dropped into the seat, Garrison poured two cups. The brew wasn't nearly as strong as he liked it, but the second cup would be. He set the pot back on the stove to keep perking and took the other chair. He slid one cup across to Mike.

"Happened yesterday about eight in the morning," Garrison explained. "I warned her about that drop-off in back of the shaft, but she was caught up looking at the web of gold in the ceiling and I didn't notice 'til too late—"

"My Lord, she fell? Down that steep incline?"

Garrison nodded. "Yes, she did. I was too far away. I couldn't stop her."

Mike's cold-flushed face had gone serious. The nostrils of his flat nose flared. "How is she?"

Garrison gestured helplessly. "She broke a rib. Bone sliced through the chest wall. I set it and been tending it as best I am able, but she needs a doctor. Bad, too. I know it's asking a lot on a day like this, but can you—"

"Hell, of course, I can! I'll bring Doc Smithers back. I might have to poke a gun barrel down his left ear to get his attention, but he'll come all right."

"Thanks, Mike."

Mike's eyes moved thoughtfully for a moment. "Unless it's snowing too bad, Garry. If it is, not even threatening his life will get that squint-eyed no account up here. You know that, don't you?"

"I do. We'll make out best we can 'til you get back—whenever that is."

Garrison lifted his cup and sipped the scalding black brew. Tasted weak, but good nonetheless. Steam condensed in his mustache and beard. The drops sparkled in the faint gleam of the oil lamp. He had turned the wick low before he'd drifted off to sleep, but only a shallow pool of kerosene remained in the glass base. It would be gone in half an hour and he'd have to refill it from the jug beneath his bed.

"What made you ride up?" Garrison asked.

Mike gripped his cup in gloved hands. "Macey Runkles had the spunk to come get me out of bed last evening. She waited as long as she could, then she bundled up that boy, hitched the buggy and drove hell-for-leather for my house to tell me that Mrs. Hale had not come home. She was downright crazy with fear. Said something cryptic about how Mrs. Hale was scared of some fella, but she didn't know who. But wasn't nothing I could do last night, snow was falling too thick in town. I told her I'd leave as soon as the storm let up." Mike took a drink of his coffee and winced when it burned a pathway down his throat.

They both peered at Mrs. Hale. She hadn't moved, but her breathing seemed more rapid, causing the blanket to puff up and down as if a small frightened animal huddled beneath it. Garrison shook his head. So, she'd told Macey about the man pursuing her. Interesting.

The cabin had heated up quickly. Already Garrison's faded blue shirt clung to his sides in sweaty patches.

"There's something else, Garry," Mike said.

Garrison frowned. Mike's voice had taken on a somber tone. "What?"

"Blaine Harding delivered a special edition of the *Rocky Mountain News* yesterday afternoon. The stage driver had whipped his horses half to death to get them up the mountain."

Hathaway reached into the pocket of his green shirt and pulled out a newspaper. Without a word, he unfolded it and laid it in the center of the table next to the oil lamp.

The headlines struck Garrison like a blunt blow to the stomach. He bent over, unable to breathe.

PRESIDENT LINCOLN ASSASSINATED!!
NOTED THESPIAN JOHN WILKES BOOTH SOUGHT IN CRIME!

Like a deer clubbed in the head, he couldn't think, he could only stare. No, it couldn't be the same. Could it? Garrison found his voice. "Booth? Booth was the name of the assassin?"

Hathaway nodded. "I guess he was supposed to be a well-known actor in Washington City."

An actor. A stage idol. He had killed the president.

There had to be thousands of men named Booth, but . . . "Was he working alone? Who—who else was in on it with him? Was it a conspiracy?"

His memory began a horrifying answer to that question, listing the names of the accomplices: *Mrs. Sarah Slater, John Harrison Surratt, Jefferson Davis* . . . "

"The article names a few suspects." Hathaway turned the paper sideways and read: "George Atzerodt, Lewis Paine, David Herald and Mary Surratt. Those are the ones they're sure of, but I guess—"

"*Mary* Surratt," Garrison asked breathlessly. "Not John Surratt?"

Hathaway's blue eyes narrowed. He studied Garrison long and hard. Shadows filled in the wrinkles around his mouth. "The paper don't list a John Surratt. Where would you come up with that name?"

Garrison braced his elbows on the table and massaged his taut forehead. His belly had started to churn as thoughts skittered willy-nilly through his brain, but beneath the chaos of images and fragments of sentences, an agonized voice whispered, *No. No, sir. Only if Richmond falls . . . Sarah has already met with Booth . . . he'll send his theatrical costumes . . . hide on shores of the Potomac . . .* And he'd be waiting for a steamer named the *Harriet de Ford,* manned by a Confederate crew, to pick him up and take him to the Bahamas.

Dear God, I'm sheltering one of the conspirators in my cabin.

Garrison peered across the room at Mrs. Hale's pale beautiful face. She looked like a wounded angel, her head tilted toward him. One naked shoulder lay exposed.

No, no, it just wasn't possible.

Swallowing down a constricted throat, Garrison said, as casually as he could, "Is there any concern about a Confederate plot?"

"How'd you know that?" Hathaway asked. "Secretary of War Stanton is screaming it to the high heavens! He claims Jeff Davis himself was behind it. What would make *you* think of that?"

"Anybody with sense would wonder, Mike," he answered reasonably, and attempted to maintain his casual demeanor. "I mean, after Lee's surrender, assassination would be the South's only hope of bleeding the heart out of the Union."

He fiddled with his sleeve cuffs, pulling them down over his wrists, rubbing the threadbare blue fabric, then he gripped his coffee cup with both hands.

Like most other former Union officers, the mere mention of Lincoln's name engendered reverence in Garrison. For four long years, the tall, sallow-faced lawyer from Illinois had presided over a crumbling nation, fought valiantly and desperately to pick up the pieces . . . and been murdered for his noble efforts. The fact left Garrison feeling as hollow as a rusty old bucket. Anger mixed with his welling grief and exhaustion, leaving him shaky. He released his coffee cup and folded his hands in his lap.

"Goddamn, I'm tired," he whispered.

"That makes two of us," Hathaway said. "Sorry I had to be the one to bring you the news, but I figured you'd want to know right off."

"You were right."

They looked at each other steadily and in silence.

"You ain't gonna tell me how you knew them things, are you?"

"No. Not 'til I . . . I know more, Mike. I need to read every word in the paper and ponder on it for a time."

"Uh-huh." Hathaway stretched his legs out across the floor and heaved a ragged breath. Snow had melted off his boots. The sizable pool that had formed under the chair glittered and winked in the lamplight. "Who, may I ask, is John Surratt? Somebody you know?"

Garrison shook his head. "No."

"Well, then, how do you—"

"Mike," he interrupted. "I said I needed time to think on it, and I meant it."

"But what's there to think on? I mean either you know something or you don't, and if you do—"

"Damn it, Mike! I'll tell you when I'm ready, and I ain't ready!"

"All right," Mike said and held up a hand defensively. "In that case, I'd best finish my coffee and get moving down the trail. I should be back by nightfall." He stood up and rebuttoned his coat.

"I—I didn't mean to sound so crazy, Mike," Garrison apologized. "I'm just . . . I ain't of a mind to discuss—"

"That's your business, Garry, but I hope you'll talk more with me later," he said and genuine concern laced his voice. "Because if you know something about this—for whatever reason—we'd damn well better telegraph the information to Washington and *pronto.*"

Garrison lowered his eyes to stare at the table top while he ground his teeth.

Hathaway walked toward the door, casting a curious look at Mrs. Hale. Before he walked out into the snow, he stopped, tugged on his hat brim, and added, "I want you to think on something, Garry."

Garrison looked up, frowning. "And that is?"

"You don't want to be accused of abetting a thing like this—and withholding information would be abetting—because Washington is certainly going to hang anybody and everybody they can point a finger at."

I am in Tennessee and Charles lies dead at my feet. Men are shouting and screaming orders. Through tears I watch the rain falling, pattering in the small puddles around Charles' tall body.

The pillar of strength upon which I have relied for six years is gone . . . Nowhere in the world is there anyone I can turn to. I have never been this alone.

My mind travels back through the years to a windswept pine grove near the ocean. Sumter has just fallen. Black smoke curls from the fort and Charles stands next to me, holding our infant son in his arms. His voice is agonized, "I can't believe it's happened. The damned fools. This wanton act will bring nothing but despair and death!"

I say nothing.

I am afraid of dying, afraid of watching things die, but being dead, that is a prospect I have often contemplated with strange longing.

Some nights, in the aftermath of battle, when the cries of the wounded rose all around me, the word "death" tasted unutterably sweet on my tongue.

As I look down upon Charles, so quiet and still in the Tennessee mud, that sweetness returns to taunt me. Dear God, how desperately I wish he were here with me . . . or I there with him.

I could be . . . couldn't I?

Out there, somewhere very close, is terrible pain.

If I just let go . . .

The thought makes me feel scattered, stunned, the fragment of heart left in me filled with self-hatred.

I hear Jeremy crying. Crying and crying my name . . .

Robin, groggy, murmured as she climbed through the layers of slumber to wakefulness. Silver daylight streamed through the cabin windows and onto her face. When she opened her eyes, the log walls looked unfamiliar. She blinked. Her heart began to pound. Snow fell outside, but through the white veil, she saw mountains. The majestic scenery belonged to a foreign country for all she knew. Panic blended with the searing pain in her chest. She turned her head, and saw a tall man with curly brown hair and a long beard sitting at the table with a newspaper spread before him.

Memories flooded back . . . the mine shaft, her fall, Mr. Parker's horrified face.

Robin lifted a trembling hand to smooth tousled hair from her eyes and noticed she was dressed in one of his red and black checkered shirts. The flannel rested warmly on her arms. He had undressed her. She lowered her hand and felt the thick bandage that wrapped her chest. It was good work, a fine sturdy field dressing. Obviously he had carried her here, tended her wound, put her in his bed, and been staying up to watch over her—at least his haggard face suggested as much.

"Mr. Parker?" Robin said in a scratchy voice.

He sprinted across the room to look down on her with bloodshot eyes as he put a hand on her forehead. Robin shivered, conscious of the deft lightness of his touch. "Thank God," he said. "Your fever's broke."

"I owe you . . . a very great deal. Thank you."

Mr. Parker sank down on the chair at her bedside. "How are you feeling?"

"Like I've run a thousand miles." Indeed, her arms and legs had turned as heavy as granite.

"You ought to. You had a rough go of it." He studied every line in her face. "But you look better. You've got a little more color in your cheeks today."

Robin gazed at the ceiling. "How long have I been out?"

"About a day and a half," Garrison answered. "It's been snowing the whole time. We have got about two feet of fresh powder."

"My horse?"

"He's out there with Honey. They seem to have become fast friends." He patted her arm tenderly. "Are you hungry?"

"Yes. I am."

His chair creaked as he rose and walked to a cast-iron pot on the stove to dip out a tin cup of liquid. He returned to sit on the edge of her bed, stirring it with a spoon. "Here, try some of this broth."

Gently, he lifted her hand and put the cup in it, but took it back when he found her fingers too weak to hold it. "I'm going to lift you up a little so you can take a sip. You ready?"

"Yes."

He slipped an arm beneath her shoulders and raised her up about three inches, then tipped the cup to her mouth. She sipped the warm liquid cautiously at first, then hungrily.

"Not too fast, Mrs. Hale. 'Less you want it to come right back up."

The broth left a warm glow in her stomach that filtered down to her toes and out to the tips of her fingers. When the cup was finished, he lowered her head to the pillow again.

"That was very good, Garrison . . . oh, please forgive me, Mr. Parker. I didn't mean to be so familiar. I just—"

"I'd be very pleased if you would call me Garrison, Mrs. Hale."

She inclined her head. "You are very kind. I would also be pleased if you would call me Rose . . . The soup—it tasted rich and sweet, like wild game. Was it?"

The cup clinked as he set it on the floor. "Elk. With a few onions and some salt. There ain't nothing better to give you back your strength."

She smiled, and a glimmer lit his eyes, but the warmth died quickly, replaced by a darker emotion. His jaw set, as if he were appraising her anew and wasn't sure he liked what he saw.

"What's wrong?"

"Nothing." He tried to smile. "I just . . . I'm glad to see you awake. That's all."

As if anxious to be on his feet, he rose and walked to the table to turn up the wick on the lamp, then moved to the stove to shift the broth pot to a new position. His shadow streamed long and dark behind him.

Robin frowned. He seemed . . . nervous. He marched to the window, where he stood watching the snow fall with a contemplative frown on his face. At last, he returned to stand at her bedside.

Quietly, Robin said, "Tell me."

"I don't think I will. Not yet."

"Something's . . . bothering you. What is it?"

He spread his feet, folded his arms across his broad chest, and started to speak, but stopped, hesitant. His hazel eyes shone unusually green in the clear radiance of the oil lamp. In them, Robin read signs of struggle—pain and confusion, a strange sort of fascination.

Without a word, he walked to the table, retrieved the newspaper, and brought it back, handing it to her before he dropped into the chair again.

It took a great deal of strength to steady the paper while she read the headlines.

She let her head fall back to her pillow.

So . . .

Six months ago, it might have made a difference, but after Appomattox? Why had Davis gone through with the plan? Or had it been Davis? Perhaps not. The Confederate Congress, after all, had fled Richmond and was on the run. Norris? In the chaos, he might have been unable to contact the president. In that case, the Confederate Secret Service director might have authorized the project himself, figuring it his nation's last best hope.

Quietly, Garrison asked, "Is this the project Sarah Slater was involved in?"

Robin closed her eyes. She couldn't breathe. "Who?"

"Sarah Slater."

"I . . . I don't know that name. I—"

"Don't you? Well, that's good, Mrs. Ha—R-Rose. It had me worried. It sounded like you were the one who recommended her to Davis."

The fever. I must have been delirious . . . jabbering like a . . . a fool . . .

"What are you talking about, Garrison?"

His lips pursed into a bloodless line. "Never mind. I shouldn't have opened my mouth, not so soon. You need your rest, we'll talk about it more when you're—"

"No. No, tell me." Robin *had* to know. "Did I . . . say things during my fever?"

He took a deep breath, as if to fortify himself for her answers. "Quite a few things. They were in fragments, though. So I ain't sure if I put them together right."

"What fragments?"

"You talked about Slater, and about how you set up the transportation for Booth's escape on the *Harriet de Ford*. Or will it be that Canadian ship, the *Octavia?*" He sounded angry now and a little frightened.

Robin weakly turned to meet his eyes. He ran a hand through his curly hair, shook his head, and rose to pace the floor. The wood creaked beneath his feet.

After several moments, he stopped pacing and turned his head ever so slightly to look at Robin. The golden gleam of lamplight haloed his beard and glinted in his right eye. His face might have been chiseled from marble.

"Where on the Potomac is Booth hiding?" he asked.

Robin shook her head. "Who?"

"The assassin. The man who murdered the president."

"Oh . . ." she whispered. "The man named in the paper."

"When is he supposed to be picked up?"

"Garrison, I don't—"

"*When!*" His voice was still quiet, but the word was an order.

Robin placed her hands over her bandages and probed her injury, wincing at the pain. Her voice came out so low it was barely audible. "I don't know the answer to that, Garrison. I'm sorry, I—"

"Where are John Harrison Surratt and Mrs. Slater?"

"Who? Who are they?"

"Are they out of the country?" Garrison stroked his beard and his eyes slitted. "Is that why you're being pursued? The *federales* suspected—"

"*Federales?*" she asked.

"Mexican term, means federal officers. Did the Union suspect you were involved in this plot to kill the President and assigned a Secret Service..."

Dear God, I told him about Corley!

Robin's stomach heaved so suddenly, she couldn't stop it. She thrashed to get her head over the edge of the bed, and Garrison lunged to hold her steady while she vomited onto the floor. His arm around her shoulders felt cool and strong. When her stomach had emptied itself, dry heaves racked her. Shivering, tears streaking her face, Robin could only lie in his arms and endure the spasms while they ran their course. With each convulsion, her broken rib thrust against the bandages, struggling to cut its way out.

It would be so easy... he could turn me over to Corley, report the details about the assassination plot that I revealed, and...

A black haze wavered at the periphery of her vision, closing in, blotting out the world. She gripped Garrison's arm and struggled to pull herself to a sitting position. He sat beside her on the bed, supporting her.

"I... I'm all right," she murmured.

Garrison eased her back onto the sheets and drew the blanket up to cover her chest, then he sat down in the chair, wrung out the rag that lay in the washbasin on the floor, and mopped her face. Robin just lay there, breathing hard, staring up at him. Like fine Indian beadwork, sweat glittered across his forehead and followed the smooth curve of his temple down his cheek. His hands worked gently, soothingly.

"You've done this before," she said in a shaking voice. "I can tell."

"Can you?"

She nodded. "Yes, Major Parker," and she managed a thin smile. "Just as I can tell that you used to interrogate prisoners during the war. I—"

"Nobody near as dangerous as you, Mrs...." he paused, but continued washing her face and neck. "What is your name, anyway?"

When she said nothing, he angrily threw the rag into the basin, stood, and went to the stove. Grabbing a towel, he returned to begin cleaning up her mess. Her eyes followed him as he knelt, wiped the floor, rinsed out the towel in the washbasin, wiped again, rinsed. A log broke in the woodstove and a brief flare of light sheathed the log walls with an orange gleam. The smell of pine tar scented the room.

"Garrison," she said. "I don't know what I told you when I was delirious, but . . . you must believe that I would never be engaged in a plot to assassinate the president. No matter . . ."

He rose and walked away.

She noted the battle raging on his face. He wanted to believe her, but couldn't quite convince himself. So . . . she had told him a very great deal. Enough to make him bitter and confused, and to doubt every word she had just said to him.

Crouching, he jerked a bucket from beneath the woodstove and threw the towel on top of the rest of his dirty clothing, then he shoved it back— awaiting wash day. When he straightened, he propped his hands on his hips.

"There's one thing I have got to know, Rose," he said through a taut exhalation. "And you'd better give me the truth."

"What is it, Garrison?"

"Tell me if you've quit 'em."

"Quit?"

"Are you still working for the Confederate Secret Service? Are you on assignment in Colorado?"

Robin frowned. If he were smart, he'd be wondering what the hell to do with her right now. Wondering whether or not to turn her over to the authorities, or just let her die and bury her out here in some abandoned mine shaft, so he wouldn't be implicated in this mess. She had to tell him something, but just what sort of lie would work?

Robin tugged at her blanket. "I was never an agent for the Confederacy, Garrison," she said. "Though I . . . I knew quite a few. My husband was an officer in the Secret Service, so naturally I know things—"

"Who's the man chasing you?" The question was harsh, impatient. He knew he was getting a runaround.

A breath of wind slipped around the window and made the lamp flicker. Garrison's shadow leaped and wavered on the wall beside Robin as if alive and running, running . . . She couldn't look at it. She focused on the brass buttons on his shirt cuffs where tiny flares of gold danced in reflected brilliance.

"I'm sorry, Garrison. I don't know who you mean. What man?"

"It has nothing to do with Lincoln's assassination? Tell me that."

"I . . . I don't . . ."

Robin's stomach cramped. Outside, there came a sharp startled snort, then a rapid slamming of hooves as horse and mule raced by the cabin. Robin caught sight of them as they passed, two black shapes fleeing into the paler darkness beyond. Playing. Running together. "Please, Garrison—"

"Are you telling me the truth? You didn't have nothing to do with the president's death? You don't know nothing about it? For God's sake, Rose—"

"I don't know anything about it," she said. "I—I don't."

Maybe it was just the way he stood, with his back to the source of light, but his pupils seemed to have dilated, leaving only thin rings of green around deep dark pits. Distrust showed plainly on his face.

"Garrison," she said, "have you ever been delirious?"

"I have."

"Then . . ." she let out a halting breath. "Then you should know that when the body is really hurt, the mind conjures up fantasies, hooks bits of information together that don't belong together, puts people in places they never were, or . . . or ever will be. The mind does . . . anything it can to escape pain."

"That still means, Rose, that you got those bits of information from somewhere and I can't just stand here—!"

"Please." She groped for the paper. It fluttered to the floor at his feet. "Is there any mention of a woman named Slater in those pages?"

"No."

"Or a . . . a steamer named—what did you say? The—"

"The *Harriet de Ford.* No. No mention."

"How about a Canadian ship?"

"No mention of the *Octavia,* neither. No." His square jaw hardened. "But Goddamn, Rose, if Booth was the murderer and he escapes—"

"Garrison." Robin struggled to find the strength to go on speaking. The overwhelming need to sleep plagued her. "Will you . . . give me a chance?"

"I'm trying, Rose. You don't know how hard."

"Surely you realize that . . . every vessel on the Potomac is now under Federal surveillance."

His eyes narrowed. "Go on."

"I'm asking that you *think.* Even if it was a Confederate plot. Even if I . . . if I was involved. *And I was not.* The assassin has no chance of escaping. Andrew Johnson can't afford to let him. Not now." She swallowed and winced at the pain it caused. "Let me speak straightly," she said. "If Davis had authorized such a lunatic mission, such a last ditch effort, he would never have arranged passage . . . not for the assassin. He would want the man dead, and the quicker the better. Think. The war *is* over, and Davis must know it. Which means he also knows that the end will go much harder for the South if the Union discovers that the assassination was a Confederate plan. Do you see what I mean? This Booth would be dead before he ever had a chance to betray the Confederacy. There would be no . . . no passage. No escape for him."

In the amber gleam, every tight muscle around Garrison's deep-set eyes showed. He shifted his weight from one foot to the other.

"You must have been damned good, Rose," he said. "You've even got me believing you." He shoved his hands into his pants pockets as if straining against his own distrust.

Robin waited. Watched. He turned to face the window so he didn't have to look at her. A gap opened in the clouds and cold white light streamed into the cabin, wrapping his tall body, from the shoulders down, in a pewter cloak. It bleached his blue shirt to a bleak chalky color. He seemed to sense her gaze upon his back, because his hands moved restlessly in his pockets, fists tightening and relaxing.

Robin slid her shoulders over an inch, trying to find a position that didn't hurt so much. Nothing helped. The pain was far more violent today than it had been when she'd first broken the rib swimming to shore outside of St. Louis. Had osteomylitis set in? Fear washed her veins, making her shiver. She tugged at the blanket to pull it more tightly about her.

"By the way, Garrison," she said through gritted teeth. "Why do I smell like a distillery?"

"Whisky."

"Whisky?"

"I use it for everything from sore throats to saddle sores. I don't know why it works, but I've spilled it on cuts often enough to know that it does. Wounds heal faster when you pour whisky on 'em."

"So . . . so, you poured whisky on my broken rib?"

"I did. The good stuff, too."

Robin nodded. "I thank you for being extravagant."

A bare smile moved his lips.

"Garrison," she said, "I hate to trouble you, but . . . may I have some water?"

"Oh, of course. I'm sorry."

He hurried to the tea kettle on the warming plate and poured water out into a tin cup. He returned and, kneeling, slipped an arm beneath her head and lifted her so she could drink. But for a long while, she didn't drink, she just let herself rest against him while she looked vulnerably up into his hazel eyes. Their gazes held. She saw more there than, perhaps, he wanted her to. She saw his attraction for her and his loneliness. He even let her glimpse the hurt he had buried deep inside.

Robin closed her eyes and drank the water. It tasted sweet and earthy, like melted snow.

He wanted to care about her . . .

When she had finished drinking and he took the cup away, Robin gazed up at him again. How much did he want to care? Enough that he might forget what he'd heard her say during her delirium?

"Garrison," she said in an intimate voice. "You must believe me. I had nothing to do with Lincoln's death."

Very gently, he let her head down to the pillow, slipped his arm out, then got to his feet. "I hope to God that ain't a lie, Rose. If it is, and I find out . . ."

He didn't finish.

He walked to the table, turned off the lamp, then went back to the window and stood watching the snow fall.

CHAPTER 23

As the golden hues of afternoon waned, every tree and hill on the plains cast a long shadow. They stretched before Owen's horse like pointing fingers, guiding him eastward down the slope toward Colorado City, which sat like a glistening gem in the distance. Already Owen could hear music. A piano and, more faintly, a fiddle. He glanced at Corley, wondering if he heard them, too.

The man sat his black gelding like a Greek god, chin up, back ramrod straight. Pale blue eyes focused on the space between his horse's ears. He seemed to hear nothing. The lavender gleam of dusk accentuated his thin-lipped mouth and lean face, but had softened the brightness of his red hair. He'd pinned so many medals to his uniform front that a tinkling symphony erupted every time his horse broke into a trot. He wore a new cap bedecked with gold braid. More braid looped his cuffs and sleeves. During the war, Owen had heard soldiers refer to the gaudy accoutrements as "chicken guts," and thought it an appropriate appellation, but he wondered at the suddenness of Corley's change of style. They had been riding together for more than a week and, until this morning, the "Colonel" had not tricked himself out in such ostentatious detail.

"Looks like we'll have a good supper tonight," Owen said as he maneuvered his horse alongside Corley's. The clip-clopping of hooves intermixed with the croaking of frogs and chur of insects coming from the silver ribbon of water to his left. The scents of river plants rose as the evening deepened, bathing Owen's face in a sweet earthy coolness.

"I wouldn't be so certain, if I were you," Corley answered. "In my experience, these pathetic western towns offer little more than venison and beans, or beans and venison."

"Don't be such a pessimist."

Owen stood up in his stirrups to peer down at the town. It looked damned near deserted. Dilapidated shanties marked the outskirts of town, roofs collapsed, some with whole walls missing, as if they'd been scavenged for firewood. Worse, several of the buildings on Main Street were windowless and doorless, testaments to a fading mining boom. Decline was the rule, of course, not the exception. Mineral towns went through booms and busts, and the bust just came faster to some than others, but it came to *all* eventually. Colorado City had already seen its finest hour. Twenty or thirty horses stood tied around a three-story building that announced in huge red letters: TAVERN, GAMBLING HELL, AND HOTEL.

Owen sat back in his saddle and smiled. His empty stomach growled in anticipation. "On second thought, Colonel, you may be right. But I have to keep up my hopes. Those desiccated army rations we've been eating the past two days have given me one hellacious bellyache."

Corley answered, "Without my rations, Mr. Fontaine, you would have been forced to hunt for your dinner, and you don't look like the sort to work so hard."

Owen grinned. "Quite correct, Colonel, I have never been one to 'work' for something when I could pay someone else—"

"If you'd fought in the war you'd have far more gratitude for a full belly, not to mention the fact that your palate wouldn't be near so sensitive."

"That is, I dare say, another of the many unexpected virtues of cowardice."

Corley gave him a cold look and straightened in his saddle to gaze down at the town, grimacing at the saloon's sign. "I believe the order of that list says a great deal about the quality of the western character. Are you certain you weren't born in this region, Fontaine?"

"I wasn't, but I admit that I share many western sentiments. For example—"

"That's right, you said you were born in London, didn't you?"

Owen's heart stopped. "Did I?"

Corley shrugged. "Doesn't matter. Please, go on, *which* western sentiments do you proclaim?"

Owen shifted in his saddle. How did the man know his birthplace? His thoughts ran wild, trying to find the solution. Had Owen been talking in his sleep and fallen into his youthful accent? Years ago, in Paris, a very expensive courtesan had informed him that he did that. Or had Corley been doing some investigative research? *Dear God. Undoubtedly. He's a secret service officer. What else does he know about me?*

Owen smiled. "For example, that sign makes perfect sense to me. It certainly represents the proper order of my activities tonight."

"Obviously, you are no gentleman, sir."

"A fact I'm proud of, Colonel."

"Can nothing I say insult you, Fontaine? I'm trying so diligently."

Owen shrugged and laughed. "Enough of me, Colonel. Let's talk about you. You're not exactly the energetic, persevering officer you pretend to be, are you? I've met George Sharpe, and I know for a fact that he would never send a *needed* officer out here with the war situation as critical as it was three months ago. So what is this mission you're on? Punishment? What did you do to deserve being banished to Colorado Territory?" *Or did Sharpe just want to be rid of you?*"

Corley kept his eyes straight ahead for long seconds, but his cheeks reddened.

Owen lifted a brow in anticipation.

But as quickly as Corley's flush had begun, it vanished. It now appeared that Owen's words had made no more impression upon Corley than mist on air. A strange remoteness slackened his freckled face. Even his voice sounded different, distant, mechanical. "So you're planning on drinking and gambling all night?" Corley asked.

"Drinking, gambling, and *eating*," Owen corrected. "And what about you, Colonel? Going straight to bed?"

Corley turned. Though his gaze pinioned Owen, he didn't seem to see him at all. Corley was staring at some far-off image in his mind, not quite able to make out the fuzzy lines of the face, but trying very hard. He tilted his head sideways at an odd angle. "I don't know yet."

A cryptic statement if ever Owen heard one. He waited for more, but when nothing came, he sighed, "I see." He kicked his horse, galloping down toward the saloon to put as much room between himself and Corley as possible. Dust sprouted behind him, encircling Corley in an ethereal gray haze.

As Owen rode up, he heard raucous laughter coming from the saloon, accompanied by the notes of an out-of-tune piano playing *The Battle Cry of Freedom*. A few drunken male voices bellowed the chorus:

> *The Union forever, hurrah! boys, hurrah!*
> *Down with the traitor, up with the star,*
> *While we rally round the flag, boys,*

Rally once again,
Shouting the battle cry of Freedom!

Owen was humming it himself when he dismounted. "Whoa, boy. Good boy."
He stroked his horse's buckskin-colored nose, uncoiled the lead rope from
its tether on his saddlehorn, and tied the horse to the crowded hitching rail.

Stars had just begun to pop out across the slate blue undercoat of evening,
creating a dazzling display overhead. A few puffs of cloud floated like dark
lonely wayfarers in their midst. Owen lost sight of them when he stepped
onto the wooden sidewalk and into the amber light pouring from the windows.
As he neared the saloon door, the smells of roasting meat and wood smoke
grew stronger.

Good Lord, how he missed the comforts of civilization. What he would
give for a fine glass of port, a huge beefsteak, and a soft feather bed to work
out the kinks in his back. No matter where he'd ventured east of the Mississippi, he'd always been near a town with at least one fine dining establishment.
But out here . . . Well, the best a man could hope for was a place to eat, period.
They were few and far between in this vast empty land.

Corley rode up, surveyed the hotel with obvious dislike, and dismounted.

"I'll meet you inside, Colonel," Owen called.

Corley didn't answer, and it was as if he hadn't heard. He stood fussing
with his reins, checking the breastcollar on his horse.

"Colonel?" Owen tried again.

Corley ran his hand down his horse's shoulder and leg and checked the
hoof for a very long time.

"I'll be at the bar!" Owen called, and opened the door to the saloon.

The roar struck him like a gale, filled with laughter, song, the sound of
cards being shuffled, and husky female voices.

Though only thirty by thirty feet, the room was nearly splitting at the
seams. There had to be fifty men and women packed in here. Sawdust covered
the plank floor, and men had been taking advantage of it, because brown
rings of tobacco juice encircled each of the ten tables. Poker games were in
full swing. Heavily rouged doves draped themselves over the men with the
most money stacked before them, smiling and whispering encouragements.
But not a single empty chair met Owen's searching gaze.

His face fell. He'd been hoping for a nice corner booth and a leisurely
meal.

Corley entered and stood like a giant to Owen's left. The noise level
diminished when people turned to stare at his gaudy uniform. Some eyes

widened in awe, especially those of the "ladies," but most men glared. Corley seemed oblivious. His pale eyes moved about the room, stopping there, searching, moving on, stopping again . . . looking for . . . what?

Owen shouldered through the crowd, saying, "Forgive me," and "Oh, I'm so sorry. Pardon me," as he headed toward the long bar in the rear, where a very fat, pink-cheeked woman in a low-cut green gown stood serving drinks as fast as she could pour them. Owen lifted a hand, and she gave him an irritated look. She finished the drink she was making and tramped down the bar. He could almost feel the floor shaking beneath her weight. Around five feet tall, she had to weigh two hundred pounds. She leaned toward him and yelled, "My name's Margaret! What can I bring you?"

"Your best whisky, please."

She did a doubletake at the "please," smiled faintly, and walked away.

While he waited, Owen propped a black boot on the brass footrail. Corley continued to stand near the door with a stern, anxious look on his face. As if crowds panicked him, he'd clenched his hands into huge fists. Men seemed to grasp the latent threat and parted before him when he started across the room, like the Red Sea opening at the touch of Moses' staff—or was that Aaron? Well, whatever, Corley frightened people. Just the cold inhuman look in his eyes was enough to make most stouthearted men blink.

Owen certainly did. He knew very little about Corley, just that he had been born in Ohio, had two sisters, had graduated from West Point in 1844, and had spent his entire adult life in the army. More than these basics, Corley would not reveal. Nonetheless, Owen was most assuredly at the head of the line when it came to fearing him. There was something just plain "wrong" about Corley.

The first night on the trail, Owen had thrown out his bedroll on the ground, and been surprised when he heard the snick of a pistol hammer being pulled back. The Major, it seemed, did not sleep out in the open. No. He would only sleep "inside." He had forced Owen to move his bedroll into an old dugout swarming with upset packrats. The next night, Corley had insisted they sleep in an abandoned, flea-infested wolf's den! To make matters worse, the Major had vivid nightmares. He didn't just talk in his sleep, either. He crawled, screamed, and fired his pistol at anything that moved. Owen could make out only one word during the entire tirade, and that was *Michael.* Corley screamed that name over and over again.

Flashbacks from the war, no doubt, but the insight didn't help Owen's indigestion any. The third night, he'd waited until Corley went to sleep, then he'd risen and carried his bedroll out of the cave, and up a hill, where he could look down on Corley silhouetted in the cave's firelight. The man had ghosts. Potent ones. And Owen wanted to be far out of range when Corley spied one to shoot.

The next day, after a very long night, Corley had been silent and hostile, jumping at every sound, jerking his pistol from its holster at the slightest provocation. He hadn't exchanged one word with Owen, though Owen had tried several times to engage him in conversation. That night, Owen had attempted to run. He'd saddled up his horse in a gentle rain shower, and was in the process of tying on his bedroll when Corley emerged from the run-down cabin. In the darkness, Owen hadn't been able to make out any of his facial features, but he could sense that malignant stare.

"That was a pleasant rain shower, wasn't it, Fontaine?"

"Uh . . . yes." His hands went stone still where he had begun a knot.

"I've always appreciated the rain. It makes tracking easy."

"Does it?"

"*Very* easy."

"I see."

"Good. Did I ever tell you about the note I carry in my jacket pocket?"

Owen had shifted uncomfortably. "What note?"

"It begins, 'Dear Mr. Fontaine, I regret that I will be unable to keep our breakfast engagement . . .' Need I go on?"

Owen felt numb. Of course. How had he been so blind! His head began to throb, just as it had that bright afternoon in St. Louis after he'd been way-laid. So . . . Corley knew about his treasonous activities. Rose's own words echoed in his mind: "Our glorious Union has judged treason to be a hanging offense." Corley could murder Owen and no one would so much as ask "why?"

Corley went back into the cabin.

Owen had, of course, unsaddled his horse. It didn't take much of a threat to make him back down. There was nothing more important to him than his life. He was selfish that way.

Since then, Owen had been waiting, biding his time until he could slip away cleanly, safely.

He smiled. He might have learned very little about Corley, but the things Corley had told him about Mrs. Heatherton had been worth every despicable moment on the trail. Indeed, he had developed an unnatural fascination with his darling Rosie and her glorious exploits. She had begun to fill his dreams like one of the mythical sirens.

Margaret returned with his drink and sat it on the bar. "That'll be one dollar."

Owen reached into the pocket of his black overcoat, drew out his wallet and removed a five-dollar bill. "I'd appreciate it if you could tell me where I can buy a meal, and whether or not you have a room available for tonight?"

Margaret pointed to the east wall. "Dining room's on the second floor, up the stairs through that door, and I got three rooms left. Seventy-five cents a night, that includes a bath in the morning. How long you staying?"

"Just one night, thank you. What will my room number be?"

"Take number nine. It's on the third floor and has a good view of the river."

"I appreciate that." He shoved the five dollars toward her, and added, "I plan on having this whisky gone in mere moments. Please bring me another, a double, and keep the change for yourself."

Her toothy smile broadened. "Sweet Jesus, you're a gent. I thank you, mister."

She started to tuck the bill between her huge breasts, but halted midway when Corley strode up and slid a tanned hand across the bar. She scrutinized his icy expression, his flamboyant uniform, and her grin metamorphosed into a scowl. "What do you want?"

"Brandy."

She walked away several paces, glanced back, then tucked the bill down her dress front.

Owen took a hearty swallow of his drink and groaned, "Oh, my Lord, this is bad whisky, but it tastes magnificent. Which shows you, Colonel, how far my palate has degenerated on this trip. In another week I may even find desiccated rations tasty. God forbid."

Corley said nothing. His attention was riveted on the crowd. When Margaret returned with Owen's double whisky and Corley's brandy, Corley handed her exactly one dollar.

"Oh, you're an army officer, all right," Margaret said with a rigid smile. She sniffed indignantly before she walked away.

Owen stifled a smirk, but Corley either hadn't understood the caustic remark or didn't care about it. What a curious fellow. Or maybe just plain crazy.

Owen finished his first glass of whisky and started on his second. A warm tingle had already begun in his belly and he wanted to encourage it. The piano player, a young mulatto woman with dark skin and green eyes began her next tune, and Owen nodded in approval. Mozart! And in a godforsaken wilderness like Colorado. What would these barbarians discover next? Champagne, perhaps?

Corley leaned back against the bar and swirled his brandy in his glass while he examined a woman on the far side of the room. What a beauty. Owen wondered why he hadn't noticed her first. She'd been sitting beside a burly poker player with lambchop whiskers and flabby jowls. Corley lifted his glass to her and she gave him a coy smile. He smiled back.

Owen watched the interchange with amusement. Corley was anything but a ladies' man, yet he knew how to signal a soiled dove when he wanted to do business.

Corley whispered, "Tell me something, Fontaine. Do you dream about her?"

"Who?" Owen said in confusion.

"Robin Heatherton. Do you . . . does she fill your dreams?"

Owen laughed. "Of course! What healthy man wouldn't have dreams about her?"

"Yes," Corley whispered, "what healthy male wouldn't . . . she fills mine, too, you know. Every night. Dream after dream. As if she were a demon succubus and not a living breathing woman. She tries to do things to me . . . in my dreams . . . to my—my manhood. Things you would not believe."

Corley's voice had gone husky, raw. As if to ease some inner pain, he shoved away from the bar and lifted a hand to the dove. She smiled knowingly and patted the shoulder of the gambler she'd been clinging to. Seductively, she started toward Corley. Her blue gown accentuated every female curve. The colonel shifted positions, as if he were readying himself to spring.

He leaned closer to Owen. "How tall do you think she is?"

Owen shrugged. "I don't know. Five feet seven, I'd guess. Tall for a woman."

"Yes." Corley nodded.

"She's gorgeous, too. That wealth of black hair—"

"But the way she has it pinned up makes it appear curly. Do you think it's naturally straight?"

"How should I know? Women spend half their lives twisting their hair into unnatural shapes. Ask her." Owen sipped his whisky.

Corley had begun to breathe rapidly, like a male dog near a female in heat. The medals on his chest flashed with each inhalation.

As the "lady" got closer, Corley seemed to fall to pieces. He downed his brandy, set the glass on the bar, then wiped his mouth with the back of his hand. His pale eyes had gone wide with what seemed to be fear or shock. "My God," he breathed, almost too low for Owen to hear. "She's *perfect.*"

"I told you she was gorgeous."

The woman strolled up, took Corley's arm, and plastered herself against his side. "Hello, darlin'. How are you tonight?"

A shudder went through Corley, which she must have taken for excitement. She smiled. Corley stared at her hard, taking in her oval face, the delicate arch of her eyebrows, her straight nose and wide cheekbones.

"What's your name, Colonel?" she asked.

Corley's mouth trembled when he opened it to say, "Tom. My name's Tom."

"Well, I am pleased to meet you, Tom. I'm Lily. I don't suppose you're interested in having a little fun with me tonight, are you?"

"Oh, yes," he answered. "Yes, I'm very interested."

"Well, come along then, darlin.' The night's wasting." Lily tugged on his arm.

Corley never took his eyes from her as the dove led him across the room, through the eastern door and up the stairs. He hadn't had the common courtesy to say goodnight to Owen before he left. Not that Owen minded. He was frankly glad to have Corley gone.

He frowned down into his whisky. Rather than being buoyed by the alcohol, he felt exhausted. Every muscle in his body ached. He rotated his right shoulder and winced. His legs and lower back hurt even worse. He wasn't accustomed to riding a horse for fifteen hours a day. He'd discovered muscles in his buttocks he hadn't even known he possessed.

Perhaps he would pass on the poker game tonight, have dinner brought up to his room, and, for the first time in days, just get a good night's rest. Yes, the more he thought about it, the better it sounded.

Owen made his way through the bustling crowd, carrying his whisky protectively.

Deputy Frank Neville sprinted up the back stairs of Margaret's hotel, taking them three at a time, panting from the effort. A cold pre-dawn breeze blew down the stairwell, carrying the scent of cheap perfume and other musky odors he didn't want to think about. The draft tormented the candles in their brass holders on wall, coaxing their gleam into waltzing over the carved pine handrail, the bawdy paintings of naked women on the walls, and the faded blue rug that ran the length of the stairs. The slippered feet of two whores patted on the second floor steps beneath him. Lindsay's weeping irritated him. Blonde and fourteen years old, she ought to be off in school somewhere, not here, for God's sake.

Damn, he hated cases like this, and they were all too common in these mining towns. He'd seen enough to know, from Grasshopper Diggings, Montana, to Virginia City, Nevada. It made him long for the logical insanity of his Texas boyhood. In cattle towns, at least you could understand why crimes were committed. Assaults occurred because of rustling, infidelity, and unsavory insults. And, on occasion, just because men got joy from hitting each other with their fists.

When he set foot on the landing, Frank pulled his tan leather vest down over his white shirt. The cotton felt crisp and clean against his sweating skin. His dear Joan kept his clothes all washed and ironed, just in case he had to dress rapidly in the middle of the night. She'd been born in Texas, too. She didn't understand this Colorado lunacy any better than he did. Frank sincerely hoped that the good Lord would give Sam Houston what he deserved for forcing their grand Republic to join the Union.

At the end of the hall ahead, his assistant deputy, James Lange, stood beside Margaret outside an open door. Her mousy brown hair hung down to the collar of her "tent" dress, a red one this morning, trimmed with white rickrack. Through the entry he could see lace curtains billowing in the wind.

"Well, tell me what the hell is going on, Jimmy," he said gruffly as he strode forward.

Jimmy, young and dark-haired, wet his lips nervously. His face looked as white as chalk against his black shirt. "Come and see fer yerself, Frank. I ain't even gonna try and—"

"Damn, Jimmy, when are you going to learn to gather information? I been trying to teach you—"

Jimmy flapped his arms. "I ain't never seen nothing like this, Frank! I don't know what to tell you!"

Margaret put out a hand when Frank tried to shoulder around her and into room. "Listen here, Frank," her voice had gone hoarse. "I want you to take a good look and start turning this town upside down. I won't have this happen in my place and have the man what done it get away. I won't be able to get no more girls to work for me. Not a one. You hear me?"

"Of course, I hear you, Margaret," he replied indignantly. "You think I'm deaf? If you'll get yourself out of my way, I'll get to work."

Margaret stepped aside and gestured for him to go in. Behind him, he heard the other whores come up the stairs and start running down the hall toward him. Lindsay's sobbing grew shrill.

Frank stepped into the room.

What he saw made him sick to his stomach. He shoved his brown hat back on his head and propped his hands on his hips. It made breathing a little easier.

Lily lay on the bed in a mass of rumpled pink and white quilts. She was on her back, and her long black hair had been plaited into two braids that draped over her breasts. Her naked body had clearly been arranged, arms folded over her stomach, long legs together. Two pillows had been shoved against her knees in an effort to keep her legs from parting in the relaxation of muscles that accompanied death. The bruises on her throat and the blue pallor of her face left little doubt about the cause of her demise.

"Blessed Jesus . . ." Frank murmured.

"What'd I tell you, Frank?" Jimmy said. "It ain't like nothing I ever—"

"Jimmy," he interrupted and exhaled. "Go get the sheriff out of bed. We need Jonathan to see this. This ain't an ordinary murder."

"But shouldn't I bring Doc Rainsford first, I mean she might still be—"

"Don't argue with me at a time like this, boy! Get the sheriff."

The reality seemed to sink in. Jimmy backed away and trotted down the hall, but when he passed the third door, it opened and a blond man peered out. Bare-chested, dressed only in tan trousers, he looked like the ruckus had roused him from a sound sleep. A thin nose dominated his oval face, and a large diamond ring adorned the right hand that gripped the door knob.

The man rubbed his eyes, and said, "Would you be kind enough to tell me—"

Jimmy answered, "It's all right, mister. Don't worry. One of the girls got killed last night, but—"

"We don't know for sure she's dead, Jimmy!" Lindsay yelled, and pulled her lacy wrap more tightly about her shoulders. Tears streaked her cheeks. "You ought not to be saying until we—"

"Shut up, Lindsay," Frank ordered. "Jimmy's right. Lily's dead. Get it through your head right now, 'cause that's the way it is."

"Lily?" the man in the doorway said. "The . . . the tall woman? The one with black hair—"

"That's right." Frank answered and walked down the hall to stand beside Jimmy. "She was strangled last night. Do you know something about this?"

"I don't know. I was—"

Margaret drew in a sudden breath. "Hold on, Frank," she said in a stern voice. "This fella rode in with that colonel, the man that Lily went upstairs with. I'd know him anywhere. He—"

"Yes, you're right," the blond answered. "I did ride in with him."

Whores flocked around Frank with their eyes narrowing and mouths gaping. He let his hand rest on the holstered revolver on his hip. The man seemed to take the hint.

"Please don't jump to conclusions," he said defensively. "I am completely innocent in this matter." He opened the door wider and handed a derringer out, butt first, to Frank.

"That's a good start," Frank said as he shoved it into his belt. "You can keep helping me by telling me your name and the name of the colonel."

"I am Owen Fontaine. The officer is . . ."

Fontaine hesitated and Frank gritted his teeth. He'd seen that look many times before, a man afraid for his own hide, weighing truth against a decorous lie. "What's the officer's name, Mister Fontaine?"

"Major Frederick Marley."

"That's a lie!" Lindsay declared. "He was a colonel, I saw—"

"No. Please, take my word for it," Fontaine said. "Marley is a major. He's just fond of disguises."

"Uh-huh," Frank grunted. "Well, his rank don't make no difference to me, mister. I just want to know where this Marley is now."

Fontaine shook his head. "I haven't the slightest idea. The last time I saw him, he was leaving the bar with Lily."

"Did you hear anything last night? Screams or—"

"I heard absolutely nothing, deputy. I had dinner, finished a glass of whisky, and went right to sleep. I wouldn't be awake yet if it weren't for the commotion out here in the hallway."

Frank thought it over. "Well, I imagine you if you had been involved in the killing, you'd be long gone, just like Major Marley, but—"

"He's gone? You mean he left town? You're certain?"

Relief animated Fontaine's face and something else, but Frank couldn't quite figure it out. He did, however, know that the emotion was blood kin to elation.

"I take it the major wasn't exactly a friend of yours?"

"Not at all. In fact, I was more his prisoner than anything else. He forced me to ride south with him from Denver."

Frank frowned. "Well, we'll get to the reasons for your coming here later, but first off, don't get too excited about him being gone. I ain't sure he is. He might still be in Colorado City, which is one of the reasons I need you to stay around. To identify him just in case we find him. In the meantime, I'll want you to tell me everything you know about this Major Marley."

Fontaine ran a hand through his hair and said, "You'll need to telegraph the Bureau of Military Information in Washington City. I suspect they are the only people—"

"Military Information?"

"That's right. Marley is a secret service agent."

The women began whispering to each other, sounding just like a passel of hissing cats. Frank shushed them with a rough wave of his hand. "That's right interesting. But I don't get it. The war's over. Why would the Bureau send a man to Colorado Territory? What's he looking for? Or who—"

"Those are all fine questions, deputy. Make sure you address them to Colonel George Sharpe when you send your wire. He's in charge of the Bureau. He ought to have an answer for you. I don't."

Frank gazed at Fontaine long and hard. He seemed to be telling the truth. That, or he was a damned good liar. "I'll do that, Mister Fontaine. Now, why don't you finish getting dressed, and sit tight until the sheriff gets here? I'm sure he'll have more questions for you."

Frank turned to Jimmy who stood there with his eyes wide. "What the hell are you still doing here? I told you to run and fetch Jonathan!"

CHAPTER 24

Robin lay on her back, blinking wearily at the dark ceiling and listening to Garrison talk in his sleep. It was more like moaning really, punctuated by dry sobs. Occasionally she caught a word ... Apache ... Wheeling ... Canby. General Canby undoubtedly.

He had wrapped himself in a blanket and stretched out on the floor before the woodstove. The eerie red light cast by the coals wavered over his bearded face, playing in his curly hair and shaggy eyebrows. His mouth twitched in the depths of the dream. One of his arms curved over his head and the fingers moved, as if he were grasping for something, or someone, and couldn't quite reach it. He made a soft frantic sound.

Robin's gaze drifted to the window where snow fell and fell. A hazy white veil eddied and spun beyond the thin pane of glass. It had stormed for four long days. Over three feet of snow had mounded up outside the cabin. At dusk, she'd watched her horse plow through the white ocean, following behind Honey in search of grass. They looked so pitiful, their backs glistening with ice, while they pawed at the hard crust.

Garrison's legs twitched. His deep moan brimmed with fear. Though she could not make out a single word, she knew that tone. It was the voice of a man who had suddenly found himself alone on a battlefield, all around him the bodies of his friends. It was a helpless, lost voice.

A terror familiar to Robin.

"Garrison?" she called. "Garrison, wake up."

He didn't hear her, or if he did, he'd placed her in the context of the dream. A pained sob worked its way to his closed lips.

"Garrison? ... Garrison, listen to me, you're having a bad dream. Wake up. You're in Colorado Territory and the year is 1865. You've got an injured woman in your cabin who's trying to sleep, and you're keeping her awake."

Which wasn't true. Even if he hadn't been talking in his sleep, she would have been staring at the ceiling, worried sick about Jeremy. Her fear had soured to desperation. She *had* to see her son. Soon. To make certain he was all right. "Come back, Garrison. The cabin's cold and it's snowing outside. I'm Rose Hale—"

He just continued making those frantic sounds.

"Garrison? Garrison Parker, you're in Colorado. Safe. You're safe, Garrison. There's nothing to fear, except this blasted winter storm that won't quit. Come home, Garrison. Come home and put more wood in the stove. It's starting to get chilly. Garrison—"

"I . . . I'm awake, Rose." He murmured. He braced a hand on the wood floor and sat up. The crimson light escaping through the cracks in the old stove gilded every curl in his brown hair. Sweat glued wisps to his temples and forehead. "I'm sorry, I—"

"Don't apologize. That sounded like a bad one."

He threw off his blanket and leaned forward, propping his elbows on his drawn up knees. Sweat glistened on his straight nose. He rubbed his face briskly. "Where'd you . . . you learn that trick?" he asked, voice quaking.

"What trick?"

"Talking gentle like that to wake somebody from a bad dream."

"Practice," she answered.

He looked up at her and his hazel eyes glinted blue in the dim firelight. "Spying's damn sure a hell of a life."

Robin tilted her head. Did he mean because it had given her "practice" or . . . "Is that what you were doing when Will Wheeling died? Trying to get a message through to Canby? Or was the message from Canby to somebody else?"

He let out a long breath. "To Canby."

"How long ago did it happen?"

He shook his head, as if he didn't want to think about it, but he answered, "Not long enough. Almost three years."

"Sounds like a long time, though, doesn't it?" She spoke in a soothing tone, hoping to give him time to escape the terrible dreamscape. It always took her several minutes to crawl out of that past world and believe in this world. "Most people would think of three years as an eternity. But you're right. It's not long enough for powerful memories to even dim."

"No," he whispered. "It ain't."

He propped his forehead on his knees, hiding his face from her, but before he'd ducked his head, he'd looked embarrassed, or maybe ashamed of his behavior, and Robin wondered how many people had been allowed to see him so vulnerable. The woman who had hurt him, at least. She'd shared his bed. But how many others?

He was probably afraid.

"Well, Garrison," she said gently. "I want you to know how glad I am that you were involved in espionage, even if it was only delivering messages. It makes me feel closer to you. You didn't have to hide the message in your bosom, did you? Or maybe sewn into your petticoat? How about concealed in a false lock of hair?"

He lifted his head. He had a blank expression on his face. "I put it in my shirt pocket, Rose."

"My, how creative. Did you at least have it inscribed in cipher?"

"I had it inscribed in English."

"I see. So you ate it before you were captured?"

"What makes you think I was captured?"

"The way you talked about Fort Fillmore didn't make it sound like a luxury hotel."

He blinked. "Did I tell you how many times a year I wash my underwear?"

"Did you eat it?"

"The message, you mean? Hell, yes. Didn't have no choice."

Robin arched an eyebrow. "You're a true patriot. However, if you'd used a good Virgenere Tableau cipher, Garrison, you wouldn't have had to."

His mouth quirked into a lopsided grin. Lifting a hand, he ruffled his curly hair.

Robin smiled. "Could you please put some wood in the stove, Garrison? It's getting awfully cold in here."

"Yes, ma'am," he said and got up. After he stretched his back muscles, he shoved two pieces of split pine into the firebox. Flames crackled and popped, sending sparks whirling toward the ceiling.

Robin observed their winking dance.

Garrison wandered around the cabin aimlessly for a time, his stocking feet silent, but the floorboards creaked. Finally, he poured himself a cup of old coffee and went to sit at the table. He fiddled with the crystal base of the lamp, turning it around and around. He hadn't stopped shaking. The lamp base struck the table lightly, erratically, making a *clink-clinkty-clink* sound.

"Go ahead and light it, Garrison, if it will help drive the ghosts away. It won't disturb me."

He hastily got up, walked over and pulled a twig from the woodpile, then stuck it in the stove until the tip caught fire. Carefully, he returned to the table and touched the twig to the lamp's wick. A beautiful unwavering flame was born. Robin heard him sigh as he blew out the twig and slumped into a chair.

"Better?" she asked.

"No. No, Rose, I won't be for a time."

"Would you like to talk about it?"

"I'd rather that you went to sleep. You need the rest more than I need the talk."

"I have the strength, Garrison. I may not be able to do much else, but I can listen."

She did feel better, more alive, though it still hurt to breathe. She'd spent most of the past four days sleeping and the extent of her healing surprised even her. Undoubtedly the secret lay in Garrison's unorthodox use of whisky. "What are you blaming yourself for? His death?"

"Whose death?"

"Will Wheeling's." She saw him close his eyes. "Garrison, I'm sure it wasn't your fault."

"I got different feelings inside of me, Rose."

"I'm sure you do, but are they justified? Did you shoot Wheeling, or turn him over to his enemies, or sacrifice him so you could escape?"

"Hell, no, Rose, but . . . well . . . I didn't help him neither." He massaged his forehead. "And he called my name over and over, begging me to. He was my friend. I should have done something. But I . . . I just . . ."

He hunched over the table and used one finger to circle every pine knot in the top, staring down at the golden wood with his brow furrowed. His broad chest moved with swift shallow breaths. Robin frowned. He looked like a man facing God on Judgment Day with no words to defend himself, knowing full well that the silence would condemn him.

She looked away. The small cabin heated up quickly, and sweet contentment began to fill her as her fingers and toes warmed up. It was strange the way a soldier's mind worked. That powerful bond created by guarding each other's backs left no excuses for failure. Failure to protect his friend was the same thing as betraying him outright. Wheeling's ghost would never forgive Garrison until he forgave himself.

"I heard you mention the Apache. Were you caught in an Indian attack?"

He tilted his head as if reluctant to tell her about it, and the amber gleam from the lamp flowed into his beard like liquid gold, glimmering from each hair. His tanned face resembled burnished copper, which accentuated the straight lines of his nose and shadowed the crow's-feet around his eyes. They looked deep and dark.

Robin continued, "Were you ambushed? While you were trying to deliver the message to Canby?"

A swallow worked its way down his throat, as if he were trying to keep the words from coming out, but they did anyway. "I should have kept to the ridges, not followed the damned trails, but we had orders to ride fast and hard, and rocky terrain would have slowed us down, so I . . . I . . . ."

"So you followed orders. You took the fastest route."

"But Rose, don't you see that—"

"Yes, I do see," she interrupted to spare him from having to explain it. "If you'd disobeyed orders and kept to the highest ridges where you could view miles of open country, the Apache couldn't have ambushed you, and Will Wheeling wouldn't be dead."

"That's right," he responded softly.

That familiar ache began in her heart, and Robin said, "Did I tell you my mother was Cherokee? She claimed she could see the future, and sometimes I truly believed her. I remember once when she dreamed my uncle's death. Two days later word came that he'd died in his sleep on the very night of her dream. I did not receive that same gift, but how I wish I had." She fought to keep the pain from her voice when she continued, "My husband wouldn't be dead. Nor A. P. Hill. And if I could have foreseen Grant's strategy at the Battle of the Wilderness I would have advised General Lee not to fight there, to bide our time and wait for a better place. I could have saved thousands, *tens of thousands*, Garrison. . . . But that's not the way the world works." She let out a taut breath. "I pray that God has a reason for keeping us blind and for tormenting us with all the 'if onlys'."

Garrison sat quietly for a moment, then got up and carried his chair to the middle of the room where he set it down in front of the woodstove. " 'If onlys'?" he asked as he dropped to the seat again. With the lamp behind him, much of his face had been thrown into shadow. Only the faint glow of the fire sparkled in his eyes. "You mean 'if only I had done this?' or 'if only I hadn't done that?' "

"Yes."

"I reckon you're right about that," he said, his voice calmer now, steady. "That's where the guilt comes from. Do you feel it, too? The guilt?"

"Yes," she answered and a sudden tingle of anger went through her, not that she was angry with him, but with herself. She couldn't seem to shake her guilt. All the comforting things she had just said to Garrison to ease his guilt had had no effect on her own. It was as if she refused to admit that she wasn't the cause of Charles' death, that the guilt served some purpose . . . and, after all, maybe it did. Like a bridge across a deep chasm, it had kept her mind occupied long enough for the terrible pain of loss to fade to a color that didn't hurt so much to look at. But Charles had been dead for six months. Couldn't she let the guilt go now? She had crossed that bridge . . . even the content of her dreams said so. He was no longer a lion when he came to visit her, but a man. The man she had known and loved.

"I feel it," she answered. "Sometimes I can't even breathe, and I think it's drowning me." Robin toyed with the corner of the white sheet, creasing it between her fingers. Garrison didn't move, but she felt him watching her.

"It's a bit different for me. I wake up a couple of times a month with my heart pounding so hard I worry it's gonna jump out of my chest and hop around the floor." A faint smile eased the hard lines of his face. "Why do you think human beings do that? Torment themselves so about things they can't change?"

"Because they wish so hard they could."

"Reckon so."

She hesitated, then went ahead and asked, "Garrison, where were you when Will Wheeling died?"

He sucked in a breath, held it, then let it out. "Up in the rocks, pinned down by Apache bullets. Every time I lifted my head, some warrior took a shot at me. I . . . I lay there for three days, Rose, listening to Will's screams." His mouth tightened. He couldn't say anything for a time. "The Apache are experts at torture. They know how to keep a man hovering at the edge of death, but still alive enough to feel the pain."

"Did you have supplies?"

"Food and water ran out on the first day. By the end of the third, I was half-crazy from thirst and lack of sleep. With the Apache out there, I couldn't let myself doze for more than a few minutes."

Robin remembered all the times when she had suffered from lack of sleep. The delusions after days of it had been fascinating and terrifying. She had been unable to tell whether she was awake or dreaming. Many of the terrors must have been hallucinations, but she still did not know for certain and never would. They had seemed *so* real.

"Are you sure Will was calling your name, Garrison? Or did you imagine it? Lack of sleep can do strange things—"

"Don't matter," he answered. "I thought I heard him. But you're right to question. I thought I heard lots of other things, too, train whistles, water falls . . . my mother's voice."

"Your mother?"

He nodded. "There was one point where I saw her sitting in front of me, smiling, and I thought I was dying and she'd come to take me with her. Instead, she told me to get up off my fat arse and make a run for it before the Apache came up and plucked me off them rocks. She was right, too. I was getting awful close to giving in to sleep."

Robin smiled. "She sounds like a lady I would have liked."

"I think you would have, she was a feisty woman, though I don't remember her very well. She died when I was just about Jeremy's age.

Jeremy . . . Robin's stomach cramped. She winced. "I'm sorry, Garrison."

"Don't be. It ain't like it still hurts." Then he peered at her questioningly. "Or . . . you worried about Jeremy?" he asked.

"Worried sick."

Garrison leaned forward and braced his elbows on his knees, then clasped his hands before him in a prayerful position. "I'd go fetch him for you, Rose, but you must know the only thing that would keep Mike Hathaway from getting here with the doctor is the fact that that trail is plumb impassable. Jeremy's safe, Macey will see to it."

Robin shook her head. Corley would stop at nothing to hurt her, to make her pay for what had happened to his brother. "You can say that, Garrison, because you didn't see the wild hatred in his eyes the day . . . Charles . . ."

She halted in mid-sentence, her mouth hanging open, before she closed it, and began fussing with her sheet, pulling it up over the plaid shirt she wore, tucking it in around her sides. *Good Lord, what did I almost do?*

Garrison brought his clasped hands up and propped his chin on them. "Who?"

"Hmm?"

"If you felt comfortable enough to almost slip, Rose, why don't you just go ahead and tell me? I *am* trustworthy. Did you mean the man who's hunting you? He was there when Charles died? Did he . . ." Garrison waved a hand as if searching for the connection. "Did this man kill Charles?"

Robin gripped two handfuls of blanket and pulled it up to cover her shoulders, then folded the edge of the sheet over the top of the blanket.

Garrison's clasped fingers tightened until the tendons stood out on the backs of his hands. "Goddamn, Rose. I wish to hell you'd told me this before!"

"Told you what? I haven't told you—"

"The hell you haven't! You think I don't know what it means when you start fussing with the bedding? I been watching you up close for days!" He lurched to his feet and stood like a wrathful god. "Damn it. If that fella would kill your husband and track you halfway across the country, he ain't on no military mission. Jeremy might be in danger! No wonder you ain't been sleeping. Well, we've got to do something to get that boy up here where we can protect him, *and you!*"

He'd said the last angrily, as though anticipating a retort from her. He folded his arms over his chest and hugged himself while he paced before the stove. "I—I'll rig up some snowshoes. I ain't never done it, but I'll figure it out. Can't be that hard. A willow hoop and some rawhide lacings. Something to tie them on with. I'll go down, talk to the sheriff, then—"

"No!" she blurted. "No. Not the sheriff. Please don't do that."

He stopped pacing. "But Rose, what if this fella shows up in town asking about you? If we don't tell—"

"He won't ask about me. Not under . . ." She started to fuss with the blanket and forced her hands to be still, then she braced herself for what she was about to do. She looked up and met his intent gaze squarely. "He won't be looking for me under the name of Rose Hale, Garrison. I'm telling you this so you won't be so worried, but I don't want you to ask me any questions. Please. The only way he'll be able to track me is by my description. I . . . I'm afraid I haven't been very careful in that regard. I was sick for a while and reckless with my appearance."

Garrison walked over to her, staring down, and Robin prepared herself for his shouts and suspicions. They seemed unavoidable. He stroked his beard and continued staring. She waited.

"Go on," he said.

"Isn't that enough? I just told you I use aliases, and I change my appearance. What more do you need to know?"

"I already knew your name wasn't Rose Hale. The only thing I really need to know is *his* name."

"Garrison, I can't . . . I don't think that's wise. I—"

"Then for God's sake at least tell me what he looks like!"

Their gazes held.

He lowered his hands to his sides and clenched them into fists.

From the corner of her eye, she glimpsed snow falling and falling, straight down, as light and airy as tiny white feathers. The wind had stopped. Drafts did not even stir the lamp on the table. The flame stood like a pillar of gold beneath its transparent globe, and threw a bright aura around Garrison, sil-

houetting his broad shoulders, following the V to his narrow waist, then out-
lining his long legs.

His voice came out strained. "Rose, I want you to listen to me. Don't
argue, just listen . . ."

Her mind froze at those words. Where had she heard them before? The
shiver began at the base of her spine and worked its way through her whole
body. The tone, even the inflection was the same. In the forbidden depths of
her soul, she could hear Charles, lying in the grass on the rainy terrace above
the Tennessee river: . . . *listen to me. Don't argue just listen. If anything hap-*
pens to me I want you to forget the war. Go home, grab Jeremy, and get the hell
out of the South. Disappear. You know how to do that . . .

All of her weariness and desperation flooded to the surface and her throat
went tight. She squeezed her eyes closed to cut off the tide of grief.

Somewhere out in the dark snowy mountains a wolf howled, the sound
low and mournful. Then it barked and howled again, as if pleading. Robin let
herself float on that woeful cry, rising and falling like a wave on the ocean.

The wood floor creaked as Garrison came across it and sat down in the
chair at her bedside. He laid a warm hand atop hers.

"You've got to tell me, Rose," he said. "There ain't no way around it. If
you don't, I won't be able—"

"Garrison, he won't look the same. The only thing he can't change will
be his eyes. And they're odd eyes. Pale blue. Cold, like a dead animal's."

"How tall is he? That's another thing he can't change."

"Very tall. Around six feet six inches, I'd guess."

"He was an agent. Like you?"

"I . . ." She hadn't told the truth in so long that the adrenaline pumping
in her veins made her light-headed. "Yes."

"Why's he hunting you?"

"I—I'm not sure. I've heard he thinks I'm responsible for his brother's
death at the battle of Ball's Bluff."

"Because of information you provided?"

"Yes."

He squeezed her hand tenderly, and she looked up into his face. His
troubled expression softened when he met her eyes, and she could tell he
was diligently trying to project confidence.

"Is there anything I can get you, Rose? A cup of coffee or a glass of water?
Something to help you sleep?"

"A shot of whisky would help."

He smiled. "It's a wonder I didn't think of that myself. But I can't waste it on drinking. I have to save it for your next bandage change. How 'bout a swig of beer instead?"

"No. Thanks. I guess water will do."

Rising, he went to pour two cups. He came back, handed her cup to her, and sat down again.

She used a fist to position her pillow just right, then sipped the cool liquid. It had picked up the sweet coppery flavor of the tea kettle. Her jangled nerves seemed to heave a sigh at the taste.

Garrison propped his cup on his belly, crossed his legs and leaned his head back against the log wall, staring up at the dance of shadows on the ceiling. He looked dead tired.

They sat in amiable silence for ten or fifteen minutes. Then Robin said, "Garrison, I would tell you his name, but . . . but I'm sure he's changed it, too, so it wouldn't matter. Do you understand?"

He didn't so much as uncross his legs. He just answered, "No, I don't. If it don't matter, then why don't you just tell me? What would it hurt if I knew?"

"It's not because I don't trust you, Garrison. I do."

"Do you?"

"Well . . ."

"That's what I figured. It's all right, Rose. You *will*. I just hope it don't take so long that you tie my hands behind my back."

CHAPTER 25

*D*uring the past week, I have often awakened to find his hand, large but very gentle, touching my face or patting my arm comfortingly, but this morning he did something I would never have anticipated.

He made me a cup of coffee, then helped me to sit up for the first time since my fall. After propping pillows around me, he informed me he was going to brush my hair. When I started to protest, he explained, very practically, that it needed to be done, and it would hurt too much if I tried to do it myself, since I'd have to raise my arms.

But it did not feel like a purely pragmatic deed. His heavily calloused hands touched my hair reverently, taking long slow strokes with the brush. It felt so soothing, I shamelessly yielded to this tender loverlike act.

It required more than an hour for him to comb out all of the tangles and knots, and when he'd finished, he put the brush on the floor, rose, and walked a few paces away to admire his work.

He stood for some time looking down, and a soft smile came to his face. Barely there. Just enough to cause his mouth to move and the lines around his eyes to crinkle.

I smiled and said, "Thank you, Garrison. I feel better."

"I wanted you to. I'm glad."

Gradually, as if he did not even realize the metamorphosis was occurring, his smile faded. When it had gone, he looked very vulnerable. Perhaps the intensity of his feelings frightened him. His eyes searched my face.

And looking at him standing there, I felt sad. He was pouring his heart out to me without a word, and I could give him nothing in return.

Nothing.

It is afternoon now. He left hours ago on his makeshift snowshoes.
It is still snowing, lightly, but continually. He piled blankets and elk
hides on top of me before he left, to keep me warm in case he doesn't
make it back tonight to tend the woodstove.

He set food, water, and a bottle of whisky on the chair at my bedside,
and ordered me to pour the whisky on my bandage at sunset. But, Lord
knows, I just might drink it instead.

I keep asking myself, "What shall I do about this?" and "How shall
I handle this?"

I know only that the task will be made harder because some cold
lonely part of me is attracted to his warmth.

I reach for the whisky, and uncork the bottle, promising myself I'll
save enough for my bandages.

By the time Garrison finished picking up supplies from the mercantile
the sun perched like a glowing crimson ball on the western horizon. In the
cold, crisp air, the orb rippled, seemed to turn liquid, then melted and flowed
down into the layers of thin clouds that hovered below the summits of the
mountains; they burned with a luminescent fire. It painted a glorious picture,
the ice blue peaks and the red filaments of cloud.

His pack of supplies over one arm and his snowshoes over the other,
Garrison made his way down the icy street toward Mike Hathaway's office.
Nobody walked the streets but him. With the fragmenting of the cloud cover,
the temperature had plummeted to around ten degrees. It was blasted cold.
His breath spun a shimmering fog before him as he walked.

In the road, wagon ruts and hoofprints glittered with frost, and though
torrid light sheathed the tops of the false-fronted buildings, the lower halves
were in shadow. Garrison shoved his gloved hands deep into the pockets of
his buffalo coat and broke into a trot to keep his teeth from chattering.

When he peered through the window and saw Mike sitting alone at his
desk, Garrison didn't bother to knock, but just opened the door and walked
in.

Hathaway looked up. His eyes went wide, and he lurched to his feet.
"Good God Almighty! How in the world did you get here?"

"Wasn't easy, I can tell you that for a fact. I rigged up some snowshoes."
He pointed to the pair on his back.

Hathaway leaned sideways to scrutinize them. "Well, I'll be . . . How's
Mrs. Hale?"

"Alive," he said as he leaned his pack and shoes against the wall, then removed his gloves and extended his hands to the warmth of the old potbellied stove. A vibrant tingle went through him, coaxing a shiver from his weary muscles. It felt good. "She's all right, Mike. I have been surprised by her gumption."

Hathaway heaved a relieved breath. "Well, I am happy to hear that. I tried to get Doc Smithers to ride up with me that day, but he patently refused. You'd think if a gun barrel in his ear wouldn't convince him, ten dollars in gold would. But nothing worked. I been feeling downright poorly leaving you alone with her sick and all, but I—"

"We made out fine, Mike. I thank you for trying," Garrison said as he rubbed his hands together. His damp buffalo coat had started to steam, releasing odors of mule and sweat. He shivered. "Damn, it's cold out there."

Mike came around and sat on the corner of his desk. His red hair gleamed. "You got a place to stay tonight? I know Ginny would be happy to fix you dinner and turn down the covers in the spare bedroom. If you—"

"No, thanks. I'm heading back up the mountain as soon as I get warmed up."

Hathaway's face tensed. "Don't be a fool, Garry. With these temperatures? You can't—"

"Oh, yes, I can." He nodded to Hathaway. "I stopped by Doc Smithers' and picked up a bottle of quinine and two rolls of clean bandages. So long as I'm moving, I ain't cold at all. I'll make it, don't worry. But I don't think I can risk bringing Jeremy with me. I was going to go get him, but—"

Hathaway stood up. "Goddamn, I forgot you didn't know."

Fear taunted Garrison's belly. He turned. "Know what?"

"The boy ain't at home. Not anymore, Garry. He—"

"What the hell are you talking about?" Garrison half-shouted. "Where else—"

"*Now, hold up!* Don't be getting upset." Hathaway made a calming gesture with his hands. "That boy's safe and sound. He just ain't at home. He . . . Garry, come over here and sit down so we can talk." He gestured to one of the chairs in front of his desk.

Garrison frowned at it. "I can talk just fine standing up. Tell me, Mike."

Hathaway hesitated a minute, gathering his thoughts, then he said, "There's a fella in town asking a lot of questions about a woman with long black hair. A tall woman. Says she goes by a number of different names, Heathe, Chamberlain, Heatherton. He got in two days ago—"

"Where's Jeremy?" Garrison's heart thundered. His extended fingers curled into fists and dropped to his sides. *Where is he? Did Macey—*

"Macey did. When she got wind of this fella, she packed the boy's bags and hauled him down to stay with Clara Brown in Black Hawk."

The sudden relief left him feeling weak. "Thank God. Aunt Clara agreed to—"

"Hell, yes. You know how that woman loves children. And the man that tries to hurt that boy will do it over her dead body—and Macey Runkle's, too, I wager. She seems mighty attached to the little fella."

Garrison forced his fear away so he could think. Aunt Clara Brown was a former slave who had purchased her freedom in 1857 and arrived in Black Hawk during the gold rush of '59. Her talents as a midwife, laundress, and cook had gained her the respect of the entire community. Not to mention the fact that anybody who needed a helping hand always found Aunt Clara's open.

Garrison's anxiety lessened. Jeremy and Macey would probably be safer there than anywhere, including his cabin. Few white men would think to look for Rose's son in the home of a black woman. At least, he hoped that was true.

He lifted his gaze to Mike. "And this fella? Where is he?"

"He's staying down at Mabel's Hotel, but I heard tell that during the day he's been patronizing every bar in the gulch and paying good money for answers to his questions." Hathaway's eyes narrowed. "If I was you—"

"What does this fella look like?"

Hathaway leaned forward, his blue eyes glinting. "Tall. Blond hair. Wears fancy clothes, I hear. But, Garry, I don't think you ought to try—"

"Much obliged, Mike." Garrison buttoned his coat, put on his gloves, slung his pack and shoes over his shoulders, and turned for the door. "If I wind up spending too long in town, is that offer for a meal and a warm bed still good?"

"Of course it is."

"Thanks, Mike."

He opened the door and stepped out onto the street. A man looking for Rose . . . It *must* be. The cold air stung his face. The sun had sunk below the mountains, leaving the world in dusky gloom. Mauve shadows cloaked every building. Icicles hung from eaves like sharp teeth. His chest ached.

"Goddamn it," he murmured to himself.

A faint breeze eddied along the sidewalk, bearing on its icy breath the fragrances of the night, woodsmoke and wet horses.

He sprinted up the steep hill, dodging patches of glare ice. The snow had ceased, but flakes blew off the roofs and swirled around him in glittering wreaths. When he hit the top of the hill, he broke into a dead run, lungs panting, legs pumping. As businesses closed for the night, clerks hung out "CLOSED" signs, blew out lamps, and banged doors behind them before they flooded onto the streets, going home. Garrison veered around them, not even bothering to apologize when he nearly knocked someone over.

Yellow light spilled through the front windows of Mabel's hotel and onto the street. Garrison halted his mad run. Men and women sat at tables inside.

Garrison braced a hand against a brick wall and took deep breaths to steady himself. In his dreams last night, he had done this same thing, gone to meet with the man pursuing Rose, to work out a deal. And when it had become clear that the man would settle for nothing but her pretty head, Garrison had killed him. Quickly. Cleanly. Without remorse. Images of blood and grasping hands still flitted in his memory. He couldn't quite piece them together and didn't want to. The only thing that mattered was that the man leave her alone. Garrison could convince him to do that.

He threw open the door and walked into the hotel. Familiar green tablecloths and fragrant oil lamps greeted him. People looked up, then went back to their conversations.

When Mabel saw him, she hurried across the floor, her fat cheeks jiggling. She wore a pink gingham dress and white apron, and looked hostile.

"Garrison Parker . . ." she began.

"I ain't here for fun and games, Mabel," he said sternly. "I'm looking for the fella who's asking questions around town. Heard he got in two days ago. Where is he? Can you point him out to me?"

At the serious tone in his voice, she frowned and wiped her hands on her apron. "He ain't here, Garry. He came in about an hour ago, had an early dinner, and said he was heading out to Luke's saloon for the evening. Do you want me to leave him a message—"

"No, Mabel, but thanks."

Garrison tipped his ice-encrusted hat, looked around one final time, and left. Shoving his hands into his pockets, he walked fast, down the street, around the corner, and up the hill. He could hear laughter and singing.

When he pulled back the door latch and stepped inside, he knew immediately he had found his man. Everybody else in the place dressed like a miner, businessman, or soldier, but this fella looked like an eastern dandy cast adrift in the wilderness. He sat alone at a table in the rear, pouring whisky from a bottle into a glass. His tan waistcoat, pants, ruffled white shirt, and black string tie had all been perfectly coordinated. He had a sour look on his face.

Garrison shut the door, laid his pack and snowshoes against the wall, and waved a hand to Luke, who stood behind the bar.

Luke yelled, "Where you been, Garry?"

"I holed up in my cabin 'til this storm blew over," he shouted back. "Which means I am more than eager for one of your amber ales, Luke!"

Luke grinned, showing his two top teeth, and grabbed a mug to fill.

Garrison shouldered through the crowd of singing Irishmen until he stood next to the table where the man sat. The blond looked up through narrowed eyes.

"I hear you're looking for a woman," Garrison said.

The man straightened in his chair. His thin nose and pointed chin gave him an almost effeminate look. The big ring on his finger didn't do anything to lessen the prissiness either. "I am. Please sit down. May I buy you a drink?"

Garrison shrugged out of his coat and draped it over the back of the chair before he dropped into the seat. "No, thanks. I got a beer coming," he said.

The man nodded. "Where did you hear I was looking for a woman?"

"Folks ain't talking about much else. Small towns are like that. Stranger comes in and news gets around fast. Tell me about this woman you're hunting. Is she—"

"Here you go, Garry," Luke said as he delivered the mug of amber ale. "How the hell you been? Mike came in a week ago and said you and Mrs.—"

"I ain't in a mood for chitchat," Garrison cut him off, and felt bad when Luke's face fell. The bartender wet his lips and took a step backward. Garrison dug in his pocket and tossed Luke a coin. "Sorry, Luke. I didn't mean it. I'm just here on business and don't want to be disturbed. You got that?"

"I got it, Garry. Sure. That ain't no problem. You just lift a hand if you need another beer, or something, and I'll—"

"I will. Thanks."

Luke nodded and melted into the crowd. Garrison turned back to the blond and found the man examining him carefully, like a cat at a mousehole.

"I'm Owen Fontaine," the man said and extended a hand. "What was your name?"

"Parker. Garrison Parker."

Fontaine's eyes sparkled. Garrison gripped his smooth white fingers. The man shook, but when he brought his hand back he wiped it on his pant leg, as if feeling soiled by Garrison's rough hands.

"What do you do, Mr. Parker?"

"I'm a miner. I got a claim up to Banta Hill."

"Well, isn't that a coincidence? The woman I'm looking for has a claim up there, too."

Garrison tipped up his mug and took a long drink of the sweet ale, then wiped his mouth on the sleeve of his tattered blue army shirt. "Really? Which one?"

"I don't know for certain. The former owner of the claim was Terrence Collier, he—"

"So you're looking for Rose Hale, is that right?"

Fontaine leaned back in his chair and nodded. "Yes, I think so. At least, that's what my information suggests. Do you know where she is?"

Garrison braced his forearm on the table and smiled. "I might."

The man reached into his pocket, pulled out a twenty-dollar gold piece and placed it in the middle of the table. Garrison scooped it up, figuring it would cover some of today's charges. Fontaine poured himself another whisky. "Is your memory better now?"

"A bit. Why are you looking for her?"

"I own ten percent of her claim."

Garrison stared unblinking. "How would you get part of her claim?"

Fontaine steepled his fingers beneath his pointed chin. He had an intent expression, as if intrigued by the entire discussion. "I got her into the poker game where she won it. But I thought you'd know that?"

Garrison's brows lowered. His attention was distracted when four Irishmen broke into jigs in the middle of the floor. Reeling drunk, they sang *Peg in a low-backed car*, at the tops of their lungs and off-key. Their dance steps seemed totally unrelated to their tune.

"Poker, eh? That's mighty interesting," Garrison said, turning back to Fontaine. "Why would you do that for a stranger?"

"You think that's any of your business?"

Garrison lifted a shoulder. "Just curious."

"If you've met her, you already know."

"You mean you figured you might get paid back in more interesting ways, is that it?"

Fontaine smiled. "It seemed a likely prospect at the time."

"Did you?" A tinge of anger touched his voice before he could bite it back.

Fontaine studied Garrison. "No. Afraid not. In fact, she left me in the lurch on a riverboat outside of St. Louis, and I—"

"And you followed her out West."

"Of course. I have business interests to protect."

Garrison tipped his chair back on two legs and crossed his arms defensively. His shirt already dripped with sweat. "Well, I ain't seen her, mister, but I have heard of her. I heard she lost her mine, on account of she didn't have no proof of it having been worked last year, and she headed back East. For New York, if I recall right."

Fontaine swirled his whisky and gave Garrison a vaguely antagonistic appraisal. "Are you in love with her, Parker?"

Garrison sat still for a long moment, then eased the front legs of his chair to the floor again. He didn't know the answer to that himself. "I beg your pardon?"

Fontaine looked darkly amused. "You wouldn't be the first man she's won with her substantial charms. But I wonder how much you know about her?"

"Mister, you must not have heard one word I—"

"Did she tell you she's running from a provost marshal? That he has a warrant for her arrest on charges of war crimes?" He took a sip of his drink and smiled when he saw the look on Garrison's face. Fontaine seemed to be enjoying this. "Did she tell you her real name is Robin Walkingstick Heatherton? Or that she was responsible for the deaths of thousands of Union soldiers? At Bull Run? Ball's Bluff? Chancellorsville? The Wilderness? Hmm? No? Well, I'm not surprised."

Garrison felt sands shifting beneath his feet, as if everything he'd been building his hopes upon was crumbling. He had the overwhelming urge to knock Fontaine out of that chair and kick him around the floor until he was senseless. Which surprised Garrison. Generally, he made a habit of not hitting people who told him the truth, no matter how much he didn't want to hear it. "Espionage was just part of the game, Mr. Fontaine. What war crimes is she being accused of?"

Fontaine shrugged. "I really don't know."

"Well, if you don't know that, how do you know the rest of the things you claim to? You—"

"I know. Trust me."

Garrison smoothed his beard. "That ain't something I'm likely to do any time in the near future. First off, your diamond ring tells me you ain't had to really work for a living in a long time, and second—"

"I don't give a good Goddamn what you think!" Fontaine stood so quickly his chair struck the wall and fell over on its side. Fontaine didn't even seem to notice. He braced a hand on the table and leaned down, staring Garrison hard in the eyes. "I've been told she's staying in your cabin, Parker. Now that's neither here nor there. What you and she do together is your business, but if she is there, I want you to tell her something for me."

". . . What?"

Fontaine's eyes shone like polished steel. "Tell her I'm not leaving until I see her and we work out this 'misunderstanding' about that claim, and . . ." He was breathing hard. He stabbed a finger at Garrison. "You tell her I said she'd better be thinking long and hard about how she can run our mine from hell, because I met Thomas Corley in Denver, and he most certainly wants to kill her!"

When Garrison tiptoed into the cabin around midnight, he found her asleep with her head pillowed on one arm and black hair cascading over the side of the bed onto the floor. A pang went through him when he remembered the softness of those glistening strands. They had felt like the finest Chinese silk. The whisky bottle lay on its side on the chair seat, empty, but the water hadn't been touched. The cabin felt like ice. Garrison went to the stove and loaded it with wood, then lit the lamp on the table. A bright golden glow suffused the room.

He shrugged off his pack and laid it on the table, then slipped his arms out of his buffalo coat and draped it over a chair back. For a long time, he stood watching her sleep. Her beautiful face was serene, as though she were dreaming of pleasant things for a change. Her chest moved in slow rhythms. It made a heartrending sight . . . Rose dressed in his plaid shirt, which was much too big for her, her head tilted innocently on the feather pillow, a hand on her stomach, palm up, the fingers curled.

He quietly unloaded his pack, pulling out two bottles of whisky, quinine, ten eggs wrapped in newspaper, one pound of bacon, a loaf of bread, and three precious potatoes.

When she got well enough to leave, he would miss her, miss taking care of her. Very much. Just the thought made him hurt deep down. "You're a Goddamned fool, Garrison Parker," he whispered to himself.

Angrily, he went to the stove, took the empty coffeepot off the warming shelf and filled it with water and grounds, then set it over the firebox to boil.

Next, he took down a water glass, uncorked a bottle of whisky and poured it full, *yes, by God, full.* By the time the coffee got ready, he'd be ready for it.

He frowned at her. The fire had burned down. She must be cold. He went to her and pulled the Hudson's Bay blanket up over her shoulders. She half woke and said, "Garrison?"

"I'm here, Rose."

She opened her dark eyes and smiled at him. "Where . . . where's Jeremy? I know it's been snowing all day, but I had hoped—"

"He's safe. Don't worry." Turning his back on her, he walked to the table and slumped down beside his whisky. He propped his bearded cheek on his fist. "There's other things we need to talk about."

She glanced at the full glass, and her face darkened. "What's wrong?"

He tipped the glass up, feeling the whisky burn all the way down his throat and spark a fire in his belly. Garrison drank the way he used to, when he was young and fighting a war he believed in, filled with pride. And even later, when he'd watched men dying all around him while he lived—while he wallowed in guilt with the coppery tang of blood drenching his nightmares . . .

He drank and drank, and studied her lying in his bed across the room. Her face had paled with worry. But she seemed to realize that she shouldn't ask him any more questions, not yet.

By the time he'd finished his glass, the coffee was perking. He got up, swayed, and went to pull the pot to a cooler spot. The rich brew smelled good. He poured himself a cup and turned to look at her.

"You want some?" His words came out slurred.

"Yes, thank you, Garrison."

Even the soft sound of her voice made him ache. He filled a cup for her and concentrated on not spilling it as he made his way across the floor to set it down on the chair by her bed, *his* bed. It had been so long since he'd had a woman in his bed. He set his own cup beside hers and slumped to the floor, sitting cross-legged.

The edges of his vision blurred. He wrapped his arms around his knees and let his head fall forward so that he saw only the wood plank floor. Confusion and dread throbbed in his chest. "I wish . . ." he said softly, "that you could have trusted me. I needed to know . . . things . . . and now . . . I don't know what to do."

"What happened, Garrison?"

He lifted his head and peered at her. "What do you want me to call you? Rose? Or Robin?"

Her fear was suddenly palpable. Her eyes tightened. "Please, call me Robin, Garrison."

"Robin," he whispered the name, feeling it on his tongue, letting the sound move through him like a cold autumn wind. He shook his head. "Robin Walkingstick Heatherton."

"Yes." She swallowed hard.

He gripped two handfuls of his curly hair just to remind himself that he was alive. "That provost marshal has a warrant for your arrest. Do you know that?"

"No . . . no, I didn't," she replied in a shaking voice. "But it doesn't surprise me. What are they accusing me of?"

"War crimes."

She tipped her chin up and her gaze moved over the boards in the ceiling, scrutinizing each one, the knotholes, the cracks. Her white throat gleamed silver in the firelight. "Which crimes?"

"Does it matter?"

"Yes, it does, Garrison. Sooner or later, the new president will be forced to issue an amnesty proclamation, and when he does, most Confederate 'criminals' will be granted clemency. But . . . but not all. So what they're accusing me of makes a very great difference. Do you understand?"

Her eyes pleaded with him, and he felt half-sick. "Of course, I do," he replied. "But I can't answer that, Ro—Robin. He wouldn't tell me."

A faint nod moved her head. She lowered her eyes. "You must be feeling as if I've betrayed you. I'm sorry, Garrison, I never meant—"

"How the hell would you know what I'm feeling?"

Her mouth pursed vulnerably. "I am truly sorry. I never meant to get you involved in this. I will leave here as quickly as I am able and Jeremy and I will vanish. I promise you that. I–"

"Goddamn it! I don't want you to leave. *That's the last thing in the world that I want!*"

He stumbled to his feet and folded his arms tightly across his chest, straining at his own impotence, wondering what in the hell she would make of that statement—wondering what in the hell he'd meant by it.

In sheer frustration he kicked the stove and yelled, "Do you know that Fontaine accused me of being in love with you?"

"Wh—what?" she asked breathlessly and raised herself up on one elbow.

"That's right! He accused me of being in love—"

"Did you say *Fontaine?* I thought you'd met . . . Are y—you telling me that you spent the afternoon with Owen Fontaine?"

"I am," he answered, and clenched his hands into fists. "Hell of a Goddamn fella, too. He—"

Robin fell back against her pillow and let out a groan of sheer relief. She closed her eyes and breathed for a few seconds, then she started laughing, softly at first, then harder. "Dear God!" she said. "Garrison, come over here and sit down. You had me scared to death!"

He lowered his hands to his sides and walked over to sit on the edge of the bed. Tears fringed her lashes. She smiled up at him. He was just drunk enough to reach down, pick up one of her hands, and clutch it. The bones felt frail in his grip, her skin smooth as satin. She did not try to pull away, which surprised him.

"You ought to be," he said gently. "Fontaine asked me to tell you that he met Thomas Corley in Denver and—and he said Corley most certainly wants to kill you."

Her hand started shaking and he tightened his grip. "Don't, Robin. We'll figure something out. I just need some time to—"

"Garrison," she said. The words came slowly and with difficulty, as if it hurt her to utter them. *"Where* is Jeremy? Tell me quickly."

CHAPTER 26

When Clara and little Janie eased open the door and entered the log house, Macey looked up from where she sat in the rocker by the fireplace. Jeremy lay in her arms, almost asleep. The low flames threw a wavering amber glow over the scene. Macey put a finger to her lips. Clara nodded, nudged Janie, and they both took off their worn coats and bonnets and hung them on pegs on the wall. Barely sixteen, Janie had to be the skinniest girl alive. She had an angular face with a hooked nose and blue-black skin. She watched Macey through huge dark eyes. Beneath the coat, she wore a plain brown dress, just like Clara's. Now that Macey thought about it, it probably was Clara's. Janie had come to Black Hawk from the city of Golden, hungry and scared. She had possessed one dress—and it wasn't the sort of thing a decent woman would wear to town. Clara hadn't told Macey the exact circumstances of Janie's rapid departure from Golden, but Macey could pretty well guess. The "crime" showed on the girl's bruised face. Some man had hurt her and she'd killed him. *Good for her.*

Clara glanced at Macey as she smoothed her windblown hair back into place. A cameo was pinned at her throat. Clara stood five feet seven inches tall and had wide shoulders that narrowed to a tiny waist. Macey figured her for about forty-five. As she moved about the house, folding newspapers, straightening up, she began whispering prayers. Her face had an expression of urgency, but Macey couldn't take the chance right now of asking what Clara had learned in town this afternoon.

She peered down at the little black-haired boy in her arms.

He'd sobbed for half the day and spent the other half scurrying around the house like a scared rabbit. Twenty minutes ago, his eyelids had started to droop, closing for seconds at a time, only to jerk open to survey the strange surroundings; then they would fall closed again. This time he'd been "asleep" for nearly five minutes straight.

Macey's eyes drifted over the delicate pink flowers on the wallpaper and took in the lace curtains. A pretty red braided rug lay in front of the door. Though the house was small, barely fifteen by twenty feet, it possessed a feeling of warmth and even elegance. A fat Bible with frayed leather binding sat on the table beside the rocker. It had been read a thousand times. Despite the short time Macey had known Clara, she already understood a good deal about her. A God-fearing Methodist, Clara was naturally soft-spoken, but she could deliver a hellfire-damnation lecture at the top of her lungs if the occasion required. Which was the one thing that bothered Macey. Oh, she believed in God, all right, but she'd just as soon not have to listen to somebody always saying "The Lord this," and "The Lord that." A twinge of guilt ate at her. Clara opened her arms to anybody in need—which was mighty lucky for Macey and Jeremy. And Janie. Macey guessed a little preaching wouldn't hurt her.

Macey pulled the paisley throw up over Jeremy's chest, covering both him and Traveller. That horse had not been out of his hands for a single moment all week. He'd clutched it to his belly like a bandage pressed over a bleeding wound.

Macey pulled her arm from beneath Jeremy's shoulders and stuffed a pillow in its place. Her fingers prickled. The boy seemed oblivious to her movements.

Macey whispered, "I am truly glad to see the two of you back. I been fretting all day. Did you find out anything?"

"Oh, my. Yes, we did, honey. I got a heap to tell you," Clara said. She pulled a chair up in front of the fireplace and sat down. Deep wrinkles formed around her wide mouth. "And you ain' gonna like to hear any of it."

"Liking's got nothing to do with it. What did you learn?"

Janie came over and sat on the floor by Macey's feet. She wet her lips anxiously. "It's bad, Macey. *Real* bad."

"Well, then, quit stalling and tell me about it!"

Clara leaned forward, glanced at Jeremy to make certain he was indeed asleep, then murmured, "That man is shady awright. I watched him talking real friendly-like with that no account Colonel Chivington."

Macey's eyes narrowed. Chivington, who most folks called a hero, had been involved in slaughtering a camp of Indians down on Sand Creek, south of Denver, about five months before—after the army had promised the Indians they would be safe if they camped there. Rumor had it that one of the chiefs had run out waving a white flag when he spied Chivington's horde

descending upon his people. Chivington had ignored the surrender and ordered his men to kill every man, woman, and child. Supposedly Congress
was investigating the massacre, but Macey didn't expect anything to come of
it. Indians were treated worse than Negroes in this part of the country.

"What was that fella talking to Chivington about?" Macey asked.

Clara breathed, *"Guns.* He promised the colonel that if the army cut off
his supply of weapons, he wouldn't have no trouble getting plenty from elsewhere. Fontaine tole him he could get Chivington any kind of military supplies
he needed to go on killing Injuns. I am telling the truth, as the Lord is my
witness. That's what he said. Fontaine tole the colonel all he had to do was
ask."

"Ask and pay!" Janie whispered. "You should've seen it, Macey. Me and
Clara was hiding in the kitchen at Mabel's listening to the two men talk and
I swear I ain't never heard the like. They was certainly scallawags, both of
'em. Fontaine asked for more money than I ever knew existed in the whole
wide world! Why—"

"Janie." Clara put a hand on the girl's shoulder to silence her. "Macey's
already upset. Don't go making it worse. Neither one of us knows a thing
'bout the cost of weapons, and the good Lord wouldn't want us to—"

"For Goodness sakes!" Macey hissed. "Will you tell me what you heard!
I'm gonna be old and gray before you finish the story!"

Janie hurried to answer. "Well, lemme tell you this, honey. That Fontaine—"

She'd said the last word a little too loudly, and Jeremy moaned and twisted
in Macey's lap.

"Janie," Clara said sternly. "Hush. Macey and I are gonna sit here before
the fire and have a nice quiet chat. I would 'preciate it if you would go on out
back and dip us up some cold water from the well, so as we can make a cup
of tea. Now go on, don't be arguing with me. Fetch us least half a bucket.
Enough to fill the kettle."

Janie morosely rose and went through the doorway into the kitchen. Macey heard metal clattering, then the back door opening and slamming closed.
Jeremy buried his face against Macey's bosom and heaved a sleepy sigh.

Neither Clara nor Macey spoke for a few minutes, letting the boy fall
back into a deep sleep again.

Then Clara said, "That well is so deep and the windlass so rusty, it ought
to take Janie a good fifteen minutes to get back in here. That's how long we
got to talk alone, Macey, so let's get at it."

"So this Fontaine is a gunrunner?"

"I reckon. I talked to a passel of people today, and they all tole me he was a blackguard of the worst sort."

"Well, why's he here hunting Miss Rose?"

Clara sat back in her chair and folded her hands in her lap. "Claims he owns part of her mine."

"What? How could that be?"

Clara shrugged. "I dint have no chance to ask nobody. But that's what he's been telling folks. Says he owns part and aims to get it if he has to 'wring her pretty neck.' "

Macey's brows drew together, "Landsakes, what does that mean? He's going to kill her if she thinks different?"

"Sure sounds like it."

Jeremy moved in Macey's arms, turning over onto his left side, and Macey recovered him with the paisley throw. Traveller's white head poked from between Jeremy's fingers. She wondered how he could keep clutching the toy even when deeply asleep. Not that it mattered. If that's what it took to keep him sane, well so be it. Everybody needed something. Jeremy had his toy horse, and she had her books. There wasn't no difference. His little face had relaxed, shedding the terrified look he'd worn all day.

Clara whispered, "And listen, Macey. Five days ago the newspaper run a story 'bout a killing down to Colorado City. A dove named Lily Solomay was murdered. Somebody choked her to death."

Macey's soul chilled. Horrifying images of Andre Guillard and her last night in Denver rose. She suppressed a shudder. "Did they catch the fella what done it?"

Clara shook her head. "No. Leastways they hadn't at that time. But this here Fontaine fella was mentioned in the article. I guess they questioned him good, 'cause he rode in with the army officer that was suspected of killing that poor girl."

"An army officer done it?" Heart thumping, Macey shook her head. "Why didn't they keep Fontaine in Colorado City then, 'til they caught that fella?"

"Guess they dint have no evidence against Fontaine."

"Hmph," Macey grunted. "That or he paid somebody off."

"Wouldn't doubt it one bit. Folks say he's mighty rich. Been paying hundreds of dollars to any man who'll tell him a word or two 'bout the whereabouts of Rose Hale."

"Has anybody coughed up the truth yet?"

"Lots of folks. Nobody knew in the beginning what he was up to, so they dint try to hide nothing. Fontaine's ridden his horse by Mrs. Hale's house a dozen times, I guess. Then Mist' Garrison was down yesterday and—"

"*He was?*" Macey asked, hoping for worst. "What happened?"

"The story is he cornered Fontaine in Luke's bar and gave him one whale of a talkin' to. Luke hisself tole me that Fontaine was madder'n a boxed badger when Mist' Garrison left the bar. Luke even said he'd heard Mist' Garrison threatened to kill that Fontaine."

"What did Fontaine do?"

"Luke said he screamed and hollered like a stuck hog and called Mist' Garrison some fierce names. Afterward, Mist' Garrison pulled his pistol and shoved it square into Fontaine's chest and tole him he was gonna blow a hole in him big 'nuff for a train to go through."

"And?"

"That's all Luke knew. But I figure Mist' Garrison must've been talking to people all day so when he met with Fontaine he knew a heap about him— which is why he threatened to kill him right off."

"Mercy," Macey said, disappointed. If Parker had just gone ahead and killed Fontaine everybody would have felt better. Justice was justice and, in Macey's book, Fontaine deserved it just for riding around with a murderer.

She used the tips of her bare toes to set the chair rocking again. It made a soft creaking sound, soothing her as much as it had Jeremy. Thank God there weren't any men in the house. Men spent half their lives greasing things, or nailing on them, to get them to be silent, which irritated her. She'd rocked many a child to sleep in furniture that talked back and had loved every companionable groan and shriek.

"No wonder Miss Rose is scared silly of him," Macey said. "I could tell from the first day we met that some man had her on the run. I just didn't know what to do about it."

"Well, Macey, honey, you done the best you could by bringing her son here," Clara replied. "The Lord won't let nothing happen to you or the boy while you are under my roof. I just know it."

Macey glanced at the Colt revolver snuggled beside her hip in the chair, the metal all shiny and the wooden grips oiled.

"The Lord's awful busy these days, Clara. If he wants to help, that's fine, but I think I'll count on myself for protection. Myself and Miss Rose. She—"

Clara pulled her head back in disbelief. "You're fooling me! That fine eastern lady knows how to use a gun?"

Macey nodded. "I'm telling you Clara, that lady can shoot better'n any man I ever saw. I don't know where she learned, but that woman is downright deadly with a gun." She adjusted Jeremy to take the weight from her numb left leg. He jerked his eyes open and stared around in terror.

Macey leaned down and whispered, "Everything's fine, Jeremy, sweetheart. I'm here and I ain't letting you go for nothing, so you go right ahead and sleep." She kissed him on the temple and stroked his dark hair away from his pink cheeks. Such handsome boy, if he just wasn't as skinny as a blade of grass.

Jeremy used his free hand to clutch a handful of her calico skirt and sleepily said, "I—I love you, Macey."

"I love you, too, baby. You go back to sleep for me now, you hear?"

He drifted off to sleep. He'd only started displaying his affection for her in the past couple of days, and it always made Macey's heart ache. She saw Clara smile.

"That boy sure sets a store by you, Macey."

"Well, I feel the same way about him. He's a mighty fine boy. He ain't never disobedient, and I don't even think it would occur to him to backtalk me. He's a little gentleman, that's what he is."

"Yes," Clara said. "I can see he is."

Macey started rocking again while she thought about this Fontaine fella and what his being in town meant for Miss Rose and Jeremy. "You think that Fontaine could've killed that dove hisself?"

Clara frowned. "Why would you think that?"

"Well, I was just recalling the look in Miss Rose's eyes that first day we met. I'd swear she was afraid for her *life*—not just her gold mine." Macey bit her lower lip. "And I know how that feels, Clara. I've been afraid for mine often enough. The look in her eyes that day was the same look I've had in mine a hundred times. I'd swear it. And if it was Fontaine she was scared of . . . well, I just wonder, that's all. He might've killed that dove and blamed it on that officer he was riding with." She gave Clara a serious look. "Did he look like the type when you saw him?"

Clara smoothed the wrinkles from her brown sleeves, then clasped her hands as if in prayer. "Can't rightly say, and I . . . I wouldn't want to judge the man without—"

"Clara, I ain't asking you to do something against the Bible, I just thought you might've noticed if he had hateful eyes, or notches on his pistol or anything of the like."

Clara bowed her head. Very softly, she answered, "I did notice he had a arrogant way 'bout him."

"How do you mean?"

"Smug. Like he owned the whole world. He was wearing a fancy black suit, and smoking a big cigar, and you know . . ." Clara lifted her eyes and frowned at Macey. "I did have a feeling he had a cruel streak. But it was just a feeling, Macey. I ain't accusing him of—"

"No, of course not, Clara. I know that. You wouldn't accuse somebody of spitting on the street if you caught 'em at it! What else did you notice?"

Clara's eyes moved, as if she were thinking. "Nothing else, 'bout his person anyway. But I can tell you this, not a single decent man in town liked him. People talked 'bout Fontaine like he was worse'n a rabid dog."

"And ought to be treated the same way," Macey announced. "With a bullet through the brain to ease everybody's distress."

"Macey!" Clara's face pinched. "I truly wish you could be more charitable. The good Lord ain't gonna let you into heaven if'n you keep saying such—"

"I'm planning on being charitable, Clara. I really am. Just as soon as I have the time. But until then—"

" 'Til then, you're gonna keep being mealymouthed. At this rate, Macey, you're gonna be bait for Satan long before Jesus has a chance to win your heart."

Macey wanted to tell Clara that she'd never met Jesus, but she and Satan were old friends. She'd seen his stony eyes and felt his hard hands in dozens of men. But saying such a thing wasn't a good idea. If Clara thought she were demon-possessed she might disown her naturally generous nature and throw Macey and Jeremy out onto the cold street. Clara believed such things, and fervently.

"Clara," Macey said. "I would really be obliged if you'd take it upon yourself to save my soul. I can use all the help I can get."

Clara studied her suspiciously. "You sure? You won't mind if I preach at you?"

"Not one bit, Clara. Though I'd be obliged if you'd give me some time to get used to the idea. In fact—"

"Time?" Clara said and smiled. "There's no time like the present, honey." She rose and went to pick up her Bible. "You just sit there watching the fire and as soon as Janie gets back, I'll get at the Lord's work. You *both* need it."

Robin stood in the open door of the cabin the next morning, wrapped in her blue cloak, watching Garrison saddle Honey. His breath smoked faintly in the starlight. The mule pawed at the snow with her front hoof and whinnied as if in irritation.

Garrison threw on the saddle blanket, adjusted it, then said, "Hell, don't tell me about it, Honey. I know it's cold! Tell that woman over there. She's the one who wants to kill herself by riding to town."

The pines on the crest of the hill behind him swayed in the scarlet gleam of dawn—they resembled dark spears floating on a sea of blood. Robin shivered. Nightmares had haunted her sleep. Her fear for Jeremy had become a living thing, spawning images that chilled her soul. She pulled her blue hood closed at her throat. Already her knees were trembling.

"I have no intention of dying, Garrison."

"Intentions ain't got much to do with it," he said. "Leastways, I never noticed no direct connection, and I knew a heap of fellas who—"

"I get the idea."

He gave her a disgruntled look, lifted her saddle and swung it up on Honey's back. His buffalo coat and beard bore a dusting of wind-blown snow. It glittered when he moved. Reaching under the mule's belly, he cinched up the first strap, and as he reached to buckle the second, he added, "All Honey has to do is slip on one patch of ice *that we can't see 'cause you wanted to leave in the damned dark,* and when you hit the ground on your head, we may as well call the undertaker."

"Central City doesn't have an undertaker."

"You checked into it, eh? You got seers in your family? If you knew you were going kill yourself and cause me problems, and you didn't see fit to tell me—"

"Garrison," she replied, enunciating each syllable in his name. "I *can* hold on."

He stared at her. "Well, I am glad to hear it, Robin, since it appeared to me that you could barely stand up."

She exhaled a silvered breath. "I have to get to town. You know it." Once the words were out, she leaned heavily against the doorframe to prop herself up.

His eyes tightened. "I do know it. But I do *not* know that you have to do it today. Look at you? You're shaking all over and you've only been on your feet for five minutes!"

"I'll make it."

"When you can't even—!"

"I *must* see Jeremy, Garrison. And . . . and I have to speak with Mr. Fontaine."

The wind moaned through the pines and waffled the brim of Garrison's hat. He tugged it lower over his eyes, propped his hands on his hips, then shook his head. "Well, Goddamn it," he said and waved her forward. "Come on. Let's get moving, then. I ain't of a mind to argue with you all morning."

"Aren't you going to saddle my horse first? I thought you wanted me on Honey because she was more surefooted, and that you'd be riding—"

"No, I ain't. Now, come on!"

Her boots crunched in the deep snow as she stepped outside. Garrison tramped forward. His hazel eyes reflected the starlight like mirrors, becoming gray and glistening.

"Grab on to the doorframe," he instructed. "I want you steady when I pick you up."

"All right. I'm ready."

He slipped an arm beneath her knees and one around her back, and very carefully carried her to Honey. Then he lifted her into the saddle and held Honey's halter while Robin arranged herself.

"You all right?" he asked.

"I'm fine, thank you." She picked up the reins.

"Put down those reins," he ordered. "You ain't 'riding.' I'm gonna lead Honey down the mountain. That way maybe I'll slip on the ice first and kill myself, instead of Honey slipping and killing you."

"That's not necessary, Garrison. I can—"

He grabbed the reins, jerked them out of Robin's hands, and slowly guided Honey down the mountain. Robin threw him murderous looks, but he ignored her. She held tight to the saddlehorn. As the day lightened, she could see just how deep the snow was. With every step, Garrison sank past his knees and, on occasion, past his hips. Picking a safe path was no easy task. It required that he put one foot down, test the snow, then put the other foot down. Even then, he often fell, and had to lead Honey around to a new trail.

When the sun rose above the peaks and golden light flooded the slopes, Central City came into sight. The buildings of downtown sparkled with an amber hue. Robin said, "Garrison, could you stop for a moment?"

He immediately complied, then ran back around to peer up at her anxiously. "What's wrong? You all right? You need to rest?"

"No. I'm fine," she lied. Her chest ached as if a fire raged in her heart. "I just wanted to ask you something."

"What?"

"I want you to manage the Banta Hill mine. I think you're perfect the job and that way you can keep your cabin. Are you interested in the position?"

He didn't move. His head stayed cocked at the same angle. "Well—I—I don't . . . know. I . . ." His mouth hung open.

"Speak up! Do you want the job or not?"

He answered, "There ain't no way I can get along with Fontaine, Robin."

"For heaven's sake! I own the blasted mine! The only person you have to get along with is me!"

"Well, I reckon that'll require heroism in and of itself, but—"

"Don't insult me!"

Honey sidestepped and tossed her head at the loud voices, and Garrison grabbed for her halter, soothing, "Whoa, Honey. It's all right, girl. Whoa up, there. Good girl." He scratched Honey's neck, and she breathed out a frosty breath, and quieted down.

"Well?" Robin demanded, more subdued.

"Fontaine does own ten percent of the claim, Robin, and I want you to know straight off that I ain't taking orders from no eastern dandy. Worse, if he tries to give me an order, likely as not, I'll kill him just to soothe myself. You see what I'm saying?"

"You mean you don't think you're right for the position."

"Well, it sure as hell ain't easy to make a living once word gets around that you're a murderer."

"Don't be silly! I won't fire you."

His brows lowered. He blinked once. "Well, all right, then. We'll talk about it as we get along down the mountain."

He gathered up the reins, clucked to Honey, and they set off.

A short while later, he tipped his face to the sunshine, and said, "I *do* like the idea of keeping my cabin."

CHAPTER 27

Garrison sat in Robin's dining room, drumming his fingers on the table, listening to the wind hurling itself against the house. Macey sat opposite him, with her chin propped on her hand. Her high-collared lavender dress was the perfect image of propriety. Her oiled hair was combed back into a bun. Both of them stared out the bay window, waiting.

The rain had turned to sleet and coated the front yard with a blanket of white diamonds that shimmered in the light from the windows. Stillness gripped the house, a quiet more profound than it had been an hour before when Robin and Macey had been tiptoeing around just after they'd put Jeremy to bed. Now, nothing moved. Occasionally, Garrison heard Robin's footsteps upstairs, soft, like the faint scurrying of mice, but not often.

Garrison shifted in his chair and pulled his watch from his pants' pocket. The minutes seemed to pass so damnably slowly, like the ticking of an executioner's clock.

"What time is it?" Macey asked.

" 'Bout eight."

"Then where is he?"

Garrison shoved his gold watch back into his pocket. "He ain't late yet."

"On a night like this?" Macey said. "He ought to here early, so he can get this talking over with and be back to his hotel before the temperature drops so much it freezes his horse's hooves to the ground. *And* so Miss Rose can start resting like she ought to."

Garrison let out a breath. They'd made it down the mountain late last night, and by ten o'clock this morning, Fontaine knew she was home. He'd sent a messenger to arrange a meeting, and Robin had consented, though she could barely stand on her own two feet.

The sonofabitch.

Macey jumped, her eyes wide as she gazed out the window. "Here he comes. He's riding that buckskin horse and wearing a black overcoat and hat."

Garrison stood up. "I'll go fetch Rose. Tell him she'll be down quick enough. Just do whatever he asks, Macey."

Macey's face contorted. "I'll usher him into the parlor, pretty as you please, but I ain't gonna be nice to him, Garry. Not for nobody."

He gave her a lopsided grin. "You're a fine woman, Macey."

As he trotted up the staircase, he heard Macey open the door, and say, "Come in." Then, more sharply, "Get yourself into the parlor. Mrs. Hale will be down soon."

The door slammed and Fontaine grumbled something unpleasant. His boot heels thudded into the parlor.

Garrison lifted a hand to knock at Robin's bedroom door, but hesitated. He could hear her moving about inside. Soft movements. As if each hurt. Lamplight leaked around the door frame, throwing slender spires across the wooden floor.

Garrison knocked. "Robin," he called. "Fontaine is here."

He heard her come across the floor, her steps faint, like a silk scarf drawn over wood. When she opened the door, Garrison just stared. She stood before him dressed in a black satin gown snugged at the waist with a wide cream-colored sash. Her long hair was piled on top of her head in a thousand tiny curls, and she wore a pair of diamond earbobs.

"You ready?" he asked.

"As ready as I'll ever be." She gave him a tired, but warm smile. "Thank you for staying to help me. I'm sure I couldn't have made it down and then up those stairs again—"

"Don't thank me yet. I might not be around to carry you back upstairs, on account of I might have to drag Fontaine's dead body out and bury it first."

"I appreciate the offer," she said. "I'll let you know if it's necessary."

"You promise?"

Closing the door behind her, she stepped out into the hall, and gazed up at him wryly. "Yes. But don't get too eager. I don't think he's as bad as you think he is. At our last meeting he seemed like a decent human being."

Garrison just scowled as he reached for her. Very gently, he lifted her into his arms and descended the stairs. Despite the fact that he'd been feeding her as much as he could, she felt as light as a brittle autumn leaf. At the foot of the stairs he set her on her own two feet and said, "Just remember, I'll be in the kitchen with Macey. Holler if you need me. For *anything*. You understand?"

Robin nodded. "Thank you, Garrison. But I'm sure I'll be all right."

He gave her a skeptical look and headed for the kitchen.

He found Macey seated at the table by the cook stove, a glass of brandy in front of her. She looked up and said, "Well, set yourself down. I reckon this is gonna take a while."

"I reckon so."

He slumped down in the chair on the opposite end of the table. With a flourish, Macey reached down by the table leg and pulled up a bottle of whisky. It had a glass turned over the cork. "I figured this is what you'd want."

She handed it across the table and he took it and poured some into the glass.

"Only half full?" Macey asked.

He nodded solemnly. "Murder is an act best done sober. I have to keep my wits about me tonight . . . I'd hate to miss."

"Well, I definitely would not want you to miss, neither," she replied, and knocked back her glass of brandy. "Since all I'll have to do is help you drag his body out, I reckon I can bibulate all I want to."

He smiled. The way she swayed at the table, she'd been bibulatin' for a while, fortifying herself for the evening's activities.

"Macey," he said bracing his elbows on the table, "I would like you to give me a hand piecing information together. You've been in town, I haven't. What are folks saying about this Fontaine fella?"

"You mean you don't know?" She looked shocked.

"No, I don't know. How could I?"

Bewildered, Macey lounged across the table, and said, "I thought you'd already altercated with Fontaine?"

"I was in town, and I did meet with him. But not for more than half an hour. Which ain't hardly enough time to—"

"Didn't you threaten to shoot him after he called you some rough-and-ready names?"

Garrison's bushy brows drew together over his straight nose. He took a drink of whisky and squinted at her. "Macey, you been listening to Luke Foster down at the bar? That's just the sort of grandiose hogwash he'd be circulating about me."

"Well, tarnation," she said, and pounded a fist on the table. Garrison grabbed for his glass. "I was so hoping that part was true."

*   *   *

Owen paced before the stone fireplace. Snowflakes whirled beyond the parlor's bay window. As wintry twilight had deepened the icy sleet stopped and a cold wind swept down the peaks, shoving snow before it, creating such a dense ground blizzard that Owen could barely see across the street. The ride from the hotel had been very cold. He wasn't looking forward to the return trip.

His eyes drifted over the stark room. No paintings adorned the walls. No rugs covered the polished wood floors. Atop the oak writing desk on the western wall a single oil lamp gleamed. The flickering light of the fire and the low gleam of the lamp cast a dim orange glow over the small table and high-backed couch that sat before the fireplace. A bottle of sherry and two glasses stood on the table.

Steps sounded in the next room, and Owen pulled down his black shirt sleeves and adjusted the lapels of his mustard-colored jacket. Voices murmured.

Then, she appeared in the doorway.

Owen straightened.

She walked toward him, erect, beautiful, and radiating the same beguiling charm he remembered from the riverboat. Her black satin gown was exquisite.

"My dear Mrs. Heatherton," he said, and propped his hands on his hips to glare at her. "How *very* nice to see you again."

"Don't be unkind, Mister Fontaine," she said. "From what I hear, you know very well why I had to jump ship outside of St. Louis."

"I assume," he said, "that you are referring to the illustrious Major Corley?"

She came around the opposite side of the couch and seated herself, folding her hands in her lap. "I understand you met him."

He stood staring down at her. How odd that she appeared calm. Just the mention of Corley set his blood to pumping. Owen smiled at her. Her diamond earbobs, and the pins in her hair, glittered wildly. Seeing her again soothed some of his need for the finer things in life. My God, she was beautiful.

Owen sat on the other end of the couch. "Yes," he said. "I met him. Met him, rode with him for a hundred miles and, thankfully, I lost him."

Firelight glimmered in her dark eyes. "May I pour you a sherry?"

"Yes, Mrs. Heatherton. I'd like that. Don't you want to hear more about Corley?"

She filled two glasses and handed one to him. Her hand was rock steady. "Yes, I'd be very grateful if you would tell me about your experiences, Mr. Fontaine—"

"*Do* call me Owen, Mrs. Heatherton. I can tell you're quite overjoyed to see me again, and such a welling of emotion deserves familiarity. Don't you agree?"

She nodded. "If you like."

Boldly, he let his eyes drift over her body. She responded by smiling coldly. "You're even more beautiful than I remember, Rosie, dear. Or shall I address you as Robin?"

"Mrs. Hale will be fine, thank you. That's the name I go by now."

Owen lifted his glass of sherry to examine the color in the firelight. It gleamed like burnished copper. "Oh, I don't think we need to be so formal, but since you're concerned about preserving your masquerade, I'll call you Rose. Now, dear, do tell me, how you are? The gold towns are buzzing with news of your injury—and you do look pale. Or is it just the sight me that's drained the color from your cheeks?"

"I'm still recovering from a fall down a mine shaft. I broke my rib, and I—"

"Well, if you hadn't been so anxious to evade having breakfast with me, you wouldn't have broken it the first time, and I'm sure your current injury wouldn't be half so serious."

Her graceful brows arched.

Owen crossed his legs and propped his glass on his knee. "Or perhaps your continuing illness is due to Parker's poor care? Tell me everything, dear. I'm quite concerned about your welfare."

"Are you, indeed?"

"Good heavens, yes. In fact, I've been plagued with dread. Just the thought of you alone with Parker . . . Well, with you so incapacitated, and him such a barbarian, I was certain he would take advantage of your helplessness." Owen leaned forward, and whispered, "Tell me, darling, did he *look* when he changed your bandages?"

She leaned toward him and matched his whisper, "Let me satisfy your vulgar curiosity by telling you that he did, and I enjoyed every minute of it. Is there anything else you would like to know?"

Owen had been unable to suppress the desire to ask her straightforwardly, but now he wished he hadn't. She looked serious and a pang of jealousy shot through him. He admitted to himself that he'd been hoping to establish a "warmer" rapport with her and found this news truly disconcerting. He finished his glass of sherry.

"My dear Rosie," he said. "How could you confess such a thing to me when you know I'm expiring with love for you? I should challenge Parker to a duel before he has a chance to tell anyone and tarnish your honor."

"I wouldn't if I were you," she replied matter-of-factly. "He's a very good shot, and I'd hate to see you dead."

"Would you?" Owen laughed and draped his arm over the carved back of the couch. "That makes me feel better."

A fierce gust of wind battered the house and came down the chimney, causing the low flames to crackle and pop. Carnelian threads of light reflected in the wood floor. Owen saw her shiver. She turned to gaze out the window where gray veils of snow twisted and tumbled by, some as thin as strands of silk, others quite solid, like frosty bodies moving in some eerie winter dance.

"Cold?" he asked.

"I'll be fine," she said and rubbed her arms. "Please tell me more about Corley. You rode with him, you said?"

Owen poured himself another glass of sherry. He could see her trepidation now. It seeped through her controlled facade like water through cracks in stone. Her gaze was still unperturbed, but the corners of her mouth showed the strain. Would the dam eventually break and all her hidden fears flood out? He had no idea, but the possibility intrigued him. Some perverse part of his nature wanted to see her vulnerable, longed for it, in fact. Though he couldn't say why exactly.

"Yes," he answered. "We met in Denver and he interrogated me about your whereabouts. I lied, of course." He sipped his sherry and looked up at her. She didn't seem to be breathing. He continued, "I don't know why I lied, but I did. I told him you had gone to Fort Lyon in the far southeastern corner of the territory."

He saw a swallow go down her throat, but her voice remained steady. "And what happened then?"

Owen swirled his sherry, watching the amber waves wash the crystal. "Then he forced me to ride south with him. Being the coward that I am, of course I went."

Memories of that morning in the hotel, the pounding feet, the frantic voices—he smiled to drive away the icy sensation in his chest. She sat still, watching him through dark intent eyes. "I'm not sure you want to hear what happened next. It wasn't pretty. I have never—"

"Tell me. Please. I need to learn everything about him that I can."

"Oh, well, some things are easy. He was born in Ohio, graduated from West Point in 1844, and has spent the past twenty-one years in blissful service to this confused country. He is, as you know, on the provost marshal's staff, though for the life of me, I can't see George Sharpe keeping such a madman employed. Sharpe has a good deal of common sense and he—"

"You know him?"

As she tilted her head to the right, questioningly, the glow of the fireplace flowed like honey into the tiny curls in her hair, and accentuated the smooth texture of her skin. Owen took a few moments to admire her beauty. And she knew that was what he was doing. Their gazes locked. A strengthening current, like a warm rush of water, ebbed back and forth between them.

When Owen began to feel it too strongly, he frowned down at his sherry again. "Not personally, but I know a good deal about him. And I am well acquainted with several members of his staff—though I'd never met Corley before." His brow furrowed. "Rose, did it occur to you that I might be able to help you? I have many useful friends in the military."

She bowed her head and concentrated on the laced fingers in her lap. "I assumed that your military friends were the sort who only helped themselves."

He threw back his head and laughed, amused by her sardonic comment.

"You mean," she said, "that my assumption was incorrect?"

"Well . . . not wholly. They are the sort who require proper 'incentives,' but I assure you, they would have been eager to come to my aid. I could have been of service to you. And saved myself a few bruises and sleepless nights, as well."

"I am sorry you had to endure Thomas Corley's—"

"Well, that's makes two of us among, I suspect, many more. Especially one very attractive woman in Colorado City." He grimaced at the memories. "Have you heard about that?"

"Something, yes."

"Her name was Lily Solomay. She was beautiful. Tall. Raven-haired. In fact, she looked a lot like . . ." A curious tingling invaded his gut. He sat up straighter. "She looked a lot like *you*, Rose."

"He—he killed her . . . I heard."

"Strangled her." His eyes narrowed. "Then he braided her long black hair, Indian style, and . . ." He couldn't go on. "Well, never mind the rest. You get the idea."

The muscles of her jaw hardened. It took a full minute before she answered, "Yes. I do." He heard the bitterness and anxiety in her voice.

"Did you read about it in the paper?"

She nodded. "Yes. Garrison brought me the article. And I read about you. Owen?" she asked bluntly, but without reproach. "Why did you lie to them about his name?"

"Oh, that," he breathed. "Well, when they first asked me, I had no idea where Corley was, and I knew if I told the deputy the truth and Corley found out, he would most assuredly hunt me down and kill me." Owen massaged his taut neck muscles. "Like any other fool, I assumed that if he thought I was covering for him, he would take it kindly and spare me his wrath. In short, my dear Rose, I was protecting my own skin."

A mixture of snow and sleet began drumming against the windowpanes, and Owen turned away from her penetrating gaze to study the icy night.

"It's all right, Owen," she said. "I don't blame you."

"Don't you? You should. I've been blaming myself enough."

"No, I might have done the same thing myself, if I thought it would save my life or Jeremy's."

"It's kind of you to say so."

The fire's luminescent glow gilded the smooth curves of her right cheek and sparkled in her eyes. She looked sad and a little frightened, and it went straight to his heart. "Rose," he said concernedly. "I never told him, or anyone else, the name of the place you were coming. But, you know, don't you, that eventually he will wind up here in Central City?"

She laced her fingers in her lap and squeezed them hard. "Yes, I know that."

"What are you going to do?"

"I—I don't know, Owen."

"May I give you some advice?

"Please."

He reached into the pocket of his jacket, removed the envelope she'd left for him on the riverboat, and laid it on the couch between them. "The twenty-three hundred dollars is all there. I don't want greenbacks. I want to see my interest in the mine pay off. Invest this into equipment, get the mine running, then leave. I'll take my cut at the end of every year. *Don't* stay here, Rose. It's not safe and you know it."

She got to her feet, folded her arms, and walked to stand before the fireplace. The light danced in the folds of her black satin gown. "Yes. I do know it. But you're right, Owen, I must get the mine up and running first, to secure my future. Then I can go. That shouldn't take me more than a week, maybe ten days. I believe I can maintain my charade in town for that long."

Owen leaned forward and braced his forearms on his thighs. "*I* can get the claim producing for you. I am, after all, part owner. It would be a pleasure to—"

"No. Thank you. I mean no offense, Owen, but the only person I trust with my business affairs is me."

"Indeed?" he said, and lounged back against the couch. "It seemed to me that you trusted Parker well enough, though, God knows, I'll never understand why you hired him."

"Because you dislike him, you mean?"

"Oh, it's not so much that I dislike him, though there's quite a lot to dislike. I just think we could have done better, that's all."

"Well, I *don't* think so." Her voice had become terse.

This display of loyalty amused him. "Don't you? I should be happy that you have such limited exposure to common laborers. But I met several men in Denver who had considerable experience managing large, profitable mining operations, and any one of them would have been better than Parker. Forgive me, but Parker hardly appears successful. In fact, he looks dirt poor. I'm surprised he could feed you while you were in his cabin."

Her nostrils quivered with rage and she dropped her fists to her sides. "Garrison Parker is the manager of the mine, and that's that."

"If you say so."

"I *do* say so."

"Very well. So long as he works out. How much are you paying him?"

"That's none of your concern, and I would appreciate it if you—"

"Well, then, let me tell you what I've heard. It's all over town that you offered him two hundred dollars a month and a ten percent interest in the mine. Is that correct?"

Stiffly, she replied, "It is."

Owen shook his head in exaggerated disbelief. "Good God, Rose, you could have hired the King of England for that! But what's done is done. I don't see any cause to kick and scream about it." He smiled. "There, there, calm yourself. I want to return to our former discussion. Tell me what I may do to help you get the mine running quickly and efficiently."

"Nothing. Thank you. I'll do it myself."

Owen rose and stood facing her.

"Well then, perhaps the best thing I can do," he offered, "is to telegraph some of my 'allies' in the provost marshal's office. If they are willing to dispatch investigators to apprehend Corley, you may not have to worry about leaving at all. Which will give you more time for the mine."

Hope tensed her face, desperate hope, and no small measure of suspicion and fear. "Do you . . . do you think they might be willing?"

"Maybe. It depends on how convincing I am when I detail his murderous escapades to them."

"I see." Her voice had gone quiet. "And what are you asking in exchange for this help?"

"The soul of practicality even if the depths of terror," he said, and his brows lowered. It sounded as if she were willing to negotiate a business deal. He smiled. Perhaps his suspicions about her moral elasticity would prove out after all. "I thought we could work that out along the way."

"Would a larger percentage in the mine help cover your time and expenses?"

"It might. But there are other things that would please me much more. As you so astutely pointed out weeks ago, money isn't something I particularly need."

The struggle on her face entertained him. She was obviously weighing her life and that of her son against his coarser "needs." What would she do now? Scream and shout? Call him a cad? Throw him out of her home? . . . Or would she acquiesce to his implied demands?

"Your drinking has diminished, my dear," Owen said and gestured to her untouched glass of sherry on the table. "Good for you. I'm sure the healthy glow will return to your cheeks in no time. I genuinely look forward to it. When you have the strength, I would like to get to know you *much* better."

She looked as if she'd just swallowed poison. Her back went ramrod straight. Owen walked over and playfully chucked her under the chin.

"Cheer up," he said. "If I can arrange it so the government doesn't hang you, you'll have years to exact revenge for my pointed questions and tasteless innuendoes."

"I certainly hope so."

He grinned. "I'd best be going. After all, I'll have to get down to the telegraph office early tomorrow morning so I can start trying to save your pretty hide. A hide that I would very much like to—"

"Get out Owen."

"Oh, I'm going, dear. But don't forget, I have a room at the hotel. Please feel free to call on me at your earliest convenience."

On his way out, he grabbed his coat and hat from where Macey Runkles had tossed them on the table in the dining room.

Sleet stung his face as he strode down the walkway. Would she come to his hotel? He had no idea. But just the *game* thrilled him.

He grinned as he mounted his horse and kicked it into a gallop down the cold icy street, wondering what it would be like to have such a glorious woman as his mistress.

"He said *what?*"

CHAPTER 28

Feathery clouds drifted across the sky, stroking the face of the sun with thin transparent fingers. Owen glanced at them as he guided his horse down the sharp incline above the town of Black Hawk. Weather in the high mountains was annoying as hell. Rainy and cold one instant, it could turn hot as blazes the next when the sun emerged from behind a bank of clouds. He didn't know whether to roll up his gray shirtsleeves or pull his heavy black overcoat from where he'd tied it behind his saddle—he'd been alternating every fifteen minutes.

He'd telegraphed his "friend," Major Gill, in the provost marshal's office two hours before. The immediate reply listed Rose's numerous war crimes and promised a preliminary response to Owen's charges against Corley by tomorrow morning. That's what he liked about Gill. Though the man drove a hard bargain, once the price had been settled, he could be counted upon to throw his influence around. He probably had his underlings scurrying already.

Owen could understand Gill's self-serving practicality. The telegraph company, on the other hand, was operated by sheer thieves.

The wires had only reached Central City seven months before, in October of 1864, so the owners could charge whatever they damned well pleased. And it pleased them to charge a lot. A ten-word message cost a whopping ten dollars and ten cents, and Owen's message had been thirty words! On top of the five hundred dollars he'd promised Gill, communication alone might run well over three hundred dollars. Outrageous!

Worse, a message sent from Central City had to be transferred in Denver, which meant it was almost impossible to send a query and receive a response in the same day. He'd been lucky with Gill this morning. Apparently, only a few messages were traveling the lines so early, so his had gotten through.

To give his ire a chance to cool, Owen had decided to take a ride around the mining camps.

Plumes of dust gusted by him. Ahead, the road passed through a narrow defile lined on both sides by jumbled piles of granite boulders. Wavering shadows dappled the outcrop. Owen loosened the reins a little and let the horse trot. Coolness enveloped them when they entered the defile. His horse slowed to a walk.

He'd managed three hours of sleep last night, which didn't help his mood. Dreams of Rose had kept him tossing and turning. Over and over, he'd removed the sparkling diamond pins from her hair and run his hands through that wealth of midnight strands, before undressing her. The yearning, of course, had nothing whatsoever to do with love. He barely knew Rose and, because of some of the things Corley had told him, would approach any sort of intimacy warily—but knowing he didn't love her did little to stem the tide of his lust. Simple lust. That was all. But he felt like a man who had been crawling through the desert on his belly for days without water. Calling his condition "simple" thirst didn't quite do it justice.

Owen shook his head. She had done nothing, absolutely nothing, to encourage him—except for a casual suggestion that might be taken to mean that she might be willing to use her flesh as the basis for negotiations. But with a woman as exotically beautiful as Rose, perhaps that's all it took. And if that's all it took for Owen, a mere glance might have sufficed for Corley.

His gut twisted. "For goodness sakes, stop thinking about Corley."

If things worked out the way he hoped, Corley would be behind bars in a matter of days, and Owen wouldn't have to worry about him ever again. A lingering sense of dread continued to plague him, however. Corley would never give up hunting for Rose until . . .

The buckskin suddenly leaped sideways with a snort, and Owen glimpsed the blue shadow that detached itself from the granite outcrop.

Owen cried out when the man struck him and dragged him off his horse to the ground. He landed hard, and they rolled in the dust, swinging wildly at each other.

Owen yelled, "Goddamn it, Parker! What the hell's the matter with you?"

A fist landed in the middle of Owen's face, and the pain so enraged Owen that he grabbed for the pistol on his hip.

"Don't!" Parker dove, catching Owen's elbow and shoving up hard and fast, pinning his arm over his head. Then brutally, and repeatedly, he slammed a knee into Owen's groin. White flashes of agony bolted through him.

"Jesus . . . Christ, Parker!" he gasped. Nauseated and disoriented, he let the gun drop and curled into a tight ball. "Will you tell me . . . what the hell you want?"

"I aim to talk to you," Parker replied. He grabbed Owen's pistol and stood up.

"Talk?"

"That's right, talk," he answered as he checked the revolver's cylinder to find out how many shots remained. "I just have a way with words."

Owen groaned and winced when he rolled to his side. "You certainly do, Parker."

Parker watched him, his hazel eyes hard, unyielding. Standing that way, in the slanting rays of morning sunlight, he looked damned tall and muscular in a way that only hard labor can make a man. For a brief instant Owen regretted his life of ease. He would have loved to stand up and . . . well . . . so much for fantasizing. The most maddening element of all was Parker's aplomb. He appeared perfectly calm, almost uninterested. He could have been peering down at a rock, instead of Owen's battered and bloody carcass.

Amused with himself, Owen chuckled. He had no chance against this man in a fair fight, but there were other ways of finishing an opponent. He hadn't done his own fighting in years, he'd hired it done for him, and if he lived through this, Parker would rue this day indeed. The thought buoyed Owen's spirits.

He shifted to massage his aching right kidney, and Parker, observing, commented mildly, "Be glad you're alive, Fontaine. I ought to kill you for what you said to Robin last night."

"What? What are you talking about?" Dazed, blood streaking his face, Owen's mouth gaped for a moment, then, when understanding dawned, he broke into a roar of amazed laughter. *"That's* why you attacked me? For suggesting she become my mistress? Good Lord, Parker. You sound like an actor in a bad play!"

Parker answered by delivering two sharp kicks to Owen's left kidney and saying, "I'd be much obliged if you'd get up so I can knock you down again."

"I don't think that's such a good idea."

"I didn't ask your opinion." Murderous rage glinted in his eyes, but his face showed no emotion whatsoever. "I said, *get up,* or by God, I'll—"

"All right," Owen said and held up a hand. "Just one minute. Just . . . one . . ."

Rolling to his knees, he took a few deep breaths and stood up. He shook as if with ague. He used the back of his hand to wipe away the blood that trickled down into his eyes.

"So?" Owen asked. "Now what?"

Parker tilted his head to study Owen with one eye. His brown curly hair stuck out beneath the brim of his felt hat. "You admit you said them things to her? About her coming to your hotel at her earliest convenience? About how you want to get to know her *much* better?"

"Yes! All right! I admit it. What of it? You act like a sulking school boy, Parker. What's the matter? Did I infringe on something you consider to be *yours?*" Owen's voice had risen to a shout. "I don't think she sees it that way, Parker. But maybe you should ask her yourself, I've heard she has a *great* familiarity with men, and you—"

With one swift motion, Parker swung the barrel of the pistol for Owen's skull. Owen threw up an arm to avert the blow, but the force sent him sprawling across the road again. Gravel gouged through his gray silk shirt, shredding it into strips.

"Get up!" Parker ordered. "Get up and fight, goddamn you!"

Owen braced himself on one elbow and shook his head while he laughed. "No, thank you just the same. I don't think I will."

Parker's jaw clenched. He lifted the pistol, and the sleeves of his faded blue army shirt billowed in the wind. "Get up, or I'll kill you right now."

Rage flooded Owen's veins. He fell back to the road with his arms wide, his lacerated chest exposed through the rips in his silk shirt, and he flailed back and forth in the road. "Go ahead. Shoot! I'm right here. Kill me!"

Parker just stared.

". . . Well? What are you waiting for? Afraid Rose might object to her benefactor's murder? Do you know what I spent all morning doing, Parker? Composing and sending a message that ought to chuck Thomas Corley into prison within the week." Owen lifted his head and cupped a hand to his ear as if waiting for Parker's reply. "What? No quips? No threats? Didn't she tell you that part?"

Parker's head moved in an almost imperceptible nod. "She told me." He cocked the hammer on the pistol, and leveled it dead center at Owen's head. "Hold still, now. This will be a whole lot quicker if you don't move."

"Uh . . . Parker, listen—"

"No, don't think I will. I got better things to do with my time."

Owen's eyes widened as he looked down that dark barrel. He could see Parker's finger tightening on the trigger, his knuckle going white. My God! The man was going to do it. He was going to kill him! For something as trite as insulting a woman's honor. This was too ridiculous!

"Parker! I—I'll apologize." Licking the sweat from his upper lip, he added, "Or . . . or . . . tell me what you think is appropriate penance, and I'll do it!"

"Will you?"

"Hell, yes!" Owen blurted. Parker wasn't even breathing hard. Owen could see the hazel of his eye lined up with the revolver's sights. Completely still. "L—listen, Parker. I agree that my behavior last night might have been rude, but I don't think I deserve to die for it!"

"It was a mite worse than rude, Fontaine."

"For God's sake! You think bad manners are a killing offense?"

"I reckon I do."

"This is insane! Will you wait just a blasted minute! *Listen*—"

"No. You listen," Parker said in a low clipped voice. "You made her feel small and dirty last night, Fontaine. She didn't deserve that—maybe no more'n you deserve to die right here in the road—but seeing as how such considerations didn't plague your mind none last night . . ." One of Parker's eyes squinted. "I don't see why I ought to—"

"*What can I do to make amends?*" Owen yelled. ". . . Tell me! I'll do anything!"

Parker's aim did not waver, but he looked over the sights this time, pinning Owen with a cold glare. He appeared to be thinking. "There are a few things that might help."

"What!"

"First off, you could give back your ten percent interest in the claim. The way I heard it, you said yourself that you don't need the money."

"My . . . my interest?" Owen asked. "But, Parker! I won it fair and square. If I hadn't gotten her into that game . . ."

It was a subtle motion, just a bare movement of arms raising and head lowering, lining up eye and sight. The man had a chilling expression, as if he would enjoy pulling the trigger.

Owen swallowed hard. "All right. " He nodded. "She can have the claim. I won't interfere. Is that enough? May I go now?"

Parker's jaw ground. He didn't say anything for a time, but his hazel eyes flared. "Not yet. Let's talk for a bit more. Robin's sick and she's tired. She needs time to heal . . . and time to . . . well, to be by herself. Which means seeing you will put a strain on her. You get my meaning?"

"I do." Owen indignantly leaned forward. His kidney hurt so bad, he reclined and propped a hand on the ground. "And just how long do you want me to wait, Parker, before I tell her what I've found out from the provost marshal's office?"

For the first time, real emotion tensed Parker's face. Hurt or confusion, or something even more revealing . . . desperation. "Have you found out anything yet?"

"A few things. Rather critical, I'd say."

"For example?"

Owen chuckled while he shook his head. "I learned what they're charging her with. And it isn't pretty, Parker. She—"

"What?"

Owen pointed to his horse standing twenty paces away. "May I? The telegraph wire is in my saddlebags." He started to rise, and Parker kicked his feet out from under him. He fell hard. Owen growled a string of profanities. "If you won't allow me to—"

"I'm gonna allow you. I just want you to remember something. I think killing you would be a service to America, and given your record in gunrunning, I reckon the army would agree. So, you be real careful not to give me a reason."

"Do you need a reason?"

"Not much of one."

"That's what I thought."

With great care Owen got to his feet, held his hands over his head, and walked to his saddlebags, conscious the entire time that Parker's pistol remained leveled at his head. The man walked behind him with the stealth of an assassin, his movements not even audible above the rustling of leaves in the wind.

Dressed in his red satin smoking jacket, Owen paced in the narrow space between his bed and the chest of drawers. Only about eight by ten feet, the hotel room barely gave him space to take three steps in any direction, which fueled his anger. He paced the length of the room, from the gruesome painting of Jesus on the northern wall to the washstand on the southern wall, turned, and retraced his steps. He'd thrown his overcoat across the blue bedspread, and had spent well over an hour cleaning dirt, blood, and grit from his face and chest. Already dark circles had formed beneath his eyes. Him! With two black eyes. Good Lord.

I'll do anything! he'd said, like a comedian spouting lines. And none-too-amusing ones at that. He'd been stunned by Parker's violence, and only after he'd returned here to the hotel had his shame and rage blended into one stout brew. He had just enough of his wits about him to keep from riding to the nearest bar, finding the worst hooligan he could, and hiring the man to kill Parker. Parker deserved to be killed for what he'd done. The man was arrogant and impulsive. But Rose would know the cause of Parker's death. Which meant she might do something unwise, like hiring a discreet murderer herself . . .

Yes, she had it in her to pay someone to kill Owen.

If she weren't already guilty of paying for murder, she would be some day. Owen knew how easy it was for a person with money. It could happen over nothing: An unjust accusation, a few harsh words, maybe a shove or a challenge; then the "pieces of silver" changed hands and it was done, and you could never look back.

What a burlesque. First, she leaves him stranded on a riverboat, then he meets Corley and is frightened for his life. Finally, he finds Rose again, and has to battle a hairy, uncouth barbarian over insulting her, and now he has to worry about her hiring a killer! Not only that. He'd promised to relinquish his interest in the claim!

He was furious with himself, even more so because he knew that Parker was probably gloating about it this very instant. Owen should be laughing. This was hilarious. But he didn't want to laugh, he wanted to shoot Parker just to see the smug expression drain from his bearded face.

Owen stopped pacing in front of the mirror and gazed at his reflection. His black eyes looked worse. The color had gone from blue to a deep dark purple, the shade of week-old liver. His nose had started to swell too. Fortunately the pain had gone. Now, it just felt numb. But every other square inch of his body ached to compensate.

"You stupid fool," he muttered to himself, and ran a hand through his freshly washed blond hair. "You should have guessed that she'd tell Parker everything you said last night and that he'd react exactly as he did. The man's a Texan, and they're all born idiots."

He let out a long breath, and stared at the scratches on his chest that showed through the V in his red jacket.

He wouldn't be able to show his face in town for days.

Which ought to provide him with enough time to think up a way of paying Parker back for the embarrassment.

APRIL 23, 1865

MAJOR THOMAS CORLEY—STOP—COLORADO CITY COLORADO TERRI-
TORY—STOP—IN RECEIPT OF YOUR LAST TELEGRAM REGARDING ACTIVI-

TIES OF OWEN FONTAINE—STOP—CHECKED INTO HIS BACKGROUND—STOP—MIGHT WELL BE MURDERER OF MISS SOLOMAY—STOP—FONTAINE WANTED FOR CRIMES TOO NUMEROUS TO LIST—STOP—SINCE LOCAL AUTHORITIES HAVE REQUESTED YOUR ASSISTANCE YOU ARE AUTHORIZED TO PROCEED WITH INVESTIGATION—STOP—COLONEL GEORGE SHARPE.

CHAPTER 29

Macey sat at the kitchen table, making out a list of supplies she needed to get at the mercantile and watching Jeremy from the corner of her eye. He'd been roaming the house like a small thin reflection of a child, galloping Traveller over chairs and tables and across the polished wood floors. All in silence. He now stood with his nose flattened against the frosty kitchen windowpane, looking up the rocky slope behind the house, whispering to Traveller. Sunshine bathed him in brilliance. Such a quiet boy. He never began a conversation: even when spoken to, he seemed terrified to answer. The only creature on earth that he talked to was that toy horse. His fear grew worse when Miss Rose was gone, like today. She had ridden to Banta Hill with Garry to take a look at the way he was using timbers to shore up the mine, which he vowed was about to collapse around his ears. Macey didn't expect them back until supper time.

Jeremy tapped Traveller's head against the window several times and sighed deeply. Macey put down her quill and turned.

"Jeremy, honey, I'm feeling mighty lonely today. Would you like to come and keep me company while I finish my list?"

Jeremy bit his lower lip. Quietly, he edged across the floor and climbed into the chair next to Macey's at the table. His face had blanched to the color of his white shirt, which made his dark hair seem as black as a crow's wings. Wide eyes stared at her, unblinking—like a baby rabbit's facing a wolf. He clutched Traveller to his chest.

Macey smiled at him. "Honey, what's the matter? You been roaming the house like you lost your soul somewhere and can't find it. Are you missing your mother?"

He frowned at the table top. "No."

"Jeremy, sweetheart, look at me. I'm your friend, ain't I?"

He nodded.

"You're my friend, too. I love you just like you was my own son, and I'm worried sick about you. If you can't tell me what's ailing you, who can you tell?"

Jeremy bowed his head and peered at her from beneath his lashes. After a moment, he began petting Traveller—an answer if ever she'd seen one.

Macey reached out and stroked Traveller's nose with her fingertip. "Well, thank heavens you've got Traveller to talk to. He always listens, don't he?"

"Yes."

"And he never runs off and leaves you, or yells at you, or makes you scared. That horse is a mighty fine friend to you, Jeremy."

"He's my—my *best* friend."

Macey nodded approvingly. "It's good to have a best friend. I ain't got one. Did you know that?"

Jeremy looked up, astonished. "No. No, I—I didn't know that. I thought all grownups had friends. Lots of them. Garry—"

"Oh, well, sure. Garry's just got that kind of crazy personality that draws people like flowers draw bumblebees. But I'll bet if you asked him Garry would tell you he ain't got more than two or three real friends in all the world. I used to have a best friend, down in Denver City, but she moved back to Oklahoma."

Jeremy cocked his head. "Mama has lots of friends, too. Back home, she was always going to parties, and for long trips to visit relatives, and sick friends. She had lots of sick friends during the war."

The unspoken words "and left me alone" hung in the air like the sword of Damocles, just waiting to fall and slice off their heads. So that's why he got silent and scared whenever Miss Rose left, even for a few minutes. He was afraid she wasn't coming back. After all, his daddy hadn't.

Macey braced her chin in the palm of her hand. "Well, I reckon so. My Lord, when I think about all the folks who got shot, or took sick in camp, why it makes my heart flutter. Your mama is a good person to have tried to help so many people."

Jeremy nodded, but he looked sad. "I love her."

"I know you do. I do, too. She's been plenty good to me. But I have been scared plum silly about her recently. Haven't you? I wouldn't say none of this except to my best friend. Do you think you could be my best friend for today, Jeremy?"

He looked up fearfully. "Yes."

"Thank you, honey, 'cause I got a lot of things on my mind that I need to talk to somebody about. I mean what with your mama getting hurt in the mine, then that buffoon, Fontaine, coming over and making her feel even worse, I am just plain fidgety." Macey shook her head, picked up her quill, and jotted down "1¼ pounds adamantine, or 1 pound sperm candles" on her list. The mercantile didn't always have what you wanted, so a person had to be ready to make substitutions.

In the pause, Jeremy got on his knees in his chair and propped Traveller on the table in front of him. "Macey? Why is Mama so sad? And—and Garry seems mad."

"He sure does. The other night after he carried your mama upstairs, he came down huffing and puffing like a freight train and darn near tore the front door off'n its hinges when he slammed it. Scared me, pretty good, I'll tell you. Did you hear that?"

Jeremy nodded. "It scared me, too."

Macey's heart ached. She should have gone upstairs after that just to make sure Jeremy was all right. Damn her for being so neglectful. "I'm sorry I didn't come and tuck you in again, Jeremy. That way we could have been scared together. If anything ever scares you again, and your mama's busy or gone, I want you to run down them stairs and hop in bed with me, 'cause you can bet I'm lying there worrying myself silly, too."

A frail, hopeful smile lit his face. "I will."

"Good." She ruffled his black hair. "What do make of this Fontaine fella? Do you dislike him as much as I do?"

Jeremy filled his cheeks with air, held it for a second, and blew it out in one furious exhalation. "Mama met him on the riverboat when we were going to St. Louis. I don't like him. I don't like him at all."

"Well, I don't neither. The first instant I saw him, I pegged him as a black-hearted rogue."

"Me, too," Jeremy agreed, but his brows puckered. "What's a rogue, Macey?"

"A bad man, a swindler and the like. Somebody who kicks dogs and beats horses."

At this revelation, Jeremy's mouth dropped open. He looked at Traveller with fear in his eyes. "Maybe that's why Garry's mad all the time, 'cause he knows Mr. Fontaine is a rogue."

"I reckon. And from what I hear, Garry ain't the sort of man you want to have agin' you. He was a big hero in the war, you know. Fought all the way from California to Texas. I think he was a major, if Luke Foster was telling the truth this time, and I ain't sure he was. Matter-of-fact, I ain't rightly sure

Luke would know the truth if it up and slapped him in the mouth. But, anyway," she said and waved a hand, "on occasion, Garry still wears pieces of his uniform, a blue shirt, or sky blue trousers."

She had to admit, it made her feel good when she saw Garry wearing them scraps. He'd fought for something he believed in, fought for a whole lot of people who couldn't fight for themselves.

Jeremy's face fell. He suddenly looked very unhappy. "Macey?"

"What is it, honey?"

"Was . . . Garry was a damned Yankee, wasn't he?"

"Well, I reckon some folks would call him that. But you know what, Jeremy? I figure heroes are heroes no matter what side they fought on. Takes just as much bravery to lay your life on the line fighting for the North as it did fighting for the South."

"But, Macey," Jeremy said in a hushed voice, like he was afraid Garry might hear. He braced his elbows on the table and leaned closer to her. True agony strained that young face. "The Yankees killed my pony, Freddy, and my dog, Billy, and . . . and my Daddy." His mouth trembled. "I'll never forget those things."

"And you shouldn't, neither. Why if you ever forgot what happened during the war, I swear the sun would stop shining. Nobody should ever forget. That would be just like . . . like betraying all them people who fought and died for what they believed in—which would be the same as going out and spitting on their graves."

Jeremy blinked. "My Grandmama and me used to go out and put flowers on the graves in Richmond. Macey, did you have family that got killed in the war?"

"You bet I did," she answered proudly. "My relations fought on both sides of the war. I had a uncle with the 55th Massachusetts who was commissioned a lieutenant. That was a mighty fine accomplishment for a colored soldier, Jeremy. I don't think there were more'n nine or ten Negro officers in the whole war."

Jeremy's face shone. "What happened to him?"

Macey gestured with her hand. "Well, I think he's still alive. But I had a cousin who got killed, fighting for the Confederacy in Richmond. He—"

"In *Richmond?*" Jeremy cried. "He was a colored soldier in Richmond? I didn't know we had any!"

"Well, I hope to shout you did." Miss Rose had told Macey straight out about how her husband had fought for the Confederacy and that they'd lived in Richmond for five years, and said she hoped it wouldn't bother Macey none. Course, Macey didn't hold it against her—especially since her own cousin had fought for the South.

"What was your cousin's name, Macey?"

"Slocum Reeves. President Davis passed the Negro Soldier Law on March 13th of this year, and Slocum joined right up. He was born free, you see, and let me tell you, that man considered hisself to be a Southerner. Oh, he didn't like slavery none, but he figured he was fighting for his homeland against Northern aggression. General Richard Ewell was his commanding officer. I do believe that Slocum hated Yankees worse than you Jeremy. He wrote me a letter, just about a week before he was killed, and called Yankees 'carpetbag parvenus.' I recall, because I didn't have no idea whatsoever what a parvenus was."

Jeremy sat listening so intently, he didn't seem to be breathing. "But not Garry," he said. "Garry's not a carpetbagger."

"Shucks, no, honey. People fight for what they believe in. Don't matter if nobody else sees it their way. If it makes sense to them, that's what makes the fighting honorable."

Jeremy's expression tensed. "Even if it means killing a little boy's pony . . . or . . . or his Daddy?"

Macey put a hand on Jeremy's pale cheek and gazed into his blue eyes. "Yes, even if it does. Though I expect the soldiers that did them things didn't like what they were doing, they just figured they had to."

Jeremy's gaze clung to her. "Macey, what do you think happens when a pony dies?"

Macey frowned. "You mean does the pony go to heaven or hell?"

"Yes." He wet his lips. "Nobody ever . . . ever talks about animals and God. I know good people go to heaven when they die. But what happened to my pony? He was a good boy."

The question had obviously been plaguing Jeremy's mind for some time. He started breathing heavily, as if worrying what she might answer. Macey rubbed her chin, thinking. "I don't rightly recall the Bible ever saying. But I can't imagine heaven without animals. I mean, I ain't going if the place don't have dogs, and horses, and deer, and elk. I am sure that God loves animals, just like you and me. Elsewise, why would He have created 'em in the first place? I bet your pony is running free across green meadows in heaven, Jeremy. And Billy's probably barking at his heels."

Jeremy laughed—a sudden, gay sound, and Macey laughed too. Jeremy reached out and patted her hand. "And my Daddy is riding my pony, I bet."

"I expect so," Macey said, seeing the shining light in Jeremy's eyes. "Why, I even—"

"Riding him!" Jeremy interrupted, "and combing his mane, and brushing him every night, and making sure he gets pieces of sugar candy now and then."

"You been worried about Freddy, haven't you?"

The corners of Jeremy's mouth turned down. "I—I was worried about who would take care of a pony if it didn't get to go heaven. What if a pony just had to run around in the sky, all alone? One time, my pony got sick with the croup, and I had to watch him and pet him night and day to make sure he got better."

Macey smiled. Who else but a child would think a horse's soul might be running around in the sky all by itself? "I'm sure glad Freddy had you there to protect him, Jeremy. He was a mighty lucky pony."

"I miss him."

"Well, you go ahead, but I'll bet he's just fine. Fat and sassy, feeding on wildflowers and blueberries."

Jeremy smiled, then he tilted his head in a regretful way. "I miss my Daddy, too. Sometimes, real bad."

"Oh, I surely do know how that is. I miss my Mama so bad sometimes that my stomach aches and aches. Even though she died a long time ago."

Very clearly, she saw her mother, lying in the glow of candles with peeling wallpaper behind her, wearing a beautiful green dress that Macey's labors had bought. In the gray frame of her hair, the long hooked nose, the full lips, and closed eyelids, seemed overlain with a web of sixty or seventy years— more than twice the true number.

Macey had stood by the door greeting the mourners who came to pay their respects, her high-collared yellow dress smudged with tears. Thirty-two people had come. Mostly other "doves," and their children, but a few men, too. The smell of fresh-picked flowers had filled the room, wet and sweet with the coming of spring.

"Your mama died?" Jeremy asked, bringing her back to the present.

"Yes, twenty-five years ago, though it don't seem so long. Feels like it's been six or seven months."

"How did she die?"

Macey wondered whether or not to tell him the truth. "A man killed her. Never knew who he was. Just some fella who come in off the streets, I reckon."

Macey had always blamed herself, fearing that the man had come seeking her, and when he'd found only her ailing mother, he'd tried to force her to do the things Macey ought to have been doing. Either her mother couldn't, 'cause she was too sick, or she'd said something that set the fella off. Who knew? Sometimes there wasn't no reason for violence. It just happened.

"Macey," Jeremy murmured, his eyes on the table. "Have you . . . have you ever tried to go to heaven? You know, to talk to your mama?"

"No, honey," she answered, and looked him over carefully. He must want to talk to his daddy awful bad. "Have you ever tried it?"

Jeremy's finger drew slow designs on the table top. "Sometimes. But I— I can't get there. The stars always get in the way."

Macey picked up his hand and squeezed it. "You just keep trying. I'm sure your daddy has been feeling mighty bad about leaving you without saying goodbye."

Tears glinted in Jeremy's eyes.

Macey smiled sympathetically. "You all right, Jeremy?" When he just squeezed her hand back, she hesitated, then said, "You know what? I been thinking about baking up a wild rice pie. Does that sound good to you?"

Jeremy sniffed and wiped at his clogged nose. "I never heard of such a thing. What is it?"

"Oh, landsakes, honey! Wild rice pie's about the best eatin' this side of paradise. You beat up three eggs, pour in four ounces of maple sugar and six ounces of molasses, then blend in twelve ounces of cooked wild rice, pour it all into a pie crust and bake her good 'til she sets up. Usually 'bout forty-five minutes. Want to try it?"

"Yes, Macey. I'd like to."

"Good," she said, standing up. "Come on. We'll start making the crust."

APRIL 24, 1865

COLONEL GEORGE SHARPE—STOP—BUREAU OF MILITARY INFORMATION WASHINGTON CITY—STOP—CONTACTS IN DENVER TELEGRAPH OFFICE INFORM ME MESSAGE SENT TO YOUR OFFICE YESTERDAY MORNING FROM MISTER FONTAINE—STOP—PLEASE ADVISE AS TO CONTENT—STOP—MAJOR THOMAS CORLEY.

CHAPTER 30

Garrison and Robin came out of the mine and walked side-by-side up the steep path that led to the cabin. He'd showed her each place where he thought the shaft needed shoring up, and they had discussed what sorts of timbers to use, how much they'd cost, and how long the process would take. She had listened patiently, but her dark vigilant eyes told him that she knew he hadn't brought her all the way up here to talk about the timbers and rock strata. She was giving him time to tell her on his own, when he got good and ready—but clearly, her anxiety was building. Half an hour ago, she'd knotted her fists in the slanting side pockets of her blue riding skirt and hadn't taken them out since. Garrison could see those fists in there, clenching, moving nervously as she hiked up the winding trail.

Blinding sunshine flooded around them, sparkling on the mica in the boulders, glinting off lingering patches of snow, and shining in the silver buttons on Robin's blue jacket. She had plaited her hair into one long braid and left it hanging down the middle of her back. A matching blue slouch hat topped her head. She looked mighty pretty against the spring wildflowers that had emerged in the past three days. A crazy quilt of red, blue, yellow, and white patterned the slopes. Higher up, the wintergreen firs and pines still clutched their capes of snow, but the vast frozen mountain had at last begun to thaw. Scents of melting snow and new grass filled the air.

As they neared the cabin, she irritably said, "Garrison, I wish you'd just tell me."

"I'm fixing to."

He opened the door and gestured for her to enter. When she passed by her fragrance of lemon verbena enveloped him. Pleasant. He'd taken a bath that morning and dressed in his best black and white checked shirt and denim pants. As always when he washed his hair with good lye soap, it dried in a mass of brown curls.

"Sit down, Robin," he said. "Can I pour you a cup of leftover coffee?"

"From the way you've been acting, I suspect I'm going to need a glass of whisky."

"Sorry," he answered. "Ain't got any. I drank it all last night."

She removed her hat and set it on the table, then took one of the chairs. "In that case, coffee will do just fine. I thought you seemed awfully quiet today. Headache?"

He smiled faintly as he poured two cups of lukewarm coffee. "Not bad. I've had 'em much worse."

"And just why did you need a good drunk last night?"

Garrison walked back, set both cups of coffee down, and reached into his shirt pocket. Drawing out the folded telegram, he handed it across to her. She glanced at him as she unfolded it. The more she read, the more erratically she breathed.

Garrison sat down in the other chair and cupped his cold hands around his coffee. She wasn't just wanted for espionage, but for subverting the Congress, treason through collaboration with a foreign power, and the murders of a variety of military and secular officials. She must have read the message three or four times before she refolded it and handed it back to him. Garrison let it lie in the middle of the table.

Neither of them said anything.

She sipped her coffee, her eyes focused on some faraway place in her head, but her face had gone grim, filled with anger. A pale square of window light stretched across the plank floor and climbed half-way up her tall body. Her skirt and the bottom half of her blue jacket appeared a shade lighter, while the top remained royal blue. He ran a hand through his hair and waited.

Finally, she said, "The telegram is addressed to Owen Fontaine. How did you get it?"

"I had a talk with him. He gave it to me."

Her expression did not change one iota. She said, "Of his own free will?"

"Not exactly."

"I see . . . Is he alive?"

"Pretty much."

Robin nodded and began gruffly pulling off her black riding gloves, tugging ruthlessly on the fingers. "I don't know whether to be glad or sad about that."

"Me neither," he answered. "Though he did agree to give up his ten percent interest in the claim."

"He did?"

"Uh-huh."

". . . Uh-huh," she repeated in exactly the bored tone Garrison had used.

Her eyes drifted over the cabin, landing on the Hudson's Bay blanket on the bed and the battered coffeepot on the edge of the stove. Garrison could tell she was putting things together like a puzzle master.

Anxiously, she shoved out of her chair and strode to the woodstove where she warmed her cold hands. "Garrison, I don't ever want you to do that again."

"I don't really care what you—"

She whirled angrily. "Do you know what Owen is doing at this very moment?"

Garrison's gaze didn't waver, but he sat back in his chair and folded his hands over his stomach. "I expect he's trying to figure a way of prying open one of his eyes."

"And once he gets it open, he's going to go searching for somebody to kill you. The man has no honor! He would never fight you face to face, not even—"

"I noticed that. It was mighty irritating, too."

"Damn it, Garrison! In the future, please consult with me before you do anything so reckless."

"Consult with you?" He bushy brows arched. "You mean come to you and say, 'Robin, I'm gonna beat the hell out of Fontaine so he'll leave you alone. What do you think about that?' Is that what you mean? Something like that?" he stared at her. "Why, I reckon I could do that. Providing you promise to keep your mouth shut and not answer me."

"Do you think this is funny?"

"A little."

"I'm genuinely worried about you, Garrison."

"Are you?" he asked. "Well, then, maybe you'll answer some personal questions for me."

"Ask. Please."

He pointed to the telegram on the table. "Did you do them things?"

"Which things?"

"Did you subvert the Congress?"

Her narrow shoulders squared. "To the best of my abilities."

"Which members?"

"Several members."

"Hmm. Did you collaborate with foreign powers to overthrow the United States government?"

She leaned forward, stuck out her chin, and answered, "As many foreign powers as I could. None of them wanted to help, though. Cowards, one and all. That fat woman on the throne in England—"

"Did you murder all them people?"

Robin closed her mouth and straightened up. "Of course not. I don't even know who half those people are. *Those* charges are false, probably trumped up by some white-livered senator—"

"What about the other half?"

"What?" She scowled at him. "What other . . . oh, the other half. Well . . . Don't sound so cocky! It's not like you never killed anyone in the line of duty."

"I reckon I killed my share. You murdered anybody since you left the service?"

"No," she answered curtly, angrily.

Garrison braced his elbows on his knees and used both hands to massage his forehead. "Well, good. I was worried about that possibility."

"You shouldn't be. I only kill people who need killing."

At her matter-of-fact statement, he sat up, looked at her for a minute, and started laughing. Loudly.

"You are very irritating, Garrison. The government wants to put a noose around my neck and you're amused! How can you laugh at a time like this?"

"How can you not?" he countered, but tried to stifle his mirth, to little avail. Every time he opened his mouth, he broke into peals of laughter again. "Well, anyway," he said when he could. "We've got to do some thinking about this."

"*We?* For God's sake, I'm the one they want to hang!"

"I ain't anxious to see you swinging from the gallows, neither. I have an interest here. I'm your partner, ain't I?"

"Well, yes. Of course."

He got up, went to stand beside her, gazing down into the dark depths of her eyes. She looked mad—but more scared. Deep down scared. Like she might be on the verge of telling the world to go to hell, and hightailing it for God-only-knew-where. He sincerely hoped she was.

"What are you thinking?"

"I—I don't know," she answered. "Really . . . I just don't know."

He crossed his arms across his chest. "You ever been to Mexico?"

"What?" She looked at him as if he'd started speaking in a foreign language. "Where?"

"Mexico. You know, that big country south of Texas. It's right pretty. Lots of trees, and pure white beaches that go on forever."

The furrows in her brow deepened as understanding dawned, and a grateful smile brightened her beautiful face. "Thanks for thinking about it, but—"

"Don't decide yet. Think about it for a while. Putting the Rio Grande between yourself and harm might just be the only way to—"

"And what about our mine?"

"Sell it. It's worth a million, and the instant folks know it's up for sale, you'll have buyers crawlin' all over you. With the profits, Robin, you could set up a right nice hacienda down around Tampico, maybe raise some cattle, do a little farming. It would be a good life for you and Jeremy."

She lowered her hands, put them in her skirt pockets again, and balled her fists. The sunlight cast a saffron aura around her, sending flickers through her hair.

Garrison had thought long and hard about this last night, trying to figure a way out for her. Only Mexico made sense. He'd heard rumors that there was a growing community of ex-Confederates down there, men and women who could not, would not, give up. And men who understood very well that the Union would never forgive them their crimes.

"You know, don't you, Robin, that there ain't gonna be any amnesty for you? Not with those charges. And you're exactly the sort the government will want to make an example of, they'll—"

She lifted a hand abruptly to silence him. "Don't tell me things I already know."

She'd been laying all her hopes on a grant of amnesty. This must feel like a meathook in her belly. He stood quietly, letting her think.

"There must be another way," she said. "I can't run my whole life, and Jeremy . . ." A hollow, haunted look entered her eyes. "What of Jeremy?"

A gust of wind blew down the stovepipe and breathed cold air over them. She shivered. Instinctively, Garrison extended an arm to drape it around her shoulders in a gentlemanly gesture, and Robin took a step forward, into his arms. Surprised, uncertain of her intent, he pulled her close and stroked her back gently.

"Robin—"

"Don't ask me anything. Just . . . just hold me."

He nodded. "For as long as you want."

He let himself drown in the fragrance of her hair, in the sensation of her body pressed against his. A rush of feeling flooded him, frightening in its intensity. For a blessed timeless moment, he concentrated on the beat of her heart. He could feel it pounding against his chest. Rapid. Forceful. She must be terrified. He tightened his arms around her, hoping to make her feel safer, and not quite so alone.

"Garrison," she asked, "have you ever been to Mexico? You spoke about it as if you'd—"

"Many times. In my youth, I used to go over to help the *banditos* round up their cattle."

She backed away. "Start telling me everything you can about the place. The lay of the land, the vegetation, details about the people, their customs and language. Do you know how to speak—"

"*Si, Senora.* But you'd best sit down. This'll take a while."

I am pacing my bedroom like a caged wolf. I pull off my jacket and throw it at the foot of my bed.

Dear God, what am I going to do?

For weeks I've been harboring the same fear that I saw in Garrison's face this afternoon, wondering how I can possibly save myself if the government won't grant me amnesty. There must be a way. There must be!

Why can't I think of it?

I sit heavily on the edge of my bed and put my hands on either side of my head, pressing hard, trying to force some sense into my frantic brain.

I mustn't give up. There is a way.

But everything is so much more complicated now than it was before, and I can't seem to untangle the strands, and I—I feel so confused and tired. Corley is close. Very, very close. I can "feel" him out there, as if our minds are somehow connected across the miles.

He knows he's close.

He can sense me just as clearly as I sense him. This statement sounds ridiculous, even to me, yet . . . I believe it.

I lie back on my bed and stare at the spiderweb hanging in the far corner of the room. Intricate, perfectly woven, it glitters in the fading rays of twilight.

God. Oh, God.

I erred outrageously when I hooked up with Owen Fontaine. Corley followed Owen. And, in the end, that's how Corley will find me. I have to shake Owen.

Which means . . . I can't stay here.

I have to leave.

I roll over onto my side and bring up my knees, ignoring the mud that cakes off my boots onto my white bedspread. I curl into a ball, and try to imagine life in Mexico. I can hear Garrison's deep voice describing it. A peacefulness pervades his words. All the while, he's looking at me, silently telling me he wants to go with me, and I . . . I don't know how to answer.

I still miss Charles desperately. Any warm thoughts that I have about Garrison make me feel as if I'm being unfaithful to my husband.

But my husband is dead! He's dead!

Why can't I let him go, and get on with my life?

A rhetorical question . . .

I know the answer.

It's because Charles only died in Tennessee. Not in my heart. He still breathes inside me. The rhythm's deeper, slower than mine. And, though I feel those breaths growing fainter, I pray every day that he never stops. I can't lose him. God, not yet.

Even as I say this, I remember Garrison's arms around me, strong, so comforting. How did that happen? How did I let it happen? I treated him as more than a friend. I gave him hope.

Why did I do that?

I cannot let myself answer that question.

Not so long as I still hear Charles breathing inside me . . .

CHAPTER 31

APRIL 26, 1865

MAJOR THOMAS CORLEY—STOP—COLORADO CITY COLORADO TERRITORY—STOP—RESULT OF YOUR INQUIRY—TWO OFFICERS HERE CHARGED WITH TREASON—STOP—FONTAINE MESSAGE POINT OF ORIGIN—CENTRAL CITY COLORADO—STOP—PROCEED WITHOUT DELAY—STOP—FURTHER INSTRUCTIONS WILL AWAIT YOU THERE—STOP—YOU SHOULD ALSO KNOW THIS DAY WE RAN TO GROUND ASSASSIN OF MR LINCOLN—STOP—BOOTH DEAD AND JUSTLY SO—STOP—COLONEL GEORGE SHARPE.

George Sharpe sat at his desk massaging the back of his neck. The muscles ached from too much tension, too many days without sleep, too little food. He'd never felt this tired in his life.

Lieutenant Jonas Cyrus stood at ease before him, his sandy blond hair and neat beard touseled from the wind that had been blasting Washington City for two days straight. Even now the windowpanes in Sharpe's office rattled. A tan haze of dust so obscured the city beyond that he could just make out the golden gleam of the capitol's dome. The sight comforted him, especially after the past two weeks.

Cyrus shifted, inhaling a deep breath. His bloodshot eyes were red rimmed with exhaustion. His gray shirt and trousers bore streaks of black mud.

Sharpe crossed his legs and leaned back in his chair. "Pretty bad out there?"

"Yes, sir. Bad enough."

"Well, at least it's over." He used his finger to shove Cyrus' report across the shiny oak of his desk. "I read your report, but I want it from you. In detail. . . . And sit down, Cyrus, before you fall down."

"Yes, sir. Thank you, sir." Cyrus sank into the chair in front of Sharpe's desk and laced his fingers in his lap. "He . . ." Cyrus took a breath, "he was shot and killed by a man in the New York cavalry, sir."

"How did it happen?"

Cyrus hesitated before replying, as if he were struggling to unsee what he had seen with his own eyes. "Let me begin earlier . . . sir. So you will have the full picture."

"Please. Go ahead."

Cyrus nodded. But it took a moment for him to prepare himself. "As best we can figure, Booth and an accomplice, a slow-witted Maryland youth named David Herald, spent last week hiding in the swamps in Maryland. Booth broke his leg in the jump from President Lincoln's box at Ford's Theatre and he was in such pain that he couldn't move about too well. They crossed the Potomac about April 22nd, near Port Tobacco. Then they made their way to the Rappahannock, and stopped about twenty miles south of Fredericksburg."

Sharpe's mind filled with images of that battle, as it always did when the place was mentioned. December, 1862. The North had suffered a terrible defeat at Fredericksburg. Almost 13,000 Federal soldiers had been killed or wounded, while the South had lost a little over 4,000. General Lee had been brilliant. And would continue to be . . . until the Union blockade truly began taking its toll and Lee could no longer feed or clothe his army. Only then did the undauntable Lee seem to lose his way. *Thank God, thank God.* Sharpe bowed his head and silently offered a prayer to the Almighty for the mercies that He had bestowed upon the Union on the day the great Robert E. Lee faltered, knowing that no matter what he did, he could not win.

Cyrus cleared his throat, and Sharpe looked up to meet that hollow gaze. "And then?" he asked.

Cyrus answered, "Then Booth and Herald hid on a farm three miles south of the Rappahannock. They . . . they knew we had them surrounded. They fled into a tobacco shed. Booth's companion surrendered when we ordered him out, but Booth . . ." Cyrus swallowed hard.

Sharpe waited.

"Booth," Cyrus continued, "he refused to come out. We set the shed on fire, and still he refused. We could see him sitting in there—crippled, holding his crutch and his carbine. The flames behind him were leaping and so bright . . . I swear, Colonel, I swear I could even see the expression on his face. He—he looked . . . surprised. As though he couldn't understand why anybody would hunt him for what he had done. Colonel," Cyrus said, and peered pleadingly at Sharpe, "while Booth was sitting there silhouetted against the fire, one of our sharpshooters shot him. Right through the neck. The bullet cut holes in both sides of Booth's collar."

Cyrus shook his head and closed his eyes for a few seconds. "Even then, he was still alive when we dragged him out of the burning shed and onto the porch of the farmhouse. The bullet had struck his spine. He was paralyzed, but he . . . he looked up at me, sir. Right at me."

Cyrus' mouth hung open, and Sharpe said, "Did he speak to you?"

A weak nod moved his head. "Booth said 'I thought I did for the best,' and then, just at sunup when golden light was spilling through the forests, he asked us to lift up his hands so he could see them. We did, and he looked at them with a frown, as if he were scrutinizing the lines, the way a soothsayer does. Finally, Booth whispered, 'Useless. Useless.' Then he . . . he died, sir."

Sharpe let out the breath he'd been holding. Cyrus was so young. Nineteen. He had never been involved in actual combat. Of course the event had shocked him.

Sharpe leaned forward and braced his elbows on his cluttered desk. Papers lay canted at numerous angles, quills and ink bottles scattered amongst them. When he couldn't find a quill, or other necessary item immediately, Sharpe simply pulled another from his drawer and went on working. Only when his desk held no more quills, sheets of paper, erasers, or bottles of ink, did he reluctantly undertake the task of hunting up those hidden on the desktop and restowing them.

In a gentle voice, Sharpe said, "I would like to discuss another matter with you."

Cyrus answered, "Yes, sir."

Sharpe reached to his left, picked up a stack of letters and telegrams, and handed them across to Cyrus. "Please read the first two pages, and the last four telegrams. The rest can wait. They're reports Major Corley has been sending in for the past six months."

Cyrus whispered, "Yes, sir," and began reading.

It didn't take long, a few minutes. When Cyrus had finished he looked up and said. "I don't understand."

"Neither do I. Not fully. But, as you can see, Major Corley has been tracking this Owen Fontaine in the hopes that Fontaine would lead him to Mrs. Heatherton. Corley insists that Heatherton has, for years, been Fontaine's contact for gunrunning within the Confederacy. We've had so many more important things to work on—" he gestured in frustration—"the fall of

Richmond, General Lee's surrender, the president's assassination . . . well, we didn't take the Fontaine connection seriously until yesterday, when Corley wired that he was working on a murder case with the sheriff in Colorado City and that Fontaine was the prime suspect."

Cyrus licked his dry lips. "But Fontaine's telegram says that Major Corley was the murderer, and—" he shuffled through the pages—"Deputy Neville claims that a man named Colonel Fredrick Marley did it."

Sharpe nodded and steepled his fingers over his lips, watching Cyrus. The young man had started to fidget, shifting in his chair, crossing and uncrossing his legs. "As you will have noted, I gave Corley permission to continue working with the sheriff. But I am not at all convinced that Mister Fontaine's accusations are false. There is no Colonel Marley assigned to the West. I checked. That leaves Fontaine and Corley as the prime suspects. You spent a good deal of time with the Major last October and November. Tell me your impressions. Is Corley capable of such an act?"

"Well, I—I don't know, sir. If he were, surely he would also . . ." His voice drained away and his brows drew together.

"What were you saying?"

"Just that if, I mean, sir, that Major Corley understands secret service procedures well enough, that he could . . . well, I hate to . . ."

Sharpe finished it for him. "You mean that if Corley had committed the crime, he is an expert in obtaining and manipulating information. He could do it in such a way that, on the one hand, he could make himself appear innocent, and on the other, frame just about anybody he wanted to."

Cyrus jerked a nod. "Yes, sir, that's what I mean."

"Do you think he killed that woman?"

"I do not know, sir."

Sharpe rose and walked to the window. Cold wind whistled around the shaking panes, making him realize how much he'd been perspiring. The wet patches beneath his arms turned icy. He suppressed a shiver. He had been glad to have Corley gone. The man had always made him uneasy. But murder . . . ? Strings of high clouds twisted and tumbled over Washington City. In the distance, they blended with the blowing dust, forming a broad opaque perimeter wall.

He turned. "Let me rephrase my question, Lieutenant. In your professional judgment, after working closely with Major Corley, do you believe he possesses the disturbed kind of mind that we, in his bureau, have specifically identified as dangerous? As capable of rash violent acts? Is Corley the type of man who could ride with William Quantrill's gang of cutthroats? Is he a Jesse

James or a Cole Younger? *Is he capable of killing an innocent woman for no reason?"*

Cyrus tilted his head reluctantly. "Sir . . . I honestly cannot say."

Sharpe folded his arms. "Because your professional judgment is inadequate to the task, or because you fear betraying a fellow officer?"

Cyrus spread his hands. "May I relate a conversation I had with the Major at Ball's Bluff, sir? It distressed me at the time, but I honestly haven't thought about it since."

"Please do."

Cyrus nervously brushed dust from his trouser leg. A fine sparkling fog filled the sunlit air around him. "We were standing on the shore of the river, looking out at Harrison's Island, and Major Corley was telling me about the battle where his brother died. Did you know about that, sir?"

"Yes."

Cyrus nodded. "Well, Major Corley told me that after he watched his brother drown, he looked up on top of the bluff and he saw Mrs. Heatherton standing there. He said she was magnificent, and—"

"That's the word he used? 'Magnificent'?" Sharpe asked. Corley's hatred for the woman had been so obvious, that it seemed unlikely.

"Oh, yes, sir," Cyrus replied. "I remember because it surprised me, too. After all the terrible things I'd heard him say about Mrs. Heatherton, I couldn't believe it either. But that's what he said. *'She was magnificent.'* "

Sharpe frowned and rubbed his chin. "What else did he say?"

"Well, he said that he dreamed of her, of Mrs. Heatherton. And . . ." He suddenly lowered his gaze to his hands. His mouth tightened.

"What's wrong?"

"Sir, I am ashamed to convey the rest of the conversation to you. It was— unfit, sir."

"Continue your report, Lieutenant."

Cyrus obeyed, but in a strained voice. "Yes, sir, Major Corley said that Mrs. Heatherton was a common whore and deserved to be treated as such. He said that he had heard intimate descriptions of . . . of the sexual techniques she used to gain information from men. He said he often wondered if Mrs. Heatherton were human or a demon succubus sent to drain away men's lives."

"What about the dream? You mentioned a dream."

"Yes, sir. I did." Cyrus swiveled around in his chair to face Sharpe. The color had faded from his cheeks. "Major Corley said that in his favorite dream, he had his hands around Mrs. Heatherton's throat, choking the life from her."

Sharpe stood still, unable to move. The only sound in the room was the incessant rattling of the window. "The woman murdered in Colorado City was strangled to death."

"Yes, sir." Cyrus answered very softly. "I read that."

They stared at each other.

Sharpe started for the door. "Come, Lieutenant. We have work to do."

APRIL 27, 1865

OWEN FONTAINE—STOP—CENTRAL CITY COLORADO TERRITORY—STOP—CORLEY ARRESTED THIS MORNING—STOP—BEING HELD AT FORT LYON COLORADO TERRITORY BUT WILL LEAVE UNDER HEAVY GUARD WITHIN DAYS FOR WASHINGTON CITY—STOP—REGARDING MRS HEATHERTON—PRESIDENT JOHNSON ABOUT TO SIGN PROCLAMATION OF AMNESTY—STOP—PARDON TO BE GRANTED ALL WHO DIRECTLY OR INDIRECTLY PARTICIPATED IN REBELLION IF ACCUSED WILL TAKE OATH TO HENCEFORTH SUPPORT AND DEFEND CONSTITUTION—STOP—WILL EXPECT REMAINDER OF COMPENSATION FROM YOU SOONEST—STOP—MAJOR MILES GILL.

CHAPTER 32

Robin's boots squished in the slushy snow as she made her way down
Main Street. In the false-fronted buildings, lamps gleamed through windows scalloped with snow. The white haze whirled and spun before her. Holding her blue hood at her throat, she tilted her head to fend off the huge fluffy flakes. After several days of spring-like weather, it had turned winter again, with a vengeance. Black clouds obscured the peaks, and bitter arctic winds blasted Central City. She'd seen only two other people walking this afternoon, both hurrying to get their business done. Everyone else had driven to town in covered wagons or buggies, which cut their time out in the weather in half. But Robin walked slowly, deliberately. She inhaled deeply of the damp stone and pine, wishing the snow would soak through her cape and dress, until the icy chill lanced her bones. Maybe then, when her flesh felt as cold as her soul, she would be able to think straight. She had to.

The fear had dwindled, but it had been replaced by a dull numbing ache that made the exterior world seem distant and unreal. Only her internal calculations, point and counterpoint, mattered. *If I do this, what will happen? If I fail to do that, what will happen?*

For years, she had lived one precarious charade after another, turning from female to male, Negro to White to Indian—anything that might get her through enemy lines and close to someone who possessed critical information. She could do it again, if she had to, but a voice whispered deep in her soul, *Will you always have to be someone else? Will you condemn your son to the same fate? Will he have to worry every minute that the next knock on the door will send him fleeing for his life? . . . Isn't there a sanctuary left in the whole world? Dear God, isn't there?*

She didn't hear the jingling traces as she pulled up her long burgundy-colored skirts and stepped out onto Gregory Street to slog through the mud.

"*Jesus Christ!*" someone shouted.

A horse screamed in her ear, and when Robin spun breathlessly, the animal reared, his hooves pawing the air above her. She threw up an arm and stumbled backward, trying to get out of the way before he could split her skull with those hooves, but she tripped over the hem of her cape and fell into the mud. Black goo oozed up around her hands. For a dizzy moment, she could not fathom what had happened. Then the frightened horse brought his hooves down inches from Robin's legs, whinnied in fear and began bucking and kicking at the wagon behind him.

A man yelled, "Whoa, goddamn you! *Whoa!*"

Scrambling away on her hands and knees, she made it up onto the walk, and sat shaking, covered with mud, unable to say a word. The frightened horse continued to snort and rear. She had been so lost in her thoughts, that she had almost . . .

Doors jerked open, and people ran out pulling on coats, shouting to each other as they gathered around her. Blaine Harding, the assayer, knelt beside Robin and gripped her arm to steady her. He hadn't taken time to grab his hat and snowflakes were melting on his bald head. "Are you all right, Mrs. Hale? Is there anything I can—"

"She walked right out in front of me!" yelled the driver of the wagon, a grizzled old man with a grimy buffalo coat. "There wasn't nothing I could do! She just traipsed out like she didn't even see me!"

"Shut up, Harland!" Blaine Harding shouted back. "The way you drive that wagon it's a wonder you haven't killed somebody before now! Go on, get out of here!"

The driver tugged hard on his horse's reins, turned him and sent him galloping off down Main Street, slinging mud behind him.

Once people realized what was happening, more doors opened and a large murmuring crowd formed around Robin. She knew almost none of them, except in passing.

"Mr. Harding," she said in a shaking voice. "Please, help me up. I'm all right."

"Are you sure, Mrs. Hale. I could have somebody run and fetch the doctor for you."

"No, no, really. I'm fine. Thank you. Just help me up."

Harding put a hand on her back and held her arm as she got her feet under her. She stood there, wobbly, breathing in and out, for several moments.

"Mrs. Hale?" Mabel Wirth pushed through the crowd. She stood with her arms folded over her flowered dress to shield herself from the snow. "Why don't you come down to the hotel for a minute and have something hot to drink? You'll feel better if you do."

"You're very kind, Mrs. Wirth, but really, I—"

"I'm a doctor!" a man called. "*Excuse me*. Get out of my way! Let me by!"

Before Robin could move, a man shouldered through the gathering, his brutal rush causing people to murmur crossly as they cleared a path for him.

A hand closed around her forearm with hurtful strength.

Robin looked up into the clean-shaven face of a black-haired man . . . with ice-blue eyes . . .

"No!" she screamed and in a swift violent motion flung herself backward into the crowd, fighting to wrench her arm free from his grip, but he would not let go. She fell to the ground, flailing, kicking.

"Help me! Somebody help me! This man wants to kill me! *Please, somebody*—"

"I'm Major Thomas Corley!" he shouted. "Of the Bureau of Military Information, and this woman is under arrest! She's a Confederate spy!"

Blaine Harding, who had grabbed Robin's other arm to help her, stared down at her uncomprehendingly. "A . . . a spy? A Confederate spy?"

Mrs. Wirth looked about anxiously. "What are you talking about?" she demanded. "Mrs. Hale a spy? That can't be! She a fine woman!"

"She was involved in the conspiracy to assassinate President Lincoln!" Corley shouted. "She's guilty of treason against the United States!"

Blaine Harding released her arm and stepped back, as if afraid to even touch her. "Assassination," he whispered in horror. "Oh, my dear Lord."

"He's lying! Please, someone help me!" Robin screamed. "I swear to you I had nothing to do—"

Corley's blow came out of nowhere, taking her in the temple, snapping her head around. A white flash of pain blasted through her. Corley hauled her to her feet, and she let her knees go weak, stumbled against him, and pulled her pistol from her cape pocket. She rammed it against Corley's side, she—

"*No!*" Blaine Harding screamed and leaped for her hand. Ripping her pistol away, he threw it into the snow on the sidewalk. He stood breathing hard, his face red with confusion and anguish. "I'm sorry, Mrs. Hale! I just couldn't let you—"

"*Get out of here! All of you!*" Corley bellowed. "Before I arrest you as her accomplices! Go on, get away from us!"

"No, Mr. Harding," Robin pleaded. "*Please!* I beg you—"

"Shut your mouth!" Corley glared down into her face. He'd been drinking. The powerful scent of whisky flooded over Robin. "No one can help you. Do you understand me? No one! You are beyond saving now."

In a lightning motion, he twisted Robin around, holding one of her hands behind her back, while his other arm closed around her throat.

As Corley shoved her down the walk in front of him, Robin struggled to look over her shoulder, "Mrs. Wirth!" she choked. "Find Garrison Parker, tell him—"

The muscular arm over her throat squeezed so hard that the force lifted her feet off the ground. Robin struggled, fighting for air. The terrible strangling sounds coming from her mouth terrified her.

"Stop it!" he hissed in her ear. "Stop!"

Robin wrenched her body furiously, contorting to bring one boot up behind her. She kicked him hard in the shin, while she threw the whole weight of her body against his arm . . . and broke free!

She ran, her cape flying out, her hair tumbling around her shoulders. His steps pounded behind her as she careened around the corner and dashed down the deserted alley that led toward home, running with all her heart. Horses sidestepped and whinnied as she flew past, their bridles jingling.

She didn't make it fifty steps.

Corley tackled her around the waist and drove her body into the snow. Robin clawed at his powerful hands, screaming, "No, leave me alone! *Please, don't hurt me! Don't*—"

He gripped her chin, and wrenched her head around. The smile he gave Robin made her go cold inside, cold and desperately afraid. It was a lover's smile, soft, tender, full of warmth. Madness filled his eyes.

He gently smoothed the tousled hair away from her face. "Hurt you?" he whispered. "Tonight we'll be together, Robin Walkingstick Heatherton, and I'll be able to show you just how much I care about you."

Garrison sat, elbows on the dining room table, looking across at Macey. She wore a gray dress with pearl buttons. Her eyes were riveted on the snowy street outside. She'd been cracking her knuckles for ten minutes straight. Garrison gritted his teeth to keep from flinching. The storm had intensified, eating the mountains whole. They could have been sitting on a street in Boston for all they could see. Garrison could just barely make out Honey, tethered by the iron gate in the front yard, her long ears and back coated with snow. The railing around the broad veranda glimmered with ice. Snow fell, it melted, it froze. The roads would bear a thin crust of ice by nightfall, over six inches of slimy mud.

He shifted in his seat. "Jeremy upstairs?" he asked.

Without looking at him, Macey said, "He's taking a nap."

"R—Rose left two hours ago?" He had to constantly remind himself to call her Rose Hale in front of other people.

"Yep."

Macey cracked three more joints, and Garrison drummed his fingers on the table. "Macey?"

"What?" she turned to peer at him irritably.

"Are you sure you don't know where she went? Did she mention needing something—"

"I told you, Garry, she just said she was going for a walk. That's all. But I—I sure thought she'd be back by now, especially with the storm so bad and all."

They stared at each other, and Garrison got up and took his hat from where it lay on the floor. He pulled it low over his eyes. "I'm gonna go find her. I'll be back as quick as I can."

He strode for the door, jerking his buffalo coat off the peg. But as he was slipping his arms through the sleeves, Macey yelled, "Whoa up, Garry! Somebody's coming."

He hurried back into the dining room and found Macey squinting through the snow at the black buggy that had pulled up outside. The buggy jostled as a man in a black overcoat jumped down.

At the same moment, Macey and Garrison said, "Damn it."

"But does he have Rose with him?" Garrison asked.

Macey shook her head. "I don't see her, but I can't really tell. She could be in the buggy, taking her time—"

Fontaine flung open the iron gate and ran up the path to the veranda where he stamped snow from his boots, brushed it off his coat sleeves, and knocked.

"I'll get it, Macey," Garrison said.

"Good," she answered and folded her arms malevolently. "'Cause I wasn't gonna."

Garrison smiled. "I sure like you, Macey."

He opened the door and stared down into Fontaine's brown eyes. "What do you want?"

"First," Fontaine said. "I would like to come in out of the snow . . . if you won't object?"

Garrison opened the door wider, but grudgingly. "No, I reckon I don't object. Not yet."

Fontaine entered and looked around the parlor. His gaze landed on the blue couch in front of the roaring fireplace, then veered left toward the stairs. "I would like to speak with Rose, please."

"Why?"

Fontaine removed his black overcoat and hung it on a peg, then smoothed the sleeves of his mustard-colored waistcoat. Beneath it, he wore a black ruffled shirt and trousers. He took off his hat and hung it by his overcoat, then ran his fingers through his wet blond hair, taking his time with grooming, it seemed. When he turned back to Garrison, he said, "I don't believe that's any of your business, Parker. Where's Rose? This is important, and I don't have all day."

"She ain't here, but she ought to be back soon. Come on into the dining room." He smiled. "We can wait for her together."

Fontaine gave him a look of pure loathing. "I believe I'd rather sit in my buggy and freeze to death."

"Have it your way," Garrison said and held the front door open for him.

Fontaine looked out at the snow and snapped, "How soon will Rose be back?"

"Pretty soon."

"Well, I suppose I can stand it." He marched into the dining room.

Garrison shook his head and closed the door again. In the dining room, he found Fontaine sitting in his chair, legs crossed, fingers laced, glaring at Macey. She stood on the other side of the table, arms still folded, her mouth puckered like she'd eaten sour grapes.

"Well," Fontaine commented, looking back and forth between Macey and Garrison, "you two haven't changed a bit."

"You, neither," Macey said gruffly. " 'Cepting for them black puffy circles under your eyes."

Fontaine's brows lowered.

Garrison suppressed a smile.

Fontaine said, "Macey, while I wait, I would like a cup of coffee, if it isn't too much trouble."

"It *is* too much trouble."

"Somehow," Fontaine said, "I had the feeling it would be." He turned to Garrison, "Parker, can you give me an estimate on what 'pretty soon' means? I need to be back to my hotel by four o'clock."

Garrison spread his feet and caressed his beard. "Pretty soon means, as soon as she gets here. Which'll be soon enough, I reckon."

Fontaine rose angrily to his feet. *"Where* did Rose go. Perhaps I can catch her on her way back."

"No," Garrison replied. "I expect not."

"Damn you, Parker. Are you always so—!"

"Macey?" Garrison said in a soft voice. "Would you mind if I speak to Fontaine alone for a few minutes? Shouldn't take long."

"Not at all," Macey answered, and headed for the kitchen with her chin held high. *"Speak* to him for me, too, will you?" The kitchen door slammed behind her.

Fontaine eyed Garrison suspiciously. "What did she mean by that?"

"Oh, Macey and I read each other's minds. It's kind of like them fish on the California coast that swim upstream guided by the call of another fish miles and miles ahead."

Fontaine's eyes slitted. "Ah. Telepaths. I should have known."

"Why don't you take a seat again, Fontaine?"

Warily, he sat.

Garrison ambled over and took Macey's chair. "How are things going?"

"Why, just lovely, Parker. Couldn't be better. And how are you?"

Garrison swiveled around in his chair and put both elbows on the table so he could look straight across at Fontaine. "I guess I ain't very smart," he said. "I figured you'd have lit out for the East after our last—er—conversation. Why are you still here?"

"Because I have business here."

"What business?"

Fontaine dug into his inside coat pocket, drew out a telegram and threw it on the table in front of Garrison. *"That* business. Which I think Rose will be quite glad to hear."

Garrison unfolded the paper, held it up, and read it. Any amusement he had felt at seeing Fontaine drained away into a black abyss of fear. His heart started to pound.

He laid the wire down on the table and said, "When did you get this? I can't read the date."

"What? Is that all you're going to say?"

"When?"

The nostrils of Fontaine's thin nose flared. "What's the matter with you? Why aren't you ecstatic? I thought this news would make you jump for joy."

A terrible bubble of suspicion was swelling in Garrison's chest, making it hard to think. He desperately wanted to believe that all Robin had to do was take an oath of loyalty to the Union and she could go free.

But he couldn't believe it. Not with the charges she faced.

Fontaine leaned across the table. "Don't you think it would be appropriate to say 'Thank you, Fontaine, for saving Rose's hide,' even if you didn't mean it? You could at least—"

"I suspect your foolishness may have condemned her."

Fontaine shook his head as if he hadn't heard right. "What are you talking about?"

Garrison shoved the telegram toward him. "Who do you think really sent that wire?"

"Miles Gill! His name's on it and he's as loyal a swine as a man can buy. He's never failed me before. So long as I only pay him half in advance."

Garrison frowned out the bay window. The storm had briefly stopped. He studied the dun underbelly of the clouds that just cleared the roofs of houses. The iron-rich smell of snow pervaded the room. Beads of moisture sparkled on the veranda, and stood like transparent pearls amid the snow in the grass. There would be more snow today. The wet slushy kind that always came in spring. Where the hell was Robin? If she wasn't back in five minutes, he—

Fontaine drew a breath. "The message came from Gill. Although, I'll grant it might all be lies. He could just be telling me what I want to hear so I'll finish paying him."

Garrison didn't respond.

Fontaine added, "I take it you don't think that's likely?"

"No."

"Well, if you're so damned perceptive, Parker, please enlighten me."

Garrison leveled a hard glare. "First," he said, "there's the possibility that Gill, or someone else in the Bureau, is just being a dutiful officer. Setting up a trap—like he was ordered to do."

"A trap? For Rose?"

"Or you."

Fontaine blanched. "Me? Why me?"

"Oh, I reckon you'd know the answer to that better'n I would."

Fontaine's eyes darted around the room. "What's the second possibility?"

Garrison watched Honey pawing for grass along the fence. Her dapple-gray hide blended with the clouds and snow. The second possibility was one he would never broach with Fontaine. Mostly because he hadn't figured out all the angles yet. But, he knew something about intelligence work, and if he had been sent out to track down an enemy spy, he would have routinely sent in reports on his progress, would have detailed everything he had discovered, every person he'd interrogated, every lead he'd pursued. If Corley had half Garrison's sense, he'd have told Colonel George Sharpe about Fontaine, his best lead, immediately. After that, Sharpe would have alerted his staff to keep an eye out for information relating to the gunrunner.

But . . . Garrison's mind worked, twisting things around to see them from different viewpoints. What if Gill was *not* on Fontaine's payroll? What if the man was a good trustworthy officer? Gill would have showed Fontaine's message to Sharpe immediately. And . . . and Sharpe would have backtracked to the message's point of origin, and—"

Garrison shoved out of his chair and slammed a fist into the table, which made Fontaine jump to his feet. *"When* did you receive that telegram?"

"Four days ago! Why? What difference—"

"Four days? What did you do? Wait 'til you were pretty again before you came to deliver it? Goddamn you!"

Depending upon where Corley was when he received confirmation of Fontaine's location . . .

Garrison ran for the kitchen. *"Macey? Macey!"*

She trotted out of her bedroom with a book in her hands, her eyes wide. "What's the matter?"

"Pack a bag for Jeremy, and pack one for yourself, too. Be ready to leave when I get back."

"Why? What—"

"Rose is in danger. I've got to find her, and you've got to—"

"Go!" She shoved by him, running for the stairs.

Garrison ran the opposite direction, sprinting over the veranda, down the steps, and across the snowy yard for Honey. When he'd mounted and reined Honey around, he saw Fontaine loping across the veranda, his coat over his arm, his hat in his hands.

The truth must have finally sunk in.

Cold silence enveloped the filthy, mouse-ridden hole in the ground. The dugout had been abandoned for several months, perhaps even a year, but dusty furniture still lined the walls, and a drooping sheet of muslin hung from the ceiling. Two chairs, one with a leg missing, stood in the center of the room, near a crude, rough-hewn table. Four candleholders had been driven into each wall, and wax dripped down onto the dirt floor. A rusty woodstove sat against the eastern wall. Last night, he'd gone about gathering wood for it. Such wood as he could find in this denuded country, sticks and rotten logs, dead branches of chokecherry. But the pile would keep them warm for a few days. And that would be long enough.

He'd found this place yesterday about noon, after riding all night through a bitter windstorm that had so scoured the foothills that a tan wall of dirt-filled air had rolled down and sheathed Denver City. It had taken hours of hunting. He had ridden his horse up a series of narrow, winding, game trails, far off the roads, searching, searching . . . until he'd found this place. He'd had to make certain no one would be able to hear her screams—because only he had the right to do so. He had earned it.

The place wasn't perfect. He would have preferred a grand suite in New York City or Paris. But this would have to do. At least he'd stolen clean sheets from his last hotel room. The first thing he'd done when he'd found this place was to tuck them around the cornshuck mattress, in preparation. Her brown Indian skin contrasted sharply with that pure white. It fascinated him.

What huge dark eyes she had. He hadn't remembered that. That they were so large. Odd. He'd thought he had memorized every detail of her figure and face.

He massaged the tight muscles at the base of his skull. It was all those other women who had pretended to be her. They had confused him. Told him such lies. After they were dead, he could see the difference. The hair of the whore in Golden had not really been black; in the morning light it was auburn. The woman in Auraria had promised him her eyes were brown, but they weren't. They were hazel. He'd had to lift her lids and hold the lamp close, but he had seen the falsehood for himself. And that woman in Colorado City . . . she had been the worst. She had tried to deceive him into believing her breasts had suckled a child, but a woman who had suckled a child had enlarged brown nipples. He could see the proof right here before his eyes. *So beautiful.* All of those other women had deliberately deluded him!

But not this time.

No. Not this time.

Robin Walkingstick Heatherton lay on the narrow bed no more than ten feet away.

No more mistakes. Not ever again.

While she watched, he went about building up the fire in the stove, getting it good and hot, so it would burn all night.

Then he blew out the lamp on the table and stood before her in the dim glow that penetrated the cracks in the stove. He undressed slowly, draping each piece of clothing over the back of the chair.

She would never escape—and she knew it. He saw the truth in her eyes. He's stripped her, laid her on her back on the thin mattress, then told her to reach underneath the bed and clasp her hands. After he'd tied them securely, he'd made her spread her legs so that her feet fell over opposite sides of the bed. He'd tied one foot first, wrapping it twice, then worked the end of the rope through the mess of old newspapers, magazines and other refuse stuffed beneath the bed. Finally, he'd wrapped her other ankle twice, then run the rope around both and tied a square knot to cinch them tightly together. The bed was crude, made of rusty iron. It had four legs and two side rails. Rawhide strips wove back and forth between the rails, supporting the mattress. The narrowness of the bed combined with the thinness of the mattress made it possible for her to move enough to relieve the numbness in her hands and feet. He'd drawn the top sheet up to her waist. When he'd folded it back he stretched out on top of her naked body, pressing his flesh against hers, she screamed and struggled. Just as he had known she would. He'd seen this moment in his dreams, over and over.

He had to use both hands to hold her head still so he could kiss her, gently, leisurely. She had screamed into his mouth, and he'd kissed her even more softly, like a husband with a frightened virgin bride.

Of course, she wasn't a virgin. She was a demon incarnate . . . She had killed his brother, and a thousand, thousand other loyal Union soldiers.

"Are you ready for me, Robin?" he asked tenderly.

He wrapped his hands around her throat and began cutting off her air, slowly, expertly, because he wanted her to remain conscious for as long as she could . . . so she would remember.

CHAPTER 33

A tiny sound woke Robin, someone pouring liquid into a tin cup. She kept her eyes closed, listening. She smelled coffee. Her throat—the skin, muscles, the windpipe—all burned as if on fire. With every intake of breath, she wheezed hoarsely. Only a little air was getting through the swollen passageway to her lungs. Her head throbbed so violently she felt sick. Lack of oxygen . . . Her arms and legs, tied beneath the bed frame, ached. How long had she been unconscious? Hours? Days? Dear God, was Jeremy all right? She prayed Macey had taken him and run. Garrison would be hunting for her. Flickers of desperate hope went through her.

A chair scritched as he moved it across the dirt floor. He blew on his coffee to cool it.

Robin flexed her aching fingers. The ropes had cut into her flesh, and the movement hurt, but she had to make sure they still functioned. She fought to swallow.

"Are you awake?"

Robin didn't answer.

Blessed Jesus, throughout the war, she had been so careful. She'd never taken unnecessary chances, never left details unattended, always watched her backtrail. This error would cost her her life . . .

Corley had hunted her too long and too hard to let her win now.

Robin extended her fingers and touched the cold hardpacked dirt floor. Weak fury roused. She forced herself to think. *Think!* There had to be a way out. If she could pull herself to one side of the bed, she might be able to fray her ropes on the rusty iron side-rail of the opposite side. If he ever slept. If she had the strength. If he didn't kill her in the next five minutes.

"I have wanted to talk with you for so long, Robin," he said. "So very long."

Her logical mind ticked through the probabilities, counting them off as if on an abacus.

But she had faced such odds before.

"Are you ready for me, again, Robin?"

She opened her eyes. He sat at the table, holding his gray tin cup in both hands. Steam spiraled up around his lean freckled face. In full dress uniform, his shoulders dripped gold braid. Sweat stained the blue fabric beneath his arms, and his coal-black hair shimmered in the candlelight.

Carefully, she surveyed the small room, letting her gaze take in everything. Four candlespikes, like those Garrison had driven into the rock walls of the mine, dotted each wall. Refuse scattered the floor, old newspapers, fragments of boards, two quartz picks, a prospecting pan, a magnifying glass, and a broken rocker cradle for placer-mining the stream beds. A stack of white candles lay near the woodstove along the opposite wall.

"No one can find us, Robin," he said. "I made certain of that. We're high up in the mountains, far from the nearest town. And it's snowing again. Any tracks my horse left are long gone." He paused to sip his coffee. "I had to kill him, of course, so he wouldn't whinny and give us away. "We're alone here. Completely alone."

"Where?" she rasped.

"South of Central City. Up on top of the pass. Outside, there's a hundred-mile vista. But, of course, you'll never see it."

Corley stood, picked up his chair and came over to set it down beside her. He turned the chair around before he sat again, then laid an arm over the chair back and rested his chin upon his sleeve, looking down at her with those warm, loving eyes. Insane eyes. Beneath the thin veneer of warmth, was a colossal rage.

"You haven't answered me," he said.

"I . . . hurt."

"I'm sorry you made me do that." The words were soft, regretful. He tilted his head so that his cheek rested on his sleeve and he smiled at her.

Robin froze, as if being stalked by a killer cat. She stared unblinking into those blue inhuman eyes.

"You didn't answer my question. Are you ready for me, again?" he repeated.

She clenched her bound hands into fists and suppressed the wretched nausea that made her want to vomit. If he had only meant raping her, it would not have affected her so. The violation of the body was just that. A physical assault. She had witnessed many physical assaults far worse than quick and dirty rape—men who had been mutilated by the enemy, their bellies slit open and their intestines pulled out of their bodies so their deaths would be slow agony. But Corley used rape as an attack on his enemy's soul. He could not ejaculate unless his hands were crushing her throat, and he came only at the point just before she lost consciousness. When he could see death reflected in her eyes, then he smiled, and gasped as he climaxed.

She had to say something, anything to distract him, to redirect his thoughts.

"Tell me about . . ." she swallowed to moisten her wounded throat. "About your brother."

In a pained voice, he responded, "Michael. You killed him."

"How did it happen?"

"You know how it happened."

"No, I—I don't. Except that he died at Ball's Bluff."

Corley's lids fluttered. She saw tears on his lashes. "Yes. Drowned. And he—he had been my protector all my life."

"Your protector? From who?"

He closed his eyes. "My father."

As though to listen better, Robin slid her left leg and arm through the refuse under the bed, raising a metallic clatter and a rustling of papers, and rolled onto her left side. Her breasts, partially covered by her long hair, hung over the edge of the bed, but her hands, the binding on her hands, rested against the rusty metal rail on the back. It would have to be done cautiously, subtly.

"Why did your father want to hurt you?"

"He wanted to hurt everybody. He hurt my mother, my sisters . . . I think he hurt them even worse than he hurt Michael. I remember once, seeing my little sister, Margaret—she was six years old—undressing for her bath. She had terrible bruises, and bite marks in her private places."

"Dear God, to a six year old girl—"

"Oh, he did it to Michael and me, too. I'm sure it's because my mother had refused him her bed. They slept in separate rooms. It was all her fault. She was an evil woman." Hatred tensed his face, but his voice remained bizarrely calm, as if chronicling a story he knew only remotely. "From the time I was ten years old, I dreamed about killing her. I thought if she were gone, that my father would find another wife, one who would fill his—his 'needs' and he would leave us children alone." He frowned down into his coffee, and she could tell he was looking at his own reflection with a kind of aloof fascination.

"And Michael protected you from him?"

"Oh, yes." A fleeting smile replaced the frown. "My father always beat us first, before he . . . I always fought back, but I was so young, I didn't have my father's strength. Michael was three years older. I would scream Michael's name until he came and joined the fight, so that I could break free and run. He rescued me. Then my father would spar with Michael for a long time. He seemed to enjoy hearing his fists land."

Robin's heart raced at Corley's disoriented expression. Was he back there now? Witnessing the horrors? His face had gone blank. She worked her wrists in a slow constant rhythm, rubbing the rope against the rusty rail.

"Did you try to help Michael when your father—"

"Oh, I—I couldn't," he said defensively. "I was too small. I just ran away as fast as I could. I always found good hiding places—in holes in the ground . . . mostly."

"And when you came home?"

He clenched his cup in both hands. "I would go up to Michael's room and wash his wounds with soap and water. He always made me talk to him all night long. Until we could see the sun rising."

Corley's guilt could have filled the oceans. It showed in every anxious movement of his hands, every line in his face, the way the tendons stood out in his neck.

"What did you say to Michael, to make him feel better?"

"Anything I could think of. I told him stories about school and neighborhood gossip. I remember once I spent all night reciting poems I had written."

"You write poetry?"

"Not anymore. But I did then. Michael liked my poems. I wrote them for him." A faint tremor touched his voice. He shifted in his chair, tipping his face so that shadows filled the hollows of his eyes and nostrils, and the candlelight glittered in his wealth of gold braid.

Puzzle pieces began falling into place, creating a horrifying picture. A skinny boy, always running, looking for a place to hide, a place where he couldn't hear his brother's screams. A boy who knew he had to come home again. Home to a father who—

. . . *He's killing his mother every time he puts his hands around my throat.*

"Even after my father's death," Corley continued, "I felt him hunting for me in my dreams. He came to me often when I was at West Point."

"How did he die?"

He waved a hand. "In a wagon accident. He was run over. The wheels crushed his lungs, and he drowned in his own blood."

His queer pale blue eyes sparkled when he looked down at Robin again. "But I loved him. That's what hurt the most. I loved him so much."

"What did he say to you . . . when he—he came to you at West Point?"

He paused and sighed. "He told me he was in hell. And he said it wasn't fiery at all. It was a dark abyss, like a tunnel, and he just kept falling and falling. The fall through the darkness never ended, he said." His voice took on an eerie, disconnected quality. "Just like you and me, Robin. Oh, we're not there yet, but . . . but we're both looking into the abyss . . . now . . . standing on the edge of the precipice and below us is . . . is nothing. Just darkness. Darkness and peace, Robin Walkingstick Heatherton. You and I . . . we'll see it together."

He gave her that warm smile. But his eyes did not see her, nor the flickering shadows that danced around the dusty cluttered room, but some scene playing out on the dimly lit stage of his memory. His brows and the corners of his mouth twitched, apparently not much liking what he saw.

"You *are* ready for me, again, Robin."

He set his coffee cup on the floor.

CHAPTER 34

He's been here, Captain Wainwright!" the young lieutenant called from the plank doorway of the telegraph office. "The operator says he picked up Colonel Sharpe's wire this morning!"

"We need a description, Norris. The man is a secret service officer." The sandy-haired captain glanced at Owen, and propped his hands on his hips. "What did Major Corley look like?"

"Just a minute, sir." Norris briefly disappeared into the telegraph office, only to re-emerge and yell, "Black hair, captain! No mustache or beard. He was dressed in civilian clothing, blue shirt, denim pants."

"Very good, Norris. Get your men organized. Tell them the major is presumed armed and dangerous."

"I guarantee it." Owen folded his arms tightly across his breast.

Wainwright peered at him scornfully and walked a few paces away to confer with Norris in private.

Owen shoved his hands into the pockets of his black overcoat and studied the crowd that had gathered. Every eye had focused on him, and not one appeared amiable. The troops had ridden in less than an hour before, hauled him away from his dinner table at the hotel, and dragged him out here to stand in the cold foggy night. They hadn't even given him the time to grab his hat. Blond hair draped wetly over his ears.

In the past half hour, the entire town had coalesced along Main Street, muttering. The orange gleams of dozens of torches reflected with eerie brilliance through the fog. *It ain't fog,* someone had rudely informed him. The clouds had simply descended low enough to engulf the city. And while it resembled thick fog, it did possess its own distinct character, whirling and eddying, spinning tiny cyclones as it passed. Sometimes Owen could see the false-fronted brick and clapboard buildings across the street with perfect clarity and at other times, like now, they became ethereal specters barely visible through the mist. He recognized a few people in the mob: Mr. Hathaway from the Land Office stood next to Blaine Harding the assayer, listening to Mabel Wirth. She had pulled a brown shawl over her gray hair, which made her rosy cheeks and prominent nose all the more noticeable. Where the hell was Parker? Of all people, he ought to . . .

A ripple of silver buttons flashed as the captain turned and walked back. Maybe thirty years old, he had a triangular face and sharp green eyes. His blue cavalry hat was pushed back on his head. He said, "I warn you, Mr. Fontaine, we have a file two inches thick on your questionable activities. You are already under arrest. Please do not complicate your situation by giving me falsehoods. I—"

"Ask, Captain," Owen replied, "I'll be more than happy to tell you what I know."

Two guards came to stand behind Owen. He noted them with mild interest.

Wainwright said, "The last time you saw Major Corley—"

"Was in Colorado City. He had red hair, then, and wore a colonel's uniform. Incidentally, how do you people do that? If a secret service officer wanders into town, is the quartermaster just instructed to give him what he wants or does he have to carry several different kinds of requisition orders with him? You know, in case he wants to become a general or a private?" When the captain's mouth pursed with irritation, Owen finished, "Just wondering," and gave the man his most charming smile.

They were going to hang him from the highest tree they could find, unless he could extricate himself from this *very* unpleasant affair. The wheels were turning in the back of his mind. Army officers were bound by regulations and laws—unlike most of his business acquaintances. If he thought about it long enough, he felt certain he could use that fact.

"Mr. Fontaine, what do you know of Mrs. Heatherton? You are one of a handful of people who might be able to identify her. Are you sure she was here, in Central City?"

"Absolutely, Captain. She lived in that lovely house with the big veranda on Spruce Street."

"Have you seen her today?"

"No, I have not. I went to her home three hours ago to speak to her. But she was not there and she never returned."

"I see." Captain Wainwright's eyes narrowed. "Mr. Harding and Mrs. Wirth witnessed Mrs. Heatherton being abducted at approximately three-thirty. Who can verify your whereabouts at that time?"

"Are you suggesting I might have—good God, Captain!"

"Please answer my question? Do you have—"

"Yes, I have an alibi! I spent a horrendous fifteen minutes with Garrison Parker and Miss Macey Runkles at Mrs. Heatherton's home, between three-thirty and three-forty-five this afternoon. Does that help you, Captain?"

"Very much, sir."

"How nice," Owen responded. "There's one crime you can't charge me with."

Captain Wainwright didn't smile. He said, "There are plenty of others, Mr. Fontaine. I wouldn't be too flippant if I were you. Did you know that Major Corley had arrived in town?"

"Good heavens, no! If I had, you would not have found me here, Captain. The major is a madman, and I'm a coward. Our conversations had not been such that I yearned to see them continue." He balled his fists in his pockets and frowned.

"I see," Captain Wainwright said. The torchlight slid along the back of his right hand as he let it come to rest on his holstered pistol.

A confused din rose from the crowd when a rider came barreling down Main Street, riding hell-for-leather, his mount stretching out, flinging mud with every hoofbeat. The man's faded blue shirt showed beneath his heavy buffalo coat.

Christ, Owen said to himself, and grimaced.

Parker didn't even bother to come to a full halt. He bailed off his mule, and ran. Straight for Owen . . .

Instinctively, Owen threw himself against the wall with his arms spread. "What the hell do you want, Parker?" he shouted.

Parker's hazel eyes flared with deadly intent. He marched forward with his gaze on Owen, seemingly unaware of the military personnel in the immediate vicinity. He had his felt hat pulled low over his eyes, his brown hair sticking out over his ears like a thick curly fringe. His boots crunched in the snow.

Parker leaped up onto the wooden sidewalk, gripped the lapels of Owen's overcoat, lifted him off the ground and slammed him back against the telegraph office wall. Not once, but three times, shouting, *"Goddamn you! I've looked everywhere for her! I can't find her! . . . Did you hear me? I can't find her!"*

"That's not my fault, Parker! I don't have anything to do with this!"

"I've got to know everything. Right now! Do you hear me? *Tell me everything!* Every word he said during the time you spent with him. Every clue to the way his mind works. Every—"

"I'll be happy to tell you!" Owen shouted back. "If you'll let me go!"

Apparently just to relieve his frustration, Parker slammed Owen against the wall once more, then released him with a violent shove. Parker stood shaking, his teeth gritted. Despite the cold and fog, sweat shimmered over his face and beaded in his shaggy eyebrows.

Owen's "guards" rushed forward and reassembled around Parker with their army revolvers out and pointed at his broad chest. Captain Wainwright stalked forward, chin up, eyes wary. "Are you Garrison Parker?"

Parker nodded, but his eyes never left Owen. "I am, Captain."

"Can you verify that Mrs. Robin Walkingstick Heatherton was in Central City this morning?"

Parker took a deep breath and turned to Wainwright. The captain straightened beneath Parker's glare. If he'd had the room, Owen suspected, Wainwright would have stepped backward a few paces.

"Tell me why you're here, Captain. Who dispatched you, and what are your orders?"

Wainwright looked Parker up and down, taking in every element of his stance and clothing. "You were in the army, Mr. Parker?"

Parker lifted his arm and wiped his forehead on his buffalo sleeve. "Under General Carleton. California Volunteers."

"What was your rank?"

"Major."

Wainwright's stiff back relaxed, as if the very fact that he was addressing a former officer gave them something in common. His shoulders eased forward. "I received orders this morning, by telegraph, from Colonel George Sharpe in Washington City. He informed me that he had documented several murders in which Major Thomas Corley was implicated and ordered me to take a detachment and hunt down Corley. He said the major should be picking up a telegram here, in Central City, and that we might be able to catch him when he did."

"And your instructions concerning Mrs. Heatherton?"

Wainwright responded, "To apprehend her no matter the cost. She is suspected of conspiring with John Wilkes Booth in the assassination of President Lincoln. If captured, I am to send her back to Washington City under heavy guard for trial . . . Well, was she here?"

"I reckon so, Captain."

"Do you know where she is now?"

"No, of course, not!" Parker shouted and took a threatening step toward Wainwright, his jaw clenched. They stood facing each other, both breathing hard. "If I knew, I wouldn't be here talking to you! I'd be there!"

Wainwright said, "Major . . . if you are willing to aid us in this search, I would appreciate it. I do not know this town or the countryside, and I—"

"Goddamn it, yes!" Parker yelled. "What do you need? I'll do anything I can to find Corley as soon as possible!"

Wainwright cocked his head suspiciously, but said, "If you could provide me with a map of the terrain, and indicate possible hiding places, I would appreciate—"

Parker turned and waved to Mike Hathaway. Hathaway responded immediately, loping across the frozen road with his red hair flopping beneath the brim of his brown hat.

Hathaway glanced from Parker, to Owen, to Wainwright, to Parker, "What do you need, Garry?"

Parker took a moment to rub the back of his taut neck. "The captain has got to see a sketch of the terrain, Mike. You've got the best maps around. Can you—"

"I'll be right back!" Hathaway trotted down the street to his office, opened the door, and vanished inside.

In the interim, Parker scrutinized Wainwright and said, "Captain, I know these mountains like the backs of my hands, and I can tell you right now, that there's a *thousand* goddamned places he might be hiding her—if they're still here at all." Inhaling, he continued, "Every square inch of Gregory Diggings, that's the name for the entire region of these mountains, has been burrowed into in search of gold. If you had to search every discovery shaft, secondary shaft, tunnel, and just plain hole in the ground, it would take you *weeks!* We've got to narrow down this search or we'll never find her in time." The captain's gaze had focused contemplatively on the torch behind Parker. "Are you listening to me, Captain?" Parker demanded.

"I am, Major! I just don't know where to begin. I was hoping you might—"

Hathaway came sprinting down the walk, panting, unrolling maps as he came. People parted to leave a path for him, asking questions, gripping his coat sleeve, and he answered their questions as well as he could while pressing forward through the crowd. Parker had started pacing, head down, nostrils flaring, eyes frantic.

Owen observed him with quiet interest. No man acted this desperate unless he loved a woman to distraction. Yet when Owen had seen Rose and Parker together, the man had never so much as touched her in an intimate way. Had he told her how he felt about her? Owen's mouth quirked. Probably not. Parker was, after all, a curious breed—and no doubt on the verge of much deserved extinction.

"Here you go, Garry," Hathaway said and handed the maps to Parker.

Parker took them without a word and went to stand beside Wainwright. He held the top map up to the glow of the torches and said, "This here is an overview of Gregory Diggings, Captain. It shows you the locations of every mine and claim. What it don't show you," Parker said with a hard exhale, "is all the other holes in the area. And there's a hundred of 'em."

Wainwright's brow furrowed. "Well, then where would you suggest we begin, Major?"

Parker turned to Hathaway. "Mike, I was thinking down around Black Hawk, what do you think?"

Hathaway nodded. "I reckon that's as good a place as any to start. That way we could work our way west, and then head up over the pass and south towards Empire and Georgetown."

"Very well," Wainwright responded. "Major Parker, will you be willing to lead a detachment?"

Parker's tanned face darkened. He paused. "No, Captain. I work better alone. But I reckon that Mike—"

"Yes, I will," Hathaway said, stepping forward. "Give me four or five men and we'll start right now."

"Thank you, sir," Captain Wainwright said and lifted his chin to Lieutenant Norris. The man shouldered forward.

"Yes, Sir?"

"Lieutenant, select five men and go with Mr. Hathaway. He knows this terrain. He'll help you in your search for Major Corley."

The lieutenant saluted and trotted away to pick his five men from the swimming mob of blue uniforms.

Parker shifted, his head slowly coming around. He pinned Owen with a homicidal gaze, then walked toward him. A head taller than Owen, he cut an imposing figure. He peered down unblinking. "Are you only worried about your own hide? Don't you even care what's happened to her?"

"Of course, I care, Parker. But what am I supposed to do about it?"

Parker turned to Wainwright. "Captain? I would like to question Mr. Fontaine. Will you release him into my custody for fifteen minutes?"

Wainwright brushed sandy hair away from his forehead and strode forward. "I can't do that, Major. This man is under arrest." He gestured to the two guards. "Marks. Steele. Please escort Mr. Fontaine back to his hotel room and make sure he remains there until we've finished our search for Major Corley."

"And after that?" Parker asked.

Owen stepped forward to listen, too.

"Colonel Sharpe wants him back in Washington to stand trial with Mrs. Heatherton. Apparently there is some information to suggest the two worked together—"

"We did not!" Owen declared. "Not ever!"

"Well, Mr. Fontaine," Wainwright said. "You will have your day in court." He turned to Parker. "If you want to question him, Major, you will have to wait you turn, and there's a crowd of high-level bureaucrats ahead—"

Crazy with desperation, Parker grabbed Owen again, threw him back against the wall, and screamed into his face, "There must be something you can tell me! Did Corley have any strange habits, did he tell you about his dreams, or his experiences during the war? Did he—"

"Strange habits?" Owen shouted. "All his habits were strange, Parker! The man liked to sleep in flea-infested wolves' dens! Moldering dugouts, or any other hole he could—"

Parker's bearded face slackened. He released Owen suddenly, turned on his heel and ran for his mule.

"Major!" Wainwright called. "Where are you going? I need you—"

"I'm mounting my own search, Captain! You'll do just fine under Mike Hathaway's guidance."

"But where are you going?"

Parker ignored the question, kicked his mule, and galloped away into the mist.

"It's all right, Jeremy," Macey said. "Everything's going to be fine. You just hang on."

Jeremy gripped the saddlehorn and sank back into the hollow of Macey's stomach. Her smell was wet wool and freshly ironed cotton and baking bread, all good things, but fear ran along his arms with icy spider feet. His mother was gone. No one knew where. An hour ago, Garry had ridden by, and shouted orders at Macey. Jeremy had been upstairs, playing in his bedroom. He'd run to his window as soon as he could, but by then Garry had stopped talking and was shoving money into Macey's hand. It had scared Jeremy. That meant they were in trouble. All of them. They had to run. Getting money was all his mother had talked about when they'd been running through forests and across battlefields. People had to have money to run away. Right after that, Macey had saddled the horse, tied two small bags on the back, then bundled Jeremy up in his heavy coat and set him on the saddle in front of her.

He watched the world go by between the horse's ears: Houses, rocks, trees. All half-eaten by the swirling fog. Fullhouse was cold. His breath made white clouds thicker than the mist. They floated up in front of Jeremy's face. Ice had started to crust his eyelashes, giving him a sparkly view of the steep road down the mountain.

"Macey?" Jeremy asked. "Where are we going?"

"I'll tell you, honey, but you got to promise not to tell anybody else."

Jeremy craned his neck to peer up at her. She had dressed in a gray cloak and inside her hood, her face was the color of walnut that had been oiled over and over—like the cedar chest in Jeremy's old bedroom in his grandmama's house. "I won't tell," he answered.

"All right. We're going to a little town in New Mexico Territory. We're gonna meet Garry there."

"Is he . . . will he bring my Mama, too?"

Macey wet her lips and a tangle of baby snakes hatched inside Jeremy's stomach, writhing and biting.

"Is he?"

Macey said, "I . . . I hope so, honey."

Jeremy started to cry, but his tears were frozen inside him, and he couldn't melt them free. Just his chest cried.

"Macey?" he choked out. "Is my Mama dead?"

"Oh, honey! No. I mean . . . I don't . . . I don't want to lie to you. The truth is I just don't know. We're all praying so hard it hurts. I can't believe God would—"

"God let my Daddy die."

His words hung in the air in silver puffs, until Macey rode through them.

She bent down and kissed the top of Jeremy's head. "I know, honey. Sometimes God don't seem so reliable, does He? But this is different. Your mama . . . well, no matter what God does, she's just too danged smart to get herself killed. You understand what I'm saying?"

Jeremy swallowed down his tight throat. "I—I do. When we were running through Kentucky, she wouldn't even build a fire at night to keep us warm or to cook dinner. She was afraid the Yankees would see the light and come hurt us."

Jeremy didn't want to think about the fields of dead men, or the flapping birds, or the bitter copper taste he'd had at the back of his throat. He squeezed his eyes shut. Trying to see nothing. In Kentucky not even the trees could look out at the meadows with their eyes open.

"That sounds awful. Did you have to eat things raw?"

Jeremy shook his head. His could barely hear his own voice, "We ate dried-out old food that Mama found in the haversacks of dead solders. The meat always tasted like wood." He looked at Macey.

Her eyes were wide. "Lord Almighty," she said softly. " 'Least your mama kept you fed. There was a good sight of folks down there that weren't eating a 'tall."

The baby snakes twisted up into a big knot that made his stomach hurt. He moved a hand to rub it. "Will it be like that again, Macey? Now that we're running? Will we have to—to—"

"God, no! First off, there ain't no dead soldiers to rob. And second, I got money and a gun. What we can't buy, we'll shoot. Don't you worry none about eating. We'll be fat as hogs by the time we get to New Mexico Territory. Just you wait and see."

Fat as hogs.

Jeremy used both hands to hold onto the saddlehorn. He knew what happened to fat hogs.

They were always slaughtered.

He felt suddenly as if he were hugging a big soap bubble on a windy day, being blown higher and higher into the sky. Soon the sharp points on the stars would prick his bubble and break it . . . and he didn't have any wings.

Jeremy looked down at his coat where Traveller hid inside his undershirt. He concentrated. It always took time. He closed his eyes and found himself in a familiar black snowstorm, moving hand-to-hand along an invisible rope that tied him and Traveller together . . .

When he felt the soft white hair of Traveller's stomach, he petted it gently, then crawled inside into that warmth.

He could no longer feel the cold mist on his face or the biting snakes in his belly. Jeremy curled on his side and went to sleep in there, with Traveller's heartbeat in his ears. Slow. Steady.

From somewhere far away, he heard Macey say, "That's a good boy, Jeremy. You sleep. Time will go faster that way."

And in a little while, all the sounds of the road faded away, and he was riding Traveller through the clouds, going up, up . . .

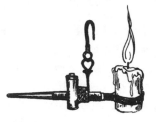

CHAPTER 35

M y darling," Corley whispered against her hair and nuzzled her cheek. He had been stretched out on top of her, sleeping, for two or three hours. "It's almost time. Are you ready?"

Dry sobs racked Robin's body as she struggled to breathe. The violence of his last assault had been so cruel she could not believe she still lived. Relief that it was over vied with despair. When he had fallen asleep, she had searched beneath the bed until she found a thin metallic object, about as long as her hand. It seemed to be some sort of pointed mining tool. She had been working her ropes against it. Sweat had pooled between their naked bodies, and turned cold with the ceasing of his movement. Robin shivered.

Corley tenderly ran his hands over her swollen throat. The concerned expression his lean freckled face terrified her. As if he did not know who could have done such a thing to her . . .

"No one will ever hurt you again," he promised. "Soon, very soon, it will all be over."

He put a bare foot on the dirt floor and stood up. What a giant of man he was. The sheen of perspiration accentuated every muscle in his stomach and chest.

"You must be cold," he murmured.

He walked to the stove and put wood in the firebox. Bright orange flashes lit the gloomy dugout. He prodded the fire with an iron poker and opened the vent all the way, so the dugout would heat up more quickly.

"There," he said. He walked back to the chair where his clothes lay and began dressing.

His eyes never left her, and Robin wept. While he was watching, she could do nothing! She could not even test her ropes to find out how far they had frayed . . .

He stepped into his blue trousers and buttoned them up, then took his time slipping on his gaudy jacket. The gold braid winked and glimmered in the candlelight. Bending down, he carefully straightened the seams of his trousers, as if he were about to attend a dress ball, and smoothed his wet black hair away from his face. Last, he put on his gunbelt and checked the holstered revolver. Then he smiled at her.

"Are you ready, Robin?"

"No, please . . ." She could barely breathe. The swelling was increasing. Soon, it would cut off her air passage altogether.

"Here," he said. "Let me soothe you."

He came over, sat on the edge of the bed, and ran his hands over her naked body, petting her with a frightening warmth. After several minutes, he began gathering up her hair, pulling locks from beneath her back. Lifting her head, he used his fingers to divide the thick blackness into two equal parts, then drew them down over her chest and smoothed them out.

"I'll start on the right side," he said.

His fingers worked expertly, separating the strands into three equal locks, braiding them tightly.

Suddenly, he hissed, *"Shh!"*

Robin halted to listen with a tormented eagerness that equaled his own. Wind whimpered. The branches of low bushes whipped against the dugout. But she heard nothing more.

"Did you hear it?" Corley whispered.

She shook her head.

"You didn't hear anything?"

"No."

"I thought I . . . I heard footsteps."

He finished braiding the right side of her hair and began working on the left, hurriedly, as if fearing he might not have the time he needed. The work turned sloppy, the plaiting loose. His pale blue eyes darted about the jumble that filled the dugout, landing on picks, shovels, the broken rocker cradle in the far corner, the candleholders on the walls. Like an artist, he arranged both braids so that they hung side-by-side between her breasts.

"It's about time, Robin."

Her mouth trembled as tears blurred her eyes. "No, please. *Please, don't!"*

He stretched out on top of her again. The buttons and braid of his uniform ate into her flesh. He kissed her face tenderly and whispered inaudible words, while he wrapped his hands around her swollen throat. Corley nodded as he began tightening his hold.

"Do you see it?" he asked. "The black abyss? Is my father there?"

Soon now, Robin thought. *The end is near. Very near.*

His thumbs gouged into her windpipe and Robin's back arched as she began choking, gasping, and pulling on the ropes that bound her hands. His blue eyes had frozen into huge unwavering moons only inches from her face.

Forcing precious breath from her lungs, Robin croaked, *"Michael? Michael, please . . . help me! Michael!"*

Corley's mouth gaped in a silent cry. He suddenly threw up his hands and sat back atop her. "Michael . . . ? Do you see him?"

Robin tugged with all her might.

A hoarse scream erupted from her throat as the ropes broke!—she flung herself forward, hauling the . . . candlespike! It was a broken candlespike!—from beneath the bed. She plunged the rusty tip into Corley's chest, withdrew it, and plunged it in again.

He fell backward and Robin, holding fast to her weapon, toppled to the dirt floor with him, her feet still bound beneath the iron bedstead, which crashed over on top of her. She threw her weight into the candlespike, forcing it deeper while she sobbed and screamed incoherently.

Corley put a huge hand in her face and brutally shoved her away. Her shoulder slammed into the sharp corner of the bedstead and sent it sliding backward into the wall. It struck so hard that it overturned, trapping Robin beneath.

She could hear Corley moving, grunting when he pulled out the candlespike. He flung it across the room. It bashed into the woodstove with a resounding clang and fell to the floor.

Robin pushed up, trying to tilt the bedstead on its side, but it fell back, slamming her to the floor.

Corley's blue pant legs appeared right before her eyes. He weaved on his feet.

He whispered, "Did he come? Did you see him?"

Horror filled Robin. "Yes," she answered. "He's here."

Corley dropped to the floor beside her and sucked in ragged breaths. "Where? . . . Where is he?" He shoved the bedstead over onto its side, so she could see, and repeated, "Where is he?" He looked back at the room.

Robin swallowed down her constricted throat. Blood gushed from his chest wound, rhythmically, bright red. She'd cut one of the main arteries . . .

Corley sagged, braced a hand on the floor, then sank to his side. Vainly, he attempted to sit up again, and the effort sent him rolling onto his back. *"Where?"* he gasped. "Tell . . . me!"

"Sitting at the table."

Blood drenched his uniform and pooled on the floor at his side. Not even the dry dirt could soak it up fast enough. The pool widened and flowed toward Robin. He moved again, shifting to stare at the table, then fell silent.

Robin slid down and slipped her bound feet over the foot of the bedstead. Desperate, unthinking, she reached over and pulled Corley's pistol from its holster, aimed at the rope between her ankles and fired. The jolt of the ropes snapping sent her toppling backward.

Bitter tears overwhelmed her. She lay on her back, clutching the pistol with both hands, and wept. Through blurred eyes, she watched the shimmering candlelight. It pulsed and swaggered, moving about the dugout as though calmly taking in the appalling scene.

Air wheezed hoarsely in and out of her lungs.

Dear God, how she longed to lie here and sleep for days, but if she didn't get up now and drag herself outside where she could pack her throat in snow to halt the swelling, she would die.

She pulled the sheet off the bed and dragged it over herself.

She could not stand.

Clutching the pistol, she crawled on her hands and knees, shoved open the door of the dugout, and fell outside into a gleaming powder of pale silver moonlight. Patches of snow shone like the purest eiderdown. Robin could make out the broad wings of a hunting owl as it skimmed over the whiteness in search of mice.

She fell on her stomach in a snowbank and began shoving handfuls into her mouth, swallowing it desperately.

The cold bit into her flesh, but she rolled to her back, packed snow around her throat, and lay staring up at the bowl of stars that arched into infinity over her head. They glittered like crushed diamonds strewn across an indigo velvet background. When she could muster the strength, she ate more snow. How sweet it tasted, and how good it felt as it went down. The fragrances of the night filtered up around her, damp earth and newborn spring flowers.

Her shivering intensified. She cocked the pistol, lifted it, and fired three shots into the night.

CHAPTER 36

The crackling of a roaring fire seeped through Robin's numb mind like smoke on a still morning, twisting around her thoughts, soft and gray, weaving warmth into the very fabric of her soul. She felt as if she were floating on that smoky wisp . . .

She opened her eyes, and saw a kinky fringe of dark brown fur, but it took a moment to realize she lay wrapped in a buffalo coat. Then she felt a man shift her in his arms, heard the chair where he sat holding her creak, and a moment of disoriented terror took hold of her. She started shaking.

"G—Garrison?"

"I'm here, Robin. I been here for hours."

Her fear receded as he clutched her against him. As usual, he did not waste effort on useless words. He was just there, always there, and his hands were warm and his voice gentle.

"I—I need—"

"Don't try to talk," he murmured. "We'll talk tomorrow. For now, just rest. Everything else can wait."

She shook her head, and he leaned closer to her to listen. He smelled of wood smoke. "What is it?" he asked.

"Jeremy?"

"He's fine. Don't you worry 'bout him."

"Take me . . ." She pulled air down her aching throat. "Take me home, Garrison. Please . . . take me home."

The lines around his hazel eyes deepened. "I can't, Robin. Soon as you're on your feet, and able, you've got to make a run for it. I've already sent Macey and Jeremy—"

"*Federales?*"

He nodded. "A hell of a lot of 'em. I believe Colonel Sharpe may have called out the whole goddamned Army of the West to search for you . . . They think you were involved in the Lincoln assasination plot."

Above him, she saw two strands of spiderweb shimmering as they blew and fluttered in the hot air rising from the woodstove. They reminded her of a ballet dancer's graceful arms.

"I wasn't. Really . . . Garrison."

But she'd been in the room when Rose O'Neal Greenhow had presented the idea to Davis. The Confederacy had just suffered a staggering defeat at Gettysburg. General Lee had offered to resign. Jefferson Davis was desperate, considering any option that might save their country.

"I believe you, Robin," Garrison said. "I never could picture you as an assassin. A soldier, yes. But not a cold-blooded killer."

The word sent a tremor through her again. "Corley . . . ?"

Garrison's shaggy eyebrows pulled together. Hatred lay just beneath his desperate concern for her. "I dragged him out of here last night, dumped his body in an old mine shaft and used Honey to jerk loose the timbers framing the door. Believe me, there ain't nobody ever gonna find him beneath all that dirt and rock."

Relief made Robin sigh. She had dreaded what the Federal government would do once they'd discovered his body. Another murder to add to the list of charges already being leveled against her.

"And," he added, "I searched his pockets before I hauled him out. I found an envelope full of greenbacks in his coat pocket. Did you—"

"Yes, I—I emptied out my bank account just before he captured me."

"Smart woman."

"Garrison?" she asked, mildly surprising herself. "You're—you're coming with me, aren't you?"

"Coming . . ." he began, then comprehension filled his eyes. A small smile touched his lips, as if her words salved a hurt deep inside him. "Yes. If you want me to. I love you, Robin . . . No, close your mouth. Don't say it. I don't want you to. It's enough for me that you asked. If you decide you can tell me more later, that's fine. But it ain't important just now. What is important is that you sleep. And don't worry. I've taken care of everything critical. Everybody you love is safe. *I promise you, I've seen to it.*"

Her skeptical nature roused and she longed to ask him just what he meant by that. How had he taken care of things? What measures had he taken to insure Jeremy's safety? But as slumber overtook her, she realized that the details didn't matter—because she believed him.

Her thoughts drifted . . . moving . . . weaving together images from the past.

Robin dreamed.

Of a cool spring morning in Virginia when a thin crescent of moon had risen above the cold mist that twined through the trees, and dew lay like tears upon the freshly tilled fields . . .

And she did not understand at all her mother's words about mirrors and dead voices.

EPILOGUE

Macey stood on the second-floor balcony of the big adobe house, holding Jeremy steady where he balanced on the wrought-iron railing. He had one hand propped on her shoulder and one fastened to the roof's support pole. Traveller perched on the edge of the round table to their right, looking down at the winding green ribbon of the Rio Grande that stretched like a snake into the heat-blurred distances. Robin walked slowly along the sandy shore with Garrison at her side. Both of them wore white, and Lord knew, in this country, they needed to. It had to be one hundred and twenty degrees today! The flowing hem of Robin's skirt billowed and flapped in the searing wind, and Garrison's shirt flattened across his broad chest. She had taken to wearing her hair the way the Mexican women did, in a single long braid that hung down her back. Since they'd crossed the border at Laredo three months ago, the two had stuck together like glue.

When the wind gusted just right, Macey could hear their conversation.

"I want to plant real trees, Garrison," Robin said. "Blue spruces and sugar maples. They'll look so beautiful around the house."

Garrison shoved his hands into his pants pockets and gave her a wry smile. "Well, you go right ahead. I reckon folks will come for miles just to watch."

"What do mean 'just to watch'? To watch what?"

"You'll see."

Robin's mouth twisted, as if perturbed. "Were you born a naysayer? Or did fate make you this way?"

"Neither," he answered. "Observation made me this way."

"Observation?"

"Never mind," he said and took a hand out of its pocket to reach for hers. She slipped her fingers into his, and he held them tightly as he walked. He seemed to be studying the strands of black hair that had freed themselves from her braid and danced in the roasting wind. A sparkle entered his eyes. "If you want to plant blue spruces, then by God, we'll plant a hundred of 'em."

Robin paused. "No, forget I suggested it. I've changed my mind," she said angrily.

"Decided you'd rather have ponderosa pines?"

"Not at all. I've decided that planting mesquite trees will provide you with fewer opportunities to entertain the neighborhood."

He seemed to be working hard to suppress a laugh. "You don't say?"

As they moved further down the shore of the shining river, Macey lost their voices.

Jeremy put his arms around Macey's neck and hugged her. "Macey, is my mama going to marry Garry?"

"Can't rightly say, Jeremy. Though I know she's asked him."

Jeremy bit his lower lip. "She did? What did he answer?"

"Oh," Macey replied, "you know how Garry is. He told your mama he wasn't gonna give her an answer 'till he was sure he knew what she wanted him to say."

Jeremy frowned and Macey patted his shoulder. "Don't fret over it. Your mama understood what he meant. That's what counts. Would you like it if she married Garry?"

Jeremy examined his mother and Garrison as they passed through the threads of shade cast by a palo verde tree. "My daddy says it will a good thing."

"Your daddy?"

"Yes," Jeremy said. "Last night Traveller took me to heaven. I found my daddy. He was sitting on a creek with grandpa, fishing. Daddy wrestled with me, and we played checkers, and we talked and talked—'till Traveller got tired and wanted to come home."

"And he told you it was all right for your mama to marry Garry, huh?"

Jeremy nodded. His eyes had not left the pair on the river bank.

"What else did he tell you?"

"Oh," Jeremy said, "we talked a lot about mama, and daddy told me how he died in Tennessee. He was shot by a firing squad. He fell in the mud, and it rained and rained on him. They didn't bury him until the next day, 'cause there was so much shooting going on. He said men were dying all around him while he lay there in the mud."

"My goodness . . ." Macey's voice had gone tight. "Your mama never told me that."

Jeremy sucked on his lower lip for a few seconds, then said, "Me either."

The squawk of a roadrunner drew their attention. They both turned to watch the bird darting across the desert, chasing an elusive cricket that hopped just out of the bird's reach. Garrison pointed at it, and his joyous laughter blended with Robin's and climbed the shimmering heat waves.

Macey glanced at Jeremy. He was smiling. The gusting wind quieted, and the silence of the desert expanded to fill the void. She shook her head.

"Lord, they sound good when they laugh together, don't they, Jeremy?"

The boy nodded again. He had his eyes focused on the roadrunner. Down along the shore of the river, the bird stopped suddenly, let out a surprised chirp, and leaped straight up into the air, landing in a puff of dust. It came up with a grasshopper in its beak. Jeremy laughed as he watched the roadrunner gulp down its prize.

Macey kissed his forehead. "Come on, youn'un. We got work to do."

"What work?"

"Making bread for dinner! You said you wanted to help me."

Jeremy yelled, "I do! I just forgot!" He jumped down from the railing. "I'll race you to the kitchen, Macey!"

"Race me? I can't keep up with you!"

"I know!" he called happily as he dashed into the house.

She could hear his steps thudding down the stairs, then a rush of childish laughter when he hit the floor and sprinted for the kitchen.

Macey turned to Traveller. The toy horse stood alone on the table, legs straight, head up, peering unblinking at the endless shimmering desert, as if eager to trot out and find adventure. Patches of white paint had peeled off its withers and neck. Traveller now resembled one of the wild pinto ponies that ran unfettered across Mexico.

Macey whispered, "You sure helped that boy, Traveller. I think he's gonna be all right now." She let her eyes drift to the freedom beyond the railing. "It won't be long," she promised, "Jeremy will be setting you free."

AFTERWORD

Sarah Slater is one of the great mysteries of the Civil War, but she did exist.

She was born in Connecticut, and later moved to New Bern, North Carolina where she met her future husband: Rowan Slater. They were married on June 12, 1861, and Rowan left for military service on June 23, 1861. He lived through the war, but he never saw her again.

We know very little about Sarah's activities until January of 1865 when she was recruited to be a spy by Confederate Secretary of War James A. Seddon. She spoke French, and he thought her the perfect choice to carry messages between Richmond and Confederate agents in Canada. Her first task was to take papers and money to Canada to be used in the defense of Confederate agents who had participated in the St. Albans, Vermont, bank robbery. The papers she conveyed convinced the Canadian judge that the men were indeed on a secret military mission, and he refused to extradite them to the United States for trial. Her task accomplished, she left Canada and met John Harrison Surratt, the chief aide of John Wilkes Booth, in Maryland. He escorted her through the countryside and made certain she arrived safely back in Richmond on February 22, 1865.

Her second mission, in March of 1865, required her to carry documents to Montreal.

She left on her last mission on April 1, 1865. Just before the fall of Richmond, the Confederacy decided to transfer the considerable funds remaining in its Canadian operation to a safer location in England. That was the job entrusted to Sarah. She stopped in Washington with the intention of visiting friends, including John Wilkes Booth, then left for New York on April 4, 1865.

And vanished.

But other information seems to fit into Sarah's "puzzle."

The Federal flotilla that took Abraham Lincoln to Richmond on April 4 was followed by a Canadian yacht named the *Octavia.* She was very persistent, refusing to be waved off. Admiral Porter had to order her to turn back or face the consequences. What she was doing on the James River is still unknown.

However, on that same day, April 4, a group of Confederates disguised as woodchoppers captured the steamer called the *Harriet de Ford,* put the passengers ashore, and ran the ship down the Chesapeake. They burned and abandoned the ship shortly thereafter for unclear reasons, although it has been speculated they heard the thunderous cannon salute in Washington announcing the fall of Richmond and got cold feet.

George Atzerodt, the member of the conspiracy who was supposed to kill Vice President Andrew Johnson, suggested another possibility. He confessed after his capture that John Harrison Surratt had told him they were supposed to hide on the shores of the Potomac and that a vessel would be picking them up to take them through the blockade.

John Wilkes Booth did hide on the shores of the Potomac for seven days after the assassination.

When Booth was killed on April 26, 1865, a bill of exchange drawn on a Montreal bank was discovered in his pocket. It was dated October 27, 1864. The same bank was used by the Confederacy in Canada. Around November 18, 1864, Booth contracted with a ship to take his theatrical costumes, prompt books, and other personal effects from Canada to the Bahamas. Curiously, the schooner was detained for legal reasons at a small town on the Saint Lawrence, and Booth's baggage and all other cargo were sold at auction to pay the salvors.

The trunk in Booth's Washington hotel room contained a copy of the Vigenere Tableau, the Confederacy's secret cipher.

By the time of Booth's death, Horace Greeley, editor of the New York *Tribune,* and other leading newspapers in the North were openly charging that the Confederates in Toronto had plotted Lincoln's murder. "Evidence" poured into the offices of Secretary Stanton, Judge Advocate General Holt and General Baker, Chief of the National Detective Force in Washington. Most of it was purely circumstantial, but one element was . . . interesting. Shortly after the shooting at Ford's Theatre, the sheriff in St. Albans, Vermont, reported that three desperate looking characters arrived, and one man dropped a handkerchief in the railroad depot with the name "J. H. Surratt" embroidered on it. John Harrison Surratt's mother, Mary, would later be hanged for her part in the conspiracy. The three men proved to be "innocent" deserters, but the handkerchief was brought back to Washington. How they obtained Surratt's handkerchief is still a mystery.

Did Sarah Slater carry the final message from Richmond to Booth telling him to go through with the assassination? Did the message promise a ship would pick him up on the shores of the Potomac and take him safely to the Bahamas where he thought his belongings would be? Was Sarah Slater on the *Octavia?* Did she make it to Canada, collect the money, and leave for Europe where she lived comfortably, if anonymously, for the rest of her life? And was John Harrison Surratt with her?

I don't know . . . What do you think?

SELECTED BIBLIOGRAPHY

Abel, Annie Heloise. *The American Indian as Slaveholder and Secessionist.* Lincoln: University of Nebraska Press, 1992.

—— *The American Indian in the Civil War, 1862–1865.* Lincoln: University of Nebraska Press, 1992.

Armitage, Susan, and Elizabeth Jameson, *The Women's West.* Norman: University of Oklahoma Press, 1987.

Athearn, Robert G. *The Coloradoans.* Albuquerque: University of New Mexico Press, 1976.

Catton, Bruce. *The Coming Fury.* New York: Washington Square Press, 1955.

——*Never Call Retreat.* New York: Washington Square Press, 1955.

——*A Stillness at Appomattox.* New York: Washington Square Press, 1955.

——*Terrible Swift Sword.* New York: Washington Square Press, 1955.

——*This Hallowed Ground.* New York: Washington Square Press, 1955.

Clinton, Catherine. *The Other Civil War. American Women in the Nineteenth Century.* New York: Hill and Wang, 1984.

Davis, Burke. *The Civil War. Strange and Fascinating Facts.* New York: Wings Books, 1960.

Foote, Shelby. *The Civil War. Fort Sumter to Perryville.* New York: Vintage Books, 1986.

——*Fredericksburg to Meridian.* New York: Vintage Books, 1986.

——*Red River to Appomattox.* New York: Vintage Books, 1986.

Gaines, Craig W. *The Confederate Cherokees. John Drew's Regiment of Mounted Rifles.* Baton Rouge: Louisiana State University Press, 1989.

Higginson, Thomas Wentworth. *Army Life in a Black Regiment.* New York, W. W. Norton and Co., 1984. (Originally published in 1869.)

Horan, James D. *Confederate Agent. A Discovery in History.* New York: Crown Publishers, Inc., 1954.

Hurst, Jack. *Nathan Bedford Forrest. A Biography.* New York: Alfred A. Knopf, 1993.

Jones, Katharine M. ed. *Heroines of Dixie.* Vols. 1 & 2. Marietta, Ga.: Mockingbird Books, 1955.

Long, E. B. *The Civil War Day by Day.* New York: Doubleday, 1971.

Luchetti, Cathy, and Carol Olwell. *Women of the West.* New York: Orion Books, 1992.

McPherson, James M. *The Negroes' Civil War.* New York: Ballantine Books, 1991.

Markle, Donald E. *Spies and Spymasters of the Civil War.* New York: Hippocrene Books, 1994.

Myers, Sandra L. *Westering Women and the Frontier Experience 1800–1915.* Albuquerque: University of New Mexico Press, 1982.

Niethammer, Carolyn. *Daughters of the Earth. The Lives and Legends of American Indian Women.* New York: Collier Books, 1977.

Oates, Stephen B. *A Woman of Valor. Clara Barton and the Civil War.* New York: The Free Press, 1994.

Peavy, Linda, and Ursula Smith. *Women in Waiting in the Westward Movement. Life on the Home Frontier.* Norman: University of Oklahoma Press, 1994.

Rhea, Gordon C. *The Battle of the Wilderness: May 5–6, 1864.* Baton Rouge: Louisiana State University Press, 1994.

Rose, Anne C. *Victorian America and the Civil War.* Cambridge: Cambridge University Press, 1992.

Ross, Ishbel. *Rebel Rose. The Life of Rose O'Neal Greenhow, Confederate Spy.* Marietta, Ga.: Mockingbird Books, 1954.

Ross, Nancy Wilson. *Westward the Women.* San Francisco: North Point Press, 1985.

Schlissel, Lillian. *Women's Diaries of the Westward Journey.* New York: Schocken Books, 1982.

Smith, Duane A. *Rocky Mountain Mining Camps. The Urban Frontier.* Lincoln: University of Nebraska Press, 1967.

Taylor, Susie King. *A Black Woman's Civil War Memoirs.* New York: Markus Wiener Publishing Co., 1992. (Originally published in 1902).

Van Doren Stern, Philip. *Secret Missions of the Civil War.* New York: Bonanza Books, 1990.

Young, Otis E., Jr. *Western Mining.* Norman: University of Oklahoma Press, 1970.